The Quest

For

Filon Bora

The Quest

For

Filon Bora

Book One in the Quest Saga

Diana Welsh

Table of Contents

A Note Regarding the Glossary

A glossary of names, places, and terms can be found at the back of this book which includes pronunciations and definitions. To minimize spoilers only the basic information is listed and any new names, places, or terms that will be encountered in future books in *The Quest Saga* are not included here, but will be added to the glossaries of said future books on an as-needed basis.

Chapter One

To the dark haired boy hiding in the shadows of the steamy alley it seems as though he has been waiting a lot longer than he has, for the smell of putrefying bodies is rather strong today, and trapped as the stench is between the walls of the renderer building and those of the inner keep it is all but unbearable. Then again it does not help that it is the hottest part of the day. Come to think about it, it is always the hottest part of the day when he comes here to the alley, for the man who summons him here says that mid-day is the best time for him to come since there are fewer people about that time of day. Probably because of the stink the boy thinks as he pulls the neck of his rather filthy shirt up over his nose and mouth. Of course that does not help much since he is wearing his alley clothes, and alley clothes never get washed. What would be the point he thinks with a smirk as he studies the gruesome expressions on the faces of the dead piled in a heap all helter-skelter near the door to the garbage renderer.

Busy day the boy silently comments with a disgusted sneer as he scoots back far enough to lean against the cool metal of the renderer building's outer wall. Yes today is the day that overlord Galwor holds his justice court, and considering the number of bodies waiting to be incinerated not too many who got caught at something had the means to buy their way out of trouble. With a frown the boy wonders if there are always as many poor souls on trial as there apparently are today, for this is the first time that he has been asked to come here on court day. Now that he has seen it with his own eyes he knows exactly why that is. It is because this court day is probably not any busier than any other court day, and with this many people around his odds of getting spotted lurking here in the alley are better than other days by far. Working that out though only makes him nervous as to what it is that is so important to his benefactor that he would ask him to risk it this time when he never would before.

Well no matter what it is the next time he asks him to come here on court day he is going to tell him no way the boy vows as he gives the insect that is feasting on his arm a disgusted glance. Court day is just too nasty even for a hardened boy like him whose gut never goes all queasy over anything he thinks. Well almost anything he adds and with that he squashes the life from the biting insect. When he looks up to his displeasure he finds the trash pile that he has been trying hard to avoid seeing staring him right in the face from across the alley, and a rather disturbing thought occurs to him. What if the child that he found in there when he first got here was the one who he was supposed to fetch out of here today? Well if she was then he has taken a whole lot of risk for nothing he thinks. She is dead and if she was his target the only thing that he can hope for now is that he still gets the promised food. After all it is not like he did anything wrong. He came when he was asked to, and he had tried to save her, but she was beyond anyone's saving he thinks as the sadness once again tries to pull at him.

...*Stop being a stupid babe Karnin...* he chastises himself as he tries to shrug off the feeling. It is not like this is the first time that he has seen someone die or anything.

"I said get out ya dirty little bugger," Karnin suddenly hears, and when he does he quickly scoots closer to the pile of rotting vegetables where he is hunkered down, for it would never do to have the wrong person find him here.

"Let go!" a youthful voice yells back.

When he hears the young boy shout Karnin's heart begins to pound in his chest, for even though he has told the other boys in his group of thieves and misfits never to come here they are a contrary lot. It is therefore possible that one of them has tried to be a hero and make a pinch for something that is not already past its prime. Luckily after listening to the young voice shout out a couple more times Karnin decides that the voice does not belong to one of his gang, for he knows every boy in it by sight, sound, and sometimes even smell. Besides, the lilt of this boy's speech is too uppity to be anyone he would even know let alone be bunking down with in a cave Karnin concludes. That comes as a big relief actually since he will not have to do anything about it now if does not want to, which at this point he does not.

As one might expect once Karnin's relief passes his natural curiosity starts to kick in and he begins to wonder who the unfortunate thief is, for it is not too often that a kid from the upper crust falls on hard times. That would explain why he got caught stealing him not having much experience at pinching and all. Not that it matters much to Karnin since he has no intention of putting his own self on the line for whoever it is. Still Karnin does sort of pity the fool, for if he has been caught with his hand in the larder of this place he will not just loose his hand his life will most likely be forfeit as well, and if he is some uppity guy's by-blow he probably will not even get a trial. No there is always some guy wanting to get even with some other guy who would jump at the chance to off the other guy's favorite child in this place. Unfortunately, a familiar man's voice rings out then, and when it does Karnin suddenly realizes that the poor boy's luck has indeed run dry.

"Tok," Karnin whispers, and then involuntarily pulls his body further back into the shadows of the heap, for Tok is a big mean bastard who is best avoided especially when he is in one of his killing moods, which from the smell of this place today he is.

"That's my mother's!" Karnin hears the unknown boy shout, and when he does he wonders if the boy is incredibly brave or hopelessly stupid.

"Yeah...well now it's mine," Karnin hears Tok reply, and then he hears the laughter of two other men, which does not surprise him much since Tok always keeps a couple of toadies around him to stroke him when he needs it.

"Shut your mouth afore Tok takes the skin off that scrawny back boy," Karnin hears one of the other men say, and then he hears the thud of a booted foot striking a body.

"You're a thief!!" Karnin hears the boy's pained voice accuse.

By this time Karnin's curiosity can no longer be quelled, for even though he is a street wise boy he is no less inquisitive than any other boy of thirteen, and so he carefully makes a small hole in a half rotted brarny fruit that is conveniently lying near the top of the pile he is hiding behind. He then puts a tentative eye to the hole, and when he discovers that he can see out to the other side of the heap through it he gives his own back a mental pat for being clever enough to think of doing it. His preening does not last long

3

however, for to his disappointment all that he can see through the stupid hole is knees to crotch, which is not something that he has the slightest wish to look at he thinks with a frown. Karnin therefore slides over and slowly peers around the side of the slimy pile just in time to see a gaunt boy with a nest of tangled golden brown hair launch himself at Tok. To Karnin's amazement and horror, the skinny boy delivers first a hard kick to Tok's shin after which he follows it up with a few well placed but ineffective hits to Tok's beefy body.

"Stupid..." Karnin whispers as he shoves a stray lock of greasy dark hair behind his ear, but still he cannot help feeling a bit of satisfaction, for he has wanted to do that to Tok for a long time.

"Why ya little bastard..." Tok mutters and then he grabs the boy by the scruff of his tattered shirt and promptly punches him square in the face, which either knocks him out or kills him, for the boy's body immediately goes limp.

"Hot-headed thing ain't he," says one of the other two men who Karnin recognizes as Tok's personal bodyguard and boot lick Bandin.

"Just like his mother," Tok says and then spits on the ground in disgust and adds, "She fought like a hellion...in the end I won a course."

"What you gonna do with him?" asks the third man, and although Karnin does not know that one's name he does recognize him as one of the house guards.

"Looks like I ain't got a do nothing with him...he's dead," Tok replies, and then he grabs a handful of the unconscious boy's tangled curls and forces his head up before he adds, "No great loss."

"What've you done Tok?!" Karnin hears a familiar voice suddenly demand, and then a rather stocky dark haired well-dressed man strides over and angrily accuses, "You told overlord Galwor they ran away!"

"Yeah well they did...found the boy lying out here... didn't get too far did he...stupid boy," Tok gives the boy's body a shake and says.

"Why not let me take him off your hands Tok...I've need of an armor boy," the man replies, and then he turns his head and looks directly at Karnin before turning his gaze back to Tok. That understandably unnerves Karnin a bit, for Boro always seems to be able to find him no matter how good he hides unlike that dope Tok who could not spot a big old bondel in a bare field.

"His mother's a faithless whore..." Karnin hears Tok say, and when he does Karnin's eyes narrow angrily, for not all whores are faithless some of them are decent women he thinks as he slowly slides a rotted unknown vegetable to the side so that he can see better.

"Aye well so was yours," Boro angrily retorts, and then gives Tok a threatening stare and adds, "Caring for the boy's part a the deal you made with the overlord."

"Yeah well deal's off Boro..." Tok informs him and after he peers into the boy's face for a minute he lets him fall to the ground like a rag doll and says, "He's dead."

"Where's his mother?" Boro softly asks as he kneels to place a hand on the boy's chest, but although Tok is too stupid to notice Karnin does not miss the moment of relief that crosses Boro's features before he quickly schools it away.

"Ah well...she come back sick...fever took her last night," Tok replies, and then he talks down his nose at Boro, "Guess that's what she got fer trying ta run off."

"I'll see to them Tok..." Boro says without looking up, which is most likely a good thing, for even though Tok is too stupid to read the message that Boro's fingers are playing on the hilt of his knife he is not quite dumb enough not to recognize the murderous expression on Boro's face.

"You'd like that wouldn't ya Boro...so's you could tell Galwor how I insulted his precious Myna's memory..." Tok accuses in a sarcastic way, and with that he turns and stomps away with his toady following close on his heels, but before he steps back inside he turns back and points a finger at Boro and warns, "I'll be your overlord one day...I'd keep that in mind before you go running to Galwor if I's you."

"Gonna off myself that day," the guardsman who had come out with Tok remarks once the door shuts behind him.

"Looney's a damn tooka," Boro angrily mumbles with a shake of his head, and then he sends the guard a stern glance and adds, "Better not let him see you talking to me or you'll find a rope round your neck next time you pull night watch."

"Yeah well it ain't right about him my lord," the guard gestures to the boy's body and says, and then he adds with a tinge of regret,

"What was he now...seven...eight...Tok'd no right ta lay a hand to him..."

"Yeah well it doesn't matter anymore does it?" Boro interrupts him to say, and then he stands and as he stares down at the motionless boy at his feet he sadly adds, "And he was nine...go on in...I'd like a minute alone with him."

"Can't my lord...Tok'll lop off my rod," the man carefully replies, for even though he fears Tok nay saying lord Boro is not wise either.

"Tok hears you calling me that title he'll toss you in the tank..." Boro says with one of those censuring one-eyed looks that Karnin knows so well.

"That ain't right neither...unlike him you got a right to it..." the man protests.

"Be silent you...you've a wife and a babe on the way...now go...you've my word that his mother won't be alone in the damn box when they burn it," Boro angrily tells him.

"Yeah okay...I trust you sir," the man replies, but the minute the door shuts on him Boro beckons to Karnin.

"There's no time to explain...take him to the cave...I'll be over later with the food," Boro tells him as he stands and begins searching the trash heaps.

"There's one over there," Karnin squints over at him and says, for he knows what Boro is trying to find and why, and so he points to the small pile of garbage nearby and says a bit too nonchalantly, "It's a girl but she's the right size."

"She alive when you got here?" Boro demands as he heads for the pile of garbage that Karnin had indicated, for despite his bravado Boro has known him long enough to see that Karnin is shaken up a bit about finding this one.

"Yeah...but she was out all night...she didn't last long..." Karnin replies with a frown, for after he had pulled some garbage over her to try to warm her a bit she had taken a few fitful breaths, and then was gone.

"Ah damn you Tok..." Boro mumbles when he pulls aside the garbage and sees the damage that had been done to the girl's body, for the child is Galwor's last remaining bastard, and so it is no mystery who it was who would have wanted her dead.

"Don't know if I can carry him all the way back Boro," Karnin comments as he watches Boro bow his head a second before he determinedly pulls the young girl's body from the rubbish and quickly slices off her long hair with his knife.

"You find a way Karnin or you'll never get anything from me again," Boro says as he levels a heated gaze on him, and after he removes his jacket and wraps the girl in it he strides away.

As the door to the inner keep slams shut behind Boro Karnin sighs, for he would rather have had an armful of food to carry than this stupid boy. Besides, if there is one thing that Karnin has learned in his young life it is that promises often amount to nothing, and so he has his doubts as to whether or not the promised food will be forthcoming today at all. Oh it will come if he takes on Boro's pet here, but that will not be tonight most likely, and if Karnin shows up with another mouth to feed and no food the other boys will most likely vote him not the leader anymore. With a curse that no boy of his age should even be familiar with let alone say Karnin fixes his angry eyes upon the unconscious boy, but he knows that he has no choice other than to find a way to get him out of here. Well not unless he wants to starve to death at any rate.

As far as what the other boys have to say about it Karnin decides that he will simply talk his way around it like he always does. With that he crouches down to peer into the boy's face, for Boro made it clear that he wanted him to stay alive, and even at the tender age of thirteen Karnin knows better than to toss away such a lucrative relationship as he has with Boro over one boy. That is a pretty good pitch Karnin thinks with an enlightened cock of his head, and with a nod he decides that he will sell bringing home another mouth to feed by telling them that Boro will probably bring them better stuff to eat now that one of his favorite lordlings is with them, for Karnin knows that the boy at his feet is a somebody. Even though he does not know who this Myna person is he can tell by the way Boro acted just now that her son is more important to him than any of the other kids that he has smuggled out he thinks as he reaches over to prod the unconscious boy, and when he does he realizes just how bony he really is.

...*Great*... Karnin thinks as he studies him, for his small size for his age coupled with the gauntness of his body tells Karnin that he is probably one of those sickly types that never live very long.

"Gonna die anyway," Karnin petulantly mumbles as he crouches down and shakes him a bit.

7

However when the boy softly moans instead of being glad that he is still alive Karnin curses, for it would have been better for Karnin if Tok's blow had killed the kid rather than having to watch another of Galwor's cast offs waste away. As it is Karnin has had to bury four of overlord Galwor's unwanted spawn to date, and this boy will make five, for he has the thick golden brown curls said to be Galwor's family trait. That and his refined lilt convince Karnin that he must be Galwor's son to whomever this Myna woman is. Probably some poor whore who did not deserve to get herself beat to death by Tok. To top it off this boy's small size and the odd color of his skin tells Karnin that he has been starved and abused for quite some time, which is not a surprise either, for overlord Galwor lets Tok get rid of whatever and whoever the overlord wants to be rid of, and Tok being the sick bastard that he is likes to drag things out for as long as he can.

Thinking on Galwor and Tok brings to mind what Boro once said about them, for from what Karnin has seen Boro was quite right when he said that they were two of a kind. They must be since Galwor seems completely comfortable with how Tok gets rid of anyone who he deems to be useless to him. Old folk, crippled up soldiers and even his own bastard children are considered disposable in the perverse world that Galwor has created since the old overlord's death or at least that is what Karnin has heard said since Galwor's father was before Karnin's time. Of course Tok is only too happy to take care of Galwor's less pleasant business, for he is truly warped. Although Tok is usually very careful to keep his hands clean by letting them die on their own, but he always beats and starves them near to death before he tosses them into this alley to make sure just like he did with that girl that Karnin found earlier.

Just like he tried to do to the boy at Karnin's feet, but this time Tok got played at his own game, and Karnin has a sneaking suspicion that Boro had a hand in that. If he did it is the first time that Karnin has seen one of Boro's plans go bad, for the only reason that the boy is still kicking is because Tok is a ham fisted bully who relies on brute strength rather than precision. The truth of it is that if Tok's blow had been just a tad more upward he would have killed this boy for sure, but like most bullies Tok has no need for any deep thinking, which is good since he is surely too stupid for it anyway. This boy is very lucky that he is, for Tok just assumed that no puny kid could survive one of his infamous killing

8

punches, and so did not check very closely to make sure that he was dead.

All things considered Karnin simply cannot figure out how someone as stupid as Tok has managed to stay alive all these years, but he guesses it is because he gets rid of anyone who he thinks might want him dead. Not this time though Karnin reminds himself. Still as Karnin watches the boy's bony chest rise and fall he wonders if it might not be best to help Tok instead of Boro this time, for this little somebody will probably be a danger to take in if Tok ever learns of it Karnin thinks, and so to bring him amongst them might very well spell disaster. He therefore tosses around the idea of giving the unfortunate creature another bash in the face, for just another small blow to the boy's nose would most likely finish him off. Karnin will just tell Boro that the new boy had up and died from that punch that Tok gave him. Boro would not be too surprised by that. After all he could not have missed noting that the kid is already pretty sick, but Karnin's decision is made for him when the boy suddenly sits up.

"I...I can't see...I can't see!!!" he shouts in a panic.

"Be quiet ...they'll hear you," Karnin urgently whispers, for the last time that he had a run in with Tok it cost him two teeth, and he would very much like to keep the ones that grew in to replace them since no more will be forthcoming.

"I'm blind!!" the boy shrieks as he gropes around, and for some inexplicable reason when he finds and latches onto Karnin's hand Karnin is overcome with an overwhelming urge to protect him.

"It'll come back...he broke your nose and your eyes're swelled shut's all," Karnin replies, and then he pulls the boy to his feet and firmly says, "Come on we got a get out a here before someone comes."

With no further conversation on it Karnin quickly tugs the boy back through the alley's obstacle course of rotting vegetables and discarded carcasses slipping from one pile of who-knows-what to the next with the expertise of someone who has done so many times before. The truth of it is that Karnin has been full-time on his own for several years now and part-time for a few years before that even. The end result is that he has acquired some rather useful skills a lot of boys his age do not have such as how to move from one side of the village to the other without ever stepping out of the shadows, for a boy on his own in the mean streets of *Filon Bora's* village who cannot become invisible eventually ends up toes up in one of the fortress's piles waiting for his turn in the garbage renderer. Karnin therefore moves along the alley in a seamless dance from one darkened nook to the next shadowy cranny.

It is not long before the two boys reach the place where the alley ends, and when they do Karnin melts into the shadows along the last building's wall taking the boy with him, for the area ahead is a major thoroughfare for those moving in and out of the inner keep's main gate. It therefore stands to reason that anyone who walks into the area is a potential target for the gate guards. Today however the area is packed with people waiting to get into the fortress, for court day brings out all the whiners and complainers who have come to seek the overlord's justice. Of course one of his minor lords deals with that sort of crap but they still do it in the inner keep. Then there are the usual gawkers and busybodies who have only come for the show. All in all it is a stroke of good luck, for with so many people milling about the gate the guards have plenty of poor souls to pick from, which makes Karnin's odds of getting across to the alley on the opposite side without being spotted better than usual.

Still they must be careful not to cause a jam up when they cut across the flow of foot traffic, for even though the guards are not really very competent they are not blind, and with so many people coming in and out Karnin expects that there will be several more guards here than usual. Sure enough he soon picks out uniformed men circulating through the crowd in groups of two. That is a problem, for even though Karnin is fairly confident that he could make it through without too much trouble he has his doubts as to whether or not his sickly charge will be able to keep up. Besides with a face like he has got now everyone will notice him. Then again maybe not Karnin corrects when a man with a bruised and battered face is led out of the inner keep by an old woman. Apparently they did not like whatever gripe he came to make Karnin supposes.

With a frustrated sigh Karnin decides that they will either have to do the 'beaten up griper' routine or back track to one of his hiding spots and wait for darkness to fall. Before he can decide though a sudden commotion erupts from somewhere inside the gate and as Karnin watches in disbelief the guards all shove their way through the throngs towards it. They soon disappear inside leaving only one lone gate guard sitting in the gatehouse, and at this point Karnin hops up and drags the boy by the sleeve into the crowd, which is actually harder to do than it sounds since everyone is now pressing towards the gate in an effort to see what poor slobs are getting beat up by the guards for disrupting things. Eventually Karnin manages to wiggle his way amongst them without losing the boy, but it was a struggle to be sure. Unfortunately his little charge is obviously running out of energy, which although it is no big surprise him being sick and all it is an inconvenient time for it to happen.

Karnin therefore considers taking a shortcut by circumventing the crowd all together. It would be quick since they are all gathered round gawking at the gate. Unfortunately it would also make it easy for the guard in the gatehouse to spot them. There is always one of those, and the rules are that he cannot leave it only call for help if he sees something Karnin recalls as he cranes his neck in an attempt to see the guardhouse through the throng. To his surprise when he finally manages to get eyes on the guard he simply cannot believe who it is, for there dozing at his post is the guardsman that he and his boys call Drunk Dim so named for his addictive ways as well as his rather dull wits. Good fortune never lasts very long though Karnin thinks with a sense of urgency as he hurriedly skirts the crowd with the boy in tow, but when at last they gain the safety of shadows in the alley on the other side Karnin pulls the tattered boy next to him and then sends him a suspicious glance, for he has to wonder if Boro's pet brat is somehow charmed.

It certainly seems as if he is Karnin thinks as he tosses things round in his head. First Tok gives him a blow that should have killed him but did not. Then a fight breaks out and clears out all but one guard who just so happens to be Drunk Dim. Everybody knows that that Drunk Dim's never on day watch especially on court day. Yes maybe he will pitch that charmed thing to the other boys Karnin thinks with a shrug, for some of them are a bit on the superstitious side, and so tossing some spooky stuff in there might go a long way. Stuff like that thing he felt when the boy grabbed his hand. If the boy is charmed that would explain it quite nicely Karnin thinks. That sort of thinking only serves to make Karnin suspect that his own wits have gone the way of Drunk Dim's, for he has never believed in such tripe as hexes and charms, and he is certainly not going to start now. With that he hauls the boy to his feet and hurries on, and when he and the boy disappear down the alley the owner of the dark eyes watching him from the fortress's roof turns away, for he has seen what he came up here to see.

11

Down in the alley Karnin is unaware that his exit with his new charge has not gone unnoticed for he is busy trying to put some logic into how he feels when it comes to Boro's pet. Unfortunately, no matter how Karnin twists it he still cannot explain the protectiveness that this new boy elicits in him any other way than as some supernatural thing. After all he is no one to him, and even though he is several years younger than him some of the others that Boro brought out of Galwor's keep were as well and Karnin didn't feel much for them. So why does he feel this way? It is totally illogical and definitely not leader-like, for good leaders do not make decisions based on feelings they decide stuff on the facts. The whole thing is just too frustrating he thinks as he taps his left hand impatiently against his thigh. He has not the luxury of caring about anyone else to this degree, but anymore thought on it is curtailed when the boy suddenly begins to resist going any further.

"Wait...please," he gasps out with a tug.

"We got a keep moving," Karnin gruffly replies and then pulls him into a narrow side street, for the narrow streets that are nearly deserted now will soon be filled with people headed home from the trials. They must be long gone by then.

"Where're you taking me?" the boy asks as he stumbles over his own feet, but Karnin quickly pulls him back up.

"To a safe place," Karnin curtly replies, and then he says as he continues on, "We got a hurry up."

"Wait," the boy says and then he digs in his heels and adds, "I got a go back and get my mother's ring!"

"You nuts or something...Tok'll kill you!" Karnin replies with an incredulous expression on his face.

"I'm not gonna let that lying bastard keep my mother's ring!" the boy argues.

"You can't even see..." Karnin smugly points out.

"I can see some now..." the boy insists as he manages to get his right eye to open a tiny slit.

"Listen you...you go back there now and you're dead," Karnin angrily tells him.

"I'm getting it back," the boy stubbornly replies, and then he heatedly adds, "Even if I got a pry it off his cold dead finger."

With that the boy yanks his arm from Karnin's grasp and slowly limps back the way they had come, but since he was lying about being able to see he runs smack into the first building that rises up in his path. When he does a slow grin spreads across Karnin's face, for he finally has his answer as to the why of it that he feels so drawn to this boy. He has balls as big as he is tall; not so good at lying apparently, but he is no cowering pansy that is for sure, and that is something that Karnin can actually relate to. Still he is probably used to telling other poor slobs what to do, but if he is to join their group then he must get it straight in his head who is the boss. Karnin therefore lets him wander about aimlessly running into this and that for a time until he grows tired of watching him fall down.

"Ballsy...but crazy's a tooka though," Karnin mumbles, as he watches the new kid pick himself up yet again and start groping along the wall that knocked him down, and with a shake of his head he sprints after him.

"You go that way you'll end up in the slaughter yard," Karnin grabs his arm and says.

"Thanks," the boy replies and then he adds, "Just point me the right way and forget about me."

"You got a plan then?" Karnin asks as he grabs the boy's sleeve and covertly turns him back the way that they had been going.

"Nope," he replies matter-of-factly as he wipes the blood from his nose with the back of his hand, and after he cleans off his hand on his pants he adds with a shrug, "But something'll come to me."

"You'll get yourself dead," Karnin tells him.

"Maybe...but I'm gonna make him dead too then," he replies and then stops to pull a small blade from his boot for Karnin's inspection.

"Why not wait until you're big enough to just make only him dead and you not dead?" Karnin inquires.

"Don't think I'll ever be big enough for that," the boy replies and then tries to squint up at him.

"One day I'm gonna have my own army," Karnin informs him, and then magnanimously offers, "I'll kill him for you then if you're still too puny to."

"Well..." the boy stops and says, and after a few seconds of contemplation, exhaustion finally overtakes the adrenaline pumping through him just as Karnin thought it eventually would, and he adds with some emotion, "Okay...but you got a do it the way I say."

"Dead's dead," Karnin replies with a shrug of his own, "What's it matter?"

"I want him to die the way my mother did."

13

"How's that?"

"Painfully slow," the boy replies, but when he reaches up to push a stray lock of hair from his face and Karnin notes the cuff bruises on his bony wrists he does not ask him anymore questions. There is no need to.

"People'll be coming back soon...we better get moving... come on," Karnin clears his throat and commands.

After he grabs the boy by the sleeve Karnin heads into another dank narrow alley, and from there to another. In this manner they traverse the remainder of the village, and are soon standing on the slight rise that lies beyond it. By now Karnin has had time to study the young boy limping beside him, and it makes him wonder how he managed to survive what Tok put him through. Not too many kids could, for judging by the numerous wounds and bruises that cover his thin body Tok was especially determined that he die a mean death. Such interest as that only adds to Karnin's growing suspicion as to his identity, for if he is one of Galwor's by-blows then that would explain why Tok hated him. Tok would see him as a threat. Then again rumor has it that Tok is the only one left of Galwor's blood. Tok might have put that rumor out too soon Karnin thinks as he slides the boy a covert glance.

Why Tok needs to kill this runt of a boy is the question. After all Tok is in a sweet place, for Galwor has no real sons and since Tok is the eldest of his bastards he will inherit Galwor's title and lands. This kid is not going to change that. So why was Tok so bent on killing him then? Whatever the reason it was important enough to make Tok get his hands dirty in a public place. Maybe Tok is afraid that this boy would kill him one day like Tok did everybody else. Or maybe somebody might kill Tok for him before Galwor dies. Somebody who knows his way round *Filon Bora* and is high enough up to get away with it.

"How much farther?" the boy suddenly asks, and when he does Karnin can see that he is pretty done in.

"Not far...just keep trudging and we'll be there before you know it," Karnin replies as they pass the now meaningless warning buoy for the broken down old security field that once defended the fortress's village.

The two boys walk along in silence then, for Karnin knows that the boy next to him is struggling just to put one foot in front of the other, and since he would rather not have to lug him he keeps his mouth shut for a time. Thankfully they do not have far to go now, for ahead is the small rise that marks the valley of holes one of which is Karnin and his gang's hideout. Well it is not really a proper hideout, for everyone knows that the valley of holes is there. Still there are a lot of holes so Karnin supposes it still qualifies as a hideout of sorts. At this point they crest the hill and see below them the shadowy v-shaped depression, and when they do Karnin thinks that he best go over his speech in his head, for when the others see that his hands are empty he will need to start talking before anyone decides to hit him. In the process of talking it out he realizes that there is one important thing that he forgot about.

"So what name do you answer to?" he asks as they descend into the small valley, for if he is to garner any support for the new boy staying he will have to make the others feel sorry for him, which is hard to do without a name.

"Torli," he replies.

"I'm Karnin and if you want a stay with us you got a agree to do what I say...cause I'm the leader here...got it?" Karnin pauses to inform him.

"So long as you promise not to punch me in the face...ever...it hurts a lot," Torli turns his head towards him and candidly replies.

"Done," Karnin agrees, and then he grabs Torli's hand and as he puts it on his shoulder he says, "Here...hang onto my shirt and don't let go...path's skinny and it's kind a far down."

With a vigorous nod Torli latches onto Karnin's shirt as if his life depends upon it, which Karnin actually gets him being sickly and almost blind at the moment and all. As he leads Torli along, the narrow winding path becomes increasingly harder to traverse, for it is pockmarked with various holes left behind by boulders that have become dislodged and now rest at the bottom of the valley. Karnin is therefore forced to slow down and pause often to help Torli around some relatively sizable hole or across an unusually narrow spot in the path. Luckily it is not too long before Karnin sees the familiar bushes and other greenery rising up to block the way ahead, but when he reaches what appears to be the end of the path he just shoves aside a few branches and keeps on walking, for he knows that the way ahead is doable he does it all the time.

Not when he is toting a skinny blind kid though, which Karnin discovers makes a whole lot of difference, and as he stops to untangle Torli's sleeve from yet another clinging branch he is very glad that the entrance to the cave that he and his boys call home is

15

not far into the thicket. So it is that after a bit of tugging and pulling they finally reach the place where Karnin knows the cave entrance to be, but no one else would since Karnin and his friends have camouflaged the entrance with a blanket that is done-up to resemble the rocks around it. Well it does when someone has not forgotten to close the thing properly Karnin corrects when he notices that the blanket is not all the way across the opening at the bottom. With a disgusted shake of his head Karnin shoves the blanket aside and then quickly pushes Torli in. Karnin then takes a quick peek round for prying eyes, and when he sees nothing untoward ducks inside as well.

When Karnin straightens up what he sees is just as it should be, for Torli is standing in the middle of the small cave desperately trying to force his right eye open so that he can see the owners of the voices who are shouting at him. All things considered Karnin thinks that it is probably just as well that Torli cannot do it. It would probably scare the crap out of him, for the other boys are preparing to tie him up, which Torli would most likely not let them do without a fight. Since that would not be a good way for everyone to meet Karnin steps next to Torli, and after he tells the other boys that Boro sent him to them he introduces Torli around. Afterwards he breaks the unfortunate news to them that Boro did not have the promised food with him, but to Karnin's surprise nobody makes too big of a fuss about it, which kind of irritates him. After all he had a pretty good pitch worked out that he will not get to use now. That is how it always goes he thinks as he strips off his alley clothes and puts on his cleaner everyday set.

In light of his empty hands Karnin calls in everyone's holdings, finds and takes for the day, and after a bit of shaming and bullying he is satisfied that everyone has turned out his pockets completely. As they stand gathered round the disappointingly small pile taking stock of what they have the boys realize that their dinner tonight will be meager indeed, but it is not the first time that has been the case nor will it be the last either they suspect. Therefore as they have done numerous times before they get down to stretching what is probably not even enough to feed one man into a meal for many hungry bellies. When all was said and done they tossed the two scrawny birds that the youngest boys managed to kill with their rock slings into their only real pot along with the wilted vegetables swiped from the crap hole digger's kitchen, added a whole lot of water, and then commenced to boiling the very essence out of it.

16

After staring at the boiling pot with their mouths watering for what seems like hours it does not take them long to divvy up the resultant soupy mush between them and slurp it down. When that is done most of the boys then opt to curl up in their blankets until Boro shows up, for they have learned from past experience that the best way to deal with a less than satisfied stomach is to go to sleep. Despite the growling of his gut Karnin finds that he is more in need of a bit of time to ponder over the day's events than to silence his belly, and so after he hands Torli his own blanket and puts him in the cozy nook in the far corner where the younger boys are curled up Karnin sits staring into the dying fire mulling things over for a time.

Patience however is not one of Karnin's better suits and so he gets tired of thinking about the same old stuff rather quickly. He therefore reaches into one of the oversized pockets that he has sewn into his pants to retrieve the hand weapon that he found in the village dump yesterday, for he has had no time to actually study it yet. Unfortunately, it is not long before he becomes bored with that too, for he knows next to nothing about hand weapons. Even so he can pretty much guess that since it was in the dump it is beyond fixing. Still it would be great if he could get it working again, for to have a hand weapon would make hunting for game possible. Well it would make hunting for game successful since it is already possible to hunt with a knife or throwing spike it is what they do now. Unfortunately bringing something down that way is rather hard, and most of the time they come home empty handed.

"So why'd you bring that new boy here anyway," a familiar gravelly voice interrupts Karnin's thoughts to ask as its owner sits down next to him.

"Boro wanted me to...and I like eating once in awhile," Karnin replies as he continues to study the weapon in his hand.

"Didn't want a say in front a the rest but he's gonna be a lot a trouble...he's pretty sick..."

"Yeah...I know Han," is all Karnin replies, for he and Han have been friends for a long time and more often than not Karnin lets him say what is on his mind, but mostly because Han is going to anyway it is just the way he is.

"If you turn that part there it'll open up," Han suddenly says and then he points a finger to the small pivot switch on the weapon in Karnin's hand.

"I suppose you know all about it," Karnin sarcastically tells him.

17

"My father taught me about hand weapons before he got killed," Han tells him.

"Yeah...I know...you told me...he traveled with the old overlord's army and fixed stuff for them," Karnin says with an impatient sigh, for Han never seems to tire of telling that tale. Then again Karnin probably would not either had it been his father, and so he dumps the weapon into Han's lap and adds a bit more kindly, "I guess you better show me then....before I break it."

"Yeah well it's already broke sorry to say," Han informs him as he takes a closer look at the piece.

"Yeah...I figured it must be," Karnin says.

"Might be able to fix it though," Han tells him, and then he explains as he turns a pivot bar on the side of the weapon, which in turn causes its nose cover to snap open, "You flip this thing here then it's ready...see...but it ain't all here...no power pack you know...it goes in that hole there."

"What's it look like?" Karnin asks, for weapons of any kind are good to have, and if this one can be fixed up they would have an advantage over most of the village's gangs.

"Small square thing about so big," Han replies and then demonstrates by holding up two fingers about two inches apart.

"That's gonna be hard to find in the dump," Karnin replies, and then he adds, "You better go look soon as the sun comes up...before they bring out new stuff."

"Me!?" Han complains, and then he asks, "Hey why'd I always got a do the dirty stuff?"

"Because I say so," Karnin retorts, and then he gives Han a sideways stare and asks, "You want a be the leader?"

"Naw," Han replies with a grin, for even though he is older than Karnin by several years Han has always known that Karnin is better suited to lead than he is. Still Han thinks that his seniority should get him something, and so he says, "Just think one a the younger ones ought a go into the heap for a change."

"Well take one a them with you then...but don't take Merl...Merl never listens," Karnin instructs.

"Yeah well...don't got a worry Merl's gone again," Han replies.

"You look around for him?" Karnin asks.

"Yeah...much as I could..." Han replies with a shrug.

"He'll turn up...he's always thinking he can do better by his self...when he finds out he can't he'll be back," Karnin says with an unconcerned shrug, for Merl has always been a bit of a loner, and

Karnin learned long ago not to waste his time and resources on people like him.

"Ah well…I'll go by me self…you know…to try an find the power pack…it's easier if it's just me anyways…in case I got a run for it," Han tells him, and then he suddenly straightens up and as he reaches for his knife he whispers, "Someone's coming."

As Han jumps up and takes a position on one side of the door Karnin quickly stashes the hand weapon under a nearby blanket, grabs his own knife, and then follows suit setting his self up on the other side of the door. As the sound of footsteps grows louder Han begins to get nervous, for there is more than one set of feet making them, and Han is not exactly good at fighting despite his father's association with the army. Karnin also notes that there is more than one person approaching, and since he is fully aware of Han's somewhat clumsy fighting methods he becomes rather anxious as well. Therefore, by the time the footsteps abruptly stop just outside the entrance to their lair both boys are tensed and poised to spring upon the first person who comes through the door.

"Don't stick me boy," a familiar voice calls out just loud enough to be heard, and with a collective sigh Karnin and Han step back into the center of the small cavern, for at least one of the two persons outside is a friend.

"Where is he?" Boro asks as he shoves the curtain aside and ducks in.

"Who?" Karnin asks with a grin, but when Boro gives him the one-eye he quickly says, "He's asleep… you know he's sick Boro…I don't know…"

"Yeah…yeah…that's why I've brought Enna here," Boro informs them and then holds the curtain aside to allow a young woman to enter before saying, "She'll take care a him until he's stronger."

"But Boro…" Karnin begins, for having some soft girl hanging around is not something that Karnin is prepared to agree to.

"But nothing…you'll not interfere with her Karnin," Boro gives him a hard stare and instructs, and then he narrows his eyes on Han who is watching Enna with a bit too much interest or so Boro thinks.

"What's in it for us then Boro," Karnin draws himself up to his full height and asks, and then for good measure he boldly fingers his blade.

"How old're you now boy?" Boro asks.

"I'm soon fourteen," Karnin haughtily replies.

"You're just turned thirteen," Boro reminds him with a snort, and then he adds, "Best to think about it hard before you try to bluff a grown man boy...he might just take you up on it."

"So why's this Torli so important anyway?" Karnin swallows his anger to ask, and then he unflinchingly adds, "You never brought a nursemaid for any a the others."

"Where's he at?" Boro sternly asks.

"Over there...with the younger ones," Karnin hooks his thumb towards the huddled forms in the far corner, and as Enna picks her way through the sleeping boys strewn about the cave floor Karnin adds, "Just so you know he's got my blanket on."

"Enna's got a couple for him so you can have it back then," Boro replies, and as he once again takes note of Han's interest in Enna he adds, "You'll get a couple more for the rest a you and some extra food if you and your band a thieves keeps quiet about Torli there."

"Only if you tell me who he is," Karnin replies, and for a second wonders if he has made a huge mistake, for he can see the glint of anger in Boro's eyes.

"Outside," Boro orders him, and then emphasizes his request by holding the curtain open for him to duck out, which after a moment of consideration Karnin does, but before Boro follows he reaches over and grabs Han by the shirt front and asks, "So how old're you then?"

"Fifteen two days ago," Han replies with an audible swallow.

"That's what I thought," Boro replies, and then he pulls Han a bit closer and says, "Listen you...Enna there's practically engaged and I've given my word to her family that she'll be safe here so if you get any ideas about her I'd advise you to forget them...you got that?"

"Got it," Han replies, and Boro can see by the embarrassed flush on Han's face that he had guessed right about his interest in his pretty young charge.

With a grunt Boro releases him with a shove for good measure and then ducks out of the dimly lit cave and into the pitch black of the night. Of course Karnin is not there by the door waiting whatever made him think that he would be? No the contrary young fool will make Boro come to him instead of the other way round as it should be considering Boro's age and rank. Karnin is rather arrogant for a damn beggar Boro thinks, but it is that same sense of self importance that makes Karnin the exact boy to groom for his purposes. Well that and who he is, for even though Karnin does not know it yet he is not exactly a nobody, which is why when Boro finally locates him he takes a calming breath before he walks over to him.

"Don't question me in front a the others again," Boro commands, and then he adds, "A leader should never set himself up for a public reprimand...it makes him appear weak."

"Rumor's gonna go round just as soon as anybody sees that hair a his..." Karnin replies, and then he adds, "I got a right to know if Tok's gonna come looking."

"You've a right to know whatever I say you do...unless you want a walk away from our little arrangement," Boro threatens.

"Maybe we'd all be doing better if I did," Karnin counters.

"Do you really think they'll follow you when you've naught to offer them but empty bellies?" Boro asks with an amused snicker.

"Look Boro...I got a think a everyone not just this Torli," Karnin replies, and although Boro does not detect an inkling of apology in his words he decides not to call him on it, for that Karnin may be thinking like a leader and not the loner that he was when Boro first found him in the streets is a milestone.

"Torli's quite brilliant Karnin...he's book learned and's got some training in the use a primitive and modern weapons," Boro replies.

"Sounds like someone's special pet," Karnin replies a bit jealously.

"He did nothing to deserve what happened to him," Boro answers, but he can tell by the dubious expression on Karnin's face that he will not be satisfied unless he tells him something more, and so he adds with a sigh, "Galwor gave his mother to Tok...but she...didn't want him... and now that she's dead Tok doesn't want a be bothered with Torli...Torli's another man's son."

"I kind a figured it was something like that," Karnin says, for even though he has not yet found an interest in women his own self he has seen enough whores servicing their customers to know what Boro means by 'she didn't want him'.

"At any rate in the end Torli's mother tried to run but Tok caught her...he chained her and Torli up and made her watch him abuse and starve Torli for weeks...and then he made Torli watch him do the same to his mother... she took the fever and died then...and through it all Torli could do nothing but try to comfort her from across the room where Tok had him shackled to the wall," Boro quietly says with a shake of his head.

21

"If you knew why didn't you save her?" Karnin asks angry that Boro let such a thing happen, for Karnin knows that Boro has his ways around things in Galwor's keep.

"Don't you dare take that tone with me boy," Boro angrily grinds out, for it is bad enough that he must live with the fact that he did not know that Myna and Torli were still there in the fortress without some snot nosed boy pushing his face in it. Myna and Torli were supposed to be on their way to the safe place that he had arranged for them, and the anger he feels over the fact that they never made it makes him grab Karnin by the front of his shirt and pulls him close to say between his clenched teeth, "You've no idea what I did or didn't do!"

Karnin can see that he has pushed Boro too far, and he can also see that he is deeply disturbed by what happened to Torli and his mother, which only serves to heighten Karnin's curiosity, for that Boro seems to be more attached to this Torli than he was to any of Galwor's other bastards who he tried to rescue puzzles Karnin. It makes him wonder if maybe Torli is not Galwor's bastard at all. That information Karnin wisely decides to milk from Torli later rather than ask Boro, for Boro is obviously in no mood for questions tonight, and so Karnin lets the silence drag on between them until he cannot take it any longer.

"Torli was gonna go back to get his mother's ring...but I stopped him...told him I'd get it back for him one day if he couldn't do it his own self," Karnin uncomfortably remarks for lack of anything better to say.

"You shouldn't make promises you can't keep Karnin...men don't follow men who do that for long," Boro warns him.

"Oh I'm gonna keep it," Karnin assures him.

"You'd 'ave to kill Tok to get that ring back boy," Boro tells him with a shake of his head.

"I know," Karnin says in a calm, calculating way that makes Boro nervously eyeball him.

"You'd better learn how to fight a bunch a men at the same time then...Tok's never gonna fight you fair," Boro informs him in an attempt to discourage Karnin from such a hair brained thing at least until he is grown enough to actually do it at any rate.

"I'll learn," Karnin replies and then pats the knife that hangs on his belt.

22

"You'll need something bigger than that puny knife," Boro retorts with a short bark of laughter, and then he adds, "You're gonna need a good plan and a damn army boy."

After giving Karnin an amused slap on the shoulder Boro turns and ducks back inside. Karnin for his part just stands there for a time trying to get his temper under control, for he does not like being made sport of. No he had gotten his fill of that sort of thing from his step father, for Mont had never tired of trying to grind him under his heel. It was his constant abuse that drove Karnin from the house that once belonged to his mother Ornea; the house that Karnin's father set her up in that should have become his when she passed not that thieving bastard's that she married after Karnin's father died. She should never have married Mont he was not very nice to her. Unfortunately she needed to have a man around to protect her and her girls, for Karnin's mother was the madam of one of the village's houses of pleasure, and so there was always some drunk guy who needed bounced out. It is how such places are.

As Karnin stands there trying to get his temper under control a cool breeze suddenly blows in and catches his hair gently lifting it up and tossing it about, and when it does Karnin can almost feel his mother's hands working the comb through it as she was wont to do every night before bed. That thought only makes Karnin all the angrier; for she should not be dead Mont should be dead. After all Mont was the bad guy. He was the bastard who made his mother go back to working the beds of her own house. He was the reason she got sick, and he was the reason she died too, for he would not even send for a healer to help her until it was too late. No if there was any real justice in the world Mont should at least be dead too, and one day Karnin is going to personally fix that.

*...And get back what should a been mine...*Karnin vows, and with a renewed sense of determination he turns and ducks back inside.

Chapter Two

As Karnin emerges from the inner keep he cannot help but pause to take in the sight before him, for everything within range of his eyes he and his motley gang created with their own hands and ingenuity. Of course more often than not it was created with someone else's stuff, but Karnin does not think that detracts from what they have accomplished in the last eight years. After all it is not like stealing what they needed made the whole thing easier quite the contrary, for they had to go out, find what they needed, and then figure out a way to pilfer it without getting caught. More often than not it was quite a challenge especially the time Han got caught making off with a big hunk of scrap shielding material. He was lucky that Ahnin was close enough to help him get away that day Karnin reminisces as he makes his way to the practice field. Yes stealing was a dangerous endeavor but it sure was a whole lot cheaper he amends with a shrug.

As he walks along the now familiar sounds of excited voices and the clang of fighting sticks coming together lulls him as no other sound could, for the sound reaffirms that he is not the only one determined to make their army the most feared in the land. That is what they will need if they want to take and hang onto *Filon Bora*, for fear is the only thing that the world understands, and nothing instills it better than a well honed army with a driving force at its heart. Contrary to what some might think Karnin knows that he is not that driving force not now at any rate. No at the moment the heart that drives their army beats in the chest of the man at the center of the group of men in the distance. Even now he is there sparring with someone who is angling for a chance to advance his position. Yes Torli has grown into a hard man to please over the years and an even tougher man to beat Karnin thinks with a perturbed expression. As it is Karnin is still waiting for that honor his own self, which is why the only way to get a place on Karnin's elite first assault team is through Torli.

Who would have thought that the sickly boy from the alley would turn out to be such an asset as he is? The answer to that question is quick to come, for Boro had always insisted that Karnin would not regret taking Torli in. As usual Boro was right although it did take Karnin many years before he was mature enough to admit that. Thinking back on the twelve years that have passed since Karnin led a blind and sick Torli to their hideout in the valley of holes makes Karnin a bit melancholy, for he never did thank Boro for all that he did for them. Then again at the time Karnin truly believed that he gave back to him in equal. Karnin now knows that he was mistaken there, but since they have not seen or heard from Boro in a very long time Karnin has never had the chance to tell him that. Hopefully the time for it has not gone the way that most things from the past have he adds.

With an impatient sigh Karnin wonders when it was that he became such a pessimist. After all Boro is well aware that Tok would like to see him dead, and Boro is much more savvy a man on a bad day than Tok is on one of his best. Besides Boro has more friends inside *Filon Bora's* walls than Tok has these days and they will help him evade the bastard's plots and plans. Unfortunately, confident thinking does not always inspire confidence, and so Karnin is still uneasy about Boro's long silence. Not even the traveling peddler who brought word to them from the south was able to say how Boro was doing. All that he could tell Karnin was that a young boy came to him with a couple tokens to cover the cost of coming north to tell the men that he would find there the news about Galwor. Karnin can only hope that it was Boro who sent the message and that he is still kicking and well, but he will have to wait and see on that. Any other choice is simply too risky he reminds himself as he reaches the men clustered round the combatants on the practice field.

"Damn it all...you've got a duck when you see the stick coming Han!" Karnin hears Torli shout.

"Yeah well believe me I would a if I'd a saw it comin'," Han's voice replies, and when he does Karnin shoulders his way through the group of men.

"I'm thinking that Han should be in charge a the transports and supplies...behind the advance," Karnin pointedly says when he emerges into the cleared area and sees Han lying on his back in the dirt.

"Agreed," Torli and Han reply in unison.

"You still need to practice your shooting Han...what if you got a defend yourself or the vehicles?" Karnin reminds him as he offers him a forearm up.

"Yeah...I know," Han replies over the men's jibes.

"Alright then...who's next!" Torli suddenly shouts.

"Me!" Karnin replies with a grin, which thoroughly redirects the men's attentions away from Han, for Torli rarely pulls his stick when he spars with Karnin, and so their matches even though short are always rather intense.

"Come on then...I got a couple minutes," Torli goads.

"So you think you can still beat me eh?" Karnin taunts as he takes the fighting stick that Han proffers to him.

"Let's see shall we?" Torli replies, and after a brief back and forth exchange Torli suddenly gives Karnin's knuckles a crack that involuntarily loosens his grip on his stick enough to allow Torli to send it flying out of his hand.

"That's twice he got you with that one there," one of the men points out.

"Yeah well...I got a hole card," Karnin retorts as he pulls his hand weapon and with a thump knocks the stick from Torli's hand.

"What're you trying to do...take off my hand?!" Torli angrily shouts.

"You a all people should a expected that," Karnin replies matter-of-factly.

"Yeah...always expect the unexpected..." someone calls out.

"Men don't always do what you think they're gonna do," another man pipes in.

"You never know..." another man begins.

"Shut up Seasle..." Torli interrupts him with an impatient gesture.

"Sorry...didn't know you's exempt from your own rules," Seasle challenges with one of his infamous dark eyed stares.

"Hey you..." Karnin warns.

"Oh yeah...commander...sir," Seasle turns to Torli and corrects with a grin that falls a tad short of respectful, but Karnin says nothing of it, for that is about as deferential a reply as anyone could hope to get from Seasle.

"You're arse's next," Torli points an angry finger at Seasle and warns, and then he turns back to Karnin and heatedly accuses, "So...honor means nothing anymore then?"

"Do you think Tok's soldiers'll fight with any kind a honor?" Karnin asks, and even though he lets Torli get away with making such a remark in front of the men Karnin sends him a look that tells him that he had best knock it off.

"No...not an honorable bone in any a them," Torli concedes with a shake of his head.

"Then it'd most likely be best to learn what to do when the fight turns mean then eh," Karnin tells him, and then he locks eyes with Torli and seriously adds, "Word's come that Galwor's dying...they doubt he'll live many more days...the time's coming quick commander."

"All right men...I've a new thing to show you!" Torli shouts after he and Karnin exchange a long knowing glance, and then he turns to a tall lanky young man with a shock of loose brown hair hanging in his face and instructs, "Bring me one Cerl."

With a hairy nod Cerl strides over to a storage box sitting near the perimeter of the practice field and pulls a second smaller metal box from. As he carries it past the crowd of men a ripple of excitement passes through their ranks, for there is no doubt that what he is carrying is a weapons' case. That usually means that the commander has built something new, for as it turns out Boro's claims of Torli's brilliance were not just spot on they were perhaps a bit understated. As it is Torli has designed several things since they came north such as the fortress's front gate mechanism and their newly built transports. He has also designed several weapons some of which are brand new designs and others remanufactured but improved versions of existing ones. Therefore, when Cerl stops in front of Torli and flips open the box's lid they all crane their necks anxious to see what new killing tool lies within the box.

"You've learned how to fire a hand weapon similar to what Tok's men've got...now you'll learn to use these," Torli says as he lifts out a small hand weapon and holds it up for their inspection.

"Sure's a bitty thing," an ogre of a man named Orn remarks, for this new weapon is half the size of the ones that he is used to firing.

"Orn'll loose the little thing in his arse crack for sure," one of the men comments.

"Yeah like he does everything else," a second man chimes in.

"Hey I can't help it if stuff don't stay where I puts it," Orn fires back with an aggravated grunt.

When Torli sees that their attention has drifted off he sighs and inclines his head for Cerl to move, which he does rather quickly, for Cerl knows exactly what the commander has in mind. So it is that as the men share a laugh at Orn's expense Torli flips the safety off, and when they cast a few more jibes Orn's way the commander points the weapon down range. By now the men are laughing it up rather loudly, and so Torli reaches up and toggles a small switch near the weapon's trigger setting it to its full strength. That should be enough to get their attention he thinks as he levels the nose of the weapon at the row of practice targets set up down field. So it is that just as Seasle spouts off some wise crack about the quantity of arse wiping paper Orn uses after his morning crap Torli squeezes the trigger.

With the distinctive thump that all weapons utilizing a force wave emit the weapon sends its concentrated surge of destruction towards Torli's intended target. However unlike the hand weapons that the men are used to using this one does not just push the long range target off its stand this one crushes it in the process. The sound of the metal target being crumpled up like so much junk apparently triggers Seasle's 'something just got mashed radar', and just as Torli thought would happen when Seasle sees the dented and misshapen target lying on the ground he nudges the man next to him who turns to see and then elbows the man standing next to him who gives the man next to him a slap on the arm. The various pokes, slaps, and elbows continue to pass through the crowd until after a few seconds Torli has their complete and undivided attention once again.

"Don't let the size fool you," Torli informs them and then levels the nose of the weapon on another target and pulls the trigger.

This time all eyes see the resultant havoc wreaked upon the target, and so Torli reaches down and returns the weapon's mode switch to its less powerful stun position. This time, when he sends his shot down range instead of mutilating the target it is only shoved up into the air to land several feet from its original position. It goes without saying that it is not as awe inspiring a shot as the one before, but even so the men are still duly impressed since the targets are designed to be similar in weight and size to a fully grown man. Of course the older larger model hand weapon could do the same on stun, but still that Torli's smaller lighter unit could produce as effective a punch is admirable especially considering its new and improved kill mode.

"As you can see this new weapon's no less powerful than the old...but unlike the old style hand weapon this one can't be deactivated by a security pulse," Torli tells them, for it is not uncommon for the innermost core of a fortress known as the inner keep to be protected by a system that renders hand weapons unusable.

"You sure a that commander...lot a guys claimed it but ain't none what lived to tell anybody it didn't work," one of the men dubiously says.

"Yeah...tested it myself," Torli replies, which pretty much satisfies them, for if Torli said that he tested something he did, and with their interest piqued Torli then rattles off, "It's capable a firing a hundred stun shots or fifty killing shots on a charge... which's about forty percent more shots than the old style hand weapon... also note that there's a lot less recoil...which'll make being able to shoot that many more shots possible."

"Each a us could take out fifty a them," a rather pale skinned dark haired young man in the crowd announces with an appreciative whistle.

"Yeah...if you could hit all fifty Gorg...which's doubtful," Torli replies, and then he adds overtop the snickers, "But even if you could...killing shots require a longer recharge time between them than stun shots...and although the variance's only a few nilos in the heat a battle a few nilos might make the difference between living or dying...which's one reason why the default for this weapon's the stun position."

"Seems kind a stupid to stun a man and have to waste my time with him again later," a somewhat disgruntled Gorg points out.

"Yeah well I promise you that the man won't be alone...and his mates'll not wait for your weapon to recharge," Karnin interjects, and then he walks over and stops in front of Gorg before he adds, "Besides not too many men can take a stun pulse and get up on their own...and it'll cut down on friendly fire casualties... some a you aren't exactly crack shots you know."

"Ah...I see what you mean Karnin," Gorg gives Orn a knowing nod and replies.

"Yeah well...the time's come for you to begin calling me sir and acting more like a soldier eh," Karnin sternly advises.

"Why not 'my lord'...yeah...lord Karnin..." Gorg sarcastically retorts, but if he thought to bait Karnin into one of his word battles he was sorely mistaken, for without a reply Karnin just swipes Gorg's feet out from under him with his foot.

"Sir or general'll do," Karnin tells him, and then turns to the group of men gathered in the practice yard and says, "You'll all start acting like disciplined soldiers or I swear I'll leave whichever one a you doesn't behind when we go...the time's run out for excuses...the lists're up...make sure you know what unit you're assigned to and who else you'll need to call sir in the future...when commander Torli's finished with you move your gear to whatever unit you're assigned to...from now on you'll eat when your unit eats...sleep when your unit sleeps...and when one a you got a piss...then you'll all go piss...by the time we set out on our first mission your unit needs to be able to function as one."

"Hear that Orn...next time you stick your woman your mates got a stick her too," one of the men in the crowd comments with a snort.

"Yeah well sorry to disappoint but from this moment on the barracks're off limits to females...wave goodbye gentlemen...you won't see them again for awhile," Karnin informs them as he inclines his head towards the line of camp women making their way to a structure that has been recently built at the opposite end of the compound.

"If I'd a known that's what you wanted it built for I'd a made sure there was a tunnel," Han remarks with a wry grin.

"From now on the day begins with the sun and ends when you master the tasks commander Torli sets you to...we got a lot to learn still and not much time to do it so most likely you'll be too tired to miss them much," Karnin replies and as he strides away he catches Torli's eye and adds, "I'd like to talk to you when you're finished here."

"Aye sir," Torli replies, and as Gorg picks himself off the ground Torli turns to him and says, "That went well eh?"

"You see..." Gorg begins.

"That wasn't really a question Gorg," Torli evenly says and then turns to the men and loudly commands, "Alright... get yourselves a weapon and form a practice line...hey you Orn...stop waving that weapon around...you shoot somebody and I'll tie your damn balls round your neck...hey you down there...you stupid or something...stand clear the target area!"

30

As Karnin walks away a smile plays across his features, for from the sound of it Torli's patience is rather thin today, which is understandable considering the task laid before him. Still no one rises to a challenge quite like Torli Karnin thinks as he walks back across the compound. As he reaches the entrance to their fortress's modest but well constructed inner keep Karnin hears the thumping of many weapons being discharged, and so he pauses with his hand hovering over the door release to listen for the telltale sound of targets being struck. When it comes he is a bit disappointed by the number, but the day is young and so he will count again later to see if they have improved before he starts fretting over it. Besides that is Torli's job he tells himself as he pushes the door release. However even as he steps inside his mind is already telling him that he could no more leave Torli to worry over whether or not the men are ready for the mission to *Filon Bora* than he could have left him in that alley to die all those years ago.

With a tired sigh Karnin traverses the small well-lit sitting area to his left and then heads down the short corridor on the other side and turns into the first door. This room is Karnin's war room where he has sat with Torli and his original gang who are now his most trusted advisers hammering out the plans for their upcoming mission south. A mission that will decide their futures, for if their plans go awry most of them will most likely never live to see another day. Karnin therefore decides to go over their plan one more time just to play it safe and so after he takes a viewing device from a locked drawer along the wall he takes his customary seat at the long industrial-looking table and flips it on. As Karnin pages through the various drawings of *Filon Bora* searching for anything that he might have missed or failed to consider he finds that he has to force himself to focus on the pages, and after a few minutes of that he flips the device off in disgust.

Apparently he will not be able to concentrate until he addresses what is really bothering him Karnin thinks as he stands and restlessly strides over to open the air vent near the room's solitary window. As he takes a deep breath of the damp marsh air the muffled sounds of Torli's exasperated voice shouting commands wafts in, and Karnin is suddenly struck by a feeling that he can only define as a sort of incredulous satisfaction. Yes that is a good description of it he thinks, for how else would one classify the feeling that one gets when a group of half starved misfit boys and camp followers achieves what they have here? It is a remarkable accomplishment. Especially considering the obstacles that they have had to overcome, but they have taken on what the fates have thrown at them and persevered. Now they are poised on the very threshold of doing what they had set out to prepare for when they trekked north all those years ago.

In Karnin's mind the icing on the whole thing is that most of the original boys who had banded together with him in the beginning of things are still here to witness the end of the tyranny that killed their families and drove them from their homes. That they will prevail in the coming battle to unseat Tok Karnin has no doubt in his mind whatsoever. No Tok has gotten overconfident and lazy, and as a result *Filon Bora* is less secure now than it has ever been in its history or so Karnin's sources say. On top of that men who do not have some sort of grudge with Tok have become scarce, and so his ranks are sullen and dissatisfied. Yes everyone knows that men do not willingly die for someone they despise. In contrast Karnin and his men are well trained and focused, but above all else they are all well motivated, for each of them has a reason to feel entitled to a bit of payback on someone or the other in that place.

Karnin is no exception to that, for he has seen with his own eyes the callous disregard that Galwor and Tok have for the lives of others. As if that were not enough the peddler who brought them word of Galwor's eminent demise told him that Tok was already toasting his good fortune. Apparently Tok is so sure of things that he has no qualms about sitting his arse in Galwor's seat before the man is even dead. Karnin intends to see to it that he will not enjoy his new found power long. No just long enough to lull him into thinking that he has nothing to worry about Karnin thinks with a rather wicked grin. However no matter how much ill will that he feels for Tok Karnin knows it is nothing when compared to what festers in Torli's soul, for Tok killed Torli's mother, and then tried to do the same to Torli. As if that were not enough ever since that day twelve years ago when Tok brought Torli into the alley to die Tok has made it his mission in life to correct the fact that he did not succeed.

As it turned out a year or so after Torli joined Karnin's band of boys what Karnin feared would happen if word got back to Tok that Torli was not dead became a reality although it did not happen as Karnin had predicted with someone in the village noticing Torli's signature golden brown locks. They had shaved those off

32

first thing. No Tok had heard a rumor going round *Filon Bora's* inner keep started by those who had burned Torli's mother's body, for they insisted that it was not Torli in the box, which sent Tok into a murderous rage. Needless to say Boro became his prime suspect, but Boro simply denied it what else could he do? Besides it was up to Tok to prove that what the workers had said was true and luckily there was no way to do that since it was not common practice to keep the ashes unless it was requested before hand, and Boro had made certain that no one did that. It was therefore a case of Boro's word against the two workers who said that they had peeked into the box before shoving it into the incinerator.

The hard cold reality is that Tok was screwed no matter what he did there, for he could not bring Boro up on charges what would they be? That he made off with a dead boy? After all Tok had sworn a blood oath to Galwor that Torli had run off and was found in the ally dead. Tok was livid or so Boro had said, and Karnin feared that his benefactor would meet with some mean end because of it. As it turns out Boro is even more of a somebody than Karnin thought, for his sister was Galwor's mother, and so Tok thought it best to leave Boro be for now. Still Tok was paranoid that Torli might still be alive and so he covertly sent his spies into the village to listen and watch. After that it was inevitable that Tok would find Torli, for even though Torli's unusual hair was an easy fix his book learned ways were more difficult to hide. More than that though Torli was just a very memorable boy, for he had a way of speaking that made people want to hear what he had to say, and people like that are remembered. Understandably it was not long before talk of the bald boy who knew things found its way to Tok's ears.

The assassin Tok sent after Torli had come very close to accomplishing what Tok had failed to do previously, and they all feared that Torli would not survive the deep wound that the man managed to inflict upon him before Karnin's boys beat his brains out. They were very lucky that Tok was not only a cheap bastard, but a stupid one as well, for he had made the mistake of thinking that an amateur killer would do since they were only a gang of stray boys. Unfortunately just because the man was not the best assassin out there did not mean that he was the worst either, for even though he had not tipped his knife with poison it was still tipped, but with some kind of biological contaminant that not even Boro had seen before. Whatever it was Torli nearly died, but once again he pulled through and his doing so endeared him once and for all to those in Karnin's band. Things changed after that, for even as young as Karnin was he knew that no one hired an assassin of any caliber to go after a nobody, and so Karnin's suspicions that Torli was a somebody were pretty much confirmed although he still had no clear idea who it was that he belonged to.

Karnin had therefore told Boro that he would not keep Torli any longer unless he knew the all of his story, for he could not safeguard Torli and the other boys if he did not know how doggedly Tok would pursue him. In hindsight Karnin realizes that Boro probably knew that Karnin could no more have turned Torli out than he could have Han or one of the others, but he did not call Karnin on it most likely because he realized that the time had come for the truth. Boro therefore related who Torli was and more importantly why it would be in Karnin's best interests to protect him. It was a sobering thing that story, and Karnin never saw Torli in quite the same way after he heard it. Boro had made him swear not to repeat what he had told him until the time was right, for Torli did not know the all of it, and for reasons that Boro would not say he did not want Torli to know until Galwor was on his deathbed. That of course would be now. Karnin can only hope that Torli will not lose it when he finds out that he knew the whole story all these years but did not tell him.

Well he will just have to get over it they are too good a team to split up Karnin decides with a stubborn glare, for whereas men obey Karnin because they need and fear him men follow Torli because they love him. That is apparently the magic combination, for after Torli came to them their numbers quickly swelled. So much so that by the time Karnin turned eighteen the two of them had managed to amass a sizable following of not only homeless young boys but artisans and trained folk who had lost everything they had because of either Galwor or Tok. Not surprisingly they outgrew the valley of the holes rather quickly, and at some point it became obvious that they needed to find somewhere else to live if they wanted to stay unnoticed. Besides if they wanted to attack Tok one day they needed to train and that was simply not possible anywhere near *Filon Bora*. Therefore after much discussion they had made their plans to leave.

The night before the first of them set out Boro had come to say goodbye, and he had handed Karnin a map that he said they would be wise to follow, for it would take them to a safe place where they could do what they needed to do. The next day their exodus began, and they had snuck away a few at a time on foot and made their way to the rendezvous place to the north that they had decided upon so as not to draw attention to their going. Then ensued many days of endless plodding along and long cold nights until foot sore and weary they finally reached a place that they named *Big Rock Crack* where they were able to get some much needed rest. Eventually they set out again to the north, and made their way to the spot marked on Boro's map. Karnin still remembers the feeling that he had gotten when he first laid his eyes upon it that first time, for it was as if he had found the most valuable thing known. In a way he had.

As it turned out the place that Boro had sent them to was not just any old piece of land it was logistically perfect, for it consisted of a large flat expanse of meadow grass that was bounded on the north by dense forests, on the east by the swamps and marshes, and to the west by more forests and the foothills of a faraway mountain range. On top of that the air was fresh, the grass green, and there were no people living within a hundred miles of the place. They therefore put down roots despite even though they knew that their lives would be difficult starting with practically nothing in an area so close to the marshes, for they had not the slightest idea about the world's wetlands other than that fish people and other creepy crawly things lived in them. Oh and that Boro said not to go wading round in them lest you run into something you do not want to meet.

The reality of it is that since they would have had to steal land from someone squatting on the dry lands of a marsh overlord seemed a decent enough choice. Why would a marsh overlord care overly much about his fringe lands? They are just a buffer zone right? Karnin and his gang had to go somewhere, and even if they had the riches to trade for some they would not have been able to acquire land legally. All the known lands of the world were entailed in perpetuity to the overlords long before Karnin was even born. Stealing the land was therefore their only option. That was not their fault it was the doing of greedy men who were so locked into wanting to own it all that they fought a bitter war in which each tried to subjugate the others until the human race dangled on the rope of self-extinction. At this point they all apparently wised up and the *Pact of the Overlords* in which all the known lands were divvied up was drafted and signed ending the conflict.

35

What came in the years after the pact Karnin can only describe as the most perverse stagnation that could befall a population. As it was each overlord ruled his own territory in whatever way that he saw fit, and the way the overlords saw fit eventually morphed into whatever new pleasure they wanted fulfilled. Many of the overlords became spoiled, pampered and cruel, and over time the needs of the common folk became secondary to their own. Eventually the ordinary man was reduced to nothing more than a pathetic drone. The overlords soon found that having a population full of mindless lackeys made their own lives easier, and they wanted to make certain that it stayed that way, for it made securing their place at the top simple to do. The overlords therefore passed a series of laws that made things such as travel and communication between territories, as well as the possession of hand weapons a crime. Well only for the regular folk of course, which together with other laws designed to degrade and stifle the masses brought progress to a screeching halt.

Well at least that is how things went in the land territories, for since land folk do not go into the marshes no one really knows for certain what the marsh overlords did. There are many who say that the marsh overlords pretty much went back to the way the marshes had done business for centuries only on a more peaceful note when it came to getting along with their marsh neighbors. Boro was one of those, and he had told Karnin that the marsh overlords had long held to a system that gave the common folk rights that most regular land folk have never had. Karnin has always been rather skeptical about that since for all intents and purposes the marsh folk had cut themselves off from the land dwellers long ago. So how would Boro know what they think and do? From what Karnin has seen marsh folk are careless creatures who have little care for what they have no use for. What other conclusion can he come to when the marsh overlord upon whose land they had built their refuge never even noticed that they were here or if he did he cared so little for the land that he could not bestir his self to come kick them off it.

Be that as it may be because of the land laws that are in place Karnin and his ragtag band are not just squatters; they are fugitives as well. They had traveled from one overlord's territory to another's without the proper permits, which is a thing the law strictly forbids. The only thing that may save their necks if it comes to it is that they crossed from a land territory to a marsh territory.

That is rather moot now since that law banning travel is not the only one that they have broken. As is often the case with criminals once the proverbial line was crossed they had nothing more to lose, and so they made regular excursions into the neighboring territories to steal what they needed. In this way they eventually managed to put together a mean little place that was nothing more than a ramshackle shelter that they fondly dubbed *The Shack*. Despite its rustic appearance it was good enough to keep them warm and dry, and they were all rather proud that they had made something from practically nothing.

Over the years, by employing the same hook and crook methods they managed to improve not only themselves but *The Shack* as well. So it was that after one rather monumental upgrade project that included adding a primitive barrier wall with a gate, and a proper watch tower as they stood admiring their work they realized that *The Shack* looked rather pathetic in comparison. So after much discussion on it they had gathered in front of *The Shack* with the intentions of tearing it down and rebuilding it only to discover that they simply could not bring themselves to do it. In the end they decided to let *The Shack* stand until they had the materials to build a proper inner keep and not just a bigger version of what they already had or so they told themselves.

Still despite the lack of a suitable inner keep they did have a proper curtain wall so they decided that they had a right to name the place anyway. After some debate they settled on the name of *Onyat*, for according to Ahnin who claimed to know every language in existence the word meant 'home' in one of the old languages of the marshes. That seemed to them to be a rather appropriate name for a fortress built on the stolen lands of a marsh overlord and so *Onyat* was officially born. Picking a marsh name must have appeased the marsh gods or some such thing for after the naming their luck took a turn for the better. One day not long after despite the odds being stacked against it someone did happen upon their compound. At first Karnin and the other boys thought what anyone would think in such a situation namely 'what now', but even though it could have ended with the man running back and telling his lord of their presence here he did not. Instead, when the young man realized what they were about he asked them to let him stay, and even though there was a risk that someone might come seeking him they made him welcome anyway.

Needless to say at the time they were all quite relieved that Bro had decided that he wanted to stay, for they were still quite young and Bro was older and big for a man of only twenty-two. There was also the armored vehicle that he had come in, for they would have had a hard time keeping him from leaving if he had chosen to. Bro wanting to join them turned out to be more fortuitous than just having his strong arm added to their cause, for he did not come empty handed quite the contrary. Bro had arrived in a small transport that was filled with goods that his lord Osgo had pinched from his overlord and sent Bro out on the sly to barter. Not just any old goods but premade building materials and systems such as one would need when constructing an inner keep complete with a brand new power plant to power it with. Torli was so excited that he nearly pissed his self.

Actually Bro gave them more than that, for he had special security clearances at his old fortress *Dorelon Bodon* and so he went back a few more times to load up more stuff. Bro always said that he did not feel bad about it since the lord of *Dorelon Bodon* was a thief his own self, which is probably why his lordship never came looking for Bro. Well that and the fact that lord Osgo eventually got caught and promptly replaced by a new lord. Luckily it was not until after Bro managed to acquire the rest of the materials needed to build that proper inner keep, which they did, but they still left *The Shack* stand for reasons that nobody wanted to discuss. It goes without saying that building things without the aid of a proper lift machine made them strong in ways that the training field alone never would have. As a result by the time they were finished with what they had materials to make those chosen to climb and set were strong and lean, and those chosen to muscle things around or work the ropes were thick and sturdy. As one might expect the climbers eventually became candidates for Karnin's first assault team and the muscle for foot soldiers. It all worked out rather well.

In the years that followed the construction of the inner keep they also built many other things that an army needed such as their three technically advanced transports and a smaller light war vehicle that Torli has dubbed a 'runner'. The real beauty of it by far though is that they built them by scavenging parts from Galwor's own war machines that they found abandoned and going to ruin in a remote hangar in *Filon Bora's* village. They also created the various trappings needed to house and maintain an army on the move. All by stealing the knowledge and needed supplies more often than not from Galwor's own lands, which they found the doing of rather satisfying. They then trained and bided their time waiting for Boro to come north and tell them that the moment had come, which it has although Boro did not come personally to tell them as they had always assumed he would.

So now after nearly eight years of hard work here in the obscurity of the north the time has finally come to put all their plans and hopes on the line, for Galwor is dying, and as soon as he does they will strike. Well shortly after at any rate for they want Tok's arse to be very cozy in the overlord's seat. To Tok cozy means safe and safe means lazy and careless. There may also be a short delay depending upon how long it takes Karnin to find a way to get a message to overlord Marsle although Karnin would rather just skip over that. Unfortunately, he had promised Boro that he would personally hand *Onyat* over to the marsh overlord who technically owns it when the time came for them to march south. Now however Karnin can see how foolish it was to promise him that, but in his own defense Boro refused to give him the map until he did. He also made him promise not to tell Torli the entire truth about his own self until the time was ripe for it. They were two very stupid promises Karnin thinks with a shake of his head.

A knock on the door brings Karnin out of his musings then, and he realizes that he has been lost in his own thoughts a lot longer than he intended, for the room that was brightly lit when he went to the window is now cast in shadows. The distant rumble of thunder makes him rethink that, and after he rubs some spit on the glass of the timekeeper on his wrist so that he can see past the scratches it confirms that only an hour or so has passed. Therefore the darkening of the sun is only the day's storm building. That it rains enough to drown a man nearly every day in late summer was one of the first things that they learned after they arrived here. That and if you piss on your shoes during the hard cold they will freeze solid before you can get back inside to the damn fire he recalls as he hears the door slide open.

"They become masters a the new weapons so quickly then Torli?" Karnin asks when he hears Torli's unmistakable footfalls, for his time at Tok's hands had left him with a slight limp that is quite noticeable when he is as tired as he apparently is right now.

"If only that were true," Torli replies, and then he explains, "I've sent them to move their belongings before the storm gets here...it looks to be a good one coming today."

"You're too soft on them Torli," Karnin accuses when Torli comes to stand next to him at the window.

"And you're too hard," Torli replies with a shrug, and then he adds in a somewhat miffed tone, "And you cheat as well."

"There's no cheating in war and you'd best get that through your honorable head or you'll get yourself and them dead," Karnin replies a bit irritably.

"We can at least act with some kind a honor amongst ourselves Karnin," Torli shakes his head and replies, then he turns his angry eyes on him and says, "What else'll keep them from joining the other side if things turn against us?"

"Fear a my foot up their arses?" Karnin offers with a grin.

"I'd remind you that you've only got two feet...and you'll need both a them just for Orn's arse," Torli replies as he returns Karnin's grin.

"True," Karnin nods, and then he asks, "So you think their loyalty to one another'll be enough to keep them from deserting do you?"

"For most yeah," Torli replies.

"And for the rest that loyalty'll mean nothing to...like Gorg perhaps?"

"There'll always be some losses...some who'll find their courage lacking...but I don't think Gorg'll be one a those...he'll likely be one a the ones that's got more courage than skill."

"Which's why I put him with all the other...questionables..."

"What?"

"Haven't you seen the list?"

"No...I came straight here."

"Then have a look," Karnin replies and then goes over to the table and punches a few buttons on his patched up and tattered personal device before sliding it down the table to Torli.

"There're two schools a thought on that approach you know," Torli points out as he reads through the groups of names on the device.

"Yeah," Karnin replies, and then crosses his arms on his chest and says, "But I'm a fan a going the course with the best odds...and the odds're good that if things go wrong for us that unit a

40

'questionable' men'll most likely be too busy trying to be the first out the damn door to think a joining the other side."

"You're most likely right...and not all a them on this list're stupid...so those ones'll know that Tok's men'll never show them any mercy if they surrender," Torli agrees with a nod.

"There'll be no surrender...we're all-in on this Torli...if we fail...well...we'll be done..."

"Ah well...no one lives forever," Torli tells him with a grin.

"No but it never hurts to try," Karnin responds with a bit of a smirk, and then turns back to the window and says, "We got something important to discuss."

"Yeah...yeah... I know if you go down then I should lead the men..." Torli impatiently says as he comes to stand next to Karnin.

"No not that...something I promised Boro not to tell you until we're to this point," Karnin replies.

"Sounds serious," Torli says and then he also turns to stare out the window.

"Yeah."

"More serious than being kin to the likes a Galwor...to a man who gave over his own sister to act as his bastard son's whore?" Torli evenly asks, and then he adds, "After that not much in life seems so bad."

"Why'd you never tell me who your mother was your own self before now?"

"At first I's afraid you might not want me to stay being Galwor's kin and all...then I thought you might not like it that I got a claim to Galwor's territory..." Torli replies with a shrug.

"Why'd you think I'd even consider attacking an overlord's territory in the first place...without a claim to it the other overlords'd never let that stand...and men get executed the old fashioned way for that sort a thing," Karnin responds.

"You already knew?" Torli accuses.

"Boro asked me not to say anything..."

"So...you and Boro got it all figured out eh?" Torli softly says, but Karnin does not miss how agitated he has become.

"It's not like that."

"What's it like then?"

"He wouldn't tell me who you were until I promised not to tell you," Karnin impatiently replies.

"So...how much'd he pay you to keep me alive?" Torli belligerently asks.

41

"I'm gonna let that pass...cause we're kin," Karnin grinds out between his teeth.

"Don't do me any favors," Torli heatedly responds, and then what Karnin has just said apparently hits home, for a confused expression crosses his face and he asks, "Wait...what?"

"Now don't go off the deep end...I didn't know until Boro told me...our fathers were brothers," Karnin tells him.

"What was his name...your father's," Torli asks rather quietly.

"Debon...but I barely remember him," Karnin replies, and when he does something unreadable passes across Torli's face, and so Karnin asks, "What's the matter?"

"Don't ask me," is all Torli replies, and without any further comment he simply hurries from the room.

"That went well eh?" Karnin sarcastically mutters as he strides after Torli.

"I'd prefer to be alone...I got a think," Torli says when Karnin falls in step with him.

"I'm sorry you're disappointed to hear I'm your cousin..." Karnin clips out as he follows Torli across the small sitting area.

"Don't be stupid."

"Excuse me?" Karnin demands.

"It's not you I got a think about...it's Boro..." Torli tells him somewhat petulantly, and then he hits the door release and exits the inner keep without any other explanation.

Outside Seasle, Cerl, and Ahnin are just making their way to their new barracks near the inner keep when they see Torli storm out. They all three therefore pause to watch him, for it is obvious that he is pissed about something. Sure enough 'something' appears shortly after in the form of a red faced Karnin, and even though he does not say anything to them they can pretty much figure out for their selves what is going on. Karnin and Torli are always butting heads so much so that there is a standing bet between Cerl and Seasle as to which one's head is harder. It goes without saying that the three of them decide to sort of tag along just for fun to see how it turns out. That is until Torli presses the lock release and goes out the rear foot gate though with Karnin hot on his heels. At that point the fun evaporates, for it is not safe out there and they both know it. The three men therefore sprint across the compound and climb the ladder to the walkway along the wall where they can watch for any sign that someone is lurking about waiting for such an opportunity as this.

"Torli...stop!" Karnin calls as he emerges from the compound and to Karnin's surprise he actually does.

"I think I might be losing it Karnin," Torli blurts out as Karnin comes to stand near him.

"It's just nerves...it'll pass," Karnin responds, and then he adds, "You know in your heart that Boro wouldn't plot against you...you know that Torli."

"I know...it's just that I thought he'd be here you know...when we went," Torli tells him.

"He'll show up...you'll see," Karnin reassures him.

"You know...there's something you should know about our fathers," Torli suddenly says.

"Like what?"

"They were...well...a bit crazy."

"That so."

"Yeah...my father thought he could talk to beasts," Torli responds and when Karnin smiles in amusement he quickly says, "No really...I saw him catch a jim-jon once and ask it what cook was 'aving for mid meal."

"I's just smiling because my mother used to say that my father thought he had the spirit of a damn tooka living in his head," Karnin tells him with a grin.

"You made that up," Torli accuses.

"No..." Karnin replies with a shake of his dark head, and then he adds somewhat hesitantly, "He died when he fell off the roof a the inner keep...the village folk said he was trying to fly."

"They said mine killed his self...but Boro said he never would a done that..." Torli tells him in like kind.

"I think maybe they both got helped to the other side..." Karnin points out.

"Yeah...maybe..." Torli absently says, but then he nervously turns away as he asks, "Did Boro tell you all a what Tok did to my mother and me?"

"He did...but no one'll ever hear it from me," Karnin quietly promises, for even though Karnin has never had that particular indignity foisted upon him he can still imagine how traumatic a thing it would be to watch your mother being repeatedly raped, especially when you know that your turn is coming after.

"It took me a long time to get over that...sometimes it still haunts my dreams," Torli says, but Karnin does not reply, for he can tell that Torli is not wanting advice, and a few seconds later

Torli confirms this by saying, "I think once I kill Tok I may be able to sleep all night for the first time in as long as I can remember."

"I ain't changed my mind about that Torli," Karnin responds, for Torli can either let Karnin and his first assault team kill Tok or goad him into demanding a trial by combat, but in Karnin's mind neither option involves Torli.

"Well...you better find a way to convince yourself to...because I'm not gonna let people say I'm a coward...I won't start my overlordship that way," Torli insists, but before Karnin can respond Torli suddenly fixes his eyes on the marshes and then says with a shiver, "We'd best get back...damn marshes're giving me the creeps again."

After he takes another quick glance over his shoulder Torli turns and heads for the fortress, but before he follows Karnin pauses long enough to give the marshes an intense scan. The truth is that he feels it too, but then again he always feels uneasy this close to the water. A crack of lightening followed by the rumble of thunder sends Karnin hastening towards the compound, for the weather can turn ugly in just seconds this time of year. Getting electrocuted is not the way that Karnin would like to end this day or any other day for that matter he thinks as the wind kicks up and whips his hair loose from its bindings. Another rather large crack of thunder sounds then, and on its heels comes the rain, which not only sends Karnin and Torli scampering for the safety of the fortress, but Seasle, Cerl, and Ahnin for cover as well, but to their credit neither man moves until they see Karnin step through the gate.

So it is that none of the men see the pair of big blue eyes that suddenly appear at the surface of the marshes, for until now their owner had no reason to open them. After all he has been spying on these land men on and off for years and so he already knows what they look like. No what he came to do today was listen, for he was sent to find out what the land men are up to now that Galwor is dying. The answer will not please Marsle much, for what they are planning pretty much breaks all the rules, and if there is one thing that Marsle never does it is break the rules. Unless he can do so legally or some such interpretation of it, and even then only if doing so will get him something worthwhile that he wants. Then again is that not the way it is everywhere he adds as he sinks beneath the surface and swims away. Some time later he emerges next to his marsh machine that he has stashed in the greenery far enough away so as not to be heard by those in the fortress and after he pulls himself astride it he fires it up and heads deeper into the marshes.

Chapter Three

Deep in the northern marshes lights glow in the inky darkness, for overlord Marsle is entertaining in his fortress tonight, and so the place is all lit up like some strange glittering castle rising up from the water. Inside the fortress the overlord sits at the head of his dining table carefully scanning his guests for any sign that they are displeased by the fare served tonight, but he sees only contented faces seated down the long expanse of ornately carved and polished wood. He should not have been concerned Marsle thinks for his folk are world wise enough to realize why his table is lacking the usual fare it would normally have in early spring. As it is the rains have been unusually heavy this year, and so have delayed the breeding of many of the marsh fishes that they would normally be harvesting right now. Still Marsle feels a bit put out that his table is so very limited tonight. He is lucky that Ann is an imaginative hostess he thinks as his colorless eyes settle upon the young woman seated to his left, for she has managed to reinvent the same old thing she served yesterday with a few new sauces and such.

He will have to find something special for her when this is all over and done, for she has had her work cut out for her with all these uninvited guests he decides as he sends a brief glance to his right where overlord Oreian sits stuffing his face. As Marsle's eyes come to rest on the rather rotund marsh man and his sizable entourage they impatiently narrow, and he wishes not for the first time today that he had told the old toad to shove off when he first showed up. Unfortunately Marsle was raised with better manners than that, which is what overlord Oreian was counting on Marsle silently notes. He should have thought ahead a bit and had some polite excuse lined up to send Oreian off when he showed up Marsle chastises himself. Yes he should have known that the overlord would be coming seeing that the harvest is delayed everywhere this year.

Well almost everywhere Marsle corrects, for the *Morian Sea*, which borders Oreian's lands is never without something to pull in, but far be it for the lazy creature to actually take some initiative and build a damn boat so that he can harvest from it Marsle thinks. The man does not deserve the good fortune of having lands that border on the largest body of water in the world. The worst part of the whole thing is that just because Oreian will not bestir his self to fish the great sea does not mean that he does not wish to enjoy its bounty. No his visit was not timed the way it is for no good reason, for he would like nothing better than to exploit the lean times that Marsle is currently in by offering his assistance in the form of a fishing permit Marsle sarcastically thinks.

More like a license to steal, for Marsle has no doubt that Oreian's idea of a fair contract would be that he gets to take half of whatever Marsle's men pull in Marsle tells himself with an indignant huff. Well Oreian will be disappointed yet again, for Marsle's folk are a hardy lot who have no fondness for lazy sponges any more than Marsle does. They will therefore not be doing business together this year or any other year Marsle thinks as he watches Oreian shove more whole pickled fish into his mouth at one time than he has ever bore witness to. That explains why the man is so damn fat. Yes eating is second only to mooching in the overlord's repertoire of talents, and apparently it is what he has in common with the men he keeps round him Marsle thinks as he casts a glance down the table.

In truth Oreian's entourage is so good at feeding their faces that they are all in some stage of physical burgeoning Marsle notes although a few are a tad thinner, but then again they are also young men. Yes give it time Marsle concludes. Unfortunately their combined largess is enough to make having to repair his table necessary once they are gone, for the entire right side seems to have developed a noticeable sag Marsle jokingly adds to himself. When upon further study he realizes that the table actually does appear to be drooping he has to study his plate for a few minutes to keep his temper in check, for Marsle would like very much to point out to Oreian what their fat sloppy selves have done to his table by banging his face into it a few times so that he can get a good close look.

With a sigh Marsle asks himself whether his line in the sand that dictates when a polite welcome is allowed to expire may be a tad too low in the dirt, for that Oreian has no respect for things like the ancient table where he sits does seem to be walking a fine line between proper and improper guest behavior. Marsle realizes that his respect for the past and its artifacts is not shared by all marsh folk, but even so a guest is expected to show respect for his host's property, and the table is much more than just a place to eat it is the heart of *Laraqua* just as it was in long ago days when the place was only a marsh keep. In those days this table was an ancient tree within which the home of Marsle's ancestors was built, and it housed Marsle's ancestors high up in the safety of its branches for many years.

As is usually the case with humans the population eventually grew until it became clear that a new larger dwelling was needed, and so things were expanded and eventually the fortress known as *Laraqua* was built. They decided to keep the tree at its heart though, for in those days it was believed that it was the spirit of the tree that had brought them their prosperity. They had therefore built their new fortress around the huge tree and incorporated it into various common areas such as this one where a large gathering table was carved out complete with benches. The oddest part of the whole tale is that doing so never killed the tree and even today they tend to its roots that go deep in the marsh mud. With any luck the old tree will still be sprouting leaves in the solarium for his grand babes own children to ooh and ah over while some old man repeats the tale of the great tree Marsle thinks with a wistful expression. Well if Oreian's fat arse does not do it in that is Marsle amends to himself as he snatches up his glass from the table.

With a perturbed sigh Marsle takes a long drink of the berry brew in his cup, for even though he personally detests the sweet cloying stuff when overlord Oreian showed up Marsle had ordered his steward to move all the valuable food stuffs to the underground for safekeeping starting with their supply of spirits. It is what everyone does when they find him knocking on their gate. It is common knowledge that Oreian loves to tie one on, but having seen him drunk once was enough for Marsle. Oreian pretty much put a new spin on what the term 'sloppy drunk' means. Someone has decided to thumb her nose at his edict Marsle thinks as he slides Ann a sideways glance, for instead of the sweetness he expects he feels a bite upon his tongue. He somehow cannot fault her for it this time. No he needs a bit of spirits right now to help him avoid an inter-territorial incident he thinks as he tips his cup to her to let her know that no long lectures will be forthcoming over it later.

"So Marsle...where is Calphin tonight?" Oreian trains his beady eyes on him and asks.

"Tending to his sick wife and child most like," Marsle smoothly replies, but he can see that Oreian is rather skeptical.

"He is very devoted," Ann adds.

"Yes..." Oreian agrees as his eyes slowly rove the contours of Ann's pretty face, but just then Calphin strolls in saving Marsle the trouble of having to rescue her from the lascivious old pecker's unwanted attentions yet again.

"So how did you find Janissa tonight Calphin?!" Marsle calls out to him effectively alerting him as to what excuse it is that he has given for his lateness to table.

"She is doing much better sir," Calphin responds with one of his charming smiles.

"And Corlon...I was told that he is feeling better," Marsle comments with an amused shine in his eyes, for he has already heard that Calphin's young toddler has grown rather cranky from being confined.

"He is driving them crazy up there," Calphin responds as he slips into the empty seat next to Ann, and then he adds, "The healer says that he can resume play with the other children in a day or so...and I am not certain who was more relieved...the healer or Janissa."

"Children are such a curse at times...it is a good thing that they are so necessary or no one would even have them," Oreian proclaims, and then he slants Calphin a rather sly look and adds, "So Calphin...what interesting rumors have you heard down your way of late?"

"Ah well overlord...all the talk is of the northern rains right now," Calphin slickly replies as he ladles some of the main course into his bowl.

"Anything new going on in that female nest of horrors then?" Oreian meanly asks.

"No sir...same old same old at *Mori*" Calphin replies rather shortly, for if Calphin had had his choice Oreian would suffer a most unfortunate accident for that insult, but alas diplomacy forbids such.

"How about your squatters then Marsle?" Oreian prompts as he quickly turns away, for having those big blue eyes of Calphin's on him never fails to remind him of his unconventional mother, which always disturbs his digestion.

"Ah well Oreian...rumor has it that they have plans to go squat somewhere else...though I have no idea where," Marsle replies with a bored wave of his hand.

"Ah well...so long as they are leaving then who cares where," Oreian blurts out as he stabs a goodly sum of small brined fish from a platter being proffered round by one of the kitchen women.

"Do you think this man...this Karnin is strong enough to lay siege to one of the land fortresses overlord?" one of overlord Oreian's men asks.

"Possibly Cronen," Marsle replies cordially enough, for of all Oreian's men Cronen is the only one who has any sense at all, but then again even Oreian needs one competent man. Who would run things?

"Oh poo...poo Marsle...these men are outcasts that no one wants...how could they possibly have the intelligence let alone the equipment needed to take a land fortress?" Oreian spouts forth with a snort of amusement.

"Their leader is quite clever...and his second in command is somewhat of a genius as land men go...he has designed and built a number of things that will give them an edge if they choose to use what they have militarily," Marsle informs him.

"Yes and one day they will use it against us as well...which is your fault Marsle...you are far too accommodating," Oreian points a forkful of fish at him and says.

"Apparently so," is all Marsle replies, but even though he gives Oreian an agreeable enough nod Cronen does not miss the censoring glance that Marsle sends his overlord when he looks away.

"I for one would not advise setting yourself against them overlord Oreian...better to stay out of the affairs of land men," Calphin advises with an unconcerned shrug.

"Good advice I think," Marsle agrees, and then attempts to change the direction of the conversation by fixing his attention on a woman seated further down the table and saying in a fatherly tone, "Here now you have touched nothing on your plate girl."

"I cannot seem to...eat that...oh dear," she exclaims and then claps a hand over her mouth and flees the room.

"Your son should be here for his woman at a time like this," Oreian chastises with his mouth full, and then he waves his eating knife in the air to emphasize his words as he says, "Nothing good will come from his traveling to the southernmost marshes Marsle...the marsh folk there would not know a good idea if it rained fishes on them...is that not so Calphin?"

"Corlean will make them see that unity will be better for all marsh folk," Ann pipes in, but she quickly snaps her mouth shut and focuses her eyes on her plate when Marsle gives her a warning shake of his head.

"Do not expect too much Ann...the southernmost marshes are a different world from ours," Marsle tells her as he reaches over to give her hand a reassuring squeeze, for it is not her fault that she has caught Oreian's eye, and were it not for the rules that prohibit it the fat toad would have been treading water two seconds after he informed Marsle of it.

"Now Annitequea here would be quite different...what man would not be charmed by her eh," the fat toad informs them as he gives Ann a long perusal.

"Yes well my daughter is not for use as a bargaining chip Oreian...just because I can see a benefit to combining our resources in times of need does not mean that I would agree to a blood union that would consign any of our young women to such a life as she would find in the southernmost marshes," Marsle replies with a derisive snort, and then he spears a few more fishes off his plate, which he swallows down before he adds, "They are so very...primitive."

"If I can be excused father...I would check on Aquaous," Annitequea asks as she rises from the table.

"Yes of course...take your time...the kitchen girls will see to clearing things," Marsle tells her, and then he adds with an impatient gesture, "Make sure Aquaous eats something Ann...whatever it is that she wants see that she gets it yes?"

"Alright father...good night then overlord," she politely says to Oreian, and although Ann gives him a polite enough nod the lack of shine in her nearly colorless eyes say that it is not sincere.

After she gives her father a fond peck on the cheek Ann makes her way down the long table, and as she does she covertly checks the plates and food platters near *Laraqua's* folk seated there to make certain that there was enough put out for them, for she knows that most of them are eating sparingly in light of their guests' hearty appetites. Well they will get desert and the overlord and his clan will not she thinks with a haughty sniff as she makes her way out into the corridor, for with the exception of overlord Oreian and his gang she has had the real desert delivered to each apartment in the fortress. Still no matter her own distaste for it she had to serve something sweet to end the meal, for her father would be beside his self if she did not, but it will only be an assortment of fruits drizzled with lotsen nectar that is common in the marshes.

With any luck the old toad will be so disappointed that he will leave she tells herself as she walks down the short corridor that leads to the kitchen larder, for Cronen had made it a point to let her know how very much the overlord likes his sweets. Whether or not it was to serve his overlord's interests or his own desire to poke the big fat fish a few times Ann is not certain, for Cronen is a difficult read, which is probably how he gets on amongst Oreian and his cronies. He makes sport of them in his head the whole time. At any rate regardless of the reason why Cronen mentioned the overlord's penchant for sweets Ann has made it a point to serve only light semi-sweet desserts ever since he did. Ann did not mention it to her father though, for sometimes it is best not to tell him something even if you think that he is smart enough to notice, for her father sometimes ignores his well-bred ways if he can pretend ignorance. Well when properly motivated, which at the moment he is.

Maybe she will put a bit of tauti powder in the fat slob's sheets she thinks with a considering expression, for it would be most gratifying to see Oreian scratch his skin off. Unfortunately her father would probably think that over the line as far as things that he can turn a blind eye to she tells herself as she pauses in the corridor to enter her code in the larder room's door. Yet another thing to thank overlord Oreian for she thinks as the door slides open, for if he and his gang of gluttons were not here this door would not be locked. Oreian and his bevy of mooches are quickly forgotten when Ann enters the larder, for this is one of her favorite places in the fortress, and so she pauses for a second just to take in the ancient sights and smells of place. As she walks along fondly gazing upon its well worn shelves and standing storage vats she thinks that she could not love them more if they were made of the finest of gemstones. Actually to her they are, for this room has stood unchanged since her great-grandfather Alitin first built it.

No the larder room is unlike any room in the fortress, for here the air is kept dry, which although it is most uncomfortable for marsh folk is very necessary to store food stuffs such as herbs, spices and dried fishes. That is why in days gone by her ancestors only kept dried things in it. Now a days they keep brined things here too, for when the fortress received its most recent update her father had an automatic climate control system installed in here, and so the presence of wetter things sitting in brine is neutralized. The old wooden barrels and magnificent glass storage jars neither Ann's father nor her grandfather had touched though, for they understood the value of tradition. Therefore the beautiful old storage containers are still here doing the jobs that they have done for many generations. Hopefully for many more to come Ann adds to herself as she walks over to the long wall lined with racks of glass tube-like crucibles with stopper ends.

Now then to find something that Aquaous will not reject she thinks as she scans the jars for something different, but alas there is just nothing here that can compare to the sugared kelps that she brought to her yesterday. Well as her brother always says why change what works Ann decides and then walks down the long wall until she comes to the particular rack of crucibles that she is searching for. Well several racks to be exact, for sugared kelp is a favorite of young and old, and so Ann always has a goodly supply on hand. These ones here in the larder room are only the oldest of what they have put up with the remainder being stashed away in the cool of the underground area, but the sugared kelp is not alone down there, for the past year was also a very good year for lambis fish, and so the pickled excess is keeping the kelp company.

Ann spends a few seconds scrutinizing first one glass crucible then another for the telltale signs of a good batch, for Ann's love for the sweet treats has taught her that not all sugared kelp are the same, and although they all taste good certain ones taste much better. Those are the ones that she is seeking now. Yes only the best will do for her favorite sister-in-law especially now when she is so very unhappy and sick. Therefore, when Ann picks up the tongs she finds nearby and draws out a tubular strand one of the jars the first thing that she does is hold it up to the light turning

53

this way and that as one would do when assessing the value of some priceless gem. The strand's lackluster appearance immediately tells her that it has not taken up the sweetness well, and so she rejects it returning it to the jar. With any luck it has just not been allowed to steep long enough and in a month or so will be just right. Well or it will be the same Ann thinks for sometimes the kelp is just not the quality needed to get any better. Ann's second try yields a strand that appears quite different from the first, for when she holds this one up it glistens and shimmers as though covered with tiny green gems, which is exactly what she is hoping to see.

"Beautiful...just like it should be," she cocks her head and says to herself as she considers whether or not to eat this one and find another for Aquaous.

"You will grow fat if you keep sneaking those things," a voice behind her says, but she is not startled since she heard him coming, which was intentional since no one ever hears Calphin coming unless he wants them to.

"Maybe that old slug will stop ogling my breasts then," she replies with an unladylike snort.

"From what I hear he likes his women young and quite plump so..." Calphin points out with a knowing shrug.

"Then I shall never eat again," she replies in mock horror, and then she informs him, "This is for Aquaous...it seems that sweet is the only taste that does not make her gag right now."

"Take one of these too," he instructs and then lifts the lid of a larger more vat-like storage jar sitting on the floor to remove a large black blob and plunk it down in front of her.

"Have you lost your mind...she will toss it and me right down the nearest crap hole...or even worse...make me eat it," Annitequea wrinkles her nose at the offending object and says.

"No...really...when Janissa was growing Corlon she craved sweet too...the healer said to offer her the brined cukes because they are very nutritious...and their saltiness would taste good with the sweet," he informs her and then adds, "Turns out the healer was right...once I dared enough to try it Janissa could not get enough of them...but her breath at night...bad...made 'me' gag."

"Aquaous has not eaten anything but sweets for three days now so I am willing to give it a try...but really...a cuke...yuk," she comments with an involuntary shiver, for she has never been able to get beyond the slimy parasitical appearance of the things, and as she quickly wraps the pickled slug-like creature in a towel she says, "You know you do not have to keep Janissa and Corlon locked up Calphin...it is not contagious after all."

"That is not my doing...Janissa will not hear of anyone seeing her like she is," Calphin replies, and then he adds with a disgruntled frown, "She is still full of spots...and meaner than a snipey fish I might add."

"It is hard to believe that she did not know that she was allergic to poppy snails," Ann notes.

"She had never eaten them before...always turned her nose up to them...said they looked too much like fish lice," Calphin tells her with a smirk.

"I am surprised that she did not slit your throat for daring her to eat them," a marsh man who has come to lounge against the door frame and listen in on their conversation points out.

"Corlean!" Annitequea squeals and then excitedly flies at him.

"Hello Ann," he chokes out as she throws her arms around his neck.

"Ah the conquering hero returns," Calphin jibes.

"Not so much...the overlord Serrten wanted nothing to do with us...could not be rid of me fast enough," he replies with a frown.

"You did your best I am sure," Ann soothingly says, and then she asks, "Has Aquaous seen you yet?"

"No I have only just come...but I must see father first," he replies.

"But Corlean...she has been very sick for weeks...she cannot seem to eat much at all..." Ann tells him.

"She is not going to retch all over me or anything is she?" Corlean dubiously asks.

"Men are such idiots," Ann mutters and after she grabs up the towel and the sugared kelp she turns on her heel and stomps out.

"What did I say?" Corlean turns to Calphin and asks.

"Seemed like a perfectly reasonable question to me," Calphin replies with a shrug, and then he crosses his arms on his chest and adds, "A man has a right to prepare himself for being puked on."

"She used to be a lot more fun," Corlean remarks as he sticks his head out the door to give his sister's retreating form a curious study.

"Yes well she is exhausted from fighting off all her suitors...you missed her big day you know," Calphin informs him with a bit of censure, for when a marsh girl turns sixteen she is officially of courtable age, and that her only sibling was not there to share in it was rather upsetting for Ann.

"I know...I did not intend to still be there by then..." Corlean replies.

"Yes well at least you sent a COM...Ann was very glad to get it," Calphin informs him.

"Worst part is that I have nothing to give her," Corlean says with a sigh.

"You are not serious Corlean?" Calphin asks in disbelief, and then he adds with an amused laugh, "When you fall into the crap you do it with style eh?"

"First of all...I did not know that Aquaous was pregnant...not that it is any of your business...and I tried to find something to bring back for Ann's day from the southernmost marshes but...well ...they did not have anything there fit for my sister...for my whore perhaps...but not my innocent sister," Corlean tells him with a disturbed shake of his head, and then he pleads, "Help me out here Calphin."

"You are lucky that I like you...well...that I like Ann at any rate" Calphin responds, and then he tells him, "There is a new shipment of material from *Lanoua* that just came last night...if you hurry you can pick from it before Ann sees it."

"I owe you one...so who is Ann fighting off by the way?" Corlean asks him.

"Well Oreian for one..."

"Oreian is a shriveled up old man...besides...he has a wife," Corlean narrows his eyes and says, for that the old slug would even think to dishonor his sister so is beyond irritating.

"Not anymore...the wife went toes up a week after you left," Calphin informs him.

"And he is already trolling about for someone to replace her...six months is not even decent!" Corlean angrily retorts.

"That is what your father said after the old toad asked for her," Calphin informs him.

"My father would never even consider it...he would never give her to that shriveled up old pervert," Corlean says with a bit of venom.

"Yes well...that is exactly what your father told him...in a more diplomatic way of course...but now Oreian has sent for his son...and I cannot imagine that he has improved much since last I saw him," Calphin says with a shudder.

56

"Jonin is a twit...ah poor Ann," Corlean replies, and then he says with a sigh, "Well I for one am going to make his stay as unpleasant and short as possible."

"Now...now...you know the penalty for killing an overlord's heir apparent..." Calphin warns with a mocking lifting of his brows.

"Who said anything about killing him...you have a one track mind Calphin," Corlean accuses, but then he sighs and says, "I had best go find my father so that I can see Aquaous before she hears that I am back from someone else..."

"Come on then...I am to meet him in his conference room to tell him what those squatters are up to in private," Calphin instructs.

"They should not be up to anything," Corlean points out with a sneer, for in his opinion his father should have sent those thieves packing years ago.

"Well they are," Calphin impatiently replies, for Corlean cannot seem to get far enough past the thought that the men did not personally ask permission to squat on his father's land to see that letting them stay cost Marsle nothing, but in the end it may gain him a great deal.

The two men walk along in silence then, for Corlean knows better than to get into it with Calphin, not that he is afraid of him or anything he tells himself. It is just that Calphin is an overlord's son and heir apparent just as he is, and one cannot simply blow such a person off without consequences. Not to mention that in Calphin's case the penalty for crossing the line would most likely involve some sort of pain on Corlean's part. Besides Calphin is Aquaous's beloved brother and she would be rather upset to hear that the two of them were fighting again. Therefore for her sake he will not tell Calphin what he thinks about him butting his nose into northern marsh business Corlean decides as the two of them round the corner only to find an old woman unexpectedly blocking their path. With a surprised sound Calphin quickly throws an arm around the woman's waist and pulls her to him to keep her from being bowled over.

"What are you doing just standing there like that Nao-Nao?" Calphin chastises the old healer.

"Waiting for a handsome man to come along of course," the old woman replies with an earthy chuckle.

"I have told you time and again madam...I am a married man," Calphin answers back in mock indignation.

"Never said I was wanting to get wed…" the old woman banters as Calphin sets her on her feet, and then she gives him an ornery swat in the arse before she presents Corlean with a stern face and adds, "Good to see you can still find your way home Corlean."

"Ah Nao-Nao…you know I would not have gone had I known…" Corlean practically whines.

"Save your excuses for your poor wife," the old healer snaps out, and then promptly turns on her heal and makes her way unannounced into Marsle's conference room without another word.

"Ah Nao-Nao…please…do not be mad…" Calphin mocks.

"Shut up Calphin," Corlean angrily responds, and when Corlean shoulders his way past him Calphin yields, for he knows that Corlean's day is about to get a great deal worse.

So it is that when Corlean and Calphin emerge from the conference room a few hours later Corlean's thoughts concerning many things have changed. Not only did he learn that this Karnin person has amassed a larger army than they suspected, but also that he has managed to outfit it with the latest vehicles and armaments some of which not even the marshes could hope to stand against. Luckily they will not have to try, for the bacteria that cause the condition in land men know as 'the rot' is an effective barrier that keeps them out of the marshes. That realization only led to another more worrisome one, for if the marshes are not this Karnin's objective then who is? Thanks to Calphin's nosy ways the answer to that was confirmed to be exactly as lord Boro had told them all those years ago when he asked Corlean's father to let Karnin and his band of thieves squat. Therefore the only question still pending is when? As one might expect though all of that pales next to the implications of what the old healer had come to tell his father and him, for the news that she gave them concerning Aquaous's pregnancy was grim at best.

"I need to see her…now," is all Corlean can manage to say.

"Yes well do not go empty handed…maybe you can get her to eat something," Calphin advises, and then he motions for Corlean to follow him back to the kitchen larder where he once again pulls out a brined cuke. Instead of the sugared kelp this time he goes for the mother of all treats extracting a branch-like plant coated with a hard shell of salt and lotsen nectar that the marsh folk refer to as a sweet tree from its fancy colored glass vessel.

"Is there anything that I should...well...not do?" Corlean hesitantly asks him as he accepts the wrapped bundle that Calphin hands him.

"You should not do anything that she tells you not to do stupid," Calphin advises and then he hands him the sweet tree and says, "Do not worry...she does not hate you...actually I think that she has been pinning for you."

"Really?" Corlean asks with a pleased expression.

"Yes well do not let that go to your head...that could change in a heartbeat...now get going," Calphin says and then heads for the door, but before he exits he turns back and sagely adds, "And I do not care if she has puke in her hair and smells like yesterday's catch if you know what is good for you tell her that she is even more beautiful than you remembered."

"She is not stupid Calphin," Corlean calls after him.

"Trust me in this," his muffled voice calls back.

After Calphin's footsteps have faded Corlean sighs, for he knows that the time has come to face his wife. The problem is that he has not the slightest idea of what to say to her. He had not planned to be gone when she discovered that she was with child. Corlean had not known that it was even a possibility or he would not have gone at all. So he is somewhat nonplused by the fact that he feels so guilty, for he did not stay away on purpose. As he stands there trying to decide the best way to greet her he gets a whiff of something rather foul, and so he gives himself a tentative sniff, for it would never do if she thought he cared so little for her that he would come to her smelling of whatever it is that he is smelling. Luckily it is not himself, but then he thinks that perhaps he has stepped in something nasty, and so he tips up first one foot then the other to check, but nothing there either.

"What is that?!" he asks aloud in frustration and after a more few tentative sniffs lead him to the towel that Calphin handed him he unrolls it to reveal the brined cuke.

With a shake of his head he tosses the thing into the nearest garbage chute, for if by some off reason it does not make her puke it surely will him. Now that he has gotten rid of the offensive thing Corlean finds his self undecided as to what to replace it with, for he has been told that Aquaous has not eaten for several days now at least anything that stayed down, and he would guess that she tried her favorite foods already. He therefore assumes anything from that list will only make her remember what happened the last time

59

she tried it, and so he decides to pick something a bit more boring to contrast with the sweet tree. He therefore helps himself to a few pickled lambis fish from one of the several large jars of them sitting round the larder, for pickled lambis are a popular food and very plentiful as well thus they are put up in quantity each year.

Now that he is armed with his offerings Corlean squares his shoulders and after he takes a deep breath to calm himself he heads out the larder door and crosses to the inconspicuous stairway across the corridor that leads to the wing of the fortress that houses his and Aquaous's apartment. As he takes the stairs Corlean tells himself that everything will work out he will just force it to, for he cannot even consider any other outcome. Just thinking about a future in which Aquaous is absent is unacceptable, and so he decides that he simply will not permit it. Corlean realizes how ridiculous that sounds but for whatever reason just saying it helps. Even so when he reaches the door to their apartment he still finds himself hesitant to go in. What if she hates him for doing this to her? What will he do then?

With a shake of his dark head he reaches over and enters his code into the door, for he is acting like some nervous boy on his way to his first tryst, and that is a rather undignified way for the future overlord of the largest marsh territory in the world to behave. Besides she needs him to be strong for her he tells himself as the door silently slides open. After a cautious peek round Corlean carefully steps into the front entryway of the apartment and pauses to listen, for the healer has told him that Aquaous needs to rest, and so he does not want to wake her if she is taking a nap. Therefore, when he hears nothing but silence he tugs off his leather boots and gently eases them in the boot holder nearby before he softly pads across the sitting room to come to stand in the doorway to their sleeping chamber, and what he sees makes him recall why he was so anxious to wed her.

As it was Corlean was not anticipating meeting his father's overlord friend Bimian's daughter with any kind of enthusiasm, for he knew what they had in mind, and he had heard that Bimian's lady wife was an unruly handful, which is not surprising since she hailed from *Mori*. Since a headstrong wild woman was not what Corlean thought the future overlord of the northern marshes needed as a wife he was fully prepared to meet her and then politely tell his father no thank you in private. Corlean was therefore totally taken by surprise when he was presented to her, for she was not just beautiful she was the most beautiful woman that Corlean had ever laid eyes on. He was rendered speechless. Well more like struck dumb as in the stupid kind of dumb, but unfortunately not the silent kind of dumb. No he just kept babbling and stumbling round with his words until he finally managed to spit out some tripe about the color of her shoes, which made him seem like a fool. Why she gave him a chance to prove to her that he was not Corlean has often wondered, but he likes to think that she could not help herself. After all he is a good catch he thinks with a boyish smile as he leans against the doorjamb.

As Corlean watches her he can tell by her breathing that Aquaous is asleep, and since her back is to him he feels free to take a moment to fully appreciate the turn of her hip and the long, shapely length of her bare leg peeking out from beneath the blanket. Despite his resolve after his eyes have traveled the length of her a few times he can no longer resist the lure of her. He therefore lays his tasty offerings down then steps closer to the bed to gaze down at her face. What he sees there immediately kills any desire that he feels and replaces it with fear, for despite having already heard the healer's grim news seeing the dark circles beneath Aquaous's eyes, and the hollowness of her once full cheeks drives home the reality of their situation.

"Ah my love what have I done," he whispers as he reaches down and lifts her hair from where it has cascaded off the bed and onto the floor.

When he does she stirs a bit, and fearing that he will not be able to stop himself from touching her he quietly takes a seat in a chair on the other side of the room to wait for her to awaken on her own. As he sits there he passes the time by going over all that was said in the meeting earlier. That manages to occupy his mind for a short time at least, for Calphin's information concerning the land men at the edge of the marsh is a bit worrisome since his father's tolerance for their presence on his lands may make him appear that he is in collusion with them. If they attack another overlord the others may hold him accountable, for the truth of it is that no one goes through the trouble and expense to build and equip an army to let them sit idle.

With a soft curse Corlean wishes that he had been firmer about his objections to allowing them to settle themselves on his father's fringe lands, for perhaps his father might have reconsidered. It is too late to do anything about it now except perhaps a bit of damage control he tells himself as his eyes stray to his wife's drawn face. Yes damage control is something that he had best get good at Corlean thinks, for it is too late to do anything about Aquaous's condition except muddle through as well, which makes him feel totally incompetent. On the heels of that comes the gnawing fear that he might lose them both, and although he knows that it is probably wrong on some level he hopes that if there is a choice Aquaous will be the one to survive, but the odds of that have decreased with each month that passed.

As it is Aquaous's pregnancy has just passed the seven month period, and so to terminate her pregnancy even if she would agree to do it, which she would not, would be rather dangerous for her. According to Nao-Nao the neuro-pathways between mother and babe form at six months, and so Aquaous and the child have bonded. Therefore, Aquaous knows how the little one feels about things. She feels when it is cold or afraid, and because of this it is not unheard of for a marsh woman to lose her sanity after suffering the trauma of losing her unborn child this late in the pregnancy. Since they cannot terminate the pregnancy now the only choice left is to try to keep the babe in Aquaous's womb for as long as they can, and so if there is not a marked improvement very soon Aquaous will have to take to her bed until the babe comes.

...*This is all my fault*...he angrily thinks, for that last night before he left for the southernmost marshes he had been so desperate at the thought of not having her body again for such a long time that he did not even let her come up for air let alone do the proper meditation that a marsh woman needs to do to keep conception from taking place.

...*You are an idiot Corlean*... he chides himself, and then with a somewhat dejected sigh he lays his head back and closes his eyes intending to just rest them a bit, but he is soon fast asleep until sometime later when he hears a familiar voice.

"Corlean?"

When Aquaous's voice calls to him Corlean smiles, for in the many months that he has been gone from her he has often dreamed of her, and she has always called his name softly like this. His dreams are usually a bit less real he thinks, but perhaps he is just getting good at it he tells himself. She touches his hand then and when she does Corlean opens his eyes, but for a moment he is confused and disoriented, and he fumbles around in his mind trying to reconcile why it is that her face is so pale and drawn. She always seems so happy in his dreams. Then reality comes crashing in, and with an emotional 'ah love' he scoops her into his lap and buries his face in her hair.

"I missed you," she simply says.

"I missed you too," is all he can think to reply.

"I am sorry Corlean," she softly says, and then much to his horror she begins to weep.

"No sweet what have you to be sorry about?" Corlean asks in reply, but she only shakes her head and cries all the harder, and so he tips her face to his and searches her big blue eyes for something to say that will comfort her.

"I did not want you to see me like this...I am ugly," she tells him, and then she blurts out, "You did not even want to have a babe yet...please do not hate me."

"Aquaous listen to me," he cups her small face in his hands and gently says, and then he leans in and tenderly kisses her mouth before he adds, "You are my life...I could never hate you...and you could not be more beautiful to me than you are at this moment."

"You are such a terrible liar," she replies, and then she gives him a small smile and adds, "I look like I have been slogging in the marsh muck...and I probably smell like it too."

"Yes well you do smell a bit off my love," Corlean replies with a grin, and then he stands with her in his arms and adds as he heads for the bathing pool, "But I have a cure for that."

"You do not exactly smell like flowers yourself you know," she points out as he sets her on a stool and begins stripping her of her clothes.

"Well then I shall join you," he replies with an ornery wink, but once he has her naked and he sees the rather sizable mound where her flat belly used to be he is reminded of her condition.

"I have gotten a bit thin in some places and fat in others," she says, and then she retrieves a nearby towel and tries to cover herself.

"Do not you dare," he commands as he grabs the towel from her hands, and then he reaches down and slides his hand along her belly and gently says, "You could not be more beautiful."

"I am so glad you are home," she replies, and then lays her hand on his and says, "The healer says I may have to start keeping to my bed Corlean...I cannot possibly do that..."

"You will do as she says Aquaous...I will not lose you because you refuse to do what is best," he sternly replies and then lifts her

63

into the ornate bathing pool that encompasses nearly half of the large bathing chamber.

"But Corlean...to just lie there all day for nearly four months...it is simply not possible," she replies and he can tell by the rising pitch of her voice that she is working herself into an emotional outburst.

"You are less than a year from becoming a healer your own self...what would you prescribe?" he asks, and the small flash of anger in her eyes tells him that she would prescribe exactly what Nao-Nao had, "Well love...what does a healer do when her patient can no longer eat or drink...when her patient's body has run through all its fat stores and has begun to consume its own muscle...what does a healer do next then?"

"You...are a great...jerk!" she angrily snaps out at him and then promptly disappears beneath the surface of the water.

With a sigh Corlean stands and peers down into the clear pool, for despite the fact that he had decided against taking a headstrong woman to wife that is exactly what he did, and he has never regretted it. Especially not now he thinks as he watches Aquaous sink to the bottom of the pool, for a less spirited woman would probably not survive what is to come. Still she is difficult to manage sometimes, and Corlean has often found that the best way to convince her that he is right is simply let her think on it for a time. He can only hope that her hormones and her deteriorating physical condition are not wreaking havoc with her mind's ability to reason. Fortunately, that spark of anger just now told him that she is not so far gone that she cannot recognize a logical argument when she hears it.

Besides, the six years that she has spent learning the ways of a healer have not just evaporated into thin air. She will not ignore what the knowledge that she has worked so hard to acquire is telling her. He therefore decides against going in after her just yet, and instead strips off his clothes and then sits on the washing end of the pool where he commences to lather himself all up with one of the various body cleansers sitting nearby. When the unexpected scent of gornea flowers suddenly fills the air he picks up the jar and with a confused frown gives it a sniff, for the red jar normally contains a mixture that smells a bit more gender-neutral than this one does.

"Maybe it is the green jar?" he mumbles to himself, which is a guess that a quick sniff confirms, but instead of switching jars he only shrugs and continues washing. Why waste valuable soap? Besides she will not be able to say that he does not smell like flowers now he thinks with a grin.

After Corlean has covered every square inch of his self with the rich lather he gets up and once again goes to gaze down at Aquaous where she lies on the bottom of the pool. As he watches her he notes that her eyes are closed and he wonders if she has dosed off, which being marsh folk she could do without danger to herself, but since the reduced oxygen of doing such as that normally causes bad dreams most marsh folk tend to avoid it. Unless they are so very exhausted that they cannot help doing so Corlean thinks with a worried sigh as he absently rubs the lather around on his chest while he mulls over the pros and cons of waking her. As he stands at the edge of the pool thinking it over the decision is thankfully taken from him by a long coil of Aquaous's ebony hair that drifts over and touches her face forcing her to open her eyes to capture the offending lock. As one might expect she notices Corlean staring down at her then, and when she does her eyes widen a bit, for he is wearing nothing but lather. That combined with the distortion of looking through the water makes him look like some ravenous god of fertility, which is something that she really does not want or need right now.

"Here I come my darling," Corlean shouts.

Unfortunately, instead of returning his playful banter she gives him an angry glare and quickly rolls over and heads for the far side of the pool leaving a somewhat confused Corlean behind to wonder what it was that he did to offend her. When he comes up empty what Calphin told him flits through his mind, and Corlean thinks that this is probably one of those 'do not do anything that she tells you not to' moments. Therefore with a sigh he decides to just rinse off and see to Aquaous's needs, for she must be very exhausted not to see the humor in his joke. Perhaps it is just that she does not recall the day that she had thought it would be funny to jump upon him while he was lounging in the pool. She gave him a concussion that day, for she came in all helter-skelter and her knee banged his head into the bottom of the pool and knocked him out cold.

Then it occurs to him that she might have feared that he would actually do it. Surely she did not think that he would really have jumped on her? After all he is not an idiot! With a perturbed shake of his head he dives into the water, and as he scrubs the soap from his dark hair he makes a mental note to ask Calphin if Janissa had lost her sense of humor when she was carrying. Yes and if so how long it was before it returned, for Corlean thinks that a bit of laughter might go a long way towards easing Aquaous's fears. So thinking he pushes off and sends his body gliding on an intercept course with her, but much to his consternation, when she sees him coming she quickly hops out of the pool, and takes off across the room in what appears to be a state of panic.

"Aquaous!" he pokes his head out of the water and calls, but she does not reply, and so he quickly climbs from the pool and goes after her.

"Stop Corlean," she says when he strides into the bedroom.

"What is wrong?" he asks, and she can see by the expression on his face that he has no idea what it is that she is afraid of.

"I...cannot Corlean," she tries to explain, and when he gives her a confused look she nervously adds, "You know...I cannot...do it...I simply cannot."

"You have no choice Aquaous," he says a bit more forcefully than he probably should, but he believes that she is referring to having to stay in bed for the next four months since it was the last topic that they had been discussing, and it angers him much that she would still jeopardize her life by refusing to do so.

"Do you think to force me I will stick you Corlean," she replies and then scurries over and grabs a surgical knife from her healer's bag.

"Aquaous..." he warns as he takes a step towards her.

"How dare you!" she waves the knife in his face and shouts, and then she fixes her wide blue eyes on him and emotionally says, "How could you be so unfeeling and selfish...I am so sick Corlean."

With that her hand begins to shake, and Corlean seriously worries that she will drop the knife and cut herself. Fearing that months of worry and the demands upon her body have finally taken their toll Corlean decides not to try to reason with her, for he has no way of knowing what the delusion is that she is living, and so he quickly overpowers her and manages to take the knife without getting himself cut. Unfortunately, Aquaous continues to fight him, and at some point he decides it best to let go of her, but when he does she pulls back a puny fist and punches him in the face. When she does Corlean can clearly see that the anger and fear that she has been holding at bay has overwhelmed her, and so he does the only thing that he can think of he pulls her to him and holds her against him.

"I know you do not want to do this…and I would rather cut off my own arm than make you suffer any more than you already have," he whispers soothingly into her ear, and when she stills he adds as gently as he can, "But if taking to your bed will save your life then that is what you will do…surely you see that I love you too much to let you refuse?"

"What?" her muffled voice asks, and then she turns her face up to him and begins to laugh.

"What is so funny?" he asks a bit miffed that she did not find humor in his joke earlier, which as far as he was concerned it was quite funny, but she would laugh at something so far from humorous as this.

"You are," she replies, and then leans away from him and says, "Of course I will take to bed if I have to…but well…I thought you…ah…wanted me to…ah…well…when I saw you…ah well…you were…um…you looked…up…you know…what are you grinning at?!"

"You are blushing," he replies as his smile widens.

"I most certainly am not," she indignantly retorts.

"You are…ohh…I see," he steps back from her and says, and then he accuses, "You thought I wanted to take you…you thought that I would do that knowing how sick you are?!"

"Corlean…I am sorry…please…" she pleads, but he only turns and walks away.

When Corlean turns his back on her everything that she has suffered in the last months suddenly becomes too much to bear, for Corlean is her life and her strength, and if he leaves her now she will never survive this. That thought is quickly followed by an overwhelming feeling of fear, and although she can tell that she is causing her child undue stress and alarm she cannot seem to stop. At this point Aquaous's mind simply shuts down, for her instincts tell her to protect her unborn child, and at the moment that is the only way to do so. For a time she struggles against the darkness trying to overtake her, but when she begins to see the room fading she knows that she cannot, and that realization is terrifying.

As Aquaous fights to stay conscious an unknowing Corlean continues to walk towards the blanket that he was intending to fetch for Aquaous, for even though he is miffed that she would think him no better than a rutting beast he also knows that she is not really reasoning right now simply running on her emotions. However, before he is even halfway there an odd sound makes him glance back over his shoulder just in time to see Aquaous's body begin to crumple. With an alarmed start he bounds back across the room. As Aquaous feels herself fall she desperately tries to force her arms to move, but they do not respond and fear grips her, for she knows that her body is too weak to heal an injury if she hurts herself. The pain that she expects to come when she hits the floor never does. Instead she feels Corlean's strong arms slide about her, and as she drifts off into the darkness she hears his voice calling, but she is so tired...so very tired...

Chapter Four

As Aquaous stares up at the stars on the ceiling she finds them not in the least bit relaxing, but that is not surprising since she has been lying on her arse looking at such similar things intended to help keep her docile for over four long months. To think four months ago they feared that her babe may not stay in there long enough to grow, but now it seems that he is determined to stay in there forever, for he should have made his sojourn into the world two days ago. In the scheme of things two days is nothing to an unborn babe, but to Aquaous it has been an eternity. She therefore gently massages her distended belly while she issues a silent plea to her unborn child that he come out very soon. The babe apparently objects to that, for she instantly feels a hard kick followed by an all too familiar warm, wet feeling between her legs.

"Oh for the love of all that is..." Aquaous grinds out.

"Are you alright?" the healer's assistant asks from where she sits nearby.

"I peed myself again...I am so sorry Saleni..." Aquaous apologizes.

"Here now...what is a little pee between friends eh?" she replies with one of her good natured smiles, but when she lifts the blanket to replace the pad she suddenly stills and asks in an odd tone, "Where did you say your husband is today?"

"I sent him out to play with Calphin," Aquaous tells her with a tired sigh, for Corlean's constant hovering was grating on her nerves, but when she notices that Saleni only smoothes the blanket back down without changing the pad she says with a hopeful face, "Oh please tell me that it is not pee?"

"It is not pee," she replies, and then she pats Aquaous's leg and tells her, "I will get Nao-Nao...and have someone send for lord Corlean."

As Saleni walks away a sort of faraway feeling comes over Aquaous as if she is surrounded by glass walls that alter the perception of things by muffling the sounds and smells. A rather peaceful place she thinks as she waits for the pain that she has prepared herself for, but when it does not come within a few minutes more she begins to wonder if she is really going to birth the babe now or not. The pains should have begun with the expulsion of her fluids. Perhaps this will not be as hard as some of the births that she has attended with Nao-Nao she reasons. Then the first real labor pain starts in her back and slowly intensifies its way around to her abdomen. By the time it begins to subside she is panting and rather afraid that she might have underestimated how hard this will be, but then the pain fades, and when it does as is usual in laboring women the memory of it blurs.

"Well my girl...Saleni says the time has finally come eh?" Aquaous hears Nao-Nao's voice ask, and then the old healer walks to the foot of the bed, lifts the blanket, and promptly announces, "Why yes it has...and everything is as it should be...you can take the pad now Saleni...Nebara...you come help me with the pool."

"Yes lady healer," Saleni and Nebara respectfully reply in unison and as Saleni sets herself to the task Nao-Nao and the senior most of her apprentices Nebara go into the adjoining birthing room to make certain that the birthing pool where Aquaous will deliver is the right temperature to ease the babe's adjustment to the world.

"What about Corlean?" Aquaous asks.

"They are COM'ing him now...do not worry," Saleni reassures her.

"Oh...damn..." Aquaous manages to say through her clenched teeth as another pain suddenly hits her in the back like a knife.

"Come child...no need to panic now," the old healer says as she calmly walks back into the room.

"I am not panicking...but the pains are too hard...it is too soon Nao-Nao," Aquaous replies with a worried frown, for it is typical for laboring marsh women to have light pains that intensify over several hours time not hard pains from the start.

"It is soon...but not too soon if the babe is ready to come out...but let me take another peek," Nao-Nao calmly tells her as she gestures for Saleni and Nebara to assist her at the foot of the bed, and after the two assistants lift the blanket and push Aquaous's knees up Nao-Nao takes a good look between her legs.

"Yes but..." Aquaous begins, but Nao-Nao interrupts her.

"Saleni...go tell them to tell lord Corlean not to drag his feet yes," is all the old woman instructs as she gives Aquaous's bare leg a reassuring pat.

"Yes lady healer," Saleni replies and then hurries off to do as she has been bid.

"Corlean has gone out on the sleds with Calphin today..." Aquaous tells her as Nebara helps her rearrange her legs and then tucks her back up.

"Mindless creatures men are..." Nao-Nao mutters with a disbelieving shake of her head, for not only has the father gone off, but in the company of none other than Aquaous's brother who is Corlean's stand-in, and with a somewhat angry expression on her wizened face she calls after Saleni, "You better go to the overlord Saleni...he will know best how to fetch them back...and ask him if he will come if need be."

"What?!" Aquaous asks in alarm.

"Nothing to get upset about dear...just a precaution," Nao-Nao tells her in a soothing way.

"But Nao-Nao...I want Corlean to be the one..." Aquaous whines.

"If it comes to using a stand in Corlean will still be able to bond with the child later Aquaous...the important thing is that the child bond with a male figure," Nao-Nao reminds her.

"It is not the same and you know it!" Aquaous angrily retorts, for the first male bond the child makes will be the strongest, and so it is typically the father who makes it.

"It will have to do...but let us not get ahead of ourselves eh?" Nao-Nao cajoles in her motherly sick bed voice, and then she comes to the bedside to wipe Aquaous's forehead with a cool cloth as she tells her, "There is time yet."

Two hours later the healer thinks that perhaps there is not as much time as she first thought, for Aquaous is progressing much more quickly than is typical. She should have expected that though since nothing about Aquaous's pregnancy has gone according to the book she chastises herself. The old healer therefore makes the decision to send for the overlord, for the COM center said that Corlean and Calphin were three hours away at the deep pools when they contacted them, and so there is real doubt in Nao-Nao's mind now as to whether or not he will make it back in time. It goes without saying that Marsle wastes no time coming, but the old healer waylays him and Ann when they arrive and covertly stashes them out of Aquaous's sight in the waiting room. Seeing them would only upset Aquaous and so Nao-Nao sees no reason that she should know that they are here just yet.

Unfortunately, after another hour passes it becomes obvious to the old healer that the babe has no intention of waiting for his absent father to appear. She therefore makes the decision that Marsle will have to be his proxy, for there must be a male presence at the beginning of things, and although the father's would be best any male is better than none. With a perturbed sigh she sends Nebara out to the waiting room to tell Marsle to don the clothes that he has brought from Corlean's dirties, for that way the first scent the babe will smell will be his father's, which will later shorten the bonding time between father and child. When Marsle is ready Nao-Nao steels herself to break the news to Aquaous, and after telling the overlord and his daughter to come with her she approaches the labor bed.

"It is time to push now Aquaous," the old woman informs her.

"Where is Corlean!" Aquaous demands as another pain shoots through her lower abdomen and as it progresses through her body she snaps out, "I will kill him!"

"Yes...yes...just as he deserves...as soon as the babe is out," the healer calmly replies.

"Why would he even leave the fortress when he knew that the babe could come any day now!" Aquaous screeches out.

"You told him to go Aquaous," Ann innocently replies.

"What is he...a twit...to choose now of all moments to listen to me?!" Aquaous rages.

"Ah well dear...he is a man...men do not reason that way," Nao-Nao tells her.

"He is only a few minutes away now Aquaous..." Ann begins.

"He should not have gone so far...no matter what I said!" Aquaous snaps back, and then she gives Ann a forlorn face and tearfully says, "Oh Ann...I am so sorry."

"Here now girl...none of that...it will be alright," Marsle breaks his silence to say.

"We can wait no longer Aquaous..." the old healer says as she swings Aquaous's legs over the side of the bed.

"But Corlean will miss it," Aquaous whines as Marsle steps forward to help her waddle over to the birthing pool, but just then there is a commotion at the door and a rather disheveled Calphin bursts in.

"Wait...he is coming!" Calphin announces as he leans on his knees trying to catch his breath, for they have ridden hard and then sprinted the entire length of the fortress from the dock.

"Babes do not wait lord Calphin..." the healer clips out.

"I am here!" Corlean shouts as he rushes into the room and begins to strip off his boots and riding gear.

"Well get over here then," Marsle barks at him, and then he says, "Get into the pool."

"I hate you Corlean!" Aquaous suddenly shouts as another searing pain comes, and as Corlean wades into the shallow birthing pool she meanly tells him, "You will never touch me again!"

"Into the pool girl," the healer commands and then gives her a nudge so that she will move close enough for Corlean to lift her in and seat her in his lap.

"Now the next time you feel it you push and you do not stop do you hear," the healer stares into Aquaous's tortured eyes and calmly says, and when she does Marsle, Calphin and Ann quietly go back to the waiting room, for he has done this twice before, and so he knows that the fewer the distractions the better things will go.

"Oh...here comes another..." Aquaous suddenly announces.

"Push love," Corlean says, and then he pulls her back against him and adds, "Push hard."

"I...cannot...do this...anymore," she gasps out, and then she whines, "I am so tired."

"Yes you can... women have been doing it since the dawn of time," Nao-Nao replies, and then she firmly says, "Now push girl!"

"You can do this Aquaous...it is nearly over," Corlean whispers into her ear.

"Oh damn..." is all she is able to gasp out and then with a shriek she expels the babe into the pool amidst a blood-tinged cloud of birth fluids and it promptly wiggles away.

"You have a true son of the water," the old healer ceremoniously announces, and then she asks in an official tone, "What do you call him?"

"We shall call him...Milin," Aquaous weakly replies, and then tries to sit up a bit straighter so that she can see her babe.

"Aquaous look...he has your eyes," Corlean tells her as he props her up.

"It has only been seconds and yet his eyes have already opened," the healer notes, and then she gives Aquaous's arm a gentle squeeze and adds, "It is a good omen for his future."

With that the old woman sets about seeing to Aquaous's needs, for the babe has lived the first eleven months of his life in fluid, and so he will be just fine in the pool for a time. Besides Nao-Nao has learned in her seventy-two years as a healer that a period of calm after the birth seems to make what is coming easier for most newborn marsh babes. She can only hope that this babe is not as contrary out of the womb as he was in it. So it is that after Nao-Nao is sufficiently satisfied that Aquaous's condition is good she walks to the edge of the pool and peers down at Milin where he sits huddled in the bottom corner of the birthing pool, for she must now assess his condition, which is not so simple a thing to do as is his mother's was. Still it is possible she muses as she slowly reaches down and slaps the surface of the water, and when Milin's startled head swivels up at her she is pleased, for he is alert and aware, which is a very good sign.

"His senses are good...and those eyes well...he will charm us all," she notes, for as Corlean said the child has inherited his mother's blue *Morianite* eyes, which the healer knows will garner him a great deal of attention through the years to come.

"He shall be greatly spoiled eh Nao-Nao," Aquaous says with an exhausted smirk.

"Of course...how could he not be," the old healer replies, and a few minutes later when she sees Milin's embryonic sac has collapse and fall off she turns to Corlean and says, "Well Corlean...it is time...go and fetch your son to you...his bond with his mother was made long ago...now you must make your own."

"What if he fights me?" Corlean asks as he walks to the edge of the pool and begins descending the stairs.

"Do what your instincts tell you is right Corlean...good grief tough up man...he will not break...just do not squeeze him too hard if he struggles now get in there... slowly...do not spook him..." the healer instructs as Corlean dutifully wades in and disappears beneath the surface of the water.

After Corlean submerges in the pool he floats suspended in its warmth while he tentatively studies his son who is huddled on the bottom below him. To be honest Corlean is rather nervous about this, for his father would not say much on this part of the birth beyond advising Corlean that a father always finds what he needs to make a bond with his new babe. It goes without saying that Corlean understands the theory that each man must listen to his own counsel when it comes to this. After all he will be the one having to deal with the little creature for the rest of his days, and so it makes no sense to make a bond more suitable to someone else's mannerisms and ways of thinking. Knowing that does not help much he thinks, but then he is suddenly struck by how very small and alone Milin must feel down there, and the pain that assails him when he thinks that Milin may feel abandoned and afraid is nearly unbearable.

With his protective instincts fully engaged Corlean is no longer uncertain, and without any further hesitation he slowly swims towards his new son, for he will not allow Milin to think himself alone any longer. So thinking Corlean stops a few feet away from the boy and extends his arms to him. When Milin does not immediately come Corlean feels a brief flash of fear, for if he will not seek the comfort of his own kind it could be a sign that he is not quite right. That could spell disaster Corlean worries, but suddenly realizes that Milin's blue eyes are studying him, which is a relief to say the least. Yes he is mulling it over Corlean thinks, but then an amused glimmer reflects in his eyes, for Corlean thinks that his babe is taking his measure, which is a thing that Corlean finds oddly endearing. Much to Corlean's relief his son obviously does not find him wanting, for the child suddenly kicks off the bottom and squirms his way into Corlean's waiting arms.

"Ah," the healer suddenly says with a satisfied nod from where she stands watching at the edge of the pool, but even though Milin came readily to his father she has birthed enough marsh babes to know that the hard part is still to come.

"He has him...thank goodness," Aquaous nervously says as Corlean swims over to the stairs with Milin in his arms and begins to climb the stairs.

"And so the child born of the water did take the breath of life," the healer formally announces as she goes to stand with Aquaous where she sits bundled in a blanket on a chair near the pool's edge.

When Corlean feels his head break the water's surface he secures his grip on Milan, for the moment has come to show his son the world that awaits him above. Unfortunately, it is unlikely that Milin will understand what it is that Corlean is doing, and although it pulls at Corlean's heart he knows that no matter how much Milin chokes or struggles he must make certain that his son does not get back into the water. This moment is the *Alenio*; the transition, and although it is often a painful thing to witness for both the father and the mother it is an essential milestone that Milin must achieve. As it is unlike land folk's babes those born of marsh folk are born as humans once were in the long ago completely capable of sustaining themselves in the water, and so Milan could essentially live out his entire life underwater without ever breathing the air, which he would most likely choose to do if left to his own devices. It is therefore Corlean's job as his father to make certain that he does not.

As it is had it not been for one tragic event that took place in the long, long ago at a time when air breathing was limited to the lower forms of life all man-like creatures would still be living a life restricted to the liquid portions of the world. In those days the only time a man-like creature felt the breath of air upon his face was when he poked his head above the water's surface to satisfy his own curiosity as to what was up there. The man-like water dwelling creatures of this time period were a primitive, inquisitive lot, and it was their incessant curiosity that led a pregnant female to strand herself in a sea cave when she stayed too long admiring the shimmering rock there. Her subsequent decision to stay in the small tidal pool left behind at the rear of the cave and wait for the tide to return rather than risk crossing the sharp rocks separating her from open water turned out to be most unfortunate, for the pool dried up before the tide returned and she perished.

As often happens in such situations when her life ended the child that she was carrying was involuntarily expelled. Luckily, the pregnancy was close to term and so the child had what it needed to live outside its mother's body. The girl-child's instincts were therefore fully developed and they led her to seek out the deepest portion of the shallow pool in much the same way as Milin had just done, but unlike Milin who had not only his father and mother to protect and guide him the primitive girl-child was alone in a tidal pool that was at the mercy of the weather. That day the weather gods were most unkind, for the temperature soared and so the tidal pool quickly waned in the heat of the day until the child found herself lying in a small puddle with her body exposed to the killing dry of the air.

It was at this moment that a new type of water dweller emerged, for the child had such a drive to survive that when the moment came that she could go no longer without oxygenating sustenance she cried out and the unthinkable occurred; air came in through her mouth. Then the rudimentary lungs that had been lying dormant within her expanded, the water in them was pushed out, and the miracle of miracles happened; her body began to take what it needed from the air instead of the water. Whether or not the water dwellers had been capable of metabolizing oxygen through the lungs before that infamous day is not known, but the present day school of thought is that the lungs had existed for several generations before the cave incident occurred.

Today Milin will make that very same journey, but unlike the girl-child in the cave who had to suffer it alone Milin will have the strength of the man who fathered him to draw upon. Corlean therefore bolsters up his resolve, for this is not something that he can fail at doing, and so before he takes that last step that will take the security of the water from his son Corlean sends a silent request to the powers that be that Milin's lungs do not fail to inflate. Unfortunately such as that has been known to occur with tragic results. That simply cannot happen Corlean thinks and then he amends it with 'I will not allow it to happen'. With a determined set of his jaw Corlean makes eye contact with Aquaous and then steps from the pool, and although Corlean registers the tears sliding down Aquaous's exhausted face he remains silent. After all what can he possibly say to her at a moment like this that she would find even remotely comforting.

No she will not be comforted until she holds her son in her arms, and she will not do that until Corlean completes this one gut wrenching but all important task. Corlean therefore stands there on steps, and as the water drips from his wet clothes he waits for Milin to make the next move. After what seems to be a very long time Milin stirs in Corlean's arms, and short time later he begins to struggle, but since any alarm on his part will only serve to feed Milin's fear Corlean stands firm and forces himself to remain calm. Despite Corlean's composure Milin's efforts to free his self and get back into the water quickly become frenzied indicating that he is running out of stored oxygen. At one point Corlean is forced to wrap both his arms round him just to keep him from slipping away, and when he does his son stares up at him as if he has somehow betrayed him, which Corlean finds hard to bear.

"I love you Milin...breathe," Corlean pleads, and then he cups Milin's small head to his chest and takes a deep breath, but even though Milin stills in his arms Corlean does not feel the movement of his little lungs inflating and deflating.

"He is near the end..." the healer points out.

"Put him back...Corlean put him back!" Aquaous suddenly shrieks, and when she tries to get out of the chair Nao-Nao puts a hand on her shoulder and shoves her back into it.

"Wait!" the healer commands, for her duty now is to make certain that Milin's parents do not give in to their fears and condemn him to a short and lonely life bound to the water.

"I would rather have him live out his days in the pool than to die," Aquaous pleads.

"He will not live long in the pool...his only chance for a long fruitful life is in the air...it is his right...now wait!" the healer commands, and then she hears the telltale gurgling that she has been waiting for.

"Aquaous...he is...he is breathing," Corlean tells her in a shaky voice, and then he strides over to where she sits and goes to one knee at her feet and says, "Here see."

"Oh Corlean...thank goodness..." Aquaous manages to get out.

"Well...well...you two have produced an odd child that is of a certain...not a cough...gag or whimper," the old woman says with a chuckle, but although she seems relaxed her old eyes study Milin very carefully as Corlean places him into Aquaous's anxious arms.

"He is a very brave boy..." Aquaous coos.

"Well...he is a boy alright...knows exactly where the important parts are eh Corlean," Nao-Nao jibes with a chuckle when Milin immediately begins to root around at Aquaous's breast.

"He better learn to share..." Corlean mutters and when he does the old healer chuckles again and gives him an encouraging pat on the shoulder.

"He is beautiful Corlean," Aquaous lovingly says as the babe begins to suckle.

"How could he not be," Corlean replies, and then adds with a cocky expression, "His father is a handsome creature I hear."

"Ha!" Calphin snickers from the sitting area where he withdrew earlier with Ann and Marsle, for the birthing room's sitting area was designed to place a sight not a sound barrier between the laboring woman and those who have come to bear witness to the birth.

78

"Ah well...it appears that he is full..." Nao-Nao points out as she reaches down and gently pries Aquaous's nipple from the now sleeping Milin's mouth, and after she pulls Aquaous's blanket over her bare breast she softly calls, "Come Marsle...come greet your new grandson."

A few seconds later a rather pleased Marsle once again dressed in his own clothes peeks around the corner, and the scene that he sees makes him smile broadly, for even though Aquaous is exhausted she also has that glow about her that Marsle remembers his wife Naona had after birthing Ann and Corlean. The memory is a bitter sweet one he thinks as he walks over and plants a fond kiss to the top of Aquaous's dark head. Corlean on the other hand looks like crap Marsle thinks with an amused grin, for in truth Corlean is done in. Pleased with himself though Marsle adds as he briefly embraces Corlean as a father does his son, but once that is done Marsle slips something into Corlean's hand and pats his shoulder. Corlean for his part does not even bother to give it a glance, for it is the genetic test results done on his son's birth fluids, and so to take a peek at them would be an insult to his wife. Corlean knows that Aquaous understands the rules regarding establishing Milin's paternity beyond question, for Corlean is the heir apparent to the largest of the marsh territories, but like all those fathers before him he finds the whole thing rather distasteful.

"You have done very well for yourselves here...very well indeed..." Marsle emotionally tells them, and after he sends an unspoken question to Nao-Nao who nods in reply he then adds, "I will go prepare to make the announcements...rest while you can...the coming out will take place in six days as is custom."

"Is there any word of my parents Marsle?" Aquaous asks him.

"Not yet but Goberan is with them...try not to worry...I am certain that old clunker of a land transport has just broken down somewhere," Marsle turns back to tell her, for Bimian and Andina had detoured on their way to *Laraqua* to pay their respects to the now deceased overlord Galwor, but even though *Filon Bora* has said that they left days ago they never showed up back at the dock where their crawler is moored.

"Why have they not COM'd for help?" Aquaous asks, but when she does Marsle can see that she is close to tears, and so he crouches so that he can see her eyes when he says the next bit.

"Listen to me Aquaous...the COM system in that thing is just as antiquated as it is...you know that Goberan will not let anything happen to them..." he tells her with a certainty that he does not necessarily feel, but she is exhausted and in need of enough reassurance to ease her mind so that she can sleep, and so Marsle says nothing more only gives her hand a reassuring pat and then takes his leave.

"Oh Corlean...what if they do not make it here in time for the coming out?" Aquaous turns her distraught face up to him and asks.

"You know it cannot be delayed...too many folk have put their lives on hold to come love," Corlean gently replies even though he hates to tell her that after what she has been through, but the truth is always best.

"I know..." she replies rather sadly, and then she calls out, "Where do you think they are Calphin?"

"Knowing our mother they are probably half way to that fortress the squatters built," Calphin replies.

"Father would never allow that," Aquaous retorts with a snort.

"Telling her no is often pointless when she really wants something," Calphin says as he comes to stand nearby, and when he does Aquaous sees Ann trying to peer over his shoulder.

"Ann there you are...come and see him," Aquaous invites.

"Oh Aquaous...he is so precious," Ann coos as she walks over to view the babe.

"I had a hand in it too you know?" Corlean interjects with a disgruntled frown.

"Yes...you are precious too Corlean..." Calphin mockingly comments, which earns him one of Corlean's cool stares.

"I think that it is time for everyone but precious there to go and let them rest now," the old healer who has been standing at a discreet distance softly says, for Aquaous is visibly drooping.

With a smile Calphin gives Aquaous a brotherly peck on the cheek, and after he carefully gives his new nephew a light kiss on the head he stands and offers Ann his arm, which she accepts. As the two walk out Calphin glances back over his shoulder and gives Corlean a rather sympathetic look, for he knows from experience that his friend's life has indeed been changed forever. Nonetheless the adoring way that Corlean is gazing down upon his new son tells him that Corlean does not mind it any more than he did when his own son Corlon was born. Yes there is something about holding a creature that you created from your own body that makes a man see life from a new perspective Calphin thinks as the door slides shut behind him and Ann.

"Bring her along to bed now Corlean," the healer directs after the two have gone, and then she gently picks Milin up before she quietly tells him, "They must spend a few more days here…but now you can stay too."

"Do not forget Corlean…" Aquaous mumbles when Corlean scoops her up and follows Nao-Nao towards one of the birthing center's private rooms equipped with a bed for two and a crib.

"Forget what love?" Corlean asks in reply.

"Your father…he will be waiting with the witnesses," she tells him as he lays her down.

"Let him wait," Corlean replies and then softly kisses her brow.

"No…you will go do as you are expected to," Nao-Nao says with a shake of her head, and then she shoos him towards the door saying, "If you delay too long…that old toad Oreian will put it about that he is not yours."

"I will cut out his black heart…" Corlean throws over his shoulder as he walks out.

"Men…" the old woman remarks.

"What would women do without them Nao-Nao," Aquaous mumbles.

"A lot less," she stubbornly replies, and then she adds, "Now…you must rest…I will not have you anything but radiant as a new mother should be at Milin's coming out."

"Ummm…" she groggily replies as exhaustion finally wins out.

For the next two days Aquaous does very little besides eat, nurse her babe, and sleep. Milin on the other hand morphs into a rather boisterous and demanding babe who cannot seem to get enough of his mother's breast. It soon becomes obvious that Aquaous's strength is much too depleted to produce enough milk for her new son. The healer therefore begins to supplement his diet with a bit of donated breast milk from one of the fortress's women who is just weaning her third child, which takes much of the burden from Aquaous. As a result her condition begins to improve exponentially with each day that goes by. So much so that on the fourth day she is recovered enough to return to her own apartment where surrounded by the familiarity of her own things she spends the next two days being pampered and primped in preparation for Milin's coming out, for it is a big day for her as well.

Unfortunately, the coming celebration is a bit overshadowed by the fact that her father and mother will not be there. As it turned out just as Marsle suspected their old transport did break down and strand them for many days. Luckily, they were not too far from Marsle's squatters although why that is Aquaous will have to wait to find out, for Marsle was not very forthcoming there. At any rate Marsle's squatters of all people have agreed to send a vehicle down to help Aquaous's parents get back to their marsh crawler, which is a rather odd turn of events Aquaous thinks. After all this Karnin had made numerous requests for face time with Marsle, but the overlord has stubbornly refused to acknowledge them. Despite the insult of that when her parents got themselves into a bind Karnin was the one who answered their request for help. Life is strange sometimes Aquaous comments to herself as she dabs a bit more eye cream on what remains of the dark circles under her eyes.

Regardless of the relief that Aquaous feels knowing that her parents are safe she is still disappointed that they will not be here for Milin's coming out tonight. Well at least they are alive and well and will see Milin in a few days she consoles herself with. So long as this Karnin person does not do something dishonorable. Somehow though Aquaous feels that he will not, for even though Marsle has given Karnin the cold shoulder Aquaous knows that the overlord thinks very highly of Karnin's mentor lord Boro, and Marsle is rarely wrong about a person. She supposes that this Karnin could still have turned out bad despite having a good man advising him, but no she will not think along that line not today. Grim thoughts are not permitted today Aquaous reminds herself with a mental shake, for a sad face is no way to thank all those who have worked so hard to give her this special night. With that thought she gets up and walks into the bathing room to soak for a time before the ladies who have volunteered to dress her arrive.

Five hours and much ado later Aquaous stands powdered, primped, coifed and gowned viewing herself in the reflective glass of her dressing room. With a critical eye she turns this way and that taking in every little detail of her appearance, and when she has finished the wide smile that spreads across her face says that she is more than pleased. Thankfully her cheeks have filled out a bit now and the dark circles under her eyes are gone enough to conceal without notice. That being said most of the credit goes to the others, for the fit of her gown is impeccable, and the woman who did up her long black hair skillfully arranged it so that its many twists and woven braids actually show her face to its best advantage. Then of course there are the extras that she put in it she thinks as she notes how the shiny glass beads woven into the sweet up do piled on her head sparkle. How could anyone not be beautiful all bedecked so spectacularly she thinks as she turns and admires the way the material of the long flowing dress catches the light.

"You are magnificent," Corlean whispers into her ear as he comes up behind her and snakes his arms about her waist.

"I better after all this cost you Corlean," Aquaous replies.

"When I saw this material I had to have it for you...only you could do it justice..." Corlean gallantly tells her.

"Well spoken my lord..." Nao-Nao's voice says with a chuckle from the seating area of Corlean and Aquaous's apartment, and then she adds in a more serious tone, "It is time."

"Shall we my lady?" Corlean asks as he offers her his arm.

With a smile that warms both Corlean's heart and his loins Aquaous lays her fingers upon his proffered forearm and allows him to lead her down the various corridors and stairways to the keep's main banqueting hall where the people of *Laraqua* and its sister fortress *Lanoua* are gathering to celebrate the birth of their overlord's first grandchild. As they near the banqueting room Aquaous can hear laughter and buzzing tongues, which is not a surprise since it has been a long time since they had a celebration of this magnitude at *Laraqua*, and so its good folk have been anxiously anticipating the opportunity to don their fancy clothes and make merry. To make it all the more exciting a coming out banquet is also one of the occasions that the overlord gifts his people with a few trinkets of interest, and by tradition they must be frivolous and amusing so as to ensure that the new child is surrounded by only happy thoughts and feelings when he is presented.

This is not just any coming out though. This is the first appearance of the overlord's only son's first son, and the people therefore arrive most anxious to see what he has come up with, for he will surely want to make this moment the most memorable one that he can. Most therefore came as early as is polite and hurried to find their assigned place at table so that they might also claim their prize, and the humorous token gifts that they found waiting there were not a disappointment. So it is that when Marsle enters and takes his place at the head table the hall is filled with the sound of merriment as many giggles are shared amongst the women who flirtatiously wave their new feathered fans as well as the guffaws amongst the men as they share their sometimes bawdy ideas as to what the odd little tool at their place is supposed to be used for.

"So...what is this thing for anyway?" Calphin asks Marsle from a few seats down the table.

"No Calphin...there is to be a contest later..." Marsle begins to explain when he is rudely interrupted by a now familiar voice.

"Ah well Marsle tonight is the night eh?" Oreian says as he approaches Marsle with his son Jonin in tow.

"Yes it is," Marsle glances up from his conversation with Calphin and replies.

"So then Calphin where is your father...he has already missed the birth so I expect that he will at least be attending the coming out of his new grandchild," Oreian inquires with a shrewd narrowing of his eyes.

"Ah well I am afraid that Bimian's absence is not intentional," Marsle interjects, for the last thing that he wants tonight is for Oreian to incur Calphin's wrath. Besides Marsle is not inclined to tell him anything since that bore of a son of Oreian's has been pestering poor Ann, and so he just adds with a shrug, "I am certain that you know how it is."

"Ah...well...yes...of course..." Oreian stutters out, and then he nervously clears his throat and adds, "Yes...well...we had best find our seats...come Jonin."

With that Oreian quickly heads off to his seat at the secondary head table, for despite his rank it is more than proper not to place the overlord at the head table on a very special family oriented occasion such as this if one would rather not. Needless to say Marsle had chosen to 'rather not' the man and so Ann had given Oreian and his bloated entourage their own table although Marsle is now thinking that it could have been placed a bit further away. However, as Oreian and Jonin try to sit down Marsle takes note that when Oreian slides in the man at the end of the bench is practically shoved off, and he realizes that Ann gave them one of the smaller tables that sits ten, which would have been fine had they been ten normal sized marsh men.

"Did we run short of tables Ann?" Marsle casually asks when he hears a rather telling feminine snicker.

84

"Well…you see…the larger one was not as…sturdy father," Ann replies with an innocent blink.

"It is like trying to stuff too many lambis in a jar," Calphin comments in a low voice, which makes Ann giggle behind her hand.

"Do not encourage her Calphin," Marsle warns with as serious a stare as he can muster, but this is not a night for lectures, and besides Ann's punishment for being so rude to the overlord and his people is even now making his way over.

"Here comes pasty face," Janissa warns in a hushed voice, for the man in question has long been known by that particular nickname due to his complete lack of color, but since his mother rest her soul had the most beautiful shade of shimmering silver skin the consensus is that he is so pale because he spends his time laying about indoors.

"I could not help but overhear a rumor going round overlord…that this squatter of yours…this 'Karnin' has asked for an audience with you sir," Jonin says with a tight smile, and after he gives Ann an intense glance he adds rather smugly, "He is only a nobody after all…a homeless upstart I am told."

"Yes well this 'nobody' has managed to amass a sizable and well-appointed army to him with nothing more to offer than the promise of a full belly," Marsle retorts as he lays a hand over Ann's to remind her of her promise not to insult Jonin tonight, and after he gives it a pat he then adds, "It is always best to make friends rather than enemies where possible Jonin."

"What exactly does this Karnin intend to do with this army of his overlord Marsle?" Jonin asks as he openly ogles one of the women serving drinks, and then he cocks his head at him and adds, "I would know if we need to shore up our defenses."

"Ah well what do I care what the land folk do as long as they do it somewhere else eh?" Marsle replies politely enough, but the coolness of his eyes says otherwise as he adds, "And why would you need to worry he is squatting on my land not yours."

"From what I hear this man has not pledged his army to anyone," Jonin presses.

"Again why would that matter to you Jonin…they are land men…why would they want a damn marsh fortress?" Marsle asks somewhat impatiently.

"Ah well…they would all get the rot before they reached that new fortress of yours Jonin…congratulations by the way…I hear it is...very nice," Calphin suddenly interjects effectively directing the conversation away from the squatters.

"Yes...I have heard that *Jonlean* has six guest suits Jonin...but well I am sure that was exaggerated," Calphin's wife Janissa tosses in with a few innocent blinks to make it seem sincere, but when Jonin glances over at Ann and preens a bit Janissa rolls her eyes behind his back.

"No...that is quite correct...three guest rooms all suites with their own bathing pools as well as the master suite...kitchen and the usual large and small dining areas of course...all waiting for the right woman to put her mark upon it," Jonin replies, and then gives Ann a pointed stare, but just then the clang of a bell loudly rings out calling everyone to their seats.

"Hear all and bear witness!" the voice of the old healer suddenly rings out.

Much to the relief of those at the head table, the announcement sends the annoying Jonin scurrying back to his seat, for it would be very impolite to be standing when the lady of the day makes her grand appearance. Not even Jonin would dare to insult Marsle's daughter by marriage in his own hall. Not because he really cares much if he insults her she is that crazy Calphin's sister, but more so because it would not do much to advance his suit for Annitequea. Besides that bastard Calphin would probably blow the gate off his new fortress for it or something Jonin thinks with a sarcastic sniff as he squeezes into his seat. The old healer makes her appearance then all mystical in black as is the custom for healers to wear at such occasions as this, and mindful of Marsle's penchant for preserving the old ways the healer makes a great show of carrying an ornate ewer that contains a small amount of water drawn from the birthing pool immediately following Milin's birth to the center of the room where with a great deal of pomp she ceremoniously empties it onto the ground.

"As it was in the days gone before...wet and dry are now as one..." Nao-Nao announces.

"So it was...so it is...so it will be," the people in the room then recite in unison.

"Behold Corlean...the creator of new life," Nao-Nao then announces with a dramatic sweep of her arm, and when Corlean enters she stays him with the traditional 'waving off' and adds with a mischievous twinkle in her old eyes, "Ah...but first behold she who has chosen to allow it."

86

Without saying a word Corlean holds out his hand to his wife whom he formally and with the required flourish ushers into the room, and when he does a great sigh of appreciation ripples amongst the crowd. As well there should be Corlean thinks as he leads Aquaous round in a wide sweeping movement intended to give everyone a good look. She is beyond breathtaking all clothed in that golden gown that clings and shimmers with her every movement. It is not just the gown though it is the persona of elegance and beauty that the lady presents he decides. In reality it is also Aquaous's having made her grand entrance immediately after the black-clad healer and an elegant but simply dressed Corlean that made it seem as though a bright breath of freshness and glimmering newness blew into the room. *Laraqua's* good folk care little how the scene was painted only how well it was pulled off, and judging by their deafening applause it was beyond their expectations.

That makes Corlean feel proud and a bit relieved, for the fact of the matter is that had Aquaous shown up in a less grand outfit than she did Corlean would have been treated to a great deal of censure. Everyone knows that Aquaous had more suitors than any one girl needed, but even so she chose him to give herself and the gift of a child to. That is no small thing, for she has bound herself to Corlean in a way that cannot be undone, and for the rest of her fertile days her body will accept only his seed. The bond of egg and seed known as the *Cint Oota* is considered to be a sacred thing amongst marsh folk, and although Corlean and Aquaous made commitments to each other when they were wed either one could have gracefully bowed out of it before Milin was conceived. In reality such as that is rarely done, for marsh courtships are long and drawn out for a reason, but even so a husband or wife who decides to annul the marriage for whatever reason is not viewed with any censor as long as it is done before a child is conceived. After that an annulment is a very difficult thing to obtain, and since Corlean is Marsle's heir apparent now that Milin has been born Marsle would never agree to it.

Therefore, that Corlean do Aquaous just honor this night is extremely important. After all she has pretty much bound herself to him forever now, and so as he leads her to her seat at Marsle's right amidst the applause of those gathered he makes every effort to make certain that she remains the focal point of everyone's attention. Corlean for his part feels rather humbled by it all, for that this beautiful creature chose him when she could have had any lord in the marshes makes him feel very special. She will never regret it not while he still draws breath Corlean promises as he seats her in the place of honor at Marsle' right. Once Aquaous is settled Marsle picks up her hand and plants a fond kiss upon her fingers, for she has gifted him with his first grandchild, and to Marsle there could be no more precious a thing that anyone could have given him.

As Marsle watches his son make his way back to where the healer waits he is suddenly struck by a bit of nostalgia, for he remembers the night when he had presented Corlean for the first time. Naona had shined that night, for she was all bedazzled in a gown of shimmering silver and blue. He had given her the largest gemstone necklace ever wrought by *Laraqua's* artisans for the gift of his first child, and in return she had given him another one. A beautiful daughter followed by some of the happiest years of his life before the powers that be took her from him, but now is not the time for sadness he thinks as he turns his attention back to the ceremony.

"I am Corlean son of Marsle...grandson of Tair...great-grandson of Alitin who was the son of Grolin *King of the Northern Marsles*," Corlean formally announces, and then he adds with a great deal of emotion, "I give you Milin son of my heart."

A young woman enters then carrying a swaddled babe in her arms, but even though she is not dressed in severe black she is as custom dictates 'dressed down' in honor of the occasion. Contrary to what one might expect she does not mind forgoing the fancy clothes and partaking of the party, for she is Milin's new nanny, which is a lucrative position that many women vied to get. Yes even now she can feel those who lost out jealously eyeing her she thinks as she holds the babe up a bit to allow lord Corlean to unwrap and take him from her. When Corlean sees Milin in his finery he must admit that he puffs up a bit, for he is a stunning child of that there is no doubt, and when he turns to the crowd and holds him high for all to see the oohs, and ahs tell him that he has not just gone doting parent blind. Milin for his part does not burst into tears when he sees the crowd of unfamiliar faces staring at him as many babes do. Milin not only shows no fear of them he actually goes a step further and treats his audience to one of his dazzling dimpled smiles.

"He is so perfect," Ann coos.

"Adorable," the wife of one of *Laraqua's* guard captains says from further down the table.

"He has the lady's charmed ways overlord," Oreian calls out.

"Aye that he does," Marsle replies with pride.

"Oh can you imagine what a beautiful girl-child you two would produce," the wife of the guard captain says with a sigh.

"I do not have to imagine...I have only to gaze upon my wife to know it," Corlean walks up to where Aquaous is seated to say, and after he hands Milin to her he takes her hand and plants a kiss upon her palm.

"Well said Corlean," Marsle approves with a nod.

"You have given me the greatest of gifts," Corlean tells her, and when he goes to one knee a hush falls, for this is an important moment that no one present wants to miss, and therefore when Corlean then offers her an ornate box many necks are stretching to see inside even as he sweetly says, "Nothing I could ever give you in return could ever compare to what you have given me...but I hope that this will come close enough to please you."

As Aquaous reaches out to take the box many people towards the rear of the room stand so that they might see better, for this is Corlean's wifing gift as it is called since the birth of their child has made them man and wife in fact now. It is a very special moment and therefore wifing gifts are always as grand as the means of the couple involved can provide. In this case Aquaous's wifing gift is expected to be quite impressive. After all Corlean is the only son of the most powerful of the six marsh overlords, and Aquaous the daughter of the second most powerful so anything less than that would be the greatest of insults. Be that as it may be tradition says that tonight is Aquaous's night, and so despite their desire to see inside when Aquaous pauses to finger the box and admire its craftsmanship those gathered resist the urge to encourage a hastier reveal.

Aquaous not being the type of woman who begs for attention does not keep everyone waiting too long, and so she only takes the time to trace her finger along the words of endearment carved into the box's lid before sending Corlean an excited glance from under her lashes. Then with a graceful flourish she lifts the box's lid. However, when she peers inside she immediately gasps and snaps the lid shut again, which causes a stir of mumblings in the room. The confusion only deepens when Aquaous simply clasps Milin to her and stares unmoving into Corlean's eyes. So it is that when a tear silently makes its way down her cheek the people gathered round who were not privy to Corlean's gift ahead of time begin to get a bit indignant on Aquaous's behalf.

"Shall I bash him for you then sister?" Calphin asks even though he knows that she will not say yes, for he knows what the box contains, and that she is merely overwhelmed by the magnitude of it.

"Do not you dare," Aquaous whispers and then reaches over and strokes Corlean's face.

"So what do you think...shall you show them what it is love?" Corlean asks, for being rather proud of his gift he would like all to know of it, and with a nod she throws back the lid.

"Oh Corlean..." Aquaous whispers as she reverently lifts the metal placard from the box, for upon it is carved the eel-like fish known as a ganbe that is the symbol of her father's house entwined around the long-billed marsh bird of Marsle's house.

"Do you like the name?" Corlean asks.

"*Aqualean*...oh Corlean this is just...I have no words..." Aquaous replies as she traces the name scripted across the top of the plaque with her finger.

"It is not far away from here...but far enough to be private," Corlean says loud enough for everyone to hear, for he knows that they all recognize what the real gift is here.

In truth the placard in the box is not all that refined in appearance, but since it is only meant to represent the real gift, which by its nature could not be gift wrapped and brought to the occasion it matters little to anyone that the box that the placard came in is much better worked than it is. Everyone even those who are not fortunate enough to have one of what the placard represents knows what they are, for what Aquaous holds was created to provide the artisans with a working model from which to fashion a much larger and more ornate version from. Although such signs are used to identify various places one such as this is designed to hang upon a very specific place, and there is one thing that one must have before one could make use of it: a fortress with a gate.

"I want to see it..." Aquaous says with the enthusiasm that one might expect a woman who has just been gifted a fortress would show.

"Yes well not in the dark my dear," Marsle firmly says as he gives his steward the nod to begin serving, and when Aquaous graces him with a pout he pats her hand and adds in a doting way, "It would spoil your first sight of it...we will all go see your new home tomorrow."

Everyone begins to talk at once then, and as the noise level increases so does Milin's restlessness. Therefore, it is not long before he manages to get one of his chubby little hands in Aquaous's plate, and when he coos and reaches for her breast Corlean quickly scoops him up before he can spoil her gown. As he puts Milin in his lap and wipes his hand clean Corlean cannot help but be amused, for Milin is giving him a rather perturbed frown that he can actually sympathize with. It goes without saying that Corlean would like nothing better than to fondle one of Aquaous's breasts too. Alas he will have to wait just a bit longer, for she will be much too tired tonight. Still perhaps after she sees her new home tomorrow she will be in the mood to reward him, and although a bit of heavy petting is about all they can do yet at this point Corlean is willing to take whatever he can get.

Chapter Five

As the small vehicle clips along the road Karnin sits staring out the window going over the possible motives good and bad that overlord Bimian might have for sending his man north to *Onyat* to ask for their aid. It goes without saying that this Borsen person came prepared to be interrogated, and so was armed with a somewhat plausible explanation as to what the marsh overlord's land transport was doing so far north. The gist of it is that they were intending to take a look at the fissure that lies to the north before returning to the dock where their marsh crawler is moored when their old transport began to give them trouble. It seems that overlord Bimian has some interest in such natural phenomena. All very neat and tidy Karnin thinks but about as believable as the thought that he would just decide one day to take a walk in the marshes. No the only plausible part of the whole tale was that before contacting *Onyat* the overlord had asked for assistance from *Filon Bora*, but even though they said they would relay the overlord's request to overlord Tok no one ever came. That part Karnin has no trouble believing.

The entire story had more holes in it than Karnin cares to count. Still he can hardly pass on this opportunity, for as it turns out overlord Bimian was on his way to *Laraqua* for the birth of his daughter's first child. Since the father is none other than Marsle's son and heir helping Bimian out might just get Karnin that meeting with Marsle that he has been asking for. Not that Karnin would not have helped overlord Bimian out if it would not, but it is nice to be handed a little perk for doing the right thing once in awhile. Actually Bimian's close connection to Marsle explains how he knew that *Onyat* was even there. Apparently Marsle is more than willing to discuss *Onyat* just not with him. So now instead of dealing with just one snooty marsh overlord he must contend with two. Sometimes he wishes that he had a tad less honor. Then again it would not have mattered much since Torli has enough honor in him for both of them plus some Karnin thinks.

A few minutes later Karnin feels the runner come off speed, and when he does he gets up and flips on the bank of camera monitors mounted above the runner's control console. What he sees actually makes his mouth drop open, for there blocking the road ahead sits a relic of days long gone by. Not just any old relic either, but the largest and most cumbersome land transport ever designed and built. The signs of age tell him that it is all original and not some nostalgic replica although who in his right mind would ever want to copy that thing they only produced a handful for a reason. Even so just to have the opportunity to see one of these things up close is an unexpected treat, for as far as Karnin knows they were all repurposed many years ago. Except this one apparently he amends as Torli steps next to him. Surprisingly enough the old clunker seems to be complete Karnin thinks as he notes that the transport is still sporting its original can barrel weapons although it is fairly obvious that they are no longer operable since one of them is sitting off center in its exterior housing and the second is not fully retracted into its parking spot.

In the end even though Karnin is very glad to have seen a piece of history he is also a bit disappointed, for the condition of its gunnery would suggest that the overlord is stupid, and that is a complete let down. Yes he would have to be to leave those guns in such a state, for doing so is an invitation for someone to attack him. Although not being a military genius is not a crime, and so he could still turn out to be a decent man who is just too naïve to believe that anyone would want to attack him in the first place. Perhaps he thinks to disguise himself as a poor man. After all it is common knowledge that some overlords have picked their territories clean. Unfortunately the time period where that old ploy would have worked passed when old vehicles like the overlord's stopped being common place. Now a days that old wreck that he is driving round in will not go unnoticed it is just too damn out of place Karnin thinks.

As Karnin stands watching the object of his interest grow ever larger on the forward camera monitor he nudges Torli to get his attention, and then signs the words 'what do you think' to him in the cryptic language that they have been developing since they were boys. When he is finished Karnin glances over at overlord Bimian's man Bornan, and just as he thought would be the case the man is all eyes and ears. Frustrated ones though Karnin adds to his self, for when Torli signs back to him the words 'nice old machine' Bornan's frown deepens. Yes nothing will frustrate a man more than having to spy on guys who talk in code Karnin thinks as he turns back to the camera monitor. What did Bornan expect that they would blab like stupid boys Karnin thinks as the runner's navigational system begins to announce its arrival at the targeted coordinates.

"Take us off the road and alongside them Han," Karnin calmly commands.

"Aye sir," Han acknowledges as he takes his machine off auto, and after he guides it to the position that Karnin has requested he turns the runner in place so that its door side is facing the old transport and then cuts its drive field.

"Alright gentlemen...let's go see what we can do...get the door Seasle," Karnin directs.

"Door coming open!" Seasle calls out as he walks over and hits the door release.

"Well...lead the way Bornan," Karnin requests with a polite enough nod to overlord Bimian's man.

"Of course sir," Bornan responds and then without hesitation he walks over and hops out.

The other men follow suit but when Karnin and Torli step from the vehicle a string of curses ensues from the direction of the antiquated old transport that makes the men exchange a few dubious glances with each other, for the language is rather imaginative to say the least. As a matter of fact there are a few words and phrases that they have not even heard put together in such a way before, and so when Karnin sees Seasle give Cerl an appreciative nudge he does not bother to remind him that they are trying to appear dignified and professional. As one might expect the term 'festering old bloated carcass not fit to feed a starving dung worm' falls short of what is considered polite talk. Besides that jab that Seasle gave Cerl was actually one of admiration, for Seasle greatly admires a colorful curse. As a matter of fact that one will probably be Seasle's new phrase-of-the-day Karnin thinks with a shake of his dark head.

"I still think you should wait in the runner until we sort this out Torli...they've just come from *Filon Bora* after all," Karnin quietly mutters.

"I'm done hiding," Torli stubbornly replies.

"Bit late for him to hide anyways," Seasle points out in a subdued tone as he inclines his head towards Bornan, for he has already seen just about everything that he was sent to see or so Seasle believes.

"Yeah..." Karnin concedes with an impatient sigh, and then he reminds the other men, "Eyes and ears open...and don't do anything that's gonna embarrass us."

With that Karnin, Torli, Cerl, and Seasle follow Bornan across the open road between Karnin's runner and the disabled transport while Ahnin and Gorg step out and take up guard positions at the halfway point, for Karnin has not yet decided whether or not to trust these marsh folk. Even if he did Bimian is still an overlord, and his kind are always targets. Besides even though Bornan seems like an up-an-up guy many regular folk are, but what they also are is bound to obey the man who puts food in their bellies, and that man can often be an ambitious arse. Then there is Bimian's family ties to Marsle, which as one might think may make him a bit less inclined to treat with Karnin honorably if such as that exists anymore outside of *Onyat's* walls Karnin thinks as he notes the group of marsh men who have gathered near the disabled transport's door.

"I have brought them sir," Bornan announces when they get close enough to be heard.

"Ah well it would have been hard not to notice that already Bornan," a voice that Karnin recognizes as that of the imaginative marsh man they heard earlier replies without pausing from whatever it is that he is doing in his vehicle's power plant compartment.

"How can we be a service to you?" Karnin inquires, for the overlord would hardly be working on his own machine, and so Karnin logically assumes that this man is most likely one of the overlord's guard captains.

"Have you a big gun on that magnificent machine of yours...I should like to put this piece of crap out of its damn misery," the man cocks his head up at them and asks in reply and when he does Karnin and his men are immediately struck by his eerily translucent eyes, for until this Bornan came pounding at the gate none of them had ever seen a marsh man in person before, and so they are still trying to get used to their odd eyes and coloring.

"Ah well...maybe it's not terminal yet...how about you let my master mechanic take a peek and see if it can be saved?" Karnin offers as he gestures for Han who is waiting by the runner with the other men.

"This piece of crap is beneath him sir...give me your hand weapon Bornan...I will shoot it myself!" the man holds out his hand and demands, but when he does Bornan hesitates, and then sends a rather tall marsh man discreetly standing nearby an unspoken question.

"Now...you know that you cannot use a hand weapon for that overlord," the tall marsh man intervenes with, which surprises Karnin a bit since he would not have pegged the man with the imaginative mouth to be the overlord.

"Always the voice of reason eh?" the overlord sends the tall marsh man a disgruntled stare and asks, but since it is not really a question the tall man does not reply.

"Really Bimian do not be so rude," a woman's sultry voice suddenly calls from inside the vehicle, and after the men standing around part a pale rather shapely leg appears and a woman gracefully disembarks.

"The truth is often rude my dear..." the overlord calls and then holds out his hand in silent command that she come to him as he says, "May I present my wife the lady Andina...ah...?"

"General Karnin sir," Karnin replies.

"You must forgive my husband's foul mood...general...he has been out in the sun and heat longer than he should have been," Andina tells him as she gives her husband a rather impatient shake of her head, for he should have known better than to overstay his time outside, and then she turns to Torli and asks, "And who have we here?"

"Commander Torli lady," Torli answers with a polite nod as he struggles not to stare, for Bimian's wife is the most exotic-looking thing that he has ever laid eyes upon to date.

"I hope you gentlemen will forgive my sorry state...but it is very hot today," Andina says politely enough as she gestures to the short rather translucent shift-like dress that she is wearing.

"It's unseasonably hot for early spring I agree...but as for your state being less than it should be...I'm sure I don't know what you're talking about lady," Torli politely replies even though he thinks that she knows exactly how fetching she is with her long dark hair loose and her shapely legs out not to mention those large blue eyes.

"Perhaps we'd best continue this conversation inside out a the sun while Han sees if anything can be done with your vehicle overlord," Karnin suggests, for even though he is not certain how a marsh man seems when he is beat down by the heat he is somewhat certain that it is similar to the overlord's rather wilted posture.

"It is your time to waste master Han," Bimian concedes with a half-hearted wave of his hand.

"Stay with him Cerl...make sure he don't offend anybody," Karnin quietly instructs, and when he does Cerl nods.

"Problem general?" the tall marsh man who Karnin assumes must be the overlord's guard captain asks as they follow the overlord and his lady to the transport's door.

"If you got a broken machine Han's your man...but diplomacy...not so much..." Karnin explains with a small grin.

"Ah well...as you have seen...diplomacy is not exactly our strong suit either," the man replies with a shrug.

"Diplomacy is highly overrated!" the overlord calls over his shoulder before he climbs into his transport, and when he does the tall marsh man just smiles indulgently.

The fact that the tall marsh man obviously shares a close camaraderie with the overlord speaks much to Karnin about this man's position as well as the overlord's style of holding his men's loyalties. It says that Bimian has enough self confidence to allow such an informal bantering in front of his men. Well or that he is an incompetent nut case, but judging from the way his men are protectively sizing them up Karnin would guess the former. No the overlord is someone who men are willing to die for, and that is not something that comes easy. Actually Karnin thinks that Bimian has a style of leadership much like Torli's, which is rather convenient since he knows how to handle someone like that Karnin thinks as he steps up into the overlord's vehicle.

When Karnin steps inside Bimian's land vehicle he is immediately assailed by the smell of dampness, and although it is not unpleasant in a foul sort of way it is a bit more cloying than he would prefer. Still it is no worse than some other places that he has been and so he heads for the seat that Bimian waves him to. As he moves through the vehicle's main compartment Karnin takes note of the tangle of large pipes running across its ceiling and assumes that they are part of the environmental system, for the pipes run into and out of a large control panel on the wall. All in all though it seems like a rather slapped up and patched together system, which sort of matches everything else on the old transport Karnin decides. You would think that a man of Bimian's importance would have a better means of travel than this old relic, but he may just feel it a waste of resources being that he rarely travels by land.

Karnin's musings concerning the overlord's lack of a proper transport are rather rudely interrupted at the same moment that he discovers that the overhead piping does have a purpose that is secondary to environmental control. It is a memorable moment to say the least, for when he and Torli who is following behind him are only a few steps away from the table where Bimian and his wife have seated themselves Karnin suddenly finds his self staring into a pair of enormous yellow eyes. As he and Torli stand frozen in place the eyes look them up and down and then after staring into Karnin's face a few more seconds they disappear back into the network of piping overhead. The whole thing is so abrupt that Karnin automatically searches the ceiling for a glimpse of whatever that thing was just to reassure his self that he actually saw it.

"You must excuse my Onot...she is just curious," Andina says with an amused smile.

"What exactly's...an Onot?" Karnin asks as he and Torli nervously continue on towards the overlord's table.

"A pain in my arse that is what it is," Bimian retorts, and then adds for clarification, "And if it gets much bigger it is going back where you got it madam."

"Truthfully general Karnin we are not exactly sure what she is...I found her when she was only a tiny cute little thing, and then she just...grew!" she says with an animated gesture, and then she adds with an apologetic shrug, "I suppose we will just have to wait and see what she is when she stops."

"Aye wait and see me have to cut you out of her gut one day," Bimian shakes his head and says.

"I'd be interested to know when you find out lady...and it's just Karnin...please," Karnin replies as he takes a seat across from Bimian.

"Commander...please sit," Bimian gestures to Torli and requests, and then he adds, "As you might have surmised I do not have much patience with pomp and ceremony."

"Nor I," Karnin interjects in an attempt to redirect Bimian's attention from Torli, for the man seems to be studying him quite hard, but when that does not seem to deter him Karnin meets his eyes and says, "I'm told you and overlord Marsle're close friends sir...I got an urgent need to speak to him....but he doesn't seem interested in talking to me...perhaps you might advise me on the best way to change that."

"Ah well he will gladly talk to you...but not over a COM...Marsle likes to be able to see a man's eyes when he meets him for the first time," Bimian replies.

"I see..." Karnin replies and something about the way he says it tells Bimian that the general has a quandary.

"Let me make a deal with you general...if you give us a lift back to the dock in that fine machine of yours I will get you a meeting with Marsle," Bimian offers.

"That's very generous a you sir...but time's my concern now you see," Karnin replies.

"Yes...so I have been told...moving south I hear," Bimian prompts as he carefully watches Karnin's reaction to his words.

"Gossip mongers're often just trolling for the truth sir," is all Karnin replies.

"Is that a warning general?" Bimian asks, and when he does Karnin sees that his eyes are not actually colorless at least not when they are sparkling with anger at any rate.

"Peace sir...only a suggestion that you be careful a anything you might a heard at Galwor's mourning," Karnin replies as he watches Bimian's reaction to that.

"I would not give two seconds of serious consideration to anything that I heard in that nest of thieves...what I heard about you and your men I heard from my own sources," Bimian replies, but his experienced eyes do not miss the relief that passes between the general and his commander when he does.

"Your sources are accurate sir...we're packing to move...it's actually what I wanted to talk to overlord Marsle about," Karnin tells him.

"Well...my offer is still on the table general," Bimian tells him and because it is critical to find out if Tok knows that they are coming south Karnin takes a second or two to mull the suggestion over.

"I'm not sure I can take you up on it overlord...but that ride...that's a done deal if you need it," Karnin tells him pleasantly enough.

"That is very generous of you general...we will of course accept," Bimian replies.

"Ah well there's one catch though overlord...I can't take you to the dock...I'd rather not beg *Filon Bora* for a pass through...there a clear spot along the traveling channel to the north we might be able to make the transfer from?"

"Yes...there is a section of the traveling channel that gets fairly shallow along the shoreline...how far is that?" Bimian defers to the tall marsh man who is standing a discreet distance away.

"About one-hundred miles north of the dock overlord...but it will take our crawler longer to get there than the general's machine," the tall man replies, but before anything else can be discussed one of Bimian's guards interrupts.

"Excuse me overlord but this man wishes to speak to general Karnin," the guard tells him.

"Let him come," Bimian directs.

"What you got Han?" Karnin asks when the guard steps aside and Karnin spies him gawking around near the rear of the transport.

"Ah well sir it ain't good news...the couplings're completely gone," Han steps forward to report, and although he keeps speaking to Karnin judging by his furtive glances Bimian would guess that commander Torli is actually the one who he seems to want to talk with.

"What about the environmental generators?" Torli asks, which confirms the overlord's suspicions as to who runs what in Karnin's army.

"Generators're inoperable without the power plant...and it's completely gone...they got one battery left that ain't puking its guts all over...we could try charging it but I don't think it'll last more an two hours or so," Han informs him with a shrug.

"I did warn you that you would be wasting your time master Han," Bimian remarks.

"Wasn't all for nothing overlord...not everyday a man gets to see an antique like this up close and personal," Han replies with one of his lopsided grins.

"Yeah well we're gonna take the overlord and his people to a rendezvous point with their marsh crawler...we'll need to offload whatever we can to make room for them and their stuff...we'll leave it with a guard and pick it up on the way back," Karnin directs, and then he adds, "Looks like you're gonna get to see that big hole in the ground after all overlord...we'll do a drive by to kill some time."

"If you will loan me your COM system I will get our crawler moving general," the tall marsh man requests.

"A course...Han'll help you with that," Karnin replies and then gives Han a nod of dismissal, but before the two men walk off Karnin notices that the overlord seems to be less than happy about things, and so he asks, "Is something wrong overlord?"

"I did hear something at *Filon Bora*...something that I feel I must tell you," Bimian begins, but then he pauses a second as if considering his words before he gives Karnin a direct look and says, "The new overlord is a rather talkative fellow especially when he drinks spirits...and he spends a lot of time doing so by the way...on one such occasion he asked me whether or not Marsle controlled that fortress of yours...I am afraid that I might have...misled him a bit..."

"Oh please Bimian...you lied your arse off..." Andina breaks her silence to comment with a rather unladylike snort.

"Yes well...overlord Tok was hardly polite to us..." Bimian protests.

"He was a total ingrate...we had to sleep in this transport..." Andina indignantly tells them.

"Yes well...as it turned out that was a blessing...at any rate...I do not see what I said as lying my dear...more like...just a harmless joke," Bimian responds, and this time it is not the lady who makes an amused sound, but rather the tall marsh man who then promptly turns on his heel and follows Han out, and when he does Bimian calls after him, "That is my story and I am sticking to it!"

"What exactly did you say sir?" Karnin cannot help but ask, for he really needs to know what Bimian told Tok.

"I told him yes...last I heard from Marsle he said that he was going to put an end to his little squatter problem...I am afraid that overlord Tok may have gotten the impression that you are cooling your heals in Marsle's tank general," Bimian replies with a rather boyish grin.

"How'd he take that news?" Karnin asks with a smile that he cannot seem to keep off his face, for Bimian has inadvertently screwed Tok more than he could ever imagine.

"Seemed rather pleased by that..."

"So...do you know him...this Tok?" Andina asks Torli with a few well placed blinks of her lovely blue eyes.

"Tok's...let's just say the less you see a him the better you'll be lady," Torli replies rather abruptly or so Bimian thinks, but before he can ask him of it Karnin gets to his feet and as one might expect his commander follows suit.

"If you'll excuse us overlord...we'll go make sure things're getting done out there," Karnin tells him.

With a polite nod to Bimian and Andina Karnin and Torli then make their way towards the exit door, but when they are about half way Torli suddenly finds his way blocked by what appears to be a rather large fat tail covered in reflective scales. After sending a nervous glance to the ceiling Torli then tries to step over the thing, but the animal seems to be expecting that, for when Torli lifts his leg the creature raises its tail to match. It soon becomes apparent that the creature is doing it on purpose, for it only moves when Torli does, and then lifts its tail just enough to keep Torli from stepping over it. Karnin actually thinks that the whole thing would be rather humorous were it not so very unsettling. Besides Torli's face says that he would like to give the big tail a swift kick, which would be a foolish thing to do under the circumstances Karnin decides as he tenses to come to Torli's aid if he should decide to go that route.

"Onot stop that!" Andina chastises as she gets up and comes over, and after she grabs hold of the large tail so that Torli can step past she adds, "The nice men will leave you behind do you keep toying with them."

"No madam that is where I draw the line...I will not foist that monster upon them Andina!" Bimian irritably says.

"But Bimian...she will dry up and die this far from the marshes," Andina returns.

"It's quite alright overlord Bimian...we couldn't live with leaving the animal here to die sir," Torli says before the overlord can reply to his wife, and after he gives a grateful Andina a polite nod he and Karnin continue walking, but as they go out the door Andina hears the commander mutter, "If for no other reason than to see it."

As Torli emerges from the overlord's vehicle with Karnin the hot dry air hits him square in the face, and he feels empathy for the marsh folk who have been stuck here for days in it. After all one cannot stay inside that dark thing hour after hour without going out in the open air. Unfortunately the temperatures today are

102

oppressive even to Torli, and so he can only imagine how the marsh folk feel being out in it. Torli on the other hand will acclimate himself to it in a short amount of time, and sure enough by the time he and Karnin reach the runner neither man notices the heat much anymore. The same cannot be said for the two marsh men accompanying them, and so Karnin wastes no time giving Seasle and Cerl their instructions. So it is that a few minutes later Karnin goes off with Cerl to take stock of what cargo the marsh folk have while Torli heads towards the cargo area of the runner with Seasle and the two marsh men to help Han offload whatever they can live without for a few hours.

Torli leads the marsh men along the side of the runner with the marsh men in tow until at a seemingly random point he simply stops or so the two marsh men think as they look around for the reason for it. Their reaction pleases Torli a great deal, for to date he has not been able to test the effectiveness of his door camouflage. After all one cannot rely on the opinion of men who already know that the door is there. Therefore that the two marsh men with their supposedly superior eyesight do not see it is very compelling. It is also a bit of a relief to have one's own opinion verified especially when it concerns something as important as door security. As it is doors are the most vulnerable parts of a machine like this one, and so to keep their location as inconspicuous as possible is the usual goal. Torli's 'shadow technology' has taken that a step further, for it uses a variable light within the door's edges to eliminate the shadow that the slight gap between the door and its frame casts, which effectively makes the runner's shiny metal sides seem unbroken. Unless one knows how to ask it not to Torli adds.

"Open…" Torli quietly commands, and after a brief pause the automated security system announces that Torli's voice has been verified after which the outline of the runner's rear cargo door appears and as it silently slips open Torli turns to the two rather dumbfounded marsh men and says, "Come aboard gentlemen."

"Your vehicle is most impressive…" the younger of the two marsh men states as he steps inside the cargo hold.

"It gets us where we need to go…" Torli responds, but then he thinks that sounded rather much like a jab at their old equipment, and so he quickly adds, "Don't take that the wrong way."

"The truth is what it is," the younger man replies with a shrug.

"Yeah well...vehicles that are seldom used often develop problems," Torli generously says, but then he decides that now is the time to change the subject, and so he turns and gestures around him while he says, "This bay connects with the next through a set a roll-back doors."

"Do those roll-back doors open all the way...and can we leave them like that while we are moving?" the older marsh man asks as he surveys the room, and then he turns to Torli and explains, "Onot is rather...large."

"Yeah...we'll move whatever we cannot offload out of the first two storage areas and into the third...will a space twice this size accommodate it?" Torli asks.

"Yes commander...it will," the older marsh man replies.

"The overlord...his lady and the rest a you can ride up front in the passenger compartment...will the animal be alright back here alone?" Torli asks, for he would rather not have some crazed beast flopping around in the back of his vehicle if he can prevent it.

"Yes sir...we will leave her a pile of fish...and as long as we give her a cozy nest she will be content and sleep...Onot is exhausted from so many days of being cooped up in the transport," the older marsh man tells him.

"Alright then...you hear all that Han!" Torli calls, for he can hear Han rummaging around somewhere in one of the compartments.

"Yeah...I got it...we gonna need some kind a cage for this beast?" Han calls back.

"No...but she likes to have some place off the ground to hide master Han!" the older marsh man takes the liberty of replying.

"I got a couple nets big enough to span these two cargo bays!" Han's voice offers.

"That should be big enough," the younger marsh man interjects, and when he does Han peers around the corner.

"What kind a animal we talking about?" Han asks with a somewhat dubious expression on his face.

"Ah well Han they're not sure what it is," Torli responds.

"Uh-huh..." Han drawls out, and then he cocks his head at them and asks, "It gonna eat anybody?"

"Onot has never eaten anyone that we know of," the older marsh man assures him with an amused glint in his eyes.

"Yeah...that's what everybody says," Han sarcastically mutters as he disappears back into the next bay again, but a second later his voice asks, "This thing potty trained or's it gonna crap all over my floor back here?"

"If it does someone'll clean it up Han," Torli impatiently tells him.

"Yeah well so long's it's not me...you know how much it weighs...my nets top out at two-thousand?" Han's voice asks.

"She is big and bulky but not overly heavy...it has been a long time since she was weighed but I would say she is definitely less than two-thousand," the older marsh man replies.

"Come on back...see if you want the course nets or finer ones," Han directs, and when he does the two marsh men walk back to him, but when they do Seasle steps next to Torli, for he does not trust the marsh men much.

"Onot might put holes in that fine net," Torli and Seasle hear the younger marsh man say.

"Ain't no animal gonna a bust that net...you could blow a bomb up in the thing and the shrapnel'd still be in there when it was all said a done," Han brags.

"In that case they will do quite nicely then," the younger marsh man replies.

"Lordling..." Seasle quietly mumbles to Torli who acknowledges his observation with a nod, for Seasle never misses much despite his clowning ways, and Torli agrees that the younger man's sense of confidence places him more towards the top of the pecking pole.

"Is the main compartment ready for passengers Han?" Torli asks when he and the two marsh men walk out a few seconds later.

"Aye sir," Han assures him, for he knows that Torli wants to make certain that the control console's security covers are up before he takes anyone not cleared to see the runner's system controls inside.

"Good...if you and yours remove what you need from your vehicle my men'll help you transfer it to this one and get those nets up," Torli advises the younger of the two marsh men.

"Of course commander..." the 'lordling' replies respectfully enough.

"If one a you'll give me your environmental requirements I can start reconfiguring ours to accommodate you better," Torli says to him.

"Ah well commander...we can tolerate your environment well enough as long as it is not too hot...Onot is more the problem you see...she cannot take the dry for more than an hour or so," the 'lordling' tells him.

"It will be simpler than I thought then...do you know the beast's requirements?" Torli asks him and when he nods Torli says, "Come then...you can give them to me."

"As you wish commander," the 'lordling' replies, and after he tells the other marsh man to see to getting the nets up and getting the luggage transferred he follows Torli outside.

"What'd they call you?" Torli asks him when he falls in step with him.

"Slolar," he replies, and then he hooks a thumb over his shoulder and asks with a somewhat miffed expression, "Who is your shadow there?"

"That's Seasle," Torli tells him and when he does Seasle sends Slolar a rather ornery grin the effect of which is immediately ruined when Torli adds, "Just pretend he's not there...that's what we do."

"Boot lickin's a thankless job..." Slolar hears Seasle mutter, but somehow Slolar rather doubts that Seasle is anything even remotely as menial as that.

"Tell me Slolar...there anyone amongst you in poor health or anything?" Torli redirects the young lord's attention from Seasle by asking, for Seasle is not the best person to poke at.

"No...we are a healthy lot," Slolar shakes his head in the negative and replies.

"Good..." Torli says, and then he adds somewhat awkwardly, "I apologize for my ignorance...I's always told marsh folk needed a damper environment than us land folk."

"We can stay healthy with little humidity for quite some time with a bit of cream on the skin to protect it and a good soak daily," Slolar informs him.

"Where've you been soaking these past days?" Torli asks him, for Torli knows this area very well, and as far as he knows the closest stream is miles away.

"In the same tub of dirty water as everyone else I am sorry to admit...but it got us by," he replies with a grin.

"Slolar!" Bimian's voice suddenly shouts, and when Torli checks round he finds the overlord at the door to his broken down vehicle.

"Yes overlord," Slolar replies.

"Do not you even think to touch anything in there...I should like to get there this time!" with that he steps back inside.

"Problem?" Torli asks, for he can see by the flash of anger in Slolar's somewhat grayish tinged eyes that he would very much like to give the overlord a piece of his mind, and Torli knows that a man's tongue is often loosened by such feelings.

"Ah well my uncle sent me ahead to make certain that the contraption there was in working order so you can imagine that at the moment I am not in his good graces," Slolar replies.

"A man can only do so much with what he got," Torli responds as he files Slolar's relationship to Bimian away for future reference.

"That is exactly what I told him...but well...he is...thrifty," Slolar responds.

"Well do not feel too bad...vehicles got a mind a their own sometimes," Torli tells him, and then he gestures towards the runner and tells him with a wry grin, "The first a these I built left us sit with no power and no COM three hours from the fortress on its maiden voyage...had to walk back...general Karnin didn't speak to me for just as many days."

"That seems a bit harsh," Slolar comments with a disapproving frown.

"Ah well he would a took it better if a storm hadn't blown in when we were halfway home...had hail the size a my fist in it," Torli explains.

"Hail?" Slolar repeats and after a confused second he suddenly says, "Ah that frozen ball-like land stuff...yes I have heard of that...I have never seen it though."

"If you're lucky you never will," Torli says, and then he explains, "It comes down with a lot a force...hurts something fierce."

"I will remember that," Slolar replies with a somewhat reserved smile that Torli thinks is probably the norm for him, for even though Slolar seems friendly enough Torli suspects that he is uncomfortable with lengthy conversations.

"The environmental controls are in the main compartment...follow me," Torli instructs as they approach the runner's open side door where Bro stands guard, and when Bro moves to cut Slolar off Torli quickly says, "He's with me Bro."

"Oh aye commander," Bro responds and then dutifully steps aside, but although he yields it is obvious to Slolar that he wants him to know that he would rather not, for he gives him a long warning glare, and when Slolar stiffens his spine and glares back Bro sends him an evil grin.

107

"Bro," Torli warns without turning, for one of Bro's favorite pastimes is using his intimidating size to make others squirm, and so Torli does not need to see him to know what is going on behind his back.

"Yeah commander," Bro innocently replies.

"The lady Andina's got a pet that'll require a bit a strength to transfer...take yourself off and lend a hand," Torli instructs.

"Aye sir," Bro replies, and after he sends Slolar a challenging look he strides off.

"Can you really control that beast?" Slolar asks as he watches Bro walk away.

"No," Torli replies with a shrug, and then he adds as he enters the vehicle, "But he thinks I can...by the way exactly how large's...Onot?"

"You have not seen it all?" Slolar asks in reply, and then he adds with a satisfied grin, "I hope that ogre of yours has a twin."

"Close to it..." Torli replies, and then calls out, "Orn!"

"Aye," a voice replies from somewhere towards the back of the vehicle.

"Go help Bro get the lady's pet transferred," Torli orders.

"What kind a pet?" the voice asks in reply, and then Slolar sees a big-headed brute of a man rise up from one of the seats.

"Get to it you," Karnin's voice commands a bit testily.

"Oh aye sir I's just wondering's all," Orn replies a bit sullenly, and then makes his way towards the rear of the runner.

"Make sure you COM me when you're ready to move the animal Orn," Karnin leans his head into the aisle and requests, and as he goes back to what he is doing he mutters, "I want a see the damn thing."

"Oh aye sir," Orn grumbles as he disappears into the cargo hold.

"General Karnin may I present overlord Bimian's nephew...lord Slolar," Torli formally says as he nears Karnin's seat.

"General," Slolar acknowledges with a polite nod.

"Good to meet you...lord Slolar," Karnin stands to return the pleasantry.

"Please...it is just Slolar...my uncle hates titles and pomp," Slolar candidly informs him.

"How do you maintain the respect a your men then?" Karnin asks him with an assessing look.

"We earn it..." is Slolar's immediate reply.

"Good plan," Karnin comments with a nod, and then he turns to Torli and asks, "How much longer until we're ready to move?"

"An hour should do it I'd think," Torli replies.

"Yeah well think more towards half that...there's a storm building and it's gonna be a big one," Karnin advises him.

"Understood," Torli replies, and as he continues on towards the rear of the main compartment he calls over his shoulder, "This way Slolar."

As Karnin listens to Torli and Slolar's conversation concerning the environmental requirements needed to keep Andina's pet comfortable and quiet he carefully notes each bit of information, for Karnin would like to learn more about the impressive beast. The truth is that he would like to learn more about marsh folk too, for he has been thinking on Bimian's offer to sponsor a meet and greet with Marsle, and Karnin is starting to think that doing so might be a good move on his part. After all it could very well yield Torli and him not one but possibly two new allies, and even though they are only marsh overlords an overlord is an overlord. As cozy as that sounds before Karnin lays his neck on the chopping block of diplomacy he would like to have a bit more information about Marsle and marsh folk in general so as to know what to expect.

So it is that after ten minutes of eavesdropping Karnin has learned many things about what makes Onot tick as well as a few notable facts about marsh folk. One such fact is that even though they prefer a temperature of seventy to eighty with a humidity of seventy-five nics or so they can tolerate higher temperatures and or lower moisture ratings for extended periods of time with the proper preparation and care. All in all they are interesting tidbits of information to be certain, but unfortunately they are hardly anything very useful with respect to whether or not Marsle would hold himself to any agreement that he might make with someone who is not one of his own kind. That is the question of the day he thinks with a frown, and there is too much riding on the answer not to find it.

"Ah...Karnin...sir...?" Orn's voice suddenly calls over Karnin's COM device.

"Yeah Orn," Karnin pushes a button and replies.

"Ah...well that beast a the lady's...well... she's kind a took a liking to Bro...and well...ah... I think maybe you ought a come out...sir," Orn's somewhat hesitant voice tells him.

"On my way," Karnin replies with a nod to the man seated across from him.

"Should I bring a bigger weapon you think," Gorg inquires.

"There'll be no shooting do you understand," Karnin orders, and then he says, "This animal's important to the lady so you'll do nothing to harm it."

"As you wish," Gorg replies with a disappointed sigh.

"Where are you three going?" Karnin asks when he sees Torli, Slolar and Seasle hurrying towards him.

"It's done," Torli replies, and then he adds with an amused glint in his eye, "I'm not missing this."

"Yeah...me neither," Seasle concurs.

"Nor I," Slolar chimes in.

"Do you mean to tell me that you never seen the whole thing before," Karnin asks Slolar a bit suspiciously.

"Not when she is mating," Slolar replies with a grin, which earns him a rather impressive curse from the general who then jogs down the aisle with the other men close on his heels.

When Karnin exits the runner it does not take him long to spy the crowd gathered at the rear of Bimian's transport, and so he sprints towards them, but as the distance closes he hears lady Andina's voice saying something in a pleading tone amid a cacophony of male voices all speaking at once. The one voice that he does not hear however is the overlord's distinctive one, which Karnin finds odd. With a sigh he wonders why nothing is ever simple anymore. All those two big twits needed to do was move one gentle albeit large animal twenty feet or so: how difficult could that possibly be he reasons as he works his way through the crowd? Then the crowd parts and Karnin finds the enormity of the problem staring him in the face; literally.

"Save me..." is all Karnin can find to say when he finds Onot's now familiar yellow eyes fixed on him, for not only do they look angry, but oddly enough they seem a lot smaller now that he can see her entire head.

"Is that not the most hideous thing that you have ever seen," Bimian steps next to Karnin and remarks with a disgusted shake of his head, and then he says somewhat impatiently, "Come now Andina get back so that they can get it."

"I am not going to let anyone hurt Onot," she shouts at him and then crosses her arms and sends him a mutinous glance.

"No one wants to hurt it lady," one of the marsh men tells her as he tries to position himself between her and the animal, but he quickly finds his way blocked when Onot throws her tail in front of him.

"That big arse over there wants to cut his friend out," she complains and then sends Orn a rather hostile stare.

"Naw lady...I won't hurt it...now you go on and move afore you gets yourself hurt," Orn replies with his best woman-charming smile.

"I am sure that if everyone would just step back give her some space Onot will feel more relaxed...and he will...come out," Andina says, and when she does to Karnin's confusion she seems to be fighting to keep from laughing.

"I don't know lady...she sure seems to like him a lot," Orn dubiously says, and although he says it with a straight face Karnin can see the amusement in his eyes.

"Where exactly is Bro?" Karnin cocks his head at Orn and asks.

"She got him in her pouch like a babe," Orn replies and this time Karnin notes that Orn is not the only one having difficulty keeping a serious face, for most of the men gathered around both marsh and land suddenly seem overly interested in their boots.

"I did not even know the thing had a pouch," Bimian leans towards Karnin and mumbles.

"He still alive in there?" Torli steps closer and soberly asks.

"Oh yes she opens up so he can get some air every now and again," Andina tells him.

"I see well maybe if you step back lady he'll be able to climb out next time she does," Torli calmly says as he walks over to her, and then much to everyone's amazement he places a hand on her back and simply shoos her out of the way.

"He has his grandfather's charm I see," Bimian quietly remarks.

"I wouldn't know," Karnin tightly replies, but even though he tries to hide his surprise he is certain that Bimian's experienced eyes do not miss the fact that the comment caught him off guard.

"Yes well we will discuss what you do or do not know later eh," Bimian replies and then he gestures to the darkening sky in the distance and says, "I think we had best get your man out of there before that storm gets here."

With that Bimian seems to transform into someone else, and right before Karnin's eyes the who of what he is as well as the why of it that his men follow him becomes very clear, for he starts barking orders at his men in just the right tone to get them moving and keep them calm. At some point his wife once again tries to get involved but he makes it clear to her that he will have none of it without being too harsh on her. That she snaps her mouth shut and moves towards the sidelines as he directs tells Karnin that although Bimian may shamelessly indulge her he does so not because he is weak but because he is not. No Bimian is a damn sleeper Karnin thinks, and discovering that goes a long way towards making up Karnin's mind as to the overlord's offer of an introduction to Marsle, but Karnin's thoughts on it are interrupted when a familiar voice rings out.

"Orn you whoreson when I get ought a here I'm going to...!" Bro's head suddenly emerges from a slit near the base of Onot's tail and shouts, but the remainder of his tirade is drowned out by a sudden flash that is immediately followed by a loud crack of thunder.

Onot is so startled by the lightning and thunder that she jumps straight up into the air and hits the ground running on all four. Luckily in her panic a goo-covered Bro plops out of her pouch in a way that the other men would later describe as 'she crapped him out'. Another crack of thunder then sends Onot lapping hapless circles in an all out panic around where Bro lays on the ground trying to get his senses back, and before anyone can help him they are all forced to scatter to avoid being trampled by the stampeding beast. Unfortunately, Andina mistakenly chooses to try to get to Bro and in the process she finds herself trapped within the circle that Onot is running round him. Unable to escape Andina is quickly enveloped by the cloud of choking dust being kicked up by the panicked beast.

"Andina get out of there!" Bimian shouts, and when her small form becomes obscured by the dust he tries to push through the mayhem to reach her.

"Bimian...no...you will only get yourself trampled!" the tall marsh man who is hovering nearby shouts as he physically retrains him.

"Stay back...I will get her!" Slolar shouts as he leaps into the fray and disappears into the dust where unbeknownst to the others he pushes Andina to the ground and covers her with his own body.

"Get a hood on it!" someone shouts.

"Orn your shirt...cover its head!" Karnin barks out as he whips his shirt over his head and runs forward.

"Karnin watch out!" Torli yells and then with a curse he dodges Onot's whipping tail and rushes towards him.

"Torli cover her eyes!" Karnin shouts when he sees Torli running towards him.

Torli quickly yanks off his shirt and when Onot's head suddenly appears he leaps up and in one fluid movement throws it over Onot's head. Onot does resist, but Torli manages to hang on to both ends of the shirt. A few seconds later he is joined by one of Bimian's men who adds his strength and a wet blanket to Torli's efforts. The two are quickly joined by several others including Karnin's man Ahnin who wraps his arms round the beast's neck and begins to speak soothingly to it, but whether it is the darkness or the comfort of Ahnin's voice that quiets the beast none could afterwards say. In the end a hooded and exhausted Onot follows Ahnin peacefully enough into Karnin's vehicle and quickly clambers into the netting that has been erected for her.

"Are you alright?" Slolar asks as he climbs off Andina and lifts her to her feet.

"Yes just a bit dusty," she replies with a cough, but when another flash of lightening startles her to Slolar's dismay her eyes tear up, but Bimian is suddenly there to gather her to him.

"Here now everything is alright," Bimian reassures her, and when he does Karnin can see the relief plainly written on his face.

"She did not mean it Bimian," Andina says with a great deal of emotion.

"Yes...yes...I know," Bimian replies, and then he turns his attention to Slolar and commands, "Take care of things eh...I think we have delayed general Karnin long enough."

"Aye overlord," Slolar replies greatly relieved to know that he has redeemed himself in his uncle's eyes.

"Well...that was interesting," Karnin says to no one in particular as he pulls his shirt back over his head and walks over to where Bro has gotten to his knees, "You okay Bro?"

"Yeah...just slimed up," Bro replies as he wipes the brownish goo from his face, but when he sees Han standing behind Karnin grinning he says, "You better stop laughing Han or I'm gonna kill you when I kill Orn...the beast wanted him but he shoved me in and ran...the bastard."

"Yeah well...we'll settle that part when we get home you got it?" Karnin asks as his nose is assailed by a strong musty odor, and after he gets a begrudging nod from Bro he adds, "Make yourself scarce Orn."

"Want me to break out a wash hose?" Han asks as his nose wrinkles in disgust.

"Yeah...squirt some soap on him or something while you're at it...I want a see you when you're done Bro," Karnin instructs.

Much to Slolar's confusion Karnin then pulls his shirt back off and without a word tosses it to Torli before he walks away. As a shirtless Karnin boards the vehicle Slolar turns to thank the commander for his help with Onot, for he had put his life at risk for their sake, and Slolar is very grateful. However when he walks over to thank him the glimpse he gets of Torli's bare chest and back before he covers them with Karnin's shirt gives Slolar pause, for the commander's torso is covered with angry scars. Even though Slolar has no idea what caused the wounds he can surmise from the location and angle of the scars that they were not intended to kill him; not right away at least. Unfortunately, when Torli's head emerges from the neck of the shirt Slolar's thoughts are plainly reflected in the expression on his face, and although it is not the first time that Torli has seen someone react like this to his less than pleasant to gaze upon self he still feels a bit put out by it.

"Hail," Torli humorlessly comments, and then as he walks past Slolar on his way to the cargo bay he adds, "I told you it hurts a lot."

"What do you think?" Slolar asks the tall marsh man when he comes to stand next to him.

"Hail breaks bones and heads...he got those scars from a whip and a blade a long time ago," the man replies as he watches the efficiency with which Torli directs the loading of the remainder of Bimian's cargo, and then he adds somewhat thoughtfully, "Most grown men would find their minds broken by such as that let alone a boy."

"Which begs the question as to what a boy could have possibly done to make someone hate him as much as that," Slolar says with a disgusted shake of his head.

"Ah well some do not require an excuse to hate...it seems to be bred into them," the man replies, but he suspects that he knows exactly why someone hated Torli that much, for after spending the better part of the day sniffing around Karnin's men he thinks that

Bimian is quite right about who Torli really is, and where it is that Karnin's army is headed.

Chapter Six

Three hours after they left overlord Bimian's crippled transport, *Onyat's* runner sits idling on the shoreline near the main traveling channel between the *Northern* and *Central Marsh Territories* while the overlord's property and personnel are being transferred to the marsh crawler moored offshore. As it was the trip was relatively uneventful, and the overlord seemed to genuinely appreciate being given the opportunity to see *Big Rock Crack.* More importantly his people in general were a respectful and fun loving lot who made not one complaint the entire ride although Karnin cannot say what Onot thought about the whole thing. Not much apparently, for when they opened the rear cargo door and she got a whiff of the marshes she was out and gone without so much as a backward glance. Who would have thought that something that large and cumbersome looking could move so fast? The lady Andina did assure him that she has never seen another Onot in the marshes anywhere but even so Karnin still thinks that it is something to keep in mind if things go awry on this trip, for Karnin has decided to take Bimian up on his offer to arrange a meet and greet with Marsle for him.

As he does up the fasteners on his rather worn brown leather traveling jacket the smell of the marshes wafts in through the open runner door on the early evening breeze, which immediately reminds him of *Onyat.* Yes many have been the times that they sat on a spring's eve inhaling the odor of damp greenery mixed with the fragrance of night blooming flowers while they listened to the frogs and things chirp. Karnin has therefore come to relate that particular smell to that of home, but he does not really want to

116

think on that right now, for soon he will hand it over to Marsle. The truth is that Karnin never felt that he belonged anywhere until he came north, and thinking of returning to a life at *Filon Bora* once again leaves him feeling rather hollow inside, but that will change once Torli sits in power there he tells himself. Torli will put things to right and restore the place to its former glory.

That is why he must do this regardless of how Torli feels about it, for it may make the difference between getting Torli installed as the rightful heir to the *Eastern Central Land Territory* or not, but judging by the size of the hole that Torli's eyes are boring into his back Karnin has failed to convince him of that. Karnin understands Torli well enough to know that given enough time his head will cool and perhaps then he will start thinking on the decision that Karnin made with more logic than heart. Karnin is pretty certain that there will not be enough time for that to happen before he must leave, and so the best that he can do now for the cause is to prolong the argument brewing until the marsh men are out of earshot, for it would only make them seem weak at a time when they must appear united. He therefore stalls around by rummaging through his daypack even though he already knows exactly what is in it until the last of the overlord's people have disembarked.

"Let me save you the trouble...I'm going..." Karnin begins without turning around.

"You're out a your damn mind!" he hears Torli angrily retort.

"Don't take that tone with me," Karnin warns, and then he sighs and adds, "It's an opportunity to gain us a couple important allies...we can't just let it slip by."

"Then send me," Torli retorts.

"Ha...now who's mind's gone a beggin'..." Karnin impatiently throws at him as he tightens the day pack's cinch straps with an angry jerk, and then he turns around and heatedly adds, "Might I remind you that Bimian knows who you are?"

"All the more reason why I should go...I could ask for Marsle's support...ask him to take my complaint to the overlords...it might make me look less the wimp hiding behind you," Torli angrily tells him, and when he does Karnin can tell by the two pinpoints of color on his cheeks that his infamous temper is rearing its rather unpredictable head again.

"Yeah or he could put you in cuffs and send you back to Tok...we don't know which way the wind blows there...no...I won't risk you on an unknown Torli," Karnin responds with a shake of his dark head, and when Torli seems unconvinced he tosses in, "Don't forget who's in charge here."

"You won't be forever..." Torli threatens.

"Yeah well...I'm the man right now...that's our agreement remember...you do what I say now...you're the boss when it's done..." Karnin tells him.

"At least take Ahnin with you then," Torli insists, and then he crosses his arms on his chest and adds with a defiant stare, "No one in their right mind would expect you to agree to go alone Karnin...anyone who's anyone has at least one man along to lick his boots if for nothing else."

"Hey," Ahnin protests.

"Yeah well...I take him they'll toss us both in their tank the first time he does something weird," Karnin complains.

"I'm right here you know," Ahnin indignantly points out, but Karnin and Torli just continue on with their conversation as though he never spoke.

"Then take...Cerl..." Torli clips out with an exasperated wave of his hand, for despite his rather untidy appearance Cerl is one of the most competent fighters on Karnin's first assault team.

"His ability to play boot lick's questionable..." Karnin points out, and when he does they all nod including Torli, for Cerl is not exactly known for his diplomatic skills.

"Thank you," Cerl quips from the back of the vehicle where he is sitting.

"Then Gorg..." Torli tries.

"Listen...we stole what belonged to Marsle...showing up with a damn bodyguard's not gonna exactly make me seem...humble..." Karnin tells him.

"Good one...you humble..." Seasle jibes with an amused chuckle.

"Don't push it Seasle," Karnin returns.

"He been spyin' on us for years...he already knows you ain't humble...you'll only piss him off you play act like that," Seasle comes back with.

"Seasle's right Karnin," Ahnin tosses in.

"Alright so I won't play humble man then...but if I show up with backup Marsle's gonna get offended...he'll think I don't trust him," Karnin counters with.

"Yeah see that's the thing...you don't..." Seasle points out.

"Alright listen up...all a you...if you don't hear from me by the deadline you got my permission to come in there and get me back

118

by whatever means you see fit...until then you'll do as I say...that's it...discussion's done," Karnin firmly informs him.

With that he turns and exits the vehicle leaving Torli shaking his head in frustration, for he finds Karnin's refusal to take better care with his own safety despite his promises to do so quite maddening. Just thinking upon the level of stupidity to which this latest little gambit of his rises to sparks Torli's temper. Besides Karnin's diplomatic skills are not exactly polished, and if he has no one along to check him who knows what he might do or say if prodded at. So it is that when Han comes in and heads to the runner's controls Torli's eyes follow him, which does not go unnoticed by the other men.

"You can't..." is all Cerl gets out before Torli interrupts him.

"Han!" Torli calls and when Han turns around to everyone's horror Torli says, "Pack up your day pack."

"It's always packed," Han informs him and then punctuates his words by picking up his bag and holding it up to show him.

"You're not really gonna send Han?" Seasle asks with a disbelieving cock of his head.

"Yeah...I'm gonna send Han...then he won't do anything stupid," Torli replies.

"He Karnin or 'he' Han?" Seasle tosses back.

"He Karnin...'he' Han is pretty much a sure thing," Torli replies.

"Like saddling him with a woman," Gorg states with a thoughtful nod.

"More like a damn babe," Cerl interjects.

"Hey...I ain't stupid you know," Han belligerently complains.

"Let's go Han," Torli orders.

"Karnin'll kill you when he gets back," Cerl warns as he and the other men follow Torli and Han to the runner's door, for Torli often times does not think before he does things when Karnin pricks his temper.

"Let him," Torli mutters as he exits the vehicle with Han in tow.

As Torli steps out much to his satisfaction he sees that the sun has begun to go down in earnest now casting the marshes into shadow. Not only that but it is just at that particular moment before it is dark enough to trigger the marsh crawler's marker lights to come on, and so Han will have plenty of cover. He therefore turns to Han and instructs him to grab a storage box from the pile still awaiting transfer and carry it down to the shoreline, but to be sure to wait until all the marsh men are on their way back out so he can wade it out to the crawler. Then after he hands it off he should stall around until the other men are heading back at which time he should slip into the shadows on the right side of the crawler and make his way around to the rear and get onboard unseen. After extracting a somewhat less than enthusiastic promise to try his best Torli then follows it up with a guilt inducing 'you got a do this for Karnin' and then he quickly walks down to the shoreline where Karnin stands with the overlord and his second who is holding a rather conspicuous beautifully carved wooden box.

"Ah commander Torli," Bimian says when he spies him approaching, and then he adds with a hint of disappointment, "I wish that we had had more time to talk."

"Yeah," Torli replies, and then gives the overlord a polite smile and says, "I'd have enjoyed that overlord...perhaps the opportunity'll present itself again."

"You would be made welcome did you ever decide that you would like to pay us a visit at *Nithian* commander," he tells him, and then he says, "My lady has already gone onboard to see to that confounded beast of hers...but she asked me to extend her thanks to you and your men...and to give you this."

So saying he takes the wooden box from his second and hands it to Torli. As one might expect Torli is a bit surprised by the gift, for he was not expecting anything, and so he just stands there admiring the craftsmanship of the box. After a few seconds though Torli's good manners take over and he opens it to reveal a lovely collection of some sort of confections and a hand written note. The note sparks Torli's curiosity more than the sweets however, for technology has replaced things such as paper, and so it has become a rare and often costly commodity in the world. Torli therefore cannot resist reaching into the box to touch it. As his fingers brush across the paper's surface he discovers that it is much softer than he thought that it would be, and so he absently makes to pull it from the box. That apparently is not something that the overlord wants him to do, for Bimian reaches over and gently closes the lid pretty much forcing Torli to draw his hand back.

"The moisture will make them soggy," Bimian explains, and then he good-naturedly informs him, "My lady said to make certain that I tell you the sweets are for you and your men but the cream pot is for Bro's ah...how did she put it...ah yes his chafed man-things."

"Please tell her I said thank you on behalf a myself and my men...and Bro's chafed parts a course," Torli replies with an amused grin, for as it turned out the goo in Onot's pouch was rather irritating especially to the more delicate parts of Bro's body.

"Well Karnin we must be off...I am long past due to see my new grandchild," with that Bimian wades into the marsh and heads for the crawler surrounded by his men.

"Four days...no more...no less," Karnin locks eyes with Torli and orders.

"Aye general," Torli replies with a stony face, and although Karnin would like to tell him to stop acting like a babe he only cinches the top most straps holding up his thigh boots and then walks away.

When Karnin reaches the bank he hesitates, for the sun's last retreat happens quickly, and so everything is in deep shadows now. Torli could fix that by turning on the runner's floods, but of course he will not. No he would rather act like a child about this, and since Karnin will not ask him to and moon rise is still a time away he takes a leap of faith from the bank. To his satisfaction Karnin lands squarely on his feet in what appears to be knee high water, and as he slowly picks his way towards the dark shape in the distance he sort of wishes that he had not delayed quite as long as he did, for the gathering darkness has made it difficult to stay on course. Luckily the crawler's marker lights snap on just then giving Karnin a target to aim for, which is a good thing since there will be no chance that he will wander into the deep water that he was warned lies to the front and rear of the crawler. Not that he would drown or anything Karnin swims perfectly well but just to avoid embarrassing his self, and perhaps to keep from being eaten by whatever thing that is splashing round in the deep water he adds as he sends a nervous glance to his right.

With a shrug Karnin decides that it is probably just Onot. That conclusion does not make him feel much better though, for after what happened to Bro the thought that Andina's pet may be lurking nearby gives him little comfort. It does cause Karnin to pick up the pace a bit, for it is not like the beast is an old friend or anything, and even if it was having the she beast like you is not exactly a good thing either. Just as Karnin nears the crawler the runner's floods come on, but since Karnin was expecting something like that he does not send Torli the rather nasty hand sign hovering in his mind. After all one of them must act like a grownup. Karnin therefore climbs aboard the crawler without incident and without looking back, for he wants Torli to know that he is still peeved at him for trying to naysay him in front of the men, which is a behavior that is quite predictably Karnin-like Torli thinks as he stands smugly staring after him near the runner's side door.

"My uncle is an honorable man you know," Slolar's familiar voice interrupts Torli's thoughts to say.

"It's not your uncle I'm concerned about," Torli replies as he sees Karnin's distinct figure walk to the front of the crawler where Bimian stands, but his problems with Karnin are not Slolar's fault, and so he turns to Slolar to say a bit more civilly, "I hope we'll meet again Slolar."

"I have a feeling that we will...good luck to you commander," Slolar replies rather seriously as the low hum of an awakening power plant begins to resonate, and with a polite nod he walks off towards the marshes.

It is not long before the men standing by the runner hear the marsh crawler's hum gradually morph into a soft whirring sound, and as they stare into the darkness the marsh crawler's floods and running lights suddenly snap on and light it up. At this point Torli orders the runner's floods turned off lest they interfere with the crawler pilot's ability to navigate, but they can still tell when the marsh machine starts to move, for its lights begin to sway with a smooth rocking motion. As the thing moves away the men are mesmerized, for now that the runner's spots are off they can see the entire machine illuminated by its own lights, and the way its lifters rise and fall as it traverses the uneven marsh bed gives it the appearance of some great four-legged bug. Surprisingly enough despite its lumbering appearance it quickly eats up the open area and soon disappears from sight amongst the tall green of the scrub trees.

For a time Torli continues to stand there listening to the machine's hum, but it is not long before the droning of the crawler's lifters begins to fade, and when it becomes a whisper in the distance Torli finally decides that it is time to go home. However, before he gives the command he stares off into the darkness for a few seconds, and when he does the men simply wait, for they all know that Torli is worried about Karnin and Han. The truth is that they are all worried not necessarily about Karnin and Han as much as what Karnin will do when he discovers Han there, but in the end they console themselves with the fact that Han has always been able to get away with more than anyone else simply because he is well; Han. Torli sees a much broader picture, for he has just sent an ill prepared Han into danger, and if Marsle decides to exercise his right to punish Karnin for stealing his land Han will be an encumbrance that may cost them both their freedom if not their lives.

"Load up men!" Torli broodingly announces as he turns and boards the runner, and when he does Seasle notes the box tucked under his arm.

"What you got?" Seasle asks as he eyeballs the box.

"Some sweets for the ride back courtesy a the lady Andina," Torli replies and then slaps Seasle's hand when he tries to relieve him of his prize.

"I's only gonna carry it for you," Seasle complains.

"Ha...good one," Ahnin mockingly says.

"You trying to start somethin' weirdo?" Seasle inquires.

"Alright...let's get things back where they belong," Torli orders, and as he walks past Seasle on his way towards the rear of the runner he gestures to the box in his arms and adds, "Not to worry...I'm gonna lock these up for now."

"Why's everybody looking at me?" Seasle asks with a shrug, which earns him several snickers.

As Torli and his men set about taking down the nets in the cargo bay and making the runner ready to travel the crawler is making its way deeper into the marshes. As the machine is swallowed up by more and more greenery Karnin takes one last furtive glance in the direction of the shoreline, and when he does he suffers a moment of doubt, for no matter what his justifications he has only his own self to rely on now. He does not get much time to dwell upon that grim thought though, for Bimian quickly puts him at ease by suggesting that he take him round to familiarize him with the crawler's workings. Soon Karnin is so absorbed by the thrill of the experience that it takes him quite some time to realize that he feels perfectly at home here, which both disturbs and confuses him. After all he is a land man born and raised, and so that he feels that way is odd. Whatever the reason Karnin cannot deny that the crawler's mechanical plodding and the wildness surrounding him fills some need in him. Then again perhaps it is just the adventure of it he considers.

When the tour is over Karnin finds that he has learned many useful things about marsh folk, and one rather interesting bit of information concerning overlord Bimian, for it is obvious that Bimian is not as cheap as his wife seems to think. At least not when it involves something that he deems worthy of his funds at any rate, for the crawler is well appointed and geared for the comfort of its occupants. In addition judging by what Karnin could see of it in the dim artificial lights security has not been skimped on either although as one might expect the monitors and controls for that were not on the tour. Most likely in the smaller rear cabin if Karnin guesses, which is all he would be doing since he did not get a tour of that area either although Bimian did say that the smaller cabin housed the crawler's piloting controls. Karnin supposes that the power plant, and whatever weapons array the crawler has are in there too, for the cabin is heavily armored and sealed as one would expect the place that housed such critical components to be.

So it is that an hour or so after the journey began Karnin sits lounging in the comfort of the crawler's front deck's seating area watching the green go by in the glow cast by the crawler's lights. Much to his surprise doing so turns out to be a great deal more interesting a pastime than he thought that it would be at first, for after his senses adjusted to the new sights and sounds of the marshes he began to notice how alive the place really is even in the dark. It goes without saying that Karnin already knew that the frogs croak and the insects buzz at night in the marshes he heard them often enough at *Onyat*, but now that he is out in the thick of it he sees that there are all sorts of small creatures silently scurrying about under the cover of the night. At one point he even spotted some sort of big-eyed bird perched amongst the tangled mass of marsh scrub lining the traveling channel. All in all Karnin thinks it a remarkable experience that he is very glad not to have missed out on although it would be even more enjoyable had the circumstances been better. Still a man must take his pleasure where and how he finds it Karnin thinks as he relaxes back in his seat.

With his attention so pleasantly engaged time passes quickly, and it is not long before Karnin begins to notice a damp chill permeating the breeze. Not long after that the cold becomes rather uncomfortable, and when it does Bimian gets to his feet and after he announces that his belly is damn near eating itself he invites Karnin inside to partake of a late meal, which Karnin is only too glad to accept. As Karnin steps into the warmth of the finely decorated main cabin he is no less impressed with its beauty than he was earlier during his brief tour, for everywhere he looks there is some piece of art or trinket of interest. This time however the centerpiece of his attention is the laden down table, for what he sees there sets his mouth to watering, for there are three different types of fish laid out as well as several dishes containing things that he is not certain whether they are animal or plant. Having no wish to offend the overlord Karnin samples each of the dishes presented to him, and by the end of the meal he finds that he has eaten considerably more than he normally would this late in the day.

When the meal ends and they are all lounging about with their bellies pleasantly full Karnin thinks that he can see the beauty of going to bed in such a state, for he finds that he is feeling sluggish and content. As he lazily stares out the cabin's window he wonders if he should perhaps engage the overlord and his wife in conversation, but they seem comfortable with the silence. They are probably just happy to relax in the comfort of their own vehicle and unwind after their rather stressful journey onto the land Karnin supposes. As he stares vacantly out the cabin's window at some point it registers in Karnin's food drugged mind that there is a man standing at the railing puking, which Karnin finds rather odd since the marsh folk often travel by crawler, and so he would think that Bimian's men should be used to its swaying?

As it turns out as Karnin is just about to ask the overlord if one of his men is ill from some other thing that he might catch the larger of the world's two moons suddenly makes its appearance, and when its silvery rays fall upon the man at the rail the familiarity of his outline gives Karnin pause. It does not take long for Karnin to figure out where it is that he has seen this man before, for this is not the first time that he has seen his distinctive form illuminated in the moonlight. No he saw it damn near every time the two of them went foraging at night in *Filon Bora's* village, and even though the face has changed somewhat since then it is still basically the same old mug. As to what he is doing here well Karnin has a good idea about that too, and to say that it pisses him off is an understatement.

Karnin therefore excuses himself to the overlord and his lady saying that he thinks that he will take some air. Before he walks away Bimian tells him that he should have told them that his man could not swim, for his guard captain had to go fish him out of the deep waters before they left. Karnin of course thanks the overlord for taking care of him, but it is clear to Karnin by the amused glint in Bimian's eyes that he is well aware that Karnin had no idea that Han was onboard. Bimian then hands Karnin what appears to be a bracelet, which he then explains is a tracking device that all non-swimmers must wear while onboard his vessel to alert the crew should they fall off, and after telling him that his man out there seems reluctant to wear one Bimian asks Karnin to make certain that he puts it on and leaves it on this time. Karnin then apologizes for Han's cheek what else could he do, but as he exits the cabin his eyes narrow in anger, and he heads directly to the spot where he last saw him.

"Come out a there you sneaky bastard," Karnin demands as he peers into the shadows, for not surprisingly Han is no longer there, but Karnin knows that he will be nearby.

"Just trying to stay out a the way...sir," Han explains as he steps out from the darkness.

"So he just couldn't do it could he?" Karnin asks a bit testily, for Karnin had foolishly believed that Torli would never stoop as low as this.

"What couldn't he do?" Han innocently asks.

"You know what...I ought a toss you off that'd teach him to disobey my orders," Karnin clips out a bit childishly.

"Ah well...your logic's a bit off," Han says, and then he points out, "Tossing me off'd teach me to disobey Torli's orders next time maybe..."

"Shut up," Karnin points a finger at him and says, and then he grabs Han's arm and hooks the bracelet on, which immediately begins to elicit a soft blue glow, but Karnin is too angry to wonder on that right now, and so he only points a finger at it and snaps out, "You leave that on...and you stay out a the way."

"Gladly you testy bastard," Han mutters under his breath as he watches Karnin go back inside, but just then the lights go out and a cold breeze blows his hair, and with a shiver Han wishes that he had thought to bring a damn blanket.

"You are welcome to sit with the rest of us nobodies," a voice quietly says from out of the darkness, and although Han strains his eyes he simply cannot see its owner in the inky night.

"Over here," the voice says and then a faint light blinks on which reveals the forms of several men seated at a small table inside the partially enclosed forward steer house of the vehicle.

"Come on then the light's going to draw attention to us," another man says, and the comment makes Han decide that it might be in his best interest to go sit with them at least long enough to find out who or what it is that they do not want to notice them.

As Karnin makes his way back into the main cabin he hears the exchange between Han and the marsh men and when the man mentions putting out the light lest it be seen it only serves to prick his temper even more. What was Torli thinking to send Han who could barely cut his meat without lopping off a finger into such an unknown situation as this? Karnin for his part knows exactly why he did it, for it is not Bimian that Torli does not trust it is him. Yes Torli has been completely won over by the overlord and his charming lady and Torli fears that he will do something to offend them. So he sends Han along knowing that Karnin will not put himself in a tenuous situation lest something happen to Han. Clever Karnin admits but it is still underhanded.

"Interfering little prick..." Karnin mumbles and then takes a deep breath and tries to school his features into a nonchalant expression as best he can, for he would not have Bimian think that there is any dissention amongst his ranks.

"So what do you think of the marshes Karnin?" Bimian asks him as he sits back down at the cabin's table.

"Dark as pitch," Karnin replies.

"Ah well after a time the eyes adjust to it," Andina tells him.

"Yours perhaps...but well..." Karnin replies with a small shrug, and then he hesitantly asks, "Ah...where's...Onot?"

"Oh she is out there...somewhere," Andina replies with a rather dramatic sigh as she gestures towards the window.

"I see..." Karnin comments, but her bit of drama does not go unnoticed, and since Karnin has a good idea what it is all about he wisely decides to let it stay between the overlord and his lady.

"We are not traveling at top speed...mostly to avoid waking Marsle's folk up in the middle of the night so if you want to catch a bit of rest the first sleeping room has been set aside for you," Bimian offers, and even though he seems relaxed enough about it Karnin does not miss the perturbed glance that he gives his wife, for it is obvious that he wants her to retire.

"Ah well perhaps I shall take you up on that...it's been a long day eh," Karnin replies thinking that if he goes maybe she will, and when she only nods at him he goes so far as to get to his feet, but Andina only stays where she is.

"It has been a long week," Bimian corrects and then he too gets to his feet and says, "Come along Andina...we will need our energy when we arrive."

"Oh good grief Bimian...do you think that I am blind and stupid now?" she clips out in a somewhat exasperated tone, and then she stands and as she walks towards the rear of the vehicle she throws over her shoulder, "What were you going to do sneak back out after I had fallen asleep...come to bed when you are finished discussing whatever it is that you do not want me to hear."

"Have you a woman you call yours Karnin?" Bimian asks as he watches her go.

"I haven't the time I'm afraid," Karnin responds.

"Make the time," Bimian advises, and then he adds, "They are a great deal of trouble but...well...let us just say that it is a journey a man should begin when he is still young enough to walk the hard part."

"And that part'd be...?" Karnin urges as the overlord sits back down.

"The training part," Bimian advises as he gestures for Karnin to sit, and then he makes a snorting sound and says, "Took neigh on six years for me to relearn everything that I thought I already knew."

"Ah well I got it on good authority that I'm beyond trainable," Karnin tells him and then looks away.

"Ha...claims such as that only make a woman more determined," Bimian informs him, but even though Karnin smiles a bit at that Bimian can see that he is only being polite, and so he changes the subject by saying, "Ah well enough of small talk eh...so tell me Karnin...what exactly are your goals in life then?"

"I intend to see Torli restored to his rightful place...isn't that what you really want to know?" Karnin candidly replies.

"How old are you Karnin...I would guess not much past your majority," Bimian remarks.

"What's that to do with anything...I'm past it so what matter how far?" Karnin retorts a bit impatiently.

"Ah well I mean you no insult," Bimian says.

"I got nothing but respect for you overlord so do not take this the wrong way...but if there's something you got a say I'd rather you just out with it," Karnin says.

"Very well...what are your intentions as to commander Torli's claim to Galwor's territories...is that direct enough for you," Bimian comes back with a bit hotly, and then he holds up a hand and adds, "Do not think to feed me some magnanimous crap about how helping him regain it will be enough...you are much too ambitious for that."

"Why bother asking if you already know the answer eh...how about you tell me then...sir," Karnin sarcastically replies.

"Alright," Bimian leans forward and grinds out, and then he says in an accusing tone, "You are going to use him to make your attack on Tok appear justified...and then you will simply take it from him one way or the other."

"Were you not who you are and an old man I'd call you out for that," Karnin replies in a deadly voice.

"That would be the greatest mistake you ever made boy," Bimian heatedly answers, and then shoots to his feet.

"Oh for all that is..." Andina's voice suddenly says, and as she storms back across the room towards the two men from the doorway where she has been eavesdropping she grabs two objects and then shoves one into each man's hand and says, "Go ahead...bash each other's brains out then!"

"This is not your business Andina...and what in all that is am I to do with this!" Bimian waves the large dried fish in his hand at her and demands.

"Use your imagination," she retorts and then she tosses over her shoulder as she stomps off, "Men are so ridiculous!"

"Quite expressive isn't she?" Karnin carefully says when the silence begins to become uncomfortable.

"You have no idea..." Bimian comes back with, and then he points the fish in his hand at Karnin and says, "She is angry with me for making her let Onot go...we have an agreement that if the blasted thing follows it stays... if it does not then it does not."

"Ah I see," Karnin replies with a nod and then he adds in a matter-of-fact tone, "And she's angry because she couldn't charm you out a the agreement then eh?"

"No...no she is good to her word I will give her that...but...I have ordered all the running lights to be kept out in the hopes that the damn thing will not find us this time and of course it is 'my' fault that 'she' did not think to specify the terms of our agreement to preclude it is all."

"And yet you still keep her?" Karnin asks a bit overly loud, for from his seat he can see the lady's shadow at the doorway, and so he inclines his head towards her and adds, "You're a patient man indeed sir."

"Ha!" she fires back and a few seconds after her shadow disappears, the sound of a door slamming tells the two men that this time she has truly gone.

"I didn't come with you to make enemies overlord Bimian," Karnin looks across the table and says a few seconds later, but he thinks that perhaps it may be wise to make certain that the overlord understands the why of it that he was ready to trade blows over what was said between them, and so he carefully lays the fish on the table and explains, "I'm a bit overprotective of Torli...he got plunked into my lap when I's but a boy my own self...he's my friend and most likely the reason that I didn't grow up to be the kind a man that'd use him as you just described...or a habitual killer...maybe both."

"I see," Bimian nods, and then he asks, "Will you tell me of him?'

"If you'll tell me why you want a know?" Karnin calmly returns.

"I suspect that he is Myna's son...if he is then I can make a good guess as to why he had to leave *Filon Bora*...especially now after having met overlord Tok," Bimian replies, and then he asks, "But how did he end up with you...who exactly are you?"

"As I said before...I'm nobody," Karnin replies, but when he sees Bimian's eyes narrow on him he decides that for diplomacy's sake he must tell him something, and so he asks, "Have you any knowledge about what happened after Galwor took the overlordship?"

"Some things came across the marshes...rumors and such...but nothing with any detail beyond the fact that Galwor was a cruel tyrant and certainly nothing like his father Obron," Bimian replies.

"Couldn't say...about overlord Obron...he's before my time," Karnin comments with a little shrug, but then he continues with, "I heard the story enough times though...seems after the old overlord's death Galwor quickly ran through what capital there was...so in order to feed his appetite for the finer things he stopped paying his men and told them to find their payment in the village...needless to say they quickly stripped Galwor's village a anything a value such as vehicles, weapons, jewelry and stuff like that...and when that well ran dry they looted food sometimes leaving entire families with nothing to feed themselves with...many died in those years...not just from starvation and sickness either...for if Galwor's men discovered that even so much as a loaf a bread wasn't given over they took the offenders lives as well...sometimes burning entire families alive in their homes for the slightest thing."

"Disgusting bastards..." Bimian says, but then he cocks his head at Karnin and adds, "So how does all that explain who you are then?"

"I'm getting there...I just wanted you to understand why there were so many homeless kids roaming the streets a *Filon Bora's* village...me...I's lucky...my mother owned a pleasure house...and for whatever reason she always seemed to fly under the radar," Karnin tells him, and then he sighs and adds, "My mother eventually married...he was a big feeling bastard...I hated him and he hated me...when my mother passed I thought it best to leave."

"How old were you by then?" Bimian asks.

"I's ten...but I's already pretty street wise," Karnin replies, but then he notices that the overlord is actually disturbed by his tale, which begs the question as to why he should care what happened to a bunch of land dwellers, and so Karnin decides to press him a bit by asking, "You alright overlord?"

"Yes...well...no actually not," he snaps out, and then he rants, "I simply cannot rectify that a creature like Galwor could be Obron and Jubiet's son...they were honest...hard working...caring people."

"Yeah well now I'm finding it hard to rectify that good folk like that were Galwor's parents," Karnin tells him, and then he adds, "Maybe they weren't."

"No...Obron would never lie about something like that...especially when he started to notice how badly Galwor was turning out," Bimian replies, for any man worth anything at all would have fessed-up when faced with leaving his people to the whims of a madman, but then it occurs to Bimian that Karnin may not know the depth of the unfairness dealt to Obron and Jubiet, and so he tosses in a bit too casually or so Karnin thinks, "Unfortunately it was something in one of their bloodlines for both of Obron and Jubiet's children were not quite right."

"Galwor I know about first hand...but what problems did Myna suffer from?" Karnin looks out the window and asks, for he does not want Bimian to see the concern that he is feeling at the moment.

"She was a fey thing," a voice replies from the darkness, and the tall man that Karnin believes to be Bimian's second in command steps inside and then adds, "Harmless and fearful of neigh on everything and everyone when she was a girl."

"And you'd know that how?" Karnin asks a bit less than politely, for that Bimian has a man present is rather insulting as it speaks to his lack of trust or perhaps his lack of honor Karnin adds as he fingers the hilt of the small knife that he has concealed in his boot.

"Peace...if the overlord intended treachery I would not have let you bring your weapon aboard general Karnin or your man out there," the tall marsh man casually steps to the table and says as he holds out his hand.

"My man out there's not here by my request I assure you," Karnin informs him, and as he pulls the knife and hands it to him hilt first he adds, "I'd like to get it back then...it's the only thing I ever got a my inheritance."

"Oh I just want to see it is all...I have a sort of fascination with primitive weapons you see," the man replies, and then he cocks his head at Karnin and says in a challenging way, "I am more than capable of taking it back from you if it becomes necessary."

"Enough gentlemen...but where are my manners you two have not been properly introduced...general Karnin may I present my vassal lord Goberan," Bimian says in an official tone, and then he adds with an annoyed grunt, "He is also Slolar's father and the youngest son of my father...make no mistake of it he would not be here with us right now did he not have something to add to the conversation."

"Which's what?" Karnin asks as he watches Goberan turn the dagger over to examine the hilt.

"I knew the old lord's daughter Myna quite well...she was sweet but rather fragile in the mind...and she of all people did not deserve what I suspect happened to her," Goberan tells him, and then he adds as he hands Karnin back the knife, "But that is not what I wanted to impart to you rather that there was a young man named Dor at Obron's keep for a time...he is the son of one of the southern overlords...to make a long story short Myna took a fancy to him...and when she told me that she loved him I feared that Dor would only use her...he and Galwor were the best of friends for a reason...I told the old overlord about it...next thing I knew Myna was married off to the son of one of overlord Obron's vassals...the overlord fell ill not long after and I was sent home."

"It seems that you spent a great deal a time there lord Goberan," Karnin notes with a frown, for Karnin has never heard anything that would suggest that marsh folk could stay on land for any length of time, and given his current circumstances he is understandably concerned about the possibility.

"It was a common practice back then for the various overlords to solidify friendships by exchanging a few of their male children for a time so that they might better understand each other's cultures... I had already had my turn at it when my father traded me for Marsle a few years before and so when Obron and my father struck a friendship Goberan was sent to him and since Galwor was already traded to Dor's father Obron sent his wife's youngest brother Boro to us in exchange," Bimian explains.

"Boro," Karnin repeats with a start that he quickly tries to hide.

That his mentor had some connection to the old overlord's wife actually comes as no great surprise to Karnin, for the freedom of movement that Boro enjoyed as well as his never empty purse had always said that he had good ties to Obron's house. However, that Boro had fostered with Bimian's people is an unexpected revelation that goes a long way towards making sense of much that Boro did. Such as insisting that Karnin take his band of wayward boys to the fringe lands of the northern marshes to settle, and placing the names of several marsh men near the top of his list of persons who Karnin could trust to deal with him fairly. Yes and why Boro made him promise not to burn his bridges with overlord Marsle by simply abandoning *Onyat* without a thank you to him Karnin tosses in.

"I met Boro when we were exchanged...he seemed like a worthy young man...you know of him then?" Goberan asks even though he already knows the answer, for he would like to see if Karnin will dissemble or not.

"Yeah," Karnin replies, but then he hesitates a moment to mull over how much of this particular part of his story is wise to impart, but in the end he decides that he has little to lose now and so he tells them, "Not long after I started wandering the streets Tok caught me pinching a suit a clothes off a dead guy in killing alley...he was in the process a beating me to death when Boro interrupted things...I's able to run off while they were arguing...a few days later Han told me some fancy guy was asking about me in the village...left something for me in a box...a course someone had followed Han back...an hour or so later Boro showed up and said that if me and the other boys'd take in any kids he managed to get out a the inner keep in one piece he'd see that me and my friends were never hungry or cold again...needless to say I said yeah."

"Is that the same Han my men fished out of the water before we left the dock?" Goberan asks with a smirk.

"One and the same...the least savvy man I ever met," Karnin replies with a shake of his head, but then he sighs and says, "Who's probably not ate since early this morn."

"The men on deck always have food...and a lit burner this time of year...they will share," Goberan tells him.

"Thanks...he's our master mechanic so I appreciate you taking care a him and all," Karnin says, and when he does Goberan can see that he truly means it, but for more personal reasons than his mechanical skills.

"So what was in the box?" Bimian suddenly asks with an impatient gesture.

"More food than we'd seen in a month...and not a rotten anything amongst it...was like gifting day," Karnin tells him with a wistful expression.

"So...I am going to assume Tok's paternity has been established beyond question," Goberan inquires and when Karnin nods he then asks, "What about commander Torli's?"

"You did see him didn't you...he's got that mop a golden brown curls on his head," Karnin inquires.

"I could do that with a bottle of die and a wave kit," Goberan points out.

"I know you think that Torli might be Dor's son...but he isn't..."

"How can you be so certain?"

"Because Boro said he wasn't born out a wedlock...and his mother wasn't married to Dor," Karnin tells him with a bored face.

"It seems that you have the commander's succession all tied up then...so why have you come begging to Marsle?" Goberan inquires in like kind.

"Have I?" Karnin asks, and although he is angered by what Goberan is driving at Karnin is not so far into it not to notice that Bimian is studying him rather intently, and so he reins his emotions in a bit and simply adds, "I must admit that I done a

134

great deal a begging a one kind or another in my lifetime...you know begging for food...begging the fates for the rain to stop...or the cold to go and such things as I doubt you'd know anything about lord Goberan... so you'll just need to take my word for it when I say that if I were begging now I'd surely know it."

"Then why did you come?" Bimian calmly asks.

"Because I gave my word to Boro that I'd not move south until I thanked overlord Marsle for not tossing me and mine in his tank," Karnin retorts somewhat impatiently.

"As is fitting," Bimian says with a reproachful glance, and then he asks, "Where is lord Boro now then?"

"Word from him's long overdue," Karnin replies, and then he adds with a bit of emotion, "I'm hoping that he escaped the fortress before Galwor passed as he always planned to do...but...he's yet to turn up."

"My father liked lord Boro a great deal...he always said that he was a cunning man who would make a better friend than enemy," Goberan tells him, and then he says, "A man like that would have found a way to save himself."

"Yeah... I truly hope so," Karnin replies, but then he decides that now might be a good time to bow out of this particular conversation before it gets too personal, and so he looks across the table and says, "If you'll excuse me overlord I think perhaps I'll take you up on that bed after all."

"Of course...I am not far behind you," Bimian replies warmly enough, and with a polite nod Karnin makes his way across the cabin and into the first sleeping room, but just as soon as the door shuts behind him Bimian asks Goberan in a quiet voice, "So what do you think?"

"Well...he knows his own mind I will give him that," he answers as he takes a seat across from the overlord.

"Yes and he is not afraid to share it is he?" Bimian notes with an amused grunt.

"Even if he is sincere...which I actually think that he is...he still has no experience at leading an army or laying siege Bimian...do they even have siege guns?"

"I do not think Karnin is the siege type Goberan."

"A covert takeover is the only other way...and that is risky business...for a number of reasons..."

"Yes but imagine the fallout if they succeed?" Bimian points out with an interested glint in his eye.

"There will be fallout alright...the land overlords will order up his head on a damn pike...they will have every right to," Goberan tells him, and then he adds, "I see nothing humorous in that."

"So you like him then?"

"He is an arrogant...insufferable arse," Goberan clips out, but as he pours some spirits into his glass he adds, "Of course I like him...but the law is not in his favor in this."

"It could be..." Bimian tells him as he slides his glass closer to allow Goberan to fill it.

"Karnin is an unsworn man with a rogue army...it will not matter if his cause is just," Goberan tells him with a great deal of fervor, and then he shakes his head and adds, "I know what you are thinking...but Marsle is the only one who can legitimize this...and I have my doubts that he will."

"Time will tell," Bimian replies, and then he takes a swig from his glass before he asks, "So what did you learn from the knife?"

"An unusual crest...one that I have seen before...and unless Karnin is lying about where he got it lord Boro may be withholding a rather important fact about his and the commander's connection to each other from Marsle," Goberan replies with a pensive look.

"Whose crest is it then?" Bimian inquires, but when Goberan seems reluctant to say he adds, "Let me guess then...the commander's paternal one?"

"They are not half brothers if that is what you are thinking...the crest on Karnin's 'inheritance' is similar to commander Torli's father Edbon's...but it did not have the marker for the eldest son," Goberan tells him.

"Karnin is Debon's boy then?" Bimian asks, but then his surprise turns to enlightenment, for if Debon was Karnin's father then many things make sense, and so Bimian states, "We were wrong then."

"Yes...he is not lord Boro's son...and I am not certain if that is good news or bad," Goberan replies with a shake of his head.

"This is a complicated damn mess Goberan," Bimian comments with a bemused expression, and then he pours the two of them another drink and after he is done he says with a rather ornery grin, "Damn glad it is Marsle's mess not mine."

"I will second that," Goberan replies, and after he does the two men clink glasses and toss down the contents, but afterwards they fall silent in thought, for the truth of it is that they both know that it will not be just Marsle's mess for long.

Chapter Seven

At the same moment that Karnin is climbing into the rather posh bed assigned to him on the overlord's marsh crawler, back on the land Torli and the other men are backtracking to Bimian's crippled transport to retrieve the gear that they had offloaded. Of course once they get there not only will they have to load their gear back up they will then have to bring the two marsh men that were left behind to guard it back to where the crawler was moored to retrieve the two small watercraft known as jitties that were left behind for them. Whether Bimian's two men plan to use the jitties to go south to *Fendora* or north to *Laraqua* the overlord did not say. Either way Torli still feels rather uncomfortable about just dumping them off there in the middle of the night to fend for their selves. Unfortunately there is little else to do about it.

That particular problem as well as the need to make an extra trip back to the edge of the marshes could have been avoided had the overlord simply agreed to allow them to guard their own gear, but for some odd reason he seemed determined to leave two of his own men behind to do it. Perhaps the overlord had a few more things that he did not want to take off his transport while the land men were watching. That in and of itself would not be unusual every armored vehicle has its secret something. The runner has several. Still Bimian's decision has left him in a rather tough place where his men are concerned. Ah well at least he will get an opportunity to see those jitties up close, for he did not get to do so before they left. A bright spot in what is shaping up to be a long and rather tedious journey Torli thinks with a tired sigh, which might get even more so if he has to run those two marsh men home. Needless to say that thought gives Torli pause, for no matter how he feels about abandoning Bimian's men to their own fate he cannot tip his hand he reminds himself.

"You're right," Ahnin suddenly says from the control console where he is taking Han's place as pilot, for next to Han Ahnin is the most qualified pilot amongst them.

"Am I?" Torli asks him with as much patience as he can muster right now, for dealing with Ahnin often requires much of that since he often spouts out what seems to be nonsense at first, but in the end after a bit of explanation he is often spot on.

"Yeah...you can't take them into the marshes...you can't let them know we can do that...not yet."

"Stop doing that," Torli responds.

"Doing what...thinking?" Ahnin responds as he adjusts the runner's glide field.

"He means stop talking to the dead or selling your soul or whatever you do what makes you so good at guessing," Bro explains.

"I never guess," Ahnin indignantly retorts.

"Ah...here it comes..." Seasle complains, and sure enough a second later Ahnin pulls what appears to be a rather large dried up bird's foot from his pocket.

"Foot sees all...knows all," Ahnin recites as he waves the thing around, but when he does Seasle flicks one of the nuts that he is munching on at him and hits him square in the forehead.

"Foot should a seen that comin'," Seasle points out with an ornery grin, and when he does Ahnin takes an angry step towards him.

"No..." Torli calmly turns to Ahnin and commands, and with a begrudging wave of the foot Ahnin turns back to the controls.

"The weirdo's right you know," Cerl points out, and then he adds, "They can't know we can run this thing on water...not yet."

"Yeah...I know...but damn I hate to leave them fumbling around in the dark..." Torli responds.

"They won't be," Ahnin assures him, but when he sees their smirks of doubt he shrugs and says, "They're marsh men."

"Yeah...so...?" Seasle asks.

"Marsh men can see in the dark like it was day...and hear a bug chirp twice as far away as you and me...they're also stronger than we are and can breathe under water practically forever...so heading into the marshes after dark is nothing to them," Ahnin replies with a smug nod.

"That come to you when you's doing that wavin' thing just now or somethin'?" Seasle sarcastically asks.

"No...came to me earlier when I kissed the foot...and after I picked the weakest one amongst them out..." Ahnin mystically tells them pausing for effect, and when he sees them exchange a few uncomfortable glances with each other he adds, "I asked him...he was more an happy to brag about his superior marsh man self."

"Very funny," Bro says, and with an amused laugh Ahnin ducks and dodges the various small missiles sent his way by the other men.

"Alright...enough a that before someone hits something important," Torli calls, and then he says with an amused shake of his head, "You all better shut it and rest while you can...it's gonna be a long night."

"Gonna be a longer next two days..." Seasle points out, and when he does Torli gets up and walks to the back of the runner without a word.

"Nice move," Cerl fixes the one eye not concealed by his hair on him and says.

"What...I's just sayin'..." Seasle defends.

"Yeah...you're always just sayin'...maybe you ought a think before you do once in awhile," Cerl comes back with.

"Maybe you ought a kiss my ball sack," Seasle responds, but then he meanly adds, "Or Bro's."

"You leave my nut sack out a this it got enough damn problems already," Bro grumbles and then subconsciously scoots in his seat to rearrange his sore man parts.

As Torli's men exchange barbs the runner clips along the road back at the overlord's broken down old transport the two guards left behind to watch over the various storage boxes that Torli had off loaded had long since abandoned any pretext of professionalism. As a matter of fact, they had stopped acting the part as soon as the land men's vehicle was out of sight. They both knew that it would be hours before anyone returned, and the overlord would not expect them to continue to be so guard-like and on-the-mark when there was no audience to impress. No all in all the overlord is a reasonable enough man when it comes to things like that and since they are only guarding boxes of unimportant things and not people the overlord would only expect

139

them to be diligent enough to make certain no one comes along and walks off with them.

Besides the lady Andina had covertly slipped them a couple sweet trees before she left along with a reminder that no vehicle is worth dying over, especially this one, which pretty much told them that no one would care much if someone made off with the damn thing, and since they technically owe their allegiance to her they both decided that if anyone came along and demanded the thing they would hand it over. Just not the commander's boxes that they would have to insist they leave their fingers off. The two marsh men therefore have concentrated their attention on the only reason that they are actually still here, and so are lounging outside the land transport's door eating sweets in the cool night air as they watch both the storage boxes and the road for some sign that the land men are returning.

"Maybe they broke down," one of the marsh men suggests as he checks his time piece for the third time in as many minutes.

"If they did the overlord will crap his self," the other marsh man replies.

"No he will make someone else crap his self," the first man amends.

"At least it won't be us," the second man points out.

"Yes...I am feeling much better about getting left behind to watch boxes," the first man tells him.

"Yes well he picked us out for a reason Bornan," the second guard comments with a sage look, for the two men are Onot's primary handlers, and that the overlord overruled lady Andina and left them behind is very telling.

"He will be sending for us you mark my words...Onot will turn up at *Laraqua*...she has a sweet deal...she will not willingly let it get away," Bornan tells him, for Onot has everything that any animal could want, and so it is unlikely that she will get lost and turn wild as the overlord hopes.

"I used to think so...but after that incident with the land man I am not so certain anymore," Bornan's fellow guard points out.

"Yes...that is a good point," Bornan replies, and then he cocks his head at his friend and asks, "So why do you suppose she liked that big land man so much Tosel?"

"Probably smelled a bit off," Tosel suggests with a smirk.

"Yes well...I for one am a bit insulted," Bornan says in mock indignation.

140

"I did not know you and Onot had a thing."

"We do not...but still...that she chose a land man is rather disturbing..."

"Better him than me...that talkative one said the big ogre's balls were covered in chemical burns," Tosel tells him.

"Well...this man is going to steer clear of Onot's arse from now on," Bornan pokes his self in the chest and informs him with a nod.

"Yes me too," Tosel assures him, and then he inclines his dark head towards the stack of storage boxes nearby and asks, "So what do you think they have in there?"

"Odds are that it is nothing important," Bornan replies, and after he gets up and walks over to the pile of metal boxes he picks the top box off the pile and sits down on it before adding, "They would have left one of their own to keep an eye on them if there was anything worth taking in them."

"So...they think we are thieves then?" Tosel says with an insulted sniff.

"Last I heard most of them think that we eat our young," Bornan tells him.

"Yes well I wish that we had a couple babes right now then...my gut is pretty empty," Tosel comes back with.

"That is not even funny," Bornan retorts with a disgusted frown as Tosel walks over and pulls a box down near him to park his own arse on.

"Not any worse than that remark you made earlier..." Tosel tells him with an accusing glare.

"What remark?" Bornan demands.

"You know...about land women having hair on their crotches," Tosel reminds him.

"They do," Bornan insists, and then he adds, "And most everywhere else too."

"You are full of it Bornan...how would you know?" Tosel accuses, but then he abruptly jumps up in shock and says, "Something is moving in there."

"Right," Bornan says with a sneer.

"No really...I felt something banging on my arse," Tosel insists.

"I told you not to eat that funny looking fruit you found..." Bornan reminds him.

"I said banging 'on' my arse not in it dolt," Tosel impatiently answers back, but just then a muffled bumping sound comes from the box, and he points to it and says in a triumphant tone, "See there I told you!"

"Maybe the boxes are mined...and when you sat on it you triggered it," Bornan warns as he gingerly hops up and puts some distance between himself and the box that he was sitting on.

"Do not be stupid...bombs only bang once...well at least that is all you hear when you are getting blown up I would imagine," Tosel supposes, and then he tentatively lays an ear to the box, and after listening for a few seconds he adds, "And they do not cry either!"

With that Tosel reaches down and tries to open the box, but like the others in the pile it had been sealed by commander Torli's men prior to being left behind, and so the lid refuses to budge. With an angry curse Tosel goes to one knee in front of the box to examine its locking mechanism, for he will have to pick the lock and that will take time. However, after giving it a quick look see Tosel swears once again, for he cannot pick this lock, and so he will have to blow it, which is rather risky considering there is something alive in there. At this point Bornan realizes that Tosel is not trying to jerk his parts, and so he bends his ear closer to the box to listen, for there are lots of things that make noise many of which one should probably leave in the box. Unfortunately, the more Bornan listens the more he becomes convinced that the thing in the box is not one of them.

"Damn them!" Bornan angrily exclaims, for what he hears is crying, and from the size of the box and the sound of it he has a good idea what it is that the land folk have sealed inside it.

"We have to get it open...now," Tosel angrily says, and then he adds, "There is no way to pick it...get a thumper Bornan."

"You will break its eardrums," Bornan replies with a negative shake of his head.

"Child!" Bornan shouts at the box as he kneels down to examine the lock for his own self, and when he does Tosel sprints off and disappears inside the vehicle.

"We are going to get you out...stop crying now...it will be alright!" Bornan shouts again.

"Move Bornan," Tosel commands as he sprints back with a long pipe-like tool.

"The poor thing will be deaf for the rest of its life you do that," Bornan points out as he snatches the thumper from Tosel's hand.

"Better to be deaf than dead…how much time has passed…that child cannot have but a few minutes more air in there if that…this is a land child Bornan…they have no reserves…when the air in the box goes his little brain will be dead in a few minutes," Tosel hisses out and then snatches the thumper back from Bornan.

"Better to be neither dead nor deaf," Bornan angrily hisses in reply as he grabs the thumper from Tosel once again, but before his companion can do anything about it Bornan keys the COM device that commander Torli left with them and calls, "Broken down piece of crap to runner…you hearing me runner?"

"Runner hears you…what you need?" Ahnin's disembodied voice asks in reply.

"This is an emergency…we need the code for one of your storage boxes," Bornan requests.

"What kind a emergency?" Ahnin's voice suspiciously inquires.

"I think you have a stowaway in one of your boxes," Bornan informs him.

"Say again?"

"There is a child locked in one of your boxes man!" Bornan angrily retorts.

"Damn that boy…Torli…commander Torli!" and then the two marsh men hear a mumbled conversation.

"Box number?" Torli's voice calmly asks.

"Four…six…nine…nine…three," Tosel shouts out as Bornan keys the COM device and holds it up to him.

"You hear that?" Bornan asks.

"Yes box four, six, nine, nine, three…" Torli's voice replies, and then he quickly says, "Give it the 'open' command and then say…Torli…six…four…four…two."

"Box open," Tosel immediately turns towards the box and commands.

"Request authorization code," the box's metallic voice replies.

"Torli…six…four…four…two…" Tosel impatiently tells it.

"Authorization confirmed," the box replies and when he hears the clank of the lock being disengaged and the whoosh of the seal being released Tosel quickly throws back the lid.

"Do you got him?" Torli's voice asks, and when neither marsh man immediately replies he repeats in a more urgent tone, "Is he safe!?"

"We have him safe and sound," Bornan replies when he sees the relieved look on Tosel's face, and then he walks over and sternly locks eyes with what appears to be a young land boy peering up at him from inside the box and purposefully asks, "What do you want me to do with him?"

On the runner, when Bornan's voice says that their stowaway has been retrieved alive Torli closes his eyes in obvious relief. Then the magnitude of what could have happened had Bimian's guards not been there hits him, and his relief is quickly replaced with anger, for had this happened anywhere else Polie would most likely have died in that box. The reality of it is that the same design that makes the box able to withstand the harsh conditions of traveling renders it virtually soundproof in the process, and so none of them would have heard the boy's cries for help. It is therefore only by the dumbest of luck that the two marsh men were there with their superior marsh man hearing to discover him. Apparently that particular part of Ahnin's tale has been proven out.

Then again the boy would not be in this predicament if that bitch of a mother of his would just keep an eye on him instead of letting him run wild Torli angrily thinks as he hears Bornan's voice ask if they copied his last communication. At this point Torli does not trust himself to reply, for that he had personally told the stupid boy that he could not come combined with the anger that he feels towards his own self for not thinking to check to make certain that Polie had heeded him before they rolled out simply overwhelms him. He therefore gestures to Cerl to take over and walks away, and when he does the other men crammed around the vehicle's command console exchange a few looks, but then they seem to come to some silent consensus, for they all nod and grunt in the affirmative.

"Ah well...we'd be obliged if you'd hang onto him...we're approximately...an hour out to your position," Cerl replies, and then he adds with a bit of anger, "Oh and feel free to put him back in the damn box if you got a need to."

"Copy that," Bornan indignantly replies, for that the land men would suggest they traumatize the little one more than he already has been is outrageous, and he intends to tell them so when they get here diplomacy be damned.

"You hurt boy?" Tosel puts his hands on his hips and asks the child, but even though he thinks that he should at least give him a good tongue lashing he cannot ignore the tears sliding down the boy's cheeks long enough to do it. So he just reaches in, picks the boy out, and strides into the vehicle where he plops him in a seat.

"You hurting somewhere child?" Bornan comes inside to ask, and when the boy shakes his head no Bornan scolds, "You are lucky you know...what were you thinking to climb in there?"

"I wanted ta come an Torli said no," the boy replies in a small voice, and even though he seems a bit shaken Bornan can see by the furtive glances that the boy is sending him that he is relatively unharmed.

"What do they call you?" Tosel asks when he sees that the boy's natural curiosity has managed to win out over his fear, for he is openly studying them now.

"Polie," the boy replies, and then he adds with a nod, "An brat too."

"No doubt they do," Bornan agrees as he exchanges an amused look with Tosel.

"Well Polie...you have about an hour to think up something really good to tell commander Torli," Tosel informs him, but the boy does not even bat an eye to that, which Tosel finds quite interesting.

"So is he your father then...commander Torli?" Bornan asks.

"Nope...I got eight papas," Polie replies, and then he says with animated pride, "I'm a lucky boy."

"I see," Bornan responds and then exchanges a questioning shrug with Tosel.

"You probably do not know their names eh...after all eight is quite a lot of fathers for a babe such as yourself to remember," Tosel goads.

"I ain't no babe...I'm this many...I know all my papas," Polie holds up five fingers and indignantly retorts, and then he suddenly switches tracks and asks, "Why's your skin so shiny...you got fish skins huh?"

"No I do not," Tosel replies and then holds out his arm and instructs, "Here touch it and see."

"Oooh...it's all smooth and soft like my mamma's...nope...nope it's stiff an all...she ain't got stiff skins," Polie prattles out, and then much to Bornan's amusement he studies his booted foot and then adds with a self-assured nod, "Yep my boots's got stuffs like it...ooh I got marsh people skin boots!"

"No boy you have boots made of the leather from the skin of a beast..." Tosel attempts to inform him.

145

"Hey...you got no eyes...I seen a fishy with no eyes... it was all dead an smelly..." Polie says in a matter-of-fact manner, and then he continues with, "You got fishy eyes...hey can you swim like a fishy do...my mamma says marsh peoples likes the water...Torli says I gots a keeeen mind...but Cerl he says I gots a fresh mouff...hey...maybe I gots a keeeen fresh mind huh...or a fresh keeeen mouff huh...what's keeeen mean..."

"You hungry boy?" Bornan interrupts him to ask.

"What you got?" Polie asks, and then he says, "Oooh you got marsh people stuffs ta eat...I like marsh people stuffs ta eat."

"Now what would you be knowing about what marsh folk eat boy?" Bornan skeptically asks.

"Well...fishies lives in the water...I likes fishies...so marsh peoples likes water too so...marsh peoples got a eat fishies cause nothin else's in water cept fishies an marsh peoples...you got any fishies..."

"Save me," Tosel interjects, and then leans in to Bornan and mumbles, "I see why they thought we might want to put him back in the box."

"I will tell you what boy...I will give you one of these for every father you can name," Bornan says, and then grabs a bag off a nearby table and plunks it before Polie.

"What kind a fishies is them?" Polie asks with wide eyes when Bornan unties the bag to show him its contents, for the way the tiny dried fish in the bag sparkle in the dim light fascinates him.

"They are called lambis fish...they live in the deep marshes in groups so thick that you can just reach in and grab a whole handful of them at a time...these ones here are dried and smoked," Bornan informs him and then reaches into the bag and pops one of the fishes into his mouth before saying, "So you have a name for me then?"

"Han...he fixes stuffs," Polie instantly replies and then takes the fish that Bornan hands him, and after he tentatively sniffs it he puts it in his mouth and chews a couple of times before saying, "Hey they's all crunchy...I like crunchy stuffs."

"Yes and papa number two," Tosel inquires and then holds out another fish in front of his face.

"Seasle...he likes eatin' stuffs...he's funny...my mama don't like him much," Polie replies, and then snatches the fish and says with his mouth full, "Seasle'd sure like some a these here fishies."

146

One by one the men coax the names of three more men from Polie's mouth. So it is that they discover papa number three is a man named Cerl who always has his hair in his eyes and has legs so long that he can outrun anything. Papa number four is called Gorg who Polie thinks is a bit of a sour puss, and papa number five is the now infamous Bro who is the one who likes to fight. Then comes the one named Orn, whom Polie informs them is his mamma's favorite papa, for whenever she says his name she 'smiles real big and gets all mushy'. Papa number seven however proves to be somewhat of a sticking point, for by this time not only does Polie's small stomach get a bit full, but his attention begins to wander as well.

"So what is the next name then," Bornan prompts.

"I don't want no more fishies," Polie waves off his offering and says.

"What do you want then?" Bornan inquires with a sigh.

"What you got?"

"Well...I am probably going to regret this," Bornan says as he reaches into his pocket, and as Tosel watches in horror he pulls out a small tree like thing that he holds up to the boy.

"Have you lost your mind Bornan?" Tosel asks, for everyone knows that the last thing you give a small child this late at night is a sweet.

"Ah well...they are not all that far away now..." Bornan returns, and after Tosel nods in enlightenment Bornan locks eyes with Polie and tells him, "You have to give us the last two for this one though."

"That ain't fair," Polie protests.

"Ah but this is a sweet tree boy... it is worth probably three names at least so you are getting a bargain," Tosel cajoles.

"O...o...h," Polie drawls in reply as he eyes the sweet with a look of wonder, and then he tells them with his eyes firmly glued to the prize, "Well there's Ahnin...he's nice an he gives me his pie a lot...an...well... Karnin...but I ain't posed ta tell nobody bout him."

"I see," Bornan remarks, and as Polie takes a big bite of the sweet tree he reaches over and picks up a bottle of blue liquid that he pours into a nearby cup and says, "Here wash it down."

"Wha's dat," Polie mumbles out between his sticky lips and then giggles and says, "Ay wiss iss wike gwoo!"

"Glue...now there is an idea..." Tosel suggests with a smirk.

"Drink some out of the cup...it will help unglue you," Bornan instructs him as he holds the cup to Polie's lips and helps him take a few sips.

"Hey...it worked!" Polie says as he opens and shuts his mouth a few times.

"Oh hooray," Tosel halfheartedly replies.

"Hey!" Polie suddenly shouts and before either man can react he hops down from his seat and shoots out the door.

"Come back here boy!" Bornan calls and then quickly sprints after him, for the brat could easily get lost in the woods and who knows what might befall him then.

"Save me," Tosel mumbles as he hurriedly follows.

"I gotta get em out!" Polie exclaims when Bornan catches up with him and hauls him off his feet.

"Who?" Bornan distractedly asks, but then the meaning of the boy's remark hits him, and a new fear begins to gnaw at Bornan's gut. What if the little monster brought a friend along? He therefore dangles the boy by the back of his coat so that he can see his face while he asks, "Where is he boy?!"

"In the box...I put em in my box," Polie replies.

"There is no one else in there," Tosel replies, but then he obviously thinks better of assuming, for he walks over to the box and begins to rummage through its contents.

"He got out...let go...I got a find em!" Polie screeches and then tries to squirm from Bornan's grasp.

"Here now we will find him," Bornan gently says, for he can see that Polie is on the verge of hysterics, and so he tries to refocus the boy's attention by saying, "But we have to know what he looks like...so we know what we are searching for see?"

"I found em...he come in an I put em in the box," Polie replies, and then holds out his hands a foot or so apart and adds as though this last comment should explain everything, "He's bout this big."

"Okay..." Bornan reassuringly says, and then he blinks a few times before asking, "What color would you say he is?"

"Is he alive?" Tosel suddenly stops rummaging through the box to ask.

"Yep...he's an alive thin," Polie replies with a snort, and then he loudly whispers to Bornan, "Is he dumb?"

"Yes but we try not to say so in front of him," Bornan explains, and then grins when Tosel sends him a somewhat crude hand gesture.

"Hey what's that mean?" Polie asks.

"Ah...well...that means thanks," Bornan replies as he sends Tosel a dirty look, but any further questions concerning the mysterious missing 'he' are averted when the soft whirring sound of the runner is suddenly heard giving Bornan and Tosel no time to do much more than assume a more dignified stance before it glides in.

Inside the runner the men are gathered round anxiously watching the camera monitors, for Polie can be a rather trying creature at times, and they fear that they may indeed find him locked back in the box or worse. Therefore, when the lights from their vehicle illuminate the transport and they see Polie standing there in one piece there are a few relieved exhales. Well after a brief second of stunned silence, for when the runner's lights first hit the two marsh men their eyes shine in the dark like wild beasts do, which they find somewhat unsettling. The moment passes, and when it does there are a few snickers from within their ranks, for even though the two marsh men seem to be behaving as though nothing untoward has happened that they are both rather dirty and askew belies it. Then there is Polie's small figure hopping up and down between them like some demented wild thing to add that nice surreal touch to the scene.

"Poor bastards," Cerl mumbles.

"They're gonna need some time off," Gorg supposes.

"You best decide amongst you what you're going to do about that boy," Torli steps to the door and says in a somewhat subdued tone.

"There's two not here you know..." Gorg begins, but he is immediately silenced when Torli gives him a slashing gesture.

"Take it up with them when they return then...in the meantime since none a you really wants to know which one a you sired him than you'll all be held accountable for what he does...but I'm telling you something needs done very soon...Polie needs a legal father who can take control a him before he kills his self," Torli informs them in a tone that allows no room for argument.

"Look commander I'll take whatever punishment you got in mind for him...he's just a babe after all," Gorg steps in front of him and says.

"Step back you idiot," Torli commands, and when Gorg wisely complies Torli hits the door release button and adds, "His mother'll met out a worse punishment than I'd ever think up and I tell you if she beats him again...well...she's gonna get a taste a it her own self...you tell Bella that when you see her."

"Oh aye," Cerl agrees as he impatiently gestures for Gorg to go after him, for Gorg is supposed to be Torli's bodyguard although why he was chosen is anybody's guess Cerl thinks as he watches Gorg hop out.

"He's right you know," Seasle admits as he also hops out.

"Yeah...Bella probably ain't even noticed he's gone yet..." Bro points out as he and the other men follow Seasle out the door.

"Yeah...but she's gonna play it for all it's worth when she does," Gorg pauses outside the door to say.

"Let's go Gorg!" Torli impatiently calls, and when he does Gorg quickly hops to, for it is always best not to trifle with one of Torli's bad moods.

"Torli's never gonna turn him into a proper bodyguard," Seasle comments with a shake of his head.

"Aw...you're all too hard on Gorg...give 'em a chance," Orn interjects, for in Orn's opinion all that Gorg needs is the one thing that he has not to date been given; a fair opportunity to prove his self.

The four men file out then and stand at the ready as Torli and Gorg make their way over to where an excited Polie waits with the two marsh men. As Torli approaches he quickly scans the boxes making note that the only box that appears to have been tampered with is the same one that the guards claimed that Polie was in, for as is the usual with storage boxes containing low priority goods the code that they were given would have opened a few other boxes as well, which is a common enough practice on the land that Torli finds hard to believe would not also be employed in the marshes as well. Therefore it is to the two marsh men's credit that they did not try to open any of the other boxes. Then again maybe they were just too damn busy Torli supposes as he eyes the overly excited little boy.

"Hello commander," Bornan acknowledges with a polite nod when he comes to stand before them.

"Hello Bornan," Torli replies and then turns to Tosel and prompts, "I don't believe we were ever introduced."

"His name's To...sil...hey mander I got ta eats fishies...an heads an eyes an everythin!"

"You're supposed to be at *Onyat* with your mother right now," Torli sternly tells him, and when his face falls Torli pushes the regret that wells up in him away and says in a commanding tone, "Now thank these two men for taking such good care a your disobedient self...and then take yourself off to the runner."

"But I gotta find 'em..." Polie whines.

"Him?" Torli repeats, and then cocks his head towards Bornan.

"Well the boy here apparently found some...crawling thing...that he says he put into the box to keep that has now gone missing," Bornan replies, and then he adds, "We never did get him to say exactly what it was."

"Well Polie I'm thinking that 'he' decided he wanted to be free...perhaps he's got a family he wanted to return to eh," Torli tells him not unkindly and then he puts a hand on top of the boy's head and turns him in the direction of his waiting potential fathers.

"Oh yeah...he gots a family huh," Polie thoughtfully repeats as the other men come out to fetch him.

"He is a very...enthusiastic boy," Tosel says with a negative shake of his head as Polie's potential fathers surround him and then head back towards the vehicle, but Torli does not miss the somewhat fond glance that he sends Polie's way.

"He sort a grows on you," Torli admits.

"Hey Bor...nin...To...sil!" Torli and the two marsh men suddenly hear, and when they turn they see Polie burst out of the center of the group of men, and then promptly send them the same rather crude hand gesture that he saw Tosel use earlier followed by a smile and a goodbye wave given over Cerl's shoulder as he quickly carries him inside.

"Ah well commander he learned that by accident I am afraid...he thinks it means thanks," Bornan replies to Torli's questioning stare.

"I see...so what damages'd the brat do needs compensated for eh?" Torli asks.

"He actually did not harm anything...unless you want to count the heart attacks we nearly had when we realized that he was locked in the box," Bornan replies.

"If you do not mind commander I would like to give him something," Tosel says, and after he retrieves the bag of smoked fish from the transport he hands it to Torli and explains, "He seemed to really like them...and well no offense but he is a lot less annoying when he is busy eating."

151

"My thanks," Torli replies with a lopsided grin, and then he says, "Well then...all we need do's to load our boxes back up and we'll be off to the marshes again...you know...if you men'd rather wait until dawn to set out we'll gladly delay."

"Thank you but that will not be necessary commander," Bornan assures him.

"Very well," Torli responds, but when he does he winces slightly, and there is no mistaking the brief spark of pain in the commander's eyes.

"Are you alright sir?" Tosel asks him.

"Yeah...just a headache coming on," Torli replies, but then he seems to rally himself, for he looks up and adds with a gesture towards the runner, "Matches the pain in my arse."

"I have something for the headache if you would like it?" Bornan questions.

"Thank you but I got something..." Torli says, but then just abruptly stops talking to stare at Tosel's shoulder before he asks rather dubiously, "You got any phobias Tosel?"

"None that I am aware of," Tosel replies somewhat uncomfortably, for to him it seems like the commander is staring at something behind him.

"In that case I believe Polie's mysterious 'him' isn't lost at all," Torli informs him, and then reaches forward and removes a rather large spider from Tosel's shoulder and says, "He's just hitched a ride...this species gets very large...but its harmless enough...here take this with you Gorg...tell Cerl I said the six a you'd best...well...build it a cage or a nest or whatever the thing needs...I'll want to see it later...and it better be alive."

"But I can't leave you..."

"Get going!" Torli nearly shouts back with another wince, which quickly sends Gorg hurrying off juggling the spider from hand to hand.

"If I might be so bold but are we speaking of six of Polie's eight papas then?" Borsen asks.

"I see Polie was his usual chatty self," Torli notes, and then he replies to Bornan's question with, "Yeah we're speaking a them...and just so you know that situation doesn't 'ave my approval."

"No of course I did not mean to pry..." Borsen apologetically says but just then a few less than manly shrieks come from the direction of the vehicle, and after Borsen notes the satisfaction that briefly graces the commander's features he says, "I assume that one of the boy's papas has a phobia or two."

"Yeah he does…" Torli replies with another wince, and this time he reaches up to massage his temple a bit before he says, "Let's get these boxes loaded."

"No sir…you will take this and go rest sir…headaches that come on like that are nothing to play with," Bornan pretty much commands as he pulls a flask from his pocket.

"You carry a headache remedy with you all the time?" Torli questions, for it seems odd that he should since Slolar had led him to believe that they were all perfectly healthy.

"The lady Andina gets them…and when they come they put her down…all her men always carry some of this," Bornan replies.

"So you are the lady's guard then?" Torli asks, for that also seems strange since Bimian left them behind.

"Ah well we handle Onot sir," Tosel tells him in a rather subdued way.

"Don't take this the wrong way but…well…when?" Torli suspiciously asks, for the reason why the overlord insisted on leaving them to guard the boxes is becoming rather clear.

"Yes well…whenever the overlord has no choice sir…or he is not there…you see…he left us behind because he is hoping that Onot will run away and go back to the wild," Bornan tells him.

"I see," Torli replies with a nod of understanding, but then a blinding pain courses through his head, and the next thing that he knows Ahnin is there with his medicine, which Torli drinks down without delay.

"I'll get this…go lay down until it goes," Bornan hears the odd man that he met at *Onyat* tell the commander, and after he thanks Bornan for offering him the lady's remedy he walks off.

"What remedy?" Ahnin settles his odd eyes on Bornan and inquires.

"The lady Andina's headache remedy," Bornan replies, but before he can slip it back into his pocket Ahnin holds out his hand in silent command, and even though Bornan would later tell Tosel that he has no idea why he complied he nonetheless does.

"What's the fruity smell from?" Ahnin asks after he takes a tentative sniff.

"A marsh herb called foslinia…it is a good pain reliever," Bornan replies.

"He take any?" Ahnin asks as he hands the flask back to Bornan

153

"No...what is in your concoction there?" Bornan asks, and when he does Ahnin hands it to him, but when Bornan gives it a sniff he coughs and says with a grimace, "What is that?"

"My own special mix," Ahnin responds as Bornan sniffs the brew and gags.

"Take this...until you rethink that crap there," Bornan says as he proffers his flask to Ahnin.

"Is not crap...the stuff works...when you're hurting you don't care what it smells like," Ahnin tells him as he follows them to the pile of boxes.

"The lady's headaches make her queasy too...that stuff there would probably finish her off," Tosel comments as he watches several of the commander's men disembark and head their way.

"Yeah well...anything that don't stink don't last long around us," Ahnin replies.

"Hey magic man...the boss says you better get it in gear or he's gonna leave your arse behind," Seasle calls when he gets close enough, and then he sniffs the air like a hungry beast and asks, "Who got fruit?"

"See," Ahnin remarks, and after he sends Bornan a knowing nod he picks up one of the storage boxes and walks off towards the cargo area of the runner.

"Yes...I see," Tosel replies as he exchanges a dubious glance with Bornan.

"See what?" Seasle asks with a suspicious frown, but they just shake their heads and follow Ahnin with two more boxes, and so Seasle looks over at Gorg and says, "Fish men're weird."

"Yeah...hey...maybe magic man's part fish man," Gorg suggests.

"That'd explain a whole lot," Cerl notes, and after they share a few male grunts and nods of agreement the men pick up boxes and carry them off towards the runner.

Chapter Eight

The gentle hum of the runner's propulsion system as it speeds towards *Onyat* and home pulls at Torli as it always does, and soon he is nodding in his seat despite his attempts to stay awake. Of course Ahnin's headache remedy is not helping there, for it always leaves him played out. Still that is better than the intense pain Torli reminds himself. In truth he is beginning to wonder if he might have something going on in his head besides the stress that *Onyat's* old healer Morta says is causing his headaches. Ah well they will be home in an hour and then they will all sleep in tomorrow. Well today, for morning is not far away Torli thinks as he checks the time keeper fastened to his wrist. With a sigh he lays his head back again and closes his eyes, but his mind simply cannot stop thinking on all that has transpired today. As it was when he got up this morning he had no idea that he would be coming back without Karnin and Han, and not only is he doing so, but by now the two of them are nearly to *Laraqua*. Yes and beyond easy retrieval as well. Still there is an upside, for they learned a lot about marsh folk today, and such knowledge may one day come in handy. It might be sooner rather than later if they have to go bust Karnin and Han out of jail.

"I think I'm gonna be sick," Torli hears Seasle's voice suddenly say from the rear of the vehicle.

"You best not do it in here," Ahnin warns from where he lounges near the front controls.

"Ah you scared a puke now magic man?" Bro jibes even though he knows that he is not, for once when they were out scavenging for food Bro saw Ahnin plunge his hands into the guts of a rotting beast, and when Ahnin had smiled and triumphantly held up a slimy handful of partially digested berries it was the rest of them who either gagged or puked.

"Hey...it wasn't me who screamed like a girl over a little spider," Ahnin points out.

"That weren't no little spider...it was a damn monster," Seasle retorts, and then he moans out, "Ah damn...you got anything for a bellyache magic man?"

"Got a purge," Ahnin calls back to him.

"Don't want no damn purge," Seasle complains.

"Yeah ain't nobody what wants a damn purge for him," Orn pipes up, and then he carps, "If you's sick it's yar fault...ya ate up all the extra sweets when we's not lookin'."

"Yeah," Gorg concurs, and then he says, "Besides it ain't fair that we got a smell his crap the whole way home."

"What you want crap or puke to sniff Gorg?" Seasle testily tosses in.

"Ah...damn you Seasle...you crapped already didn't you?" Gorg demands.

"That ain't my scent...mine's more...fruity..." Seasle responds.

"Yeah...right..."

"Okay...whoever dun it better not do it no mores..." Orn warns, but the only reply he gets is a rather sinister sounding laugh.

"Cerl...you stinking bastard!" Bro suddenly accuses.

"What?" Cerl innocently parrots.

"Now I know I'm gonna be sick," Seasle moans out.

"Me too," Gorg announces.

"Ah damn...Cerl...you got a git that arse a yours seen ta...I think it's rottin' inside ta out," Orn remarks.

"For the love a...hit the button Ahnin!" Gorg practically begs.

"Hold your damn breath," Ahnin comes back with, but when the foul stench begins to permeate the entire cabin he mutters a curse and then quickly reaches over and punches a button on the control console.

The sudden whooshing sound of the emergency air evacuator drowns out everything else that gets said. Torli is too busy trying to keep the valuable paper lying on the table in front of him from being sucked away by the sudden rush of air that travels through the cabin to really care much about missing a quip or two. Luckily, when the brief surge of air subsides a brief inspection tells him that the paper is undamaged, which Torli is rather glad of since it is some of the finest paper that he has ever seen. Then there is the fact that he has yet to decipher the meaning behind what is written upon it. That only serves to focus Torli's attention back to the note that he had decided to let be for a time in the hopes that something might 'come' to him if he did. Unfortunately, reading it one more time will not make the words that are obviously 'between the lines' visible he thinks as he pushes the paper to the far side of the table.

No Torli knows that unless he gets some more information it will not matter how many times he reads the message from lady Andina's treat box he will still come up rather stupefied as to why it is that overlord Bimian seemed not to want him to read it in front of Karnin. Well except for the possibility that the overlord did not want Karnin to know that he supports their bid to oust Tok. The why of that is the question, for in the political arena of overlords despising someone is not exactly enough reason to stick one's neck out for a nobody. That leaves only one answer; Bimian does not trust Karnin. The why of that Torli refuses to examine, for Torli will neither second guess his own decisions nor let Bimian undermine his relationship with his cousin he thinks with a frustrated sigh as he picks up the paper and reads the note's words yet again.

Commander Torli,

These sweets are called 'Gonia Nona', which would mean 'Sweet Nothings' in the world's common language. In marsh custom they are a traditional gift given from one person to another in celebration of some occasion of importance or in thanks for some extraordinary favor done. We are therefore gifting this box to you and your men with the hope that this can in some small way express our gratitude to you all for assisting us in our time of need.

We would also wish to take this opportunity to tell you that our thoughts will be with you in your future endeavors, and we are very much hoping that your quest is successful, for we would like nothing better than to have you close enough to visit with us on occasion. Regardless of outcomes, if ever you find yourself requiring a safe haven, or if you simply just find yourself wanting to explore the inner marshes I hope that you will call upon us, for you shall always be welcomed on our lands and in our home.

With greatest regards,

Bimian

Overlord of the Central Marsh Territory and Fringe Lands

Andina
Lady of Mori
Lady en Tenda of the Central Marsh Territory and Fringe Lands

"*Lady a Mori...*" Torli mumbles to himself, for *Mori* is the stuff of legend and lore that until now Torli had believed to be no longer in existence especially on the level that being its lady would be treated with more importance than being an overlord's wife, and with a somewhat thoughtful expression he asks aloud, "Could it be that then?"

"What'd you say sir," Gorg asks as he comes forward and plunks down in a seat across the aisle.

"Have you ever heard a *Mori* before?" Torli asks.

"*Mori*'s just a place in a fairy tale I think," Gorg replies.

"I have," a small voice says from somewhere in the cabin.

"You're supposed to be asleep," Gorg sternly says.

"I can't...I'm hungry," Polie whines with a pathetic sniff.

"Come here Polie," Torli relents, for the boy has sat in obedient silence as he was told to do since they headed for home, which for Polie could not have been an easy thing.

"Yeah mander Torli," Polie meekly says as he comes to stand next to Torli's seat.

"Sit and tell me what you know a *Mori* then," Torli orders as he slides down a bit so that the boy can climb up next to him, which Polie is only too eager to do.

"W...e...l...l," Polie dramatically says, and then he tells him in a sing-song voice as he swings his legs, "An allll the peoples that lives on the...lan...ah...once cum...ah...up frum the...de...pe...thises a the Moo...ree...and...ah...the end."

"Ah I see..." Torli acknowledges as he and Gorg exchange amused smirks, for the ditty is an old one that speaks of the vast *Morian Sea* that covers the world and not the fortress and lands known as *Mori*. Torli decides to save the history lesson for another time though, and so he slides Tosel's gift towards Polie and says, "Here Tosel thought you might get hungry again."

"Oooh fishies," Polie replies with a bounce and then he shouts, "Hey Seasle I gots fishies!"

"What kind a fishies?" Seasle calls back.

"Crunchy ones!" Polie replies, and then giggles when Seasle suddenly pokes his head around the seat.

"Thought you were sick," Gorg dryly states.

"I'm feeling better," Seasle replies and then hangs his mouth open so that Polie can toss a fish in.

"They're crunchy alright," Seasle agrees, and then he makes a sour face.

"How comes you don't like my fishies?" Polie asks a bit crestfallen.

"Ha...just kidding you," Seasle suddenly says, and then he opens his mouth wide again so that Polie can toss in another fish.

"Hey... wanna fishy mander Torli?" Polie holds one out to him and asks.

"Ah well...I suppose I'll give one a try," Torli replies as he takes Polie's proffered fish and pops it in his mouth.

"Good huh?" Polie eagerly asks.

"Yeah well...ah..." Torli replies with a cough, for the first crunch released something mushy from inside the fish, and Torli thinks that it tastes exactly like one would suspect the rotten guts of a fish to taste, but for Polie's sake he just chews and nods.

"Hey Cerl you wanna fishy?" Polie calls.

"Ah well no thanks brat I'm still full a sweets," Cerl calls back.

"He's full a something...I wouldn't exactly call it sweet," Bro complains.

"Ha...stinky Cerl," Polie says with a giggle, and then he politely goes down the list of men present, asking each in turn if they would care to try his fish, but in the end it turns out that Seasle and Gorg are the only ones with palettes similar to his own.

"Ah I nearly forgot," Torli suddenly says, and after rummaging through his day bag for a few seconds he pulls out Andina's cream pot and calls, "The lady Andina sent this for you Bro!"

"What's in it?" Seasle asks with an interested expression.

"A special thank you for...servicing Onot I believe," Torli cryptically replies.

"Any good?" Seasle asks.

"Didn't open it...be my guest," Torli offers and then tosses him the pot of cream.

"What's it some kind a spread?" Seasle asks as he unscrews the lid and sniffs the contents, and then much to Torli's amusement Seasle does exactly what Torli expected him to do; he dips a finger in and tastes it and then says, "Pretty good...she send something to spread it on?"

"Yeah my balls idiot," Bro says as he walks up and relieves Seasle of the cream pot, and then he sends him a sarcastic glare and adds, "You can still come spread it on if you want."

"Hey…why you got ball stuffs Bro?" Polie asks, and then stuffs three fish into his mouth.

"Got sore balls boy," Bro responds and then tries to walk away before he has to explain how they got that way.

"Oh…hey…I got balls," Polie puts his head up and says, and then he adds, "Can I put some a that stuff on my balls?"

"No it's only for sore balls," Bro reluctantly replies.

"Oooh…I think my balls is hurtin," Polie dramatically says, and then stands up in his seat and tries to peer down his pants.

"Now listen up you…sore balls's nothing to play around about," Bro points a finger at the boy and says, and then sweeps the room with his eyes and adds, "And that goes for the rest a you miserable sots."

"I believe he called you a sot commander," Gorg points out, and then he asks, "You gonna let him get away with that?"

"I believe a man who's suffered such a…trauma to his balls ought a get a bit a room for his mood getting the best a his brains," Torli replies, and then he gives Gorg a sideways glance and adds, "I can remember how you got that time…"

"Not in front a the boy," Gorg warns, and with a disgruntled face he adds, "Besides that wasn't my balls if you'll recall."

"Wus it your poop hole?" Polie innocently asks, and then adds as he stuffs another fish into his mouth, "I got a sore poop hole when I ate up a bi…i…i…g rock…Mama told nanna Morta to get it out…but nana sed it'd poop out an it did."

"There…you see what you started?" Gorg says with an exasperated gesture.

"Hey Seasle!" Bro calls from the rear of the cabin.

"What!"

"Come help me out I can't reach the back!"

"Hey I think your girlfriend's following us!" Seasle jibes.

"Why you," Bro mumbles and a second later a somewhat questionable smelling sock sails up over the seat and hits Seasle squarely in the face.

"Oooh that wus a good shot!" Polie exclaims, but then he sees Torli staring intently at something and he cranes his neck and says, "Hey…how comes that thing's all blinkin'?"

160

"Alert...obstacle detected in glide route...alert...obstacle detected in glide route!" the vehicle warning system starts blaring out.

"All stop!" Torli quickly calls as he jumps up from his seat, and then he quickly rattles off, "Lock us down Ahnin...Gorg...secure the boy...the rest a you arm yourselves and secure all entry points...nobody goes out there until I say so...and kill that alarm!"

"Hey!" Polie squeaks as Gorg scoops him up under his arm, and after Bro tosses him a hand weapon he heads into the front compartment, for in an attack the safest portion of the vehicle is the place furthest from the propulsion and life support systems, which are the most likely areas that an enemy would target.

"Lock yourself in until you hear from us Gorg," Torli quietly says to him as he passes by him.

"Aye sir," Gorg replies.

"Wait...I don't wanna go..." Polie whines, but Gorg ignores him, and after he steps into the forward compartment and enters his code the door silently slides shut behind them.

"I just don't see what set it off," Ahnin says as he pans the forward cameras, but nothing is visible, and so he switches on the runner's skin sensors, but there again he finds no trace of a heat signature near the vehicle.

"How big'd it say it was?" Torli leans on the console and asks.

"Seems to be some confusion there...but it'd need to be something too big to run it over without a problem or the alarm wouldn't a sounded," Ahnin replies with a shrug.

"Unless a course it was moving...won't even let us run down a damn jim-jon without alarming," Cerl complains.

"Yeah well we're not out here to kill off the wildlife..." Torli absently replies as he studies the camera images for a time, and then he turns away and says, "It might've been a glitch or an animal...whatever it was appears to be gone now...reset the alarm and move on."

"Yeah boss," Ahnin replies as he reaches down and begins the process of clearing the motion alarm.

As Ahnin prepares to get back underway Torli turns to go back to his seat, and as he goes he reaches down to press the button on his suit's arm that will key his headset so that he can give Gorg the all clear. Before he gets a chance to do so he catches a brief flash of movement on one of the camera monitors, and so he quickly turns his attention to them just in time to see what appears to be a large eyeball staring back at him. It is gone so quickly that Torli questions whether he might have imagined it. Better safe than sorry though he thinks as he stands unmoving for a few seconds and intently peers at the monitor. When nothing shows itself again he shakes his head in disgust, for apparently he can add hallucinations with regards to the list of unpleasant things that one can expect when using Ahnin's foul tasting headache remedy. With a snort of derision he gives the bank of camera monitors one last perusal and when he does he sees the flash of another eyeball in the camera on the opposite side of the vehicle.

"Anybody see that?" Torli asks in confusion.

"That what?" Cerl asks in reply as he comes to stand next to Torli.

"Something was watching me," Torli tells him as he pivots his head between the camera monitors.

"What kind a something?" Seasle asks, and then steps over and leans in towards the bank of camera monitors searching for anything unusual, but he sees nothing and so he glances back at Torli and says with a twisted grin, "Maybe it's Onot."

"Perhaps," Torli replies, but even though he is calm something in his tone catches the attention of the others and they make their way over to him.

"What...you all gone daft or somethin'?" Seasle asks, for all of them are staring at him as though a foot has sprouted from his back.

"Look," Bro inclines his head towards the monitors and says, but when Seasle only shrugs in confusion Orn reaches one beefy arm over, and after he slaps his big paw on top of Seasle's head he twists his face back to the monitor.

"What the...!" Seasle exclaims as he jumps back, for the entire monitor in front of him is covered by one enormous eyeball.

"What'd you think's on the other end a that?" Ahnin asks, but before anyone can reply there is a loud bang on the side of the vehicle.

"I think it wants ta come in," Orn states as another bang sounds a bit further down the side, and then he adds, "Maybe it's that big she beastie after all."

"Damn well better not be," Bro threatens, but despite his bravado he subconsciously reaches down and cups his sore crotch.

"That ain't Onot..." Seasle says when another bang on the opposite side of the vehicle startles them.

"Yeah...but whatever's out there...it's either very fast on its feet..." Cerl begins.

"Or he's brought along a friend..." Torli finishes.

"Or two..." Orn chimes in.

"Damn tookas," all six men say in unison.

As the men in the cabin come to the conclusion that what has waylaid them is a flock of extremely large flightless land birds *tookapendis* or 'tookas' Gorg being isolated in the front compartment with Polie is still waiting for the all clear when the banging starts. Therefore when it becomes more insistent Gorg logically thinks that they are under attack and so he instinctively nudges Polie behind him and with his weapon in hand he backs them both against the room's most interior wall. As he stands intently listening for the telltale clinking of a hull buster or some other such sound that might forewarn him that someone is trying to blast their way in he feels Polie wrap his small arms around one of his legs. As one might expect Gorg then tries to reassure him, but instead of easing the boy's worries Gorg's 'there-there' pat only makes Polie bury his face in Gorg's pants leg and cry.

"You gotta be quiet Polie," Gorg whispers.

"I'm scared."

"Shush now...I won't let anything happen to you," Gorg promises, but just then there is a bang very close to where they are standing.

"What's that?!" Polie whispers.

"Shhh," Gorg urges with a finger to his lips.

Despite the fact that Gorg finds the knocking and banging worrisome he is rather relieved that it continues, for had someone just attached a hull buster to the runner's side they would now be running away not continuing to run up and down knocking. That begs the question as to why anyone would be announcing their presence by knocking in the first place? Perhaps to find the door he thinks, but just then the banging abruptly stops, and Gorg spends a few nervous seconds of silence wondering if they have set a charge after all. Needless to say he is glad to hear the rapping start up again, for even though it is annoying as all get out at least there is no boom coming. Still the few seconds of unknown have rattled Gorg's composure a bit.

Gorg therefore begins to scan the room for a safe place to stash Polie. That way if they do manage to breach the hull at least the boy will not get in the way. Unfortunately Gorg sees nothing but metal storage cabinets and boxes, and after Polie's recent experience with storage boxes Gorg supposes that the boy will fight him too much if he tries to shove him in one. Gorg could hardly blame him for that. Still he must protect him and so he will have to put him in one of the storage cabinets. Hopefully their larger size will not remind him of the box incident Gorg thinks as he takes Polie by the arm, pulls him over to the bank of equipment cabinets on the far wall where he throws one open and is just about to start making room in it for his charge when there is very loud bang right above their heads, which makes both man and boy swivel his eyes to the ceiling.

"Up there," Polie whispers as his hand latches onto to Grog's pants leg again.

This time no knocking follows the initial bang. Instead there is a series of clicking sounds that Gorg and Polie follow with their eyes across the roof, and back to the same spot again where whoever it is bangs one more time. The clicking across the ceiling starts all over again then, but this time it is much quicker than before. Back and forth it goes several times until it culminates in an extremely loud bang that makes both Gorg and Polie jump. As if that were not enough three more seemingly simultaneous bangs on the ceiling above them ring out, and after a bit of scratching and scraping chaos breaks out up there, for a muffled screeching sound rings out and then the clicking noise speedily shoots down the length of the vehicle's roof.

"Wut they doin up there?" Polie whispers.

"Playing *My Hill* sounds like," Gorg replies with a frown, for the whole banging, knocking, scratching, screeching, chasing thing is starting to sound familiar.

"Why they playin' on us?" Polie asks rather indignantly when whatever it is takes another lap round the runner's roof.

"Because they like high places," Gorg answers with a relieved expression, for he has seen this little game played out before although the last time it was up close and personal, but the argument that time was not over the roof of a runner.

"Torli to Gorg," Torli's voice suddenly says in Gorg's ear.

"Gorg here," he replies.

"All clear...just tookas," Torli tells him.

"Copy all clear," Gorg replies, and then says to no one in particular, "I's right."

"Bout wut?" Polie inquires.

"Bout what's up there...they're tookas," Gorg tells him.

"Wut's a tooker?" Polie asks.

"Something you don't usually see this far north," Gorg replies, but when Polie gives him a blank look Gorg scoops him up and as he carries him towards the door he adds, "You'll see...you're gonna like this."

Two and a half hours later the runner is once more on the move and Torli is once again seated at the small table with Andina's note lying before him. This time though he is not pondering the reason why Bimian was so secretive about it. Nor is he wondering why Andina's own title was given more weight than the one she carries because her husband holds the highest title that any man can aspire to. Furthermore there are no suspicious odors or crude comments coming from the rear of the vehicle, nor any small children to amuse. No exhaustion has claimed them all, which is no great surprise since it is nearly sunrise now, and no one has had any real sleep in nearly a day.

Torli is not actually asleep, for he has difficulties falling asleep in a bed let alone sitting upright in a seat, but he is resting as much as he can under the circumstances. As he sits there with his head back and his eyes closed Torli suddenly smiles, for it was actually worth the time the tookas cost them just to see the look of wonder on Polie's face. It reminded them of why it is that they are going south, for Polie and the children of his generation deserve a better life than one lived in exile on stolen lands where the fear of losing their home is always hanging over them. They deserve to have the freedom to choose what they want to do with their futures and to see the wonders that the world has to offer. Wonders that are currently closed to them unless they are lucky enough to be born to the right man or in the right place. That is what Torli hopes to accomplish when he is overlord. It is actually the only reason that he wants it as much as he does. Well that and the usual reasons like justice with a bit of revenge tossed in he cynically thinks.

With a sigh Torli wonders when he went from an enthusiastic young boy like Polie to the pessimist that he has become, but he pretty much knows the answer to that. It was somewhere between the day that the father he never knew died and the mother that he loved was murdered. Polie has no such things preying on his young mind. No he is free from all the ugliness that being a somebody in this world unleashes upon a man or woman. Then again Torli has just demanded that Polie give all that freedom up, for once the tests say who his father is he will either be a somebody or have ties to a somebody. Then the days when he could come and go unfettered will be done. Unless of course none of them are his father, which might in the long run be the best thing for Polie.

For a few more days Polie is still only a small boy with an inquisitive mind that he is free to follow, which is a good thing since Polie has a hunger for learning. A thirst for it that he never seems to be able to quench although the tookas came pretty close Torli thinks with a twisted smile. Oh at first Polie was greatly entertained by the big birds that tried to hijack them, but after an hour or so even he grew rather tired of their incessant banging, and so they had commenced in earnest to shoo them away. What ensued was one of the most aggravating situations that any of them had faced in quite some time. So much so that it nearly led to a mutiny when Torli refused to let them go out and shoot a couple of them so that the stupid things might get the point, but as always Torli managed to calm everyone down. They had then devised a solution that in the end made everyone happy. Well except for the tookas, who ended up getting their feathers singed when Ahnin diverted enough charge to the hull to send them squawking back across the open lands from whence they had come.

And so they had set out for home once again, and so far it appears that they will reach *Onyat* with no further problems, for they are only a few minutes away now. With a sigh Torli sends a request to the fates that Polie's mother Bella has passed out in her bed by now, for Torli would rather not have to speak to her again for awhile. As it is having to talk to her by COM was tiresome enough, for she was rather livid about Polie managing to stow away on as she had put it 'what you all bragged-up to be secure'. Needless to say Bella's opinion as to Torli's lack of ability to 'control those idiots a yours' made him glad that she was a long way away. There is no doubt in Torli's mind that had she been in front of him he would have made her the very first woman who he laid his hands upon in anger. Yes right round that long neck of hers Torli thinks. Even as irritating as her insults were what she said last was the most disturbing of all, for it served to point out to everyone how very untenable Polie's situation has become.

"You're all gonna be sorry for this...you're never gonna see him again..." Torli whispers in a mocking female-ish voice.

In hindsight Torli should not have been all that surprised that Bella had said that. It was her most likely response after all, for her

166

worry when she realized that Polie was gone was most likely not caused by the thought of her beloved babe being carried away into danger. She feared that her meal ticket had been lost. The reality of the situation is that Bella uses Polie as an excuse to fleece all of Polie's potential fathers on a regular basis, which is why she has resisted a paternity test. Why settle for one man to extort when she can have eight? That in and of itself would not have bothered Torli all that much if he thought that the boy was benefiting from it in some way, after all a girl's got to eat and all, but unfortunately Polie's mother has a few bad habits that often consume whatever she gleans from Polie's papas plus some.

"Maybe I'll claim him...that ought to light a fire under someone's arse," Torli mumbles with a wince as he tries to stretch the cramp from his right leg, but as usual the move only serves to send the pain into the small of his back, and with a soft curse he runs an agitated hand through his hair.

"You okay?" Cerl's voice softly inquires from where he sits across the aisle.

"Just a bit stiff...long trip," Torli quietly lies, for the pain in his back and legs right now has definitely risen beyond the level of stiff, but since there is nothing to be gained by sharing that bit of information he changes the subject by asking, "Now we know why I'm not sleeping...but why aren't you?"

"Thinking," he replies and then comes to sit across from Torli to say, "You're right about the boy...it wasn't a problem when he was too young to understand... now he's growing up and he needs a more structured life...he needs one father and one set a rules to follow...I'm just not certain what I'm gonna do if it's not me's all."

"A boy can have all the uncles he wants you know," Torli softly replies, for it is obvious that Cerl is very bothered by the thought that he may not be Polie's biological father.

"Not the same."

"Better than nothing," Torli points out.

"True...but what if it's Orn...I mean...really..."

"Then he'll need all the uncles he can get I suppose...either way we all grew up without fathers for the most part...would you 'ave Polie do the same?"

"No I wouldn't," Cerl replies as he studies his hands, and when he does his hair hangs forward away from his face and Torli realizes that there is a part of Cerl that he has never seen before

167

although he cannot actually believe that he could have overlooked it until now.

"Then the time's come to find out who's the lucky man," Torli replies as he schools the surprise from his features, for they had always assumed that Cerl wore his hair in his face to intimidate others, and so to suddenly discover that it was not the reason is somewhat disconcerting. Now is not the time nor the place to address it though Torli decides and so he says, "The tests need done now Cerl...before we leave for *Filon Bora*."

"Yeah that's what I's just thinking...I'll talk to the others...Bella'll balk you know... I'm just hoping the one she picks to kill over the box thing isn't the real papa," Cerl says.

"Ah well...at the moment she's got it in her head that it's all my fault...for not running a tighter crew and all," Torli replies with a shrug.

"That's a relief."

"Easy for you to say."

"What do you think Karnin's gonna say?" Cerl sobers and asks.

"He'll take the test...but we can't wait for him...with any luck you'll come up positive and then it won't matter," Torli tells him.

"You gonna do a test too?" Cerl cocks his head at him and asks.

"You know I'm not in the running."

"That's not what I hear."

"Really...do tell," Torli insists with a sarcastic smirk, for Cerl has obviously heard something new going round the rumor mill, and Torli is curious to know what it is.

"I know you were sick with the fever at the time Polie got made..." Cerl begins.

"I nearly died," Torli responds with a bit of emotion, for one day he had been as well as always, and the next he was too sick to even get up to tell anyone.

"Yeah I remember...you see Bella's spreading it round that there's a possible ninth papa...but she said she was so stoned at the time that she doesn't remember exactly who only that she found herself atop him and his rod was so hot it scalded her...lady parts," Cerl tells him.

"And you said that with a straight face even," Torli notes.

"Yeah well the first time I heard it I laughed my arse off and she slapped me silly so I'm sort a conditioned not to laugh at her stories," Cerl replies with a shrug.

"Yeah well her lady parts probably weren't 'scalded'...more like 'galled' from being overworked," Torli meanly remarks, for Bella is one of the original three camp girls brought from the south to service their pubescent needs, which she has done in the years that followed with a great deal of enthusiasm as Torli recalls it, and so he feels compelled to add in a more serious tone, "You know...Bella's always been...busy...so there might be other possible papas besides you eight."

"Yeah we thought a that...we all agreed a long time ago that if it ever turned out that way then we'd just keep things the same with Polie unless Bella's someone else in mind... now I'm thinking it'd be best if one a us adopts him instead," Cerl says.

"Sounds like a worthy plan," Torli replies.

"Yeah now all I got a do's find some way for us to pick who gets to be the papa that doesn't involve any kind a physical contests," Cerl answers with a wry grin and then he adds, "Maybe a contest a the mind you know...something Orn can't win."

"How about you all get the pat tests done first then we'll see," Torli advises, and then he adds in a serious tone, "Polie told the marsh men that rescued him all about his eight papas."

"Damn," Cerl mutters with a troubled frown.

"They seem to be honorable men...but men talk...and these days one can't be certain who's listening...so Polie and his annoying mother'll 'ave to move into the inner keep until we know for certain who his father is," Torli informs him with a rather stoic expression.

"It won't matter...even the possibility that he belongs to one a us'll be enough to make him a target," Cerl sits up in his chair and says, for once the word goes out that they have a viable army here there will be no shortage of persons wanting to control it, and using a favorite child to force compliance is one of the oldest tricks in the book.

"Yeah well once we know who's his father he'll 'ave a say in where the boy goes and what he does...and we can give Bella the boot back out where her annoying self belongs," Torli tells him, and then he sends Cerl a purposeful stare and stresses, "Get the testing done tomorrow Cerl."

"Will do," Cerl replies.

"Security field ahead...contact in five minutes and twenty-two seconds," Torli hears the runner's navigation system suddenly announce.

169

"Lights on...everybody up!" Torli calls, and when the lights snap on he stands and begins to gather his things off the table and pack them back into his day bag.

"*Onyat* watch tower...this's Shadow four...four...ott...two..." Torli hears Ahnin say.

"Shadow four...four...ott...two this's *Onyat* watch tower...identification verified... perimeter field coming down in three...two...one...come ahead to the gate Shadow..." *Onyat's* watch guard replies.

"Oh...and I for one'd rather Polie not know that we're running the tests...in case there's no match at all amongst us," Cerl quietly says as he gets to his feet.

"I wouldn't tell his mother either were I you," Torli softly suggests with a nod, and then he hands Cerl the sweet that he has stashed away in his pocket with a genetic swab kit and instructs, "Now go swab him...then give him the sweet so he forgets about it...and get him ready to see his doting mama...she'll be anxious to 'ave him back."

"Oh aye...she's probably had to do her own fetching and toting while he's been gone," Cerl mumbles with a disgruntled scowl, and then he moves off towards the rear where Polie is curled up sleeping with the other men.

As Cerl strides away Torli's eyes follow him with concern, for it is obvious that he wishes very much to be Polie's biological father. The odds are stacked very much against it. As it is Bella was not exactly as interested in quality as she was quantity back then, for she was ambitious, and she knew that beauty only lasts so long, which for a woman in her profession is the norm after all. Still no one ever expected her to shrivel up so soon, but an addiction to the injectors will do that. The truth is that Karnin has considered taking the boy from her more than once, and were it not for the fact that Polie would be harmed emotionally by it he would already have done so. This new rumor about her 'hot' lover is just another way she thinks to thwart Karnin, for she thinks that Torli is more likely not to take Polie away from her than any of the others, and Torli has the clout to enforce that.

"Wrong again Bella..." Torli murmurs as he feels the vehicle come off pace and slow to a stop, for he would like nothing better than to rescue young Polie from what he has not yet realized is a life of misery.

"*Onyat* watch tower we are at the gate," Torli hears Ahnin say.

"Copy that Shadow...gate coming open..." the watch guard replies, and a few seconds later he adds, "Come ahead to the courtyard...welcome home runner."

"Copy that watch tower...good to be home," Torli hears Ahnin respond as he feels the slight lunge of the runner moving forward.

As Torli waits for the vehicle to come to a stop in the courtyard he suffers a moment of regret that he has never found the right woman. Then again in retrospect that it might be for the best since the only thing that having the responsibility of a wife right now would do is to give one of his soon to be enemies a weapon to use against him, which would not bode well for anyone. Besides he and Karnin have a master plan that does not include responsibilities such as wives and children not yet at any rate, and even though Karnin is a potential father it is very unlikely that he is the man of the hour where Polie is concerned. At least that is what Karnin insists, for he always uses the methods available to prevent conception, and since he is the exacting bastard that he is Torli has no reason to doubt his certainty on it Torli thinks as he turns and walks over to wait by the runner's door.

As Torli feels the vehicle glide to a stop he prepares his mind for the coming battle, for that there will be one is a given. He therefore forces himself to calm down and assume the bored disinterested persona that he uses to put people off when he does not want to speak to them. That done he casually holds his hand out to Polie who skips over to him completely oblivious that anything untoward is about to happen. Such is the innocence of youth Torli silently notes as the blast shields roll up giving the men inside the runner their first view of *Onyat's* courtyard. As one might expect they do not see a welcoming party waiting since it is only a few hours before dawn, and so everyone is still asleep. Almost everyone Torli thinks with a sigh, for through the forward window he sees Bella laughing and yakking it up with one of Han's mechanics. Yes she is all tore up with worry Torli sarcastically thinks, but just then the door slides open, and when it does Torli sees all humor quickly fade from Bella's face.

"Polie!!!!" Bella screeches and then snatches him off the vehicle and then promptly smacks his backside.

"Ow mama!" Polie says with a squeak.

"I ought a beat your arse boy until you can't SIT!" she bends and says into the boy's face intentionally distracting the men with a view of her somewhat sunken in backside that she has thoughtfully clad in skin tight leggings.

"Now Bella he's only a child," Cerl steps around Torli to say.

"Yeah have a heart for once," Seasle more so demands than requests as he comes to stand next to the errant little boy.

"Have a heart?" Bella mockingly repeats, and then she impatiently tosses the length of her dark brown locks over her shoulder to give him a view of her cleavage before she says with a pout, "You weren't the one sittin' here not knowing where he's at!"

"Yeah well...neither was you," Seasle retorts, for he stopped trying to pacify Bella a long time ago since it never really made much difference as far as how she treated Polie.

"You're such an arse Seasle," she angrily says with a stomp of her foot.

"Listen Bella..." Bro begins with the intentions of redirecting the conversation, for Polie is hearing all this, and he does not deserve to have to witness Seasle and his mother bash each other.

"I ain't the one who should a listened...and he's gonna be real sorry he didn't," she threatens.

"Perhaps he should a listened...but I don't think he meant not to...he just got locked into the box by accident...but see he's back and in one piece...so...no harm done," Gorg tells her.

When Gorg makes his speech the other men sigh, for that he is so stupid as to say something like that to her is beyond belief. As it usually goes every unfortunate thing has an upside, and after exchanging a resigned sigh amongst their selves the other men shrug and take a step away from Gorg. After all he is already a marked man and they do not see any reason that they should go down with him. Torli on the other hand sees something quite different from his vantage point, and he thinks that Gorg's wits have not gone begging at all, for when Gorg gives Bella his damning speech Torli sees him visibly brace himself and then covertly nudge Polie towards Cerl who raises his eyebrows in surprise, for it is obvious that Gorg is deliberately trying to divert Bella's anger away from Polie. A rather selfless thing Torli thinks with a considering frown.

"No harm done Gorg?" Bella narrows her brown eyes on him and repeats, and then she angrily says with an ever increasing volume, "I got your no harm done you stupid sot...he could a been killed...then where would I be?!"

She then delivers one of the loudest slaps to the side of Gorg's face that Torli thinks he has ever heard. So hard is it that it literally cracks, and when it does everyone present recoils and rubs his own face on Gorg's behalf. Then the inevitable division between them occurs, for while Seasle and Bro simply cross their arms on their chests and wait to see if Gorg will hit her back Orn and Ahnin move closer so that they can prevent him from doing so. Cerl on the other hand could care less one way or the other so long as Polie does not witness it, and so he ushers Polie back inside the runner using the excuse that Polie forgot his fishies. Torli for his part is on the fence, but in the end Gorg does not retaliate although he does intercept her hand when she rears back for a second blow. Bella then does what she always does she issues forth a flood of fake tears intended to encourage one of the others to come to her rescue, which one of them does.

"Don't cry now Bella honey...here Gorg...let her go," Orn cajolingly says as he tries to put his arms around her and lead her away.

"Don't you honey me you lumbering idiot!" she meanly says and then kicks him in a place that puts even the strongest men down.

"For the love of all that's...what'd you do that for?" Orn asks with a groan as he clutches his crotch.

"Polie!" Bella shouts, and when the little boy obediently comes to the runner's door she walks over and roughly yanks him down.

As she storms away Polie worriedly glances back, and to his credit Orn manages to straighten up a bit and give him a reassuring wave, which obviously sets his young mind at ease, for he smiles and waves back. When Bella notices the exchange she gets her revenge for it by walking as fast as she possibly can, which forces poor Polie to run just to keep up. As the men helplessly watch Polie trips, but Bella does not even pause only drags him along until she manages to pull him back to his feet by his arm. As one might expect Bella's manhandling earns her several holes bored into her back by the eyes of every man there including Han's two mechanics who are waiting nearby to take charge of the runner. Well, except for Orn who is too busy at the moment gagging from the pain in his crotch to notice her poor treatment of her son.

"Get it done...all a you...I want an answer by tomorrow," Torli grinds out once Bella is out of earshot, and with that he steps down from the vehicle and heads for his quarters.

As Torli walks past Orn he gives his back a light pat of encouragement, and after he tells Ahnin to turn the runner over to Han's mechanics he then motions for Gorg to follow him. It goes without saying that the other men are curious, but none of them comment on it, for they can pretty much guess what the commander wants to speak to him about. It is no secret that Torli has never agreed with Karnin's assigning Gorg to that pack of losers like he did, which is why no one was really surprised when Torli brought Gorg along on this trip. Karnin being Karnin was less than pleased to find Gorg taking up space in the runner, but he got over it, for Karnin is also fair, and he would not have it said that he did not give Torli a proper chance to prove to him that Gorg is not in reality the loner that Karnin believes him to be. Actually after Gorg put himself out there for Polie the other men think that Torli is right.

"You think Karnin's gonna reassign him?" Seasle asks as he watches Torli and Gorg walk away.

"I don't know...that deal with Merl's sort a stuck in his craw," Bro reminds them, for two years ago Merl had pulled one of his infamous disappearing acts. This time was by far his worst, for he ran off when he was supposed to be on guard duty, and Karnin has never been convinced that Gorg did not know that he was going to do so since they were friends and all.

"Yeah well...I think he deserves a chance," Ahnin says, and after he pulls his foot talisman from his pocket he asks, "You want me to ask foot to give her crotch rot Orn?"

"Naw...let her...be...magic...man..." Orn replies with a rather emphatic shake of his large head.

"Maybe Orn's flock a worshipers'll off that stupid bitch when they find out she's put him out a service," Seasle says a bit jealously, for oddly enough Orn is *Onyat's* resident love machine that *Onyat's* women never seem to tire of riding upon.

"Come on...we better get him inside," Bro says as Orn tries to hobble off.

"You can do what you want...I for one'm gonna make the best a Orn being out a commission," Cerl tells them from where he is standing in the runner's open door.

"Good idea," Ahnin replies.

"Heartless...buggers," Orn gasps out as he pauses to put his hands on his knees and take a few deep breaths.

"If I's you I'd go apologize," Seasle advises Ahnin and Cerl as he walks away.

"Yeah...wouldn't want him to get his tender feelings all hurt," Cerl mockingly comes back with.

"Yeah well you hurt Orn's feelings and not even that cheesy smelling washer woman's gonna spread her legs for you," Seasle throws over his shoulder, and after a second's pause to think on that Cerl and Ahnin exchange a worried glance and then hasten off to do some sucking up to their wounded comrade.

Chapter Nine

As Karnin sits on the front deck of Bimian's swaying marsh crawler he inhales the sweet early morning scent and he thinks that if he were not headed to what might end up being a cell this would be about the most enjoyable experience that he has had since the day that he lost his virginity. As is usually the case thinking of virgins reminds him of Han, for even though he is not one he often acts the part. Today however he is playing the role of a poor wounded soul Karnin thinks as he watches Han sigh yet again. Yes Han has always been good at that particular act and today is no exception. Still it is rather childish of him, which is precisely why Karnin will not make peace with him just yet. After all how would coddling him make them both look? The answer to that is stupid at a time when he at least needs to appear competent Karnin thinks as he sees Andina come out of the cabin and pause to hand Han something. Not just any something though, but something that suspiciously resembles one of the sweets they had after the meal last night. Yes Han's poor-me act still works like a charm Karnin notes when he sees Andina give him a motherly pat to his back as she walks away.

"You cosseting my man lady?"

"Oh well...he is so dejected Karnin...how can you stand it?"

"That's just the way he looks lady...he's got one a those kind a faces," Karnin replies with a shrug.

"Really Karnin...he only did what he was commanded to do."

"I know lady...I'm gonna talk to him here in a minute," Karnin reassures her.

"Good," is all she replies as the overlord walks up to them.

176

"So Karnin…has she taught you a better way to run your own damn life yet?" Bimian asks him as he comes to stand nearby.

"You were eavesdropping," Andina accuses.

"No assuming," he comes back with, which his wife apparently decides to let pass, for she suddenly throws her arms wide in a joyous sort of way.

"I love this time of day…the sun just rising…the smell of damp mingled with that of the opening spring blooms…"

"Yes…and the silencing of all those damn bloated doodle frogs…" Bimian tosses in.

"Oh Bimian…life is too short not to appreciate all the little nuances of it," Andina chastises.

"Yes well…all that worshipping of nature is what I have you for my dear," Bimian comes back with, but when he does he reaches over and tips her face up to him, and even though the gesture is brief that it is meant to belie his words is obvious.

"*Laraqua* is just around the corner now general," Goberan tells him as he joins them.

"Oh it will be a beautiful sight this time of day…I do not think that we have ever come this early have we Bimian?" Andina inquires as she sits forward in her seat and begins to braid her long dark hair.

"I believe we have…once many years ago…but it was raining that day," Bimian replies, and then he says as if it is an afterthought, "Do not forget Marsle's rules my dear."

"Oh…Marsle is such a joyless creature," she comments with a pout, but when Bimian gives her a rather impatient stare she slides her eyes to Karnin and adds, "Marsle forbids anyone to jump from moving crawlers."

"He has a good reason for that and you know it Andina," Bimian says as though speaking to a naughty child.

"Yes…I know Bimian…" she responds, and then she simply blurts out, "It is how his wife died."

"Yes well that was very subtle dear…" Bimian tells her, but then he diplomatically moves on to something new by saying, "Pay attention now Karnin…the fortress is just ahead and the first glimpse is always the most impressive."

As Karnin stares into the swirling morning mist he notices that the greenery on either side of the crawler has suddenly begun to widen and draw away. Soon a lake-like area opens up in front of him, and there in the midst of it is one of the most intriguing structures that he has ever seen. As his eyes sweep over the all of *Laraqua* Karnin has to admit that despite the fact that Marsle's fortress does not have the usual curtain walls it is no less imposing than any land fortress that he has seen to date. Perhaps even more so Karnin decides after a more careful perusal, for the sheer size of the fortress would require that *Laraqua's* foot print be firmly set deep in the bedrock beneath the marsh to keep it from sinking. That would make undermining it just as difficult as bringing down a well constructed perimeter wall.

Actually the way the fortress's outer buildings are constructed makes it appear as if the designer intended them to function as a perimeter wall of sorts, for from Karnin's current vantage point he can see two sides of the fortress. Well one side and a partial, for the second side simply continues on and disappears in the mist so how far it goes he has no idea. Even so from what he can see *Laraqua's* outermost buildings are long, at least four stories high, and topped by what appears to be a covered walkway that runs the length of them. Then there are the towers rising up several stories higher at strategic locations that effectively negate the fact that the fortress's outer walls are scalable. Such is the downside to laying up stone. There are however other more subtle ways to secure such walls, and judging by the fact that they passed through a sensor net on the way in the place has been modernized. Therefore despite the obvious age of those outer walls Karnin would bet his best pair of boots that they are wired with a repelling system and lined with some sort of blast proof material.

All in all though the result of the builder's efforts is a structure that is beyond being just a fortress the place is a damn work of art Karnin thinks. It is the kind of place that Karnin has always dreamed of building, for it looks as though it belongs here. Like it has always been here, for its walls rise out of the water in the same natural way as do the many bent and twisted old marsh trees that Karnin sees around it. That combined with the early morning mist that is lazily creeping across the water and making the fortress's stone towers glisten in the light of the rising sun makes the place seem like some exotic water plant covered in early morning dew. In truth, Karnin is quite taken with the picture that the fortress's architect has painted and he must admit that he is quite envious of Marsle for being so fortunate as to possess this place.

"What a relief to finally arrive," Andina's voice interrupts his thoughts, and when he glances over he sees that she is winding a pretty blue tie round the length of hair that she has just finished plaiting. When that is done she stands and affectionately lays her hand on Bimian's arm and says, "I cannot wait to see our little Milin."

"Yes Calphin's last message said that his coming out was quite a success," Bimian adds.

"I have a bone to pick with Corlean for that...he could have waited..."

"Now...now Andina...you know what a stickler Marsle is for tradition," Bimian reminds her with an impatient shake of his head.

"Yes I know but...he...gave her a damn fortress Bimian...I would have liked to have been there for that," she tells him with an exasperated sigh, and then she turns her blue eyes on Karnin and asks, "What think you general...should not a man in such a high position as Marsle be a bit more flexible than to insist upon using some archaic cultural schedule?"

"I'm afraid you got me at a disadvantage lady...not only don't I know what a 'coming out' is...the only cultural tradition my men and I even hold to's that a gift giving on ones day a birth so I'm hardly qualified to give you an opinion on such," Karnin explains.

"Oh...you are good on your feet general," she slyly replies, and then she returns to the subject at hand saying, "In marsh culture a coming out is the first public appearance of a new mother and her newly born child...which...traditionally...takes place at the sixth setting of the sun following the birth...it is both a welcome for the little one and an acknowledgement of the new mother's great gift to the child's father."

"It involves a lot of complimenting and extravagant gifts...much fuss for her...much expense for him," Bimian tells him with an impatient huff.

"Fuss that she well deserves," Andina points out and then she turns to Karnin and explains, "For once a marsh woman gifts a man with a child she is well and truly stuck with him since her body will no longer quicken to the seed of any other man."

"Andina...really..."

"What...I thought I said that rather...genteelly."

"There was no need to say it at all dear."

"It is only biology...the general is hardly so innocent as to not know how babes are made for goodness sake," she defends.

179

"Ah...so marsh babes don't hatch from eggs laid in a pond then," Karnin cannot resist jibbing, for Bimian's lady is not only lively and outspoken, but her mischievous sense of humor is a thing that he finds impossible not to encourage.

"I wish they did," Andina says with a dramatic wave of her hand, and as she shoos away a bug that has lighted upon the gauzy sleeve of her tunic she asks, "Have you ever seen a babe born?"

"No lady," Karnin replies as he tries not to stare at the outline of her figure silhouetted in the sunlight, for even though she is properly clad under the filmy top the illusion that it creates begs a man to peek, and he would not have the overlord catch him ogling his wife.

"Well when you do...and I promise you somewhere along the line you will...then you will understand it when I say that you will greatly wish that babes did hatch from eggs in a pond," Bimian sagely advises, and then he grins a bit wickedly and says, "I was well and truly traumatized when our first was born."

"Ha!" the lady retorts, and then she leans over to Karnin and whispers, "He tried to run and the healer had to give him something to bolster him up."

"Ah well then I suppose you got only the one child then?" Karnin teases.

"And well you know that we have two," she answers.

"So...one does recover from it then...I'm relieved to hear it," Karnin dubiously comments.

"Eventually...but it took awhile...Calphin and Aquaous have five years between them," Bimian defensively points out.

"Oh please...that was because I wanted to wait to make another...not because you stopped trying to," Andina amends with a less than ladylike snort.

"Really Andina...you are well too free with your information at times," Bimian sends her a disapproving shake of his head and says, but if he intends to intimidate her with it he is sorely disappointed, for she just gives him one of her disarming smiles and walks forward a bit.

"Remember what I told you about taking on a woman while you are still young enough to survive it general?" Bimian asks as he stares after his wife.

"I do sir," Karnin responds.

"Make certain that she is not a boring creature...get yourself a spirited...clever woman...she will make you a better man," Bimian advises.

"I'll keep that in mind when the time comes," Karnin assures him.

Actually Karnin thinks that he will do more than just consider the overlord's wise words, for the lady Andina's timeless beauty and quick wit has altered Karnin's opinion of what a woman should be. Gone is the sweet silent nurturing picture that Karnin had of his future lady replaced by the image of a woman who is quick witted and feisty. A woman whose beauty will never fade because it radiates from within like Andina's does. Karnin is certain that even though Andina has a grown son and two grandchildren she would still turn any man's head in a room full of younger woman. In the past Karnin has always gravitated to the sweet controllable types, for he always believed that is what a woman should be. Now though he wonders if that is precisely why he has never found any woman who could hold his interest. Overlord Bimian is a very lucky man Karnin thinks. So it is that for the second time in less than an hour Karnin feels the pang of envy for something that belongs to another.

"Oh my goodness look!" Andina suddenly exclaims, and then she shoots to her feet and excitedly adds, "It is Onot!"

"Curse it all," Bimian clips out, and when Karnin follows their gazes what he sees makes him chuckle he simply cannot help himself. The overlord apparently is not in the mood for humor, for he shoots him a reproachful stare and adds, "I am glad you find humor in my dismay Karnin."

"I assure you...I'm not laughing at your pain sir...only at your situation," Karnin replies.

"Firstly do not call me sir...not one more time...it makes me feel old," Bimian settles his colorless eyes on him once again and demands, and then he adds, "You can also save that smooth talking crap for the ladies and give me some useful advice on ridding myself of the source of my discomfort instead."

"Really Bimian...you are such a poor sport," Andina declares with a smirk.

"Perhaps a short leash and a heavy ball'd ease you a bit overlord," Karnin suggests much to Andina's horror.

"Do you want me to shoot it for you overlord," Goberan asks with a lazy wave of his hand.

"Do not you dare," Andina points a finger at him and commands, and then she spreads her arms dramatically and says, "Look at her...is she not magnificent bathed in sunlight all curled around Marsle's tower?"

"Marsle is going to have the thing stuffed does she break something," Goberan informs her.

"Marsle is overly attached to that stupid fortress," she knits her brows in thought and says, and then she instructs with a casual wave of her hand, "Be a sweet and go shoo her off Goberan."

"Shoo her off?" Bimian repeats with a bit of disbelief, and then he levels an angry glare on her as he says, "You want to keep it then you go 'shoo it off'."

"Alright I will," she snaps back at him, but before she moves even an inch the overlord grabs her hand to stay her.

"You will wait until they fetch you properly...which I doubt they will be long in doing," Bimian commands.

"Not long at all uncle...master Cogen's coming out himself," Slolar says as he watches a small flat push away from the dock, and then he politely adds for Karnin's benefit, "Overlord Marsle's security master."

"Ah master Cogen...good morning to you sir," Bimian calls out pleasantly enough when the flat draws close.

"Good morning to you and welcome overlord Bimian...I have come to fetch Tosel and Bornan the why of which I am certain that you have already noticed," Cogen tells him, but when he does Karnin does not miss the assessing look that he sends his way.

"I am afraid the overlord has left them behind," Andina delights in informing him, for Bimian leaving Onot's handlers to guard the general's boxes was part of his master plan to get rid of Onot, and now that decision will cost him.

"That is...unfortunate..." Cogen replies as his eyes dart from Andina to Bimian, and then he adds, "The overlord has...well...he is not happy you see..."

"I will come Cogen...she will come down for me," Andina tells him, and when she does Karnin sees his eyes briefly turn to the overlord who gives him an almost imperceptible nod.

"Ah very good then lady," Cogen tells her as he offers her his hand.

"I will come too...perhaps I can help somehow," Slolar says after receiving another near undetectable head gesture from the overlord.

182

"You are very quiet over there Karnin," Bimian notes as they watch the flat make its way back to the dock.

"I was just wondering how my man Bro's doing," Karnin cryptically replies, but of course the overlord is not the only one who gets his point.

"Marsle truly will mount the thing on his wall does it take a liking to one of his men," Goberan tells him.

"Yes...get us anchored as soon as possible will you Goberan...we better get in there," Bimian commands, and with a nod Goberan walks towards the rear of the crawler and disappears into the auxiliary cabin.

"Thought you wanted to be rid a it overlord?" Karnin inquires in an amused way.

"Yes well...I do...but if Marsle shoots the damn thing Andina will want to shoot him back..." Bimian replies with a cock of his head and a shrug.

"Not very diplomatic..." Karnin absently remarks as he watches Andina step up onto the dock.

"Yes well...I am afraid that diplomacy is not my lady wife's strongest suit general..." Bimian tells him.

As the crawler moves towards the docking buoy near *Laraqua's* rear dock Karnin notes the flurry of activity there in preparation for its arrival, which is not surprising since Bimian is an overlord after all. Karnin supposes that having a giant scaly beasty on one of their towers makes things all the more complicated as well. Little does Karnin know that what he sees on the dock is minor when compared to the preparations that are going on behind the scenes, for Marsle being the stickler for propriety that he is will not tolerate any of the expected niceties not to be ready for his arriving guests. Then there are also the usual security issues to see to as well, for an overlord and his family is never without enemies no matter how likeable they are. Marsle's security staff has therefore increased their vigilance especially in light of the fact that Bimian is bringing some unknown land men along with him.

The concern over security is precisely why Bimian and his heir apparent traveled to *Laraqua* apart from each other, for being able to take out an overlord and his successor in one attack might be enough to temp someone to try. Calphin therefore made the trip to *Laraqua* several weeks ago with his wife and young son. Security concerns were not the only reason that Calphin came early, for Marsle also wanted Calphin to do a bit more reconnaissance on his squatters for him. As it is Marsle has used Calphin's rather odd talents to spy on Karnin and his men for many years now, which Calphin was only too happy to do being that as his father's heir he rarely gets the opportunity to use his more questionable abilities. As one might expect Bimian was not all that thrilled about his doing so, but since the risks in the north are considerably less than in the central marshes Bimian allowed it just so that Calphin might exercise his less humanitarian side.

Unfortunately, when Calphin returned from one such sojourn to the squatter's fortress some weeks ago it was to find his wife and son both laid up in bed covered in itchy red welts from head to toe. Even though they have since both recovered physically his wife Janissa's mood has remained sullen and withdrawn. At first Calphin was more than willing to overlook her behavior. Janissa has always had more than her fair share of restless energy, and so Calphin simply told himself that her mood was the result of having been closeted up in their rooms for days. When after a few days passed and she still remained rather standoffish Calphin logically began to worry. When he finally asked her about her lack of enthusiasm instead of the logical self-aware explanation that he expected to get from a woman of her intelligence and logical nature what he got was some sort of convoluted emotional accusation about being an insensitive arse, which as one might expect elicited a rather regrettable response from him.

Long story short the exchange left them both feeling righteously angered, and after several days of silence the rift between them grew ever wider until they now find themselves in a rather untenable place that neither of them knows how to extract them from. So it is that in his efforts to avoid a situation that he does not know how best to handle Calphin had neglected to inform Janissa what time his parents would be arriving this morning. Whether or not it was out of spite as his wife accused or just an oversight as Calphin insisted does not really matter, for the damage had been done. Therefore, as an already angered Calphin watches Janissa pull on her boots it suddenly dawns on him that she is taking her own sweet time at it on purpose probably to get even with him, which only serves to fan his anger more.

"Hurry up Janissa..." Calphin angrily snaps out at her when he can take it no more, but he immediately regrets it, for she flinches. He therefore tries to smooth things over a bit by adding in a more controlled tone, "Marsle's gonna crap his self if we are not there to greet them."

"Yes well...it might go a bit faster if you would bestir yourself to help me a bit," Janissa crossly replies as she kneels and begins to dress Corlon.

"All you had to do was ask," Calphin replies and then kneels down next to her.

"I should not always have to ask," she fires back at him, and although Calphin would like to tell her what a bitch she is being he would also like to get there sometime in the near future and so he holds his tongue.

"Alright then...little man," Calphin announces with a triumphant sigh when after a few tense minutes of maneuvering they finally manage to get his squirming self properly clothed, and then he asks, "Are you ready to go see nana Andina and popi Bimian?"

"Na...na...po...pee," Corlon repeats with a giggle.

"That is right," Calphin replies, and with a fond kiss to the boy's head he picks him up and as he offers Janissa an arm of truce he asks, "Are we ready?"

"As ready as I am ever going to be," she comes back with, and then with a somewhat depressed sigh she lays her hand upon his arm.

As they make their way to the dock Calphin wonders at Janissa's increasingly poor emotional state, for although she has always had her moods she has never been so out of sorts for this long a period of time. Well, not when she was not pregnant that is, which Janissa vehemently insisted that she was not when he had suggested it. Of course their spat the other day has not helped things much, and more than once in the last few days has he awoke at night to hear her weeping in the sitting room, but even though he felt that he should go to her whether she wanted him to or not he did not do so. Now he finds that he can take this no more, and even though he may have to hurt her feelings to get to the truth of what is really bothering her then so be it, for Calphin's gut says that it is more than some silly argument that has caused her to put up her walls.

"Is something troubling you love?" he asks as they navigate their way down the tower stairs.

"I am just tired is all," she replies rather shortly, but Calphin thinks that it still seems as though she would like to say something.

"Are you unhappy that we will be going home soon?" he carefully asks.

"No not really...it will be nice to be in our own home again," she replies, and then she tips her face to him and pretty much blurts out, "Calphin...what would you say if I told you that I did not want to have another baby?"

"What?" is all Calphin can find it within his self to reply to that, for Calphin has always been very open with her about wanting several children, and Janissa understood that or so he thought.

"I find that I regret it much that I did not finish my studies...and if you dare say I told you so I will smack you," she tells him in no uncertain terms.

"Then finish them...you know that I have always thought you should," Calphin replies with a shrug, and then he asks with a confused expression, "But what has that to do with having more children?"

"You are such a...a...man," she indignantly clips out, and then promptly stomps off ahead.

"What else would I be?" he murmurs.

"A smarter man perhaps?" Corlean comments behind him, and a second later he falls into step with him and adds, "But that is the down side to marrying a woman with a more gifted mind than your own."

"You should know," Calphin tells him, for Aquaous is an accomplished student of the healing arts and obviously no dummy; quite the opposite.

"Just trying to help," Corlean responds with a rather insulted sniff.

"Yes well...at least I have managed to hang onto my son..." Calphin says as he gestures to Corlean's empty arms.

"I am not the one whose wife ran from him...and I know exactly where mine is...right where I told her to be," Corlean inclines his head towards the dock and says.

"Alright then...since you are such an expert...what dumb thing have I done now?" Calphin narrows his eyes and asks.

"She wants you to say no," Corlean replies with a shrug.

"You have lost what little wits you have I think," Calphin stops and says.

"Was that the entire conversation on it...what I overheard just now?" Corlean inquires.

186

"Why yes what you eavesdropped in on was actually the all of it," Calphin sarcastically replies.

"Then what else would she have expected you to say except yes or no," Corlean tells him in a somewhat smug tone.

"Would that be yes or no to resuming her education or yes or no to having more babes then?" Calphin questions.

"Well...ah..." Corlean hesitates.

"Just as I thought...I will expect recompense for that sage advice that I did not get," Calphin quips in a mocking tone and then heads towards the dock once again.

"You had best get your nose out of Calphin's house and back into your own," Corlean hears his father's voice suddenly say, and when he turns he sees him walking a few feet behind him.

"I was just trying to help," Corlean replies.

"Then do not give advice on subjects that you know nothing about," Marsle advises, and then stops in front of him to say, "Bimian has brought along a couple of guests."

"What guests...not those squatters?" Corlean asks in disbelief, and then he angrily demands, "Why was I not told?"

"Because the last time that I checked this is my fortress not yours...now...I would remind you that this Karnin is the general of an army large enough to lay waste to most any fortress...and I would rather not end up with it camped out at my door...do not push things too far," Marsle fixes his son with one of his serious stares and warns.

"How far is too far?" Corlean asks with a smirk.

"Calphin says that this Karnin would be a worthy opponent...they are killers Corlean the lot of them...trained and tried," he tells him and then strides away, but as he goes he calls back over his shoulder, "And that damnable pet of Andina's is up on my tower."

"What...Onot?" Corlean asks in confusion, for even though Andina's animal is a rather odd thing to keep as a pet there is no reason for his father to be so very rude about it. Just then a sudden noise above him makes him shift his gaze upwards, and when he does he sees a large shiny head squeeze itself through one of the dock tower's upper walkway openings.

"Huh," Marsle grunts matter-of-factly after he stops to eyeball the beast, and then he adds as he continues on his way, "Bimian said the damn thing grew a bit."

"Grew a bit?" Corlean repeats in disbelief, and then quickly sprints towards the dock area as he barks orders to the men standing around gaping upward to get a few ropes.

When Corlean exits the tower onto the dock the first thing that he sees is Bimian's crawler approaching, and when a quick peek tells him that his mother-in-law is absent he begins searching for her on the dock, for Andina's one predictable quality is that she will get into trouble at some point or the other. There is something else that he sees on the crawler that concerns him more than Andina's quirks. Something that makes his eyes narrow in anger. So distracted is he by it that he completely forgets about Onot, for there standing next to Bimian as though they are his equals are two land men. Could it be any worse Corlean thinks? Not only does his father allow those damn squatters to squat for years on his lands free of any payment or perk, but now he has allowed Bimian to coerce him into letting them come here.

"Corlean!" he hears Aquaous call, and when he turns he sees her practically running towards him with Milin in her arms.

"Aquaous...slow down...you know you are not supposed to be exerting yourself like that yet," Corlean chastises her, for it has only been eight days since Milin was born, and after the difficult pregnancy Aquaous's strength has understandably been slow to return.

"Your father's threatening to shoot Onot down...hurry...please..." she implores as she tugs him along by his sleeve.

"Alright...alright...calm down..." Corlean tells her as he follows her along the dock towards where his father stands speaking to Andina.

"Andina ...you have gone too far this time," Corlean hears his father loudly accuse.

"She is all out of sorts Marsle," Andina calmly replies, and then she smiles up at him and says, "Surely you can have a bit of sympathy for the poor thing all lost and alone with none to care for her but me."

"The only sympathy I have is for your husband lady," Marsle replies as he clasps his hands behind his back to keep them from shaking her, and then he says with a grunt, "Which is the only reason...and I mean the absolute 'only' reason that I am going to delay shooting the damn thing for one hour...now get it off...my...tower."

"I always knew you were a kind man at heart," Andina replies, and then stretches up on her toes to give him a peck on the cheek.

"Mother!"

"Oh here are my two precious darlings," Andina coos and then embraces her daughter.

"Yes here I am," Corlean replies with a mischievous grin.

"Your husband is still delusional I see," Andina tells her as she takes Milin into her arms.

"Corlean...take the flat over and fetch the overlord and his guests to the dock...and do not start anything out there," Marsle commands, but even though Corlean dutifully nods he really has no intention of acting all polite to a thief, for if this Karnin person is not all that he is said to be the time to find out is now before he sees too much.

"They are surprisingly well mannered...these land men," Andina says as her shrewd eyes shift between Marsle and Corlean, and then she settles her eyes on Marsle and tells him, "This Karnin is intelligent...self-assured...and not to be taken lightly."

"Why mother if I did not know better I would say that you like this land man," Aquaous comments, and then nervously turns away from her mother's assessing eyes.

"I do...very much so," she replies.

"One hour Andina," Marsle warns and after he bends and gives Milin's head a kiss he turns on his heel and strides away.

"Men," Andina mutters somewhat belligerently, and then she steps closer to Aquaous to fondly smooth a stray lock from her face before she says, "I am so sorry that I was not here Aquaous...you look exhausted."

"I am alright mother," she replies, and then she brightens a bit and adds, "Corlean has hired a nanny and has given orders that no business is to be brought to me before noon...can you believe it mother...I have my own household now?"

"As well you should...I cannot wait to see it," Andina tells her, and then she bends down and kisses Milin's cheek before she holds him up to cryptically say, "May your future be as bright as your smile my beautiful boy."

"Time is passing Andina!" Marsle suddenly shouts from further down the dock.

"I see Marsle has not changed," she states, and after she reluctantly hands Milin back to his mother she tells her, "I better go get the fish...Onot likes fish...she will come down for it."

189

"We have fish mother...wait...take the flat!" Aquaous calls after her, but Andina has already gone off the dock into the water, and so Aquaous merely shakes her head and says with a sigh, "And that was your nana Andina...Milin."

Back on the crawler Karnin has finally told Han that he has forgiven him for his part in Torli's deception, and so after having gathered both his and Karnin's things Han is standing at the front of the crawler studying the design of the vehicle's forward risers while he waits to disembark with Karnin. As is usually the case when a man is admiring a beautiful thing Han is entranced by the balance and workmanship of the vehicle's sleek metal legs, and so he leans a bit closer to run a hand along one of their cool surfaces. So preoccupied is he that he does not see Andina dive from the dock, and so when she pops up near the crawler she startles him so badly that he would have gone in the water had Goberan not had the foresight to see the whole incident unfolding and grab Han by the back of his jacket.

"Oh...I am sorry Han," Andina apologizes with one of her disarming smiles, and when Han just nods like a simpleton she laughs and calls out, "Bimian toss me a fish!"

"I should toss you an anchor woman..." Bimian mumbles as he walks over and throws open one of the many deck compartments.

"What...Marsle has no rules about diving from his dock?" she protests.

"No...but he will next time we come," Bimian replies as he extracts the largest fish that Karnin or Han has ever seen from the compartment, but when he drags the heavy thing to the side he sees Karnin give him a frown and so he quickly reassures him by saying, "Stand down...I am not trying to drown her...they float."

"Ah...where exactly did this fish come from?" Karnin asks as he nervously peers down into the water, for the enormous thing has teeth; sharp, pointy teeth.

"Not from anywhere near here," Bimian replies with a bit of amusement, and then he steps aside so that Karnin can inspect the fish before he adds, "Too shallow here for a fish like this."

"That's good to know," Karnin replies as he reaches out a tentative hand and touches the impressive creature.

"This came from the inner marshes...there are a few pools there deeper than anyone really cares to know," Goberan props a foot on the rail nearby and says, and then he reaches over and relieves Bimian of the fish.

190

"A fish like that'd feed a lot a people..." Karnin points out as he watches the way Goberan effortlessly hauls the huge fish up and over the side where he lets it drop with a splash.

"You eat that you will think that your guts have run out your arse before it is all over and done," Goberan turns and informs Karnin, and then he goes to the box and hauls out a second giant fish which he also drops over the side.

"And yet you feed them to Onot," Karnin dryly states.

"Another failed effort on my part," Bimian informs him with a disgruntled huff, and then he adds, "Turns out Onot there could probably digest a jitty and not even pass wind."

"You want me to take them in for the lady overlord?" one of Bimian's crew members asks as he drags a third fish over.

"That would be appreciated Maan," Bimian replies with an approving nod.

With a nod Maan then hops over the side, and a few seconds later he and Andina swim into view shoving the three bobbing fish along in front of them. As he watches the two swim to the dock with their cargo Karnin wonders exactly where the lady plans to house the animal during their stay with Marsle. At that moment though Karnin's attention is caught by a flat that suddenly materializes out of the underside of the dock and all thoughts of the unruly Onot are put on hold, for even though he saw where the flat emerged he can see no opening through which it did. Needless to say that intrigues Karnin a great deal, for the quality of their camouflage is quite good. One can never know too much about stuff like that and so Karnin would logically like to learn how *Laraqua's* builders achieved it. Perhaps on the way in he will be able to get a closer look he decides as the man on the flat poles it towards them.

As he watches the flat approach Karnin supposes that Marsle must feel quite secure here in his watery world, for he has sent out only one man to fetch two unknown land men in. Then again master Cogen's men are everywhere, and there was that rather sophisticated sensor net on the way in so unless they are two very stupid land men they will behave since there would be no escaping this place. Besides Marsle could easily dispose of both Han and him at any time he should so choose to and none would be the wiser. Land men drown rather easily after all, but it is a bit too late now to worry about that possibility Karnin reminds himself. Therefore as the flat draws alongside the crawler Karnin uses the commotion to shoot Han a covert hand signal that tells him to be careful and to speak only when he has to.

"Ah...Corlean...how are you boy?" Karnin hears Bimian call in greeting, and when Karnin glances down he sees a rather tall, grayish eyed marsh man scowling up at him.

"I am well overlord...and yourself?" Corlean replies, but the dismissive manner in which his eyes travel over Karnin does not escape anyone's notice especially Karnin's.

"Not bad...well except for the beast that I have failed to lose yet again...which you no doubt have already noticed," Bimian replies, and then he extends a hand to him and says, "Come aboard."

"Ah well my father is a bit...impatient today," Corlean tells him as he inclines his dark head towards where Marsle waits on the dock, and then he adds, "So if you are ready I will take you in."

"Of course," Bimian replies, and then accepts Corlean's steadying arm down, but when Corlean immediately turns away he crossly says, "You forget your manners Corlean."

"My apologies..." Corlean begins intending to insult Karnin by only apologizing to Bimian, but Karnin quickly thwarts him.

"No need to apologize," Karnin interrupts him to say, and then he hops down onto the flat and with an expression on his face intended to let Corlean know that he has no desire to meet him either he says, "Come down Han...let's not keep overlord Marsle waiting."

Bimian having once been a young man recognizes a bit of chest thumping when he sees it, but he decides not to call either one of them on it. After all they are of an age with each other, and therefore equally as foolish. Besides even though Corlean can be a prick when he wants to be he knows where the boundary is that separates good from bad behavior. Well at least right now when Marsle is watching at any rate. Unfortunately, Corlean has some growing up to do yet Bimian thinks as he watches the overlord's son try to intimidate the land men with his infamous stare, but Karnin is a street wise man who would be dead right now if he was easily rattled. It will be interesting to see which one comes out on top of this bit of male posturing. Hopefully things will not get physical. That would be unfortunate for Corlean Bimian thinks with an amused glint in his eyes.

"Han," Bimian hears Karnin say and when he turns to him he sees Karnin incline his head towards the pole in Corlean's hand in silent command.

"Aye sir," Han replies, and then he steps over to Corlean and says, "If you'll allow me sir."

"Do you know how...I do not want to have to fish you out," Corlean replies a bit peeved that this Karnin has found a way to take command from him under the guise of propriety.

"Oh aye sir...I poled a flat before," Han replies pleasantly enough, for he has been passing the time with Bimian's men, and so he knows who Corlean is and why Karnin ordered him to pole them in, which Han does without any trouble at all.

"Marsle...you are a sight for sore eyes," Bimian says when Han skillfully turns the flat broadside and brings it to rest against the dock's stone face.

"I am glad to see you...but next time leave that at home eh," Marsle crooks a thumb towards the end of the dock where Andina sits feeding a now placated and secured Onot.

"Which one," Bimian good naturedly asks as he hops up onto the dock.

"Ah well both if it pleases you," Marsle replies with a grin.

"Do not be so mean," a female voice softly says, and with an expression that belies his irritated sigh, the overlord extends his hand and leads a young woman over to him.

"You old bugger..." Han murmurs, for even though he is no expert on marsh folk it is obvious that she is just barely into her womanhood, but Karnin's reprimanding stare sends him scurrying to secure the flat to the dock.

"Good grief Ann you have gotten even more beautiful than last I saw you," Bimian fondly says and then gives her a peck on the cheek.

"Quit telling her that Bimian...she will end up a vain spoiled creature...next thing I know I will have looking glasses all over my fortress," Marsle complains.

"Please stop," Ann replies a bit pleadingly, and that she is genuinely embarrassed by both men's attentions is apparent.

"Here now my manners," Marsle suddenly says, and then he shoots Corlean an unreadable gaze as he says, "Come up general Karnin...and please...bring your man as well...someone will take care of the flat."

"Overlord Marsle," Karnin says with a polite nod as he steps up onto the dock, and then he adds, "This's my man Han."

"Yes...you pole a flat quite well for a land man Han," Marsle notes.

"Thank you overlord," is all that Han replies, and then with a polite nod he respectfully steps back away from the group, but Karnin can tell from the brief disappointment that passes across the overlord's face that he had hoped Han would be a bit more talkative on the subject.

"General Karnin...may I present my daughter Annitequea," Marsle formally says.

"Lady," Karnin gives her a polite nod and says, but he must admit that he is a bit relieved that this lovely young woman is a daughter and not a wife as Han thought, for if she was the later his opinion of Marsle would be quite different from the one that he has of him now.

"Ann has recently taken the reins as lady of my house..." Marsle informs him, and then he turns to Corlean and adds, "And you have already met my son and heir apparent...Corlean..."

"Yeah overlord...we met," Karnin replies somewhat taken aback that Bimian had failed to mention that his daughter Aquaous is not just married to one of Marsle's sons, but rather to the one who will one day make her *Lady En Tenda* of the *Northern Marsh Territory and Fringe Lands.*

"Good...come then let us go and have a bit of something refreshing shall we...will that thing stay out here do you think Bimian?" Marsle gives Onot a perturbed glance and asks.

"I doubt it," Bimian candidly replies.

"Well it is a bit too big to romp around my sitting room like it did last time...we will put your things in the rear tower then," Marsle tells him, and then he adds, "It has a private entry and its own dock...where is Goberan...I thought that he would be with you?"

"He will help get Onot situated first," Bimian replies.

"Where are its handlers?" Marsle asks.

"That is a long story," Bimian replies.

"Want me to send Han to help them overlord?" Karnin asks much to Han's horror.

"No you better not...that thing is much too fond of land men," Bimian replies, and then he answers the question in Marsle's raised brows with, "Part of the same story...but I am certain that Andina will tell it far better than I ever could...Andina come now dear!"

Much to Karnin's surprise Andina not only gets up and comes to him, but she seems quite content to do so, which leaves Karnin a bit nonplussed, for she did not seem to be the type that one could train to the whistle. She is a rather canny woman though, and so she may simply find that it suits her at the moment to obey or perhaps she prefers to save her energies for more worthy battles. She is not just anyone either, for she is the lady of *Mori* in her own right although Karnin doubts that she actually exercises much control over *Mori* itself. Women simply are not given that sort of power. They are just too tenderhearted to enforce the laws necessary for people to live together with some semblance of peace.

"I would be glad to show general Karnin's man around overlord," an older man with white streaks peppering his neatly tied back hair steps up to Marsle and says.

"This is my steward...Berto," Marsle turns and informs Karnin.

"Master Berto," Karnin correctly acknowledges.

"With your permission general..." Berto responds with a short bow.

"A course," Karnin replies.

"Come all," Marsle orders, and then he suddenly turns to Ann and asks, "Did you ask our other guest to join us?"

"Of course father," she replies, and when she does she sends Karnin an interested perusal, which he assumes to be her version of polite curiosity.

"You seem worried general," Karnin hears Corlean quietly comment as Karnin watches Han walk away with Berto.

"Ah well you are mistaken I'm afraid," Karnin turns to him and replies, but he knows a condescending tone when he hears it and so he adds, "Listen...did I do something to offend you...lord Corlean?"

"Not yet," Corlean meets his eyes and replies.

"Give it time," Karnin retorts in like kind.

"Have you forgotten us Corlean," a soft voice suddenly asks startling both men out of their confrontation, and when Karnin sees her bright blue eyes he has no doubt in his mind that she is Andina's daughter.

"No...I have not," Corlean extends his hand to her and says, and then he deliberately leads her away from Karnin without an introduction, which makes Karnin seriously wonder what Bimian was thinking to wed her to such an ill tempered lout as Corlean.

...*Politics*...he thinks with a mental smirk.

195

"Corlean...what are you doing?" Aquaous quietly asks in obvious embarrassment, but when he just keeps walking she hisses, "Introduce me."

"I will not introduce my wife to some thieving nobody," Corlean remarks.

"Yeah I suppose by your standards I'm that," Karnin answers back, and although he would like to punch the insolent man in the face he clenches his jaw and manages to add with some civility, "But by my own thinking I'm a survivor...it's a matter a perspective you see."

"Ann...you and the other ladies take the babes inside...have yourselves some refreshment...we will be along shortly," Marsle quietly commands from where he stands watching the exchange, but although the disgruntled expressions on the ladies faces say that they would rather do otherwise they silently gather up the two children and head inside.

"What now Marsle?" Bimian asks.

"We take ourselves off somewhere where we can be as men and have some spirits that is what," he replies and then strides away.

"Ah...a splendid idea...come along then Karnin," Bimian directs, and then he glances over at Corlean and asks, "Where is Calphin by the way?"

"He went to fetch something," Corlean replies as he falls in next to Bimian, which pretty much forces Karnin to take the lesser position behind them.

*...One point for you...arse...*Karnin thinks as he clasps his hands behind his back and follows along.

As Karnin walks along behind the group he takes the opportunity to study Corlean a bit closer, for Karnin thinks that it would not take much to push the man over the edge. Karnin therefore thinks it prudent to gauge Corlean's abilities in case he must defend himself. It goes without saying that Karnin has no intention of throwing out the first punch, for Corlean is an overlord's son no matter how ill mannered he is, and so to smash him in his arrogant face would be a punishable offence if it were not in self-defense. Even then some overlords would still expect a man to take it and not fight back, but somehow Karnin thinks that Marsle would not be as unreasonable as that so long as Karnin did no permanent harm. In the end though Karnin thinks that Corlean is built pretty much the same as most of the other marsh men present, which is not to say that he would not be hard to beat, but still he is not like the Orn of marshes or anything.

That decided Karnin uses Corlean's rude discounting of him as an opportunity to admire the architecture of Marsle's fortress, for its interior is in keeping with its exterior, and its stone walls and narrow corridors with their arched ceilings give one the impression of great age. After studying it a bit more closely Karnin comes to the conclusion that his first thoughts were quite correct as far as *Laraqua* having been originally built a long time ago, for the stone used has real age. He was also correct in his assumptions that the fortress had been modernized, for the distinct glint of a shield lining peeking through its interior stone façade at a few difficult to conceal spots says as much. Therefore, when after traversing through several winding corridors they emerge into a cavernous area Karnin is not all that surprised to see there at the area's center a state of the art security hub.

"Good day overlord Marsle," one of the guards calls as they pass.

"That it is Rylon," Marsle returns.

"Overlord Bimian...my apologies sir...I did not see you back there," Rylon says a bit nervously.

"How are you Rylon?" Bimian graciously returns.

"Very good sir," Rylon replies, and then his eyes fall upon Corlean who he has also missed, but before he can offer yet another apology Corlean surprises Karnin by letting him off the hook.

"Have you heard from *Aqualean* today Rylon?"

"Yes lord Corlean...Anel says that all is well there sir and ready for you to come."

"Good," Corlean tells him and then gives the man a reassuring pat on the back as he passes by him.

...Alright...not a total arse then... Karnin begrudgingly thinks as he follows the group back into one of the many corridors leading away from the security hub.

The men walk a short distance more and then come to what is unmistakably one of the fortress's many towers, for when Marsle opens the door there is a short set of curved steps that lead them to a round well appointed sitting room where Karnin sees much to his surprise an old fashioned central fireplace complete with a nicely burning log. When Marsle sees Karnin admiring it the overlord invites him to come examine it more closely, and as he does so Marsle tells him the history of the hearth. It seems that

197

hearth once served as a focal point in the original marsh keep that housed Marsle's ancestors. A keep that in its entirety was no larger than this very room although Karnin has a hard time believing all of that it is a pretty story. In truth it may not be so farfetched after all Karnin decides as he takes in the huge ornate cap stones that have been darkened by the burning of fires over a very long period of time.

Overlord Marsle then gestures to a seat and then goes to sit in one of the overstuffed chairs nearby, and as Karnin takes the proffered seat Bimian seats himself in a large overstuffed chair next to Marsle then begins to converse with him about their shared grandson. As he politely waits for them to finish Karnin passes the time admiring the view from the tower's many large windows, and as he does he wonders how it is that the overlord does not worry that they might become a security risk if *Laraqua* were ever attacked. After all having a sensor net even a good one is not an uncommon thing anymore, and therefore they are at best only a deterrent for men who do not have the technology to defeat them. Then again with all the snooping around that Marsle obviously does he is well aware of that and so there must be security shutters hidden within the tower's thick walls.

Lost in his thoughts Karnin is therefore startled by the soft hissing sound that he suddenly hears, and when he searches out its source he discovers to his relief that it is only the sound of water evaporating as it is sprayed upon the hearth by what is obviously an automated humidifying system. That comes as no great surprise, for as Karnin has discovered the marsh folk like things damp as the many holes filled with standing water that they passed on their way up to Marsle's sitting room attest to, and so it would stand to reason that they would not install an open flame hearth without some way to neutralize its drying effects, which is actually something that Karnin can relate to. As it was he and his boys spent many a night in their cave with a pot of water boiling on the burner for that very same reason, but Karnin's reminiscing is interrupted when the overlord breaks the companionable silence.

"Corlean...grab the bottle and some cups," Marsle commands when Corlean goes to sit down, and so Corlean walks over to a nearby sideboard to fetch the requested items, which he dutifully takes round pausing before Karnin last.

"Pour yourself a drink Karnin...but I warn you that is no babes milk in there," Marsle lazily tells him.

"Thank you overlord but I'm afraid I don't drink spirits much," Karnin replies, and when Marsle's eyebrows go up he explains, "I done so before a course...but it seems that spirits make me a greater arse than I usually am...or so I been told."

"Ah well that is an affliction of youth I am afraid," Marsle replies, and then he adds with a wry grin, "When you get older and wiser you learn exactly how much you can consume before the great transformation occurs."

"Or you just stop caring if it does," Bimian adds with a chuckle as he pours himself and Marsle another generous helping of the dark liquid that Corlean leaves at his elbow.

"Now then general Karnin I must ask you to forgive my son's lack of manners earlier...I am afraid that he is barely into his manhood and therefore still lacking in the proper polish one would expect of a future overlord," Marsle eyes Corlean dubiously and says.

"That's understandable overlord..." Karnin replies somewhat hesitantly as he scrambles in his head to catch up with the overlord's sudden change in direction.

"Yes it should be understandable to you Karnin since you are of an age with him," Marsle agrees albeit a bit sarcastically so, and then he holds up his hand to stay whatever remark Karnin is about to make back to add, "No do not you dare get indignant with me sir...you settled yourself and those in your care upon my land without so much as a by your leave...but I allowed it because you were homeless boys and someone asked me to."

"And my men and I're very grateful sir," Karnin replies politely enough, but Marsle can see the flash of surprised anger in his dark eyes, and so the overlord decides to push it a bit further just to see how he reacts.

"Yes well...whether you realize it or not you did well and truly accept me as your overlord when you decided to put down roots upon what belongs to me and mine so do not come here and put on airs general...you are no better nor less than any of my other vassals."

"Excuse me overlord, but..."

"But it did not occur to you to come pledge yourself before now?" Marsle narrows his eyes on him and asks.

"No I got a admit...it didn't," Karnin replies, and then he fixes his eyes directly on Marsle and calmly informs him, "And I didn't come here to do so now sir."

"Explain yourself," Marsle angrily demands.

"You see just as I said...a thief," Corlean lazily states from the chair next to Karnin.

"All right then I'm a thief...there are you happy now lord Corlean," Karnin cannot help but reply.

"Have you any idea what we do with thieves Karnin?" Marsle asks a bit darkly.

"Whatever I'll suffer it then without complaint," Karnin replies, and then he says, "All I ask's that you allow my men to go south."

"Do not be hasty Karnin..." Bimian warns.

"He has confessed Bimian..." Marsle interjects with a droll wave of his hand.

"Karnin has come here under my protection," Bimian insists, and then he adds, "I will consider it a personal insult do I have to return him to his men without everything that he came with Marsle."

"The law is the law," Marsle returns with a shrug.

"It is an antiquated...ridiculous practice!"

"The law allows a second option father...tell me Karnin...how long can you hold your breath?"

"Yeah well...I'm done with this," Karnin cautiously says as he slowly rises to his feet, for something about the way Corlean's translucent eyes are studying him sets his neck to prickling.

"And just where do you think you are going eh?" Marsle asks.

"Well first I'm gonna get Han and myself back to *Onyat*," Karnin says, and as he backs towards the door he adds, "And then I'm gonna go gather up my men and clear out...oh...and leave you a rather nice well kept fortress for your kindness to us."

"And then," Marsle asks, as unbeknownst to Karnin Goberan, Slolar, and Marsle's other guest come through the doorway behind him.

"Well...once that's done I think I'll find a woman who's clean and smells nice and retire to my bed for a few days," Karnin quips as he fingers the hilt of his knife.

"Well...that part sounds doable..." Bimian comments with an amused grunt.

"Let me ask you Karnin...why did you come here if not to declare yourself to me?" Marsle asks, and then he adds, "You do not seem to be a foolish young man surely you knew that you would be at my mercy here."

"I promised a friend that I'd come," Karnin replies, and then he adds, "But I'd be remiss if I didn't warn you that my men'll come for me if I don't return as scheduled."

"Will they walk in then?" Marsle asks.

"By the time they reach you they will all be too sick with the rot to do much rescuing," Corlean remarks, and then he points to a red patch on Karnin's arm and says, "And from the looks of it there won't be much of you left to rescue either."

"How long has that been there?" a familiar voice suddenly asks, and as Karnin stands transfixed with his hand grasping the hilt of his blade the voice's owner quickly places his hand over Karnin's and commands, "Don't stick me boy."

Chapter Ten

As Karnin stands on *Laraqua's* dock watching the sun rise he cannot help but appreciate the raw beauty of this place, for if he believed in such things he would say it was an enchanted place. When he notices that the morning fog has begun to yield to the sun's warmth he takes a deep breath, and tries to memorize the smell of the inner marshes, for he wants to remember it. He wants to mark this moment in time so that it will remain unmarred by what is to come. Besides the future is an uncertain thing. That is one of the important lessons that he has learned since that fateful day that Bornan showed up at *Onyat's* gate, for Karnin never expected to be here at all let alone to be leaving a free man. He has therefore decided to enjoy what comes his way when it comes, for who knows if he will ever have the opportunity for such carefree memory-making again. In truth the direction that his life is going when he leaves today will be anything but that he thinks as he watches a long-beaked marsh bird snatch up a frog who has stayed a tad too late. How appropriate he thinks.

As it is Karnin thinks that he resembles that frog somewhat although to be fair he did not get devoured per say more like absorbed or assimilated. The upside to that more than compensated him for it though, for his odds of returning here to *Laraqua* in the near future are better than they were when he first came. As he looks out across the mooring area he cannot say that he is sorry about that little perk. All in all the past four days have been rather remarkable all tallied, for they were filled from waking to sleep with new and unusual experiences such as the jitty ride that they took to see Corlean's new fortress *Aqualean*, and the jaunt to the small artisan's village on stilts that he was told most marsh fortresses have nearby. Truthfully the only regret that Karnin has is that Torli was not here to see those things too, for he has an unquenchable thirst for new things. Hopefully Torli will be able to experience the marshes for a time once this nasty business at *Filon Bora* is finished although Torli may not be open to such as that after he learns what has transpired in his absence.

He will soon know though Karnin thinks, for today is the day and Torli is already on his way to *Laraqua* to pick him up. As it was Marsle wanted to meet the man whose bid for justice Marsle had agreed to back, and more importantly Marsle wanted to see the technology that Calphin swears he saw climb out of the marshes and speed off across the land. To his credit when Marsle requested that he bring the runner in to *Laraqua* Torli tried to pretend that it could not do it, but when Marsle told him that he knew beyond question that he could bring his vehicle in to get his three men as one might expect it gave Torli pause. As far as Torli knew only Karnin and Han were there or so he thought. It therefore goes without saying that when he found out who the third man was there was a long silence. So long that Marsle motioned for Karnin to speak to him, which Karnin did do, but Torli's only response was 'I'm coming' after which he promptly hung up.

Karnin only hopes that when Torli finds out the entirety of what he and Boro have done that he manages to hang onto the generous mood that seeing Boro again will likely instill in him. Yes Marsle's alliance came at a cost, and what he had wanted in return for not tossing everyone at *Onyat* into a cell was not a thing that Karnin even remotely thought that he would ask for when he first set out on Bimian's crawler. Despite his anger at being duped into coming here, that Boro was still around to yell at him for even thinking of not doing so had helped to take the sting out of looking the fool. In the end though Karnin was so relieved that his mentor and friend of many years was not dead that he could not even muster up enough righteous anger to tell the calculating bastard off. Of course Boro's physical condition had much to do with that too.

The truth is that once the initial shock of seeing Boro where he never expected to wore off Karnin quickly noticed how much the man had changed since he had last seen him. Needless to say when it sunk in how much the years had cost Boro Karnin could not bring himself to treat him harshly, for Boro seemed old and worn, and there was a dark brooding shadow about him that Karnin did not remember being there before. Once Boro related all that had happened to him in the last few months Karnin understood where it came from, for Galwor had fallen into a coma weeks before he died, and when he did Tok had decided to clean house in preparation for his coming to the seat. Boro being a lord and a direct relation to old Obron's wife not to mention Tok's nemesis for many years was at the top of Tok's list.

Boro had friends at *Filon Bora*, and they were quick to let him know that Tok had hired an assassin to kill him, and so Boro fled the fortress that same night with the intentions of making his way to *Onyat* as had always been the plan for him to do when Galwor passed. Surprisingly enough Tok was not so incompetent as to have hired any run-of-the-mill killer to take Boro out, for he knew that Boro was not an easy mark. Tok also figured that getting rid of Boro in a permanent way was an investment in his future, and so he dug deep into his pockets and hired an upper echelon killer from the distinguished group of killers for hire known as the *Filcet*. Since you definitely get what you pay for from them in the way of talent Tok's assassin did not fail to notice that Boro was arranging his affairs, but it suited his purposes to let Boro go. Doing so was actually an intelligent move, for it is always easier to take a more difficult target down in a place unfamiliar to him. In the cat-and-mouse game that followed Boro was forced to flee into the marshes where he somehow managed to give the man the slip, but in the process Boro had become hopelessly turned around.

Boro told Karnin that he had spent many days wandering aimlessly, and when he could go no further he had curled up in the branches of the marsh scrub and closed his eyes to wait for death to claim him. Death however did not find him that day, but rather one of its minions. As it was Calphin had run across the *Filcet* who was hunting Boro in the marshes when he was returning from one of his missions to *Onyat*. It goes without saying that Calphin did not bother to ask him what he was doing there before he killed him. Calphin knew a *Filcet* assassin of quality when he saw one and a man does not give away the element of surprise to one of their kind. Even so this particular *Filcet* was a land man and so Calphin suspected that his target must have fled into the marshes. He therefore began to search, and sometime after dark that same day he found Boro, but by then Boro was unconscious and barely alive. The lack of proper food and hydration were only partly to blame, Boro had also acquired a rather nasty flesh rot infection that nearly cost him his legs. As one might expect Boro is very grateful to the marsh folk who saved his life, but even so he is still rather bitter about having gone from a vibrant man still in his prime to a man who can barely walk without aid.

Needless to say after seeing Boro and realizing how close Tok had come to killing him Karnin had accepted that drink of spirits that Marsle had offered him earlier, and as is often the case a time spent imbibing of strong drink had loosened tongues. When all was said and done Bimian had finally gotten his answer as to Karnin's origins, but it was not until Boro had insured that his plan was securely in place, for he had cajoled and then shamed Karnin into pledging himself as Marsle's vassal first. Then Boro led the conversation in such a way that Marsle conceded that Torli was not bound to him, for if Tok had killed his way to the top then Torli was Galwor's rightful heir. Marsle therefore considered his presence at *Onyat* to be a courtesy that Marsle would expect any of his vassals to extend to anyone of Torli's status who was in need.

"Will you support Torli's bid to recover his rightful place then overlord Marsle?" Boro had asked.

"I am not so drunk as to commit to involve the marshes in a land folk's war Boro," Marsle had replied.

"Then you shouldn't 'ave accepted a land man as a vassal sir...especially one who shares a blood bond with the future overlord a the Eastern Central Land Territory," Boro had replied.

Marsle was understandably outraged, for he had opened his fortress and stuck out his neck for Boro. Marsle was therefore more than a little angry that Boro had neglected to tell him that the relationship between Torli and Karnin was more than a boyhood friendship. In all fairness Marsle's anger was actually justified, for Boro's admission had put him in a rather untenable position. As the rules go a vassal's relationship with his overlord is multifaceted in such a way that once Karnin became Marsle's vassal not only did Karnin inherit an obligation to come to Marsle's aid if need be, but Marsle took on the responsibility to aid Karnin if he or his should ever require it as well. Therefore, since Torli is Karnin's first cousin Marsle has a commitment to at minimum sanction Karnin's supporting him to regain his rightful property.

Things got a bit dicey for a time then, with much shouting and finger pointing, but in the end Boro was able to pacify Marsle into forgiving him. After all Marsle was getting a rather nicely done land fortress to protect his fringe lands out of it, and a vassal who not only had a rather well equipped army of professional fighters at his disposal, but also a first cousin who is the rightful heir to one of the most strategically placed land territories with regard to Marsle's own. Once Boro had pointed all that out even Corlean had seemed a bit more agreeable, and so Boro had gone in for the kill and revealed much to Karnin's displeasure that he would also be entitled to his fair share of the technology that had been developed at *Onyat*, which did give Marsle pause. It was only then that Karnin learned that Calphin had seen them in the marshes the day they tested the runner's capabilities on water. Needless to say Karnin was not very pleased to hear that.

Everyone seemed rather tense after all that and so they all began drinking in earnest in an attempt to soothe their rattled nerves. Soon they were a great deal more relaxed perhaps a bit too much so, for there was much jibbing of each other and ribald joke telling that Karnin thinks Marsle would not normally have taken part in quite so boisterously had he been sober, which he was not. At some point food appeared obviously sent by the ladies whom they had all stood up at the dinner table. Unfortunately acting male is apparently a universal thing that applies to all men whether they hail from land or marsh, for despite the fact that the marsh men realized that they should probably go apologize for treating the women so badly they did not do so. Instead they ate, which helped them sober up enough to get drunk all over again, and somewhere during the night they had burned out and fell asleep all over Marsle's sitting room in various odd positions.

Karnin remembers that when he opened his eyes the next morning he was lying half under Marsle's desk with another man's shirt rolled up beneath his head. He later found out from Boro whose it was, for Boro was taking too many medications to drink much, and so he remembered exactly how Karnin had acquired Corlean's shirt. Luckily it was in an honest and non-violent way. Apparently in the course of things a great deal of male bragging had ensued, and after Corlean declared that how far a man could piss was an indicator of his skill under the blankets he bet his shirt that no man amongst them could piss further than him. They had all stumbled out onto the rear dock then, and after each man had a turn at it Karnin was the only man who managed to actually hit Onot although because Bimian was motivated more than most he did come very, very close.

So it is that after a somewhat hesitant start Karnin's time at Marsle's fortress is ending today on a decent enough note, for he and Corlean had come to terms with each other, and his stay with Marsle and his people had shown him a perspective on life and living that he had never experienced before. Karnin is also leaving the marshes with a less memorable reminder of his time here, for the spot on his arm had indeed turned out to be the rot. *Laraqua's* old healer Nao-Nao has assured him that it had been treated in time to effect a total recovery, but even so the throbbing and burning is still uncomfortable enough to make him reach for the pot of cream and slather a bit more on. As he does so he once again thinks of how much pain Boro must have endured, for the spot on his own arm is nothing compared to the extensive infection that Boro had acquired before Calphin found him.

"So...you go today then?" a soft voice suddenly asks behind him.

"Yeah lady I do," Karnin replies, but he does not need to turn around to know who it is she has gone out of her way to attract his attention these last few days.

With a sigh Karnin reminds himself that Ann is too young and impulsive to understand that she should not play with men the way she does, and so he must be patient with her. That should not be too hard since he is not going to be in her company much longer. After all it was made clear to him that she was not for him and he had given the worried overlord his oath that he would not encourage this fascination that his daughter seems to have developed for land men. It goes without saying that Marsle had rattled off all the reasons why there could not be a match between them, and Karnin had to agree that all of them were valid enough. The reality of it is that the overlord need not have bothered, for even though Karnin finds Ann very alluring he would not have acted on that even had Marsle not forbade it. There is no room in Karnin's life for a steady woman right now let alone a pampered wife.

Therefore, when Marsle had told him that he hoped Ann would develop a tender for Slolar Karnin chalked up the pang of regret that he felt to just another moment of envy for something unique possessed by another. After that he had made an effort to keep Ann at a distance, which was rather difficult since she was so very persistent and resourceful as well. Actually avoiding her became a challenge, and after she had turned up in the corridor outside his room the men in her life took it upon themselves to making certain that Karnin was never alone out in the fortress. Until now that is, but he supposes that is because he is leaving today and they all figure that by the time he sees her again she will most likely be wed to someone so what matter is it now if he talks to her a bit.

"We are going too in seven or so days," she tells him, and when he turns his head to her she adds with a small coy smile, "My father is sending me to *Nithian* for a time...I think he hopes that I will change my mind about Slolar if I am around him long enough."

"Will you?" Karnin asks as he admires the way the soft light pink material of the short sleeveless shift that she is wearing accents her dark hair and pale skin.

"Maybe...but I doubt it," she replies, and then she gives him an unreadable look and adds, "He is nice and all but well...I am hoping for a bit more than just that."

"Such as?" Karnin asks, for it is obvious that she is trying to make him jealous, and the rub of it is that in a way he is, but it is not a thing of the heart but rather of the loins.

"Such as a man...not a boy," she replies as her colorless eyes suggestively sweep his male form.

"Age does not make a man a man," Karnin tells her, and then he clasps his hands behind his back and adds, "I met a few supposedly grown 'men' before who were just as silly as boys."

"Yes...but at least a man would be free to make his own choices...silly or not," she says with an intense expression.

"No one is ever really as free as that lady Ann..." Karnin tells her.

"Still...most men can come and go most times without having to ask anyone's permission," she complains with a rather endearing pout.

"So where would you go if you could go anywhere you wanted to?" Karnin humors her mood by asking.

"On a great adventure..." she replies with a faraway gaze, and then she adds as she absently fingers her long hair, "I envy you Karnin...I wish I could share in the one that you are going to."

"I'm going to war lady..." he gently tells her, and then he adds, "It's not the kind a adventure I hope you ever take."

"Will I ever see you again Karnin?" she asks, and when she turns her face to him he notes that her eyes seem to have a bit of color when swimming in unshed tears.

"One day maybe...but not for a very long time most like," he replies, and then he steels himself and says what he knows he must, "I expect you'll be long married by then."

"I will never marry a man who I do not love!" she retorts as an angry tear slides down her pale cheek.

"Then don't...you're young and got plenty a time for it," Karnin replies with a shrug.

"And you...have you no interest in what becomes of me Karnin?" she pleads.

"I'm your father's vassal now," Karnin replies, but when he sees the hope in her young face he knows that he cannot in good conscious go off and let her keep it, for no matter what his man parts say his gut knows that her future is not with him. The sooner that she realizes it the less she will be harmed by it and so he gives her a polite smile and says, "I care what becomes a all those in my overlord's household."

"Is that all I am to you then?" she asks as another tear slips out.

"There's nothing else you can be lady," he replies.

"My father has made you think that but..."

"No Ann...listen carefully...I do my own thinking," Karnin interrupts her to say, and then he puts on a kinder face and adds, "You're a charming girl with much to offer...but I'm not in the market for a wife...and you're too fine to be anything else."

"I see," she stares down at her hands and says, and then much to her credit she pulls herself up and with a nod she tells him with a miffed expression, "I hope you find what it is that you are in the market for then."

With that she turns and quickly makes her way back to the entryway. As Karnin watches her graceful form hurry away his eyes narrow angrily, for that he had to hurt her that way is something that he had hoped to avoid. As he turns his eyes away he softly curses under his breath on the lady's behalf, but then after a few seconds thought he swears again although this time because he cares that much that he hurt her feelings. With a sigh Karnin finds that he must admit the marshes have obviously changed him in ways that he did not even suspect. No before he came here he would not have felt a tug at his gut over making some silly girl cry, and part of him wishes that he could undue that particular modification to his character. That kind of guilt is a rather unpleasant thing to feel to say the least.

"So...you have sent her to cry on her bed," Corlean's voice softly asks behind him.

"She didn't give me much choice," Karnin replies.

"I know...I heard," Corlean says, and then he adds in an attempt to lighten the mood a bit, "When she has exhausted all her tears she is most likely going to spend a lot of time asking your fates to make your man-parts shrivel."

"Ah well let her hate me then if it makes her feel better," Karnin replies, and then he says in a rather bored tone, "She'll go to Bimian's and some handsome fisher's son'll catch her eye...she'll forget all about me."

"I should punch you in the face for even suggesting that," Corlean clips out, and when Karnin gives him a questioning raising of the brows he quickly adds, "Not that I would object to a fisher's son...but well...alright I am a snob then...I will not see my sister wed to someone who can offer her nothing."

"There's love..." Karnin points out.

"Yes well...she can love a man who can keep her safe and in frills just as easily as someone who cannot," Corlean retorts.

"Some things're beyond a man's control."

"Yes and some things are not...I am delivering her to Bimian's...and I assure you that I will be giving all the young men an eyeball," Corlean tells him in a matter-of-fact way.

"Why're you taking her...you two shouldn't be traveling together?"

"We have always traveled together..." Corlean says in a rather displeased way, for he does not like to be taken to task by one of his father's vassals.

"Times're changing Corlean...there're eyes everywhere these days...that *Filcet* Calphin killed in the marshes should a told you that," Karnin points out.

"I am not a fool Karnin...we will be safe enough," Corlean responds in a tone intended to make it clear to him that the debate on it is over, and then he changes the subject by saying in a lighter tone, "You do know that Ann is only going because *Nithian* is closer to *Filon Bora*?"

"You better make sure she knows about the giant man eating land worms then," Karnin says, and then he adds, "You know...the ones that eat runaway girls?"

"Ah...those worms...I will make certain to tell her," Corlean replies with a mischievous glint in his eyes, and then he pauses for a few seconds before he asks rather seriously, "Listen Karnin…I need to ask you this so do not take it the wrong way…do you have an heir or some contingency for *Onyat* should things not go well for you with this Tok?"

"I plan to leave a small contingent of men to defend the property and the civilians that reside there with us," Karnin explains, and then he adds, "There're six men that stand in line to inherit the command of *Onyat*…I'll copy the order to you before we move out."

"You know that you are a landholder now and as my father would say…boy…you are twenty and five and it is high time to get yourself a wife and make an heir," Corlean spouts forth in his best Marsle voice, but when Karnin gives him a perplexed frown he tells him, "I guess my father forgot to mention that all his vassals hold lands under their own title and by their own right…amongst our kind a leader holds the loyalty of his vassals because he earns it not because they have no choice save poverty but to give it."

"I'm…rather speechless I'm afraid," Karnin says.

"Yes well that is a first no doubt…come inside and I will give you the legal whatnots and show you the map with the new lines drawn," Corlean tells him, and then he turns and heads towards a side entrance to the fortress that Karnin has not been through before.

"Where's everyone this morning?" Karnin asks as he notes the lack of activity when they pass the door to the fortress's vast storage area, for by this time of day it is usually bustling with activity as *Laraqua's* many departments come to REC out their daily supplies.

"Ah well…my father's sent a couple patrols out…there were a few hits on the sensor net last night…you would not know anything about that would you?" Corlean inquires.

"Are you accusing?" Karnin asks somewhat defensively.

"No…should I be?" Corlean responds.

"No…you shouldn't…" Karnin assures him.

"Good because they were single hits…three of them most likely someone on foot…and if they were land men then they went the wrong way and are half way to the deep pools by now," Corlean tells him.

"Wait…" Karnin stops to say, and then with an incredulous face he asks, "So the overlord's response to a possible threat's to send all his men out searching?"

"Some are out searching...but some of the men you saw hanging around were mine...I have sent most of them home to *Aqualean* to secure it," Corlean replies, and then he adds, "The only reason that I am still here is because of you...well...and that runner of yours."

"Yeah but they're still gone you see," Karnin impatiently points out.

Corlean's reply is to pause and pull some sort of bread roll from his pocket, which in and of itself does not surprise Karnin much since Corlean always seems to have some sort of snack thing on him somewhere. However when he holds it up to Karnin as though it were the answer to Karnin's question Karnin must admit that he is understandably confused. His bemusement is quickly dealt with, for Corlean pulls back and lobs the roll over the dock towards the water, but instead of the bread becoming food for the fishes as Karnin expects it to the thing suddenly ignites and with a poof is reduced to a fine ash that slowly drifts down to float on the water's surface. As any responsible person would do before the residue even hits the water Corlean COM's the watch guard that the hit on his screen is only his demonstration of how the field works.

"You could a warned me," Karnin accuses, for apparently the sensor net is not the only security measure that *Laraqua* employs.

"I was waiting until you were done breaking my sister's heart," Corlean replies.

"Wait...you saying Ann knew that field was on?" and when Corlean shrugs Karnin comments, "I'm surprised she didn't give me a shove."

"I am sure she will regret not frying you later...when she is tired of weeping," Corlean responds.

"You know...you're pretty callous where your sister's feelings're concerned," Karnin clips out, and when he does Corlean does not miss the flash of protective anger in his eyes.

"Tell me you have not fallen for her Karnin?"

"No...but I'll tell you if I wasn't a land man...the bastard son of a second son...and in the market for a wife..."

"And would my father not strike you dead..."

"Yeah well if I wasn't all that he wouldn't..."

"True."

"Then I'd be thinking on asking for her...but I didn't survive this long by lying to myself," Karnin tells him, and then he bluntly adds, "But if she's not happily wed in five or six years...and does

212

some vaccine for this damnable rot come about then I might reconsider that."

"Fair enough...and for the record I would rather see her wed to a land man with the rot than Oreian's son Jonin," Corlean tells him as he steps up to the door, and then he punches his code into its access pad as he adds, "Oh and you are locked out too by the way."

"Thanks," Karnin replies with a disgruntled huff as he follows him inside, and then he asks, "What'd you got against this...Jonin?"

"Well for one Ann cannot stand him...for two I cannot either," Corlean replies, and then he adds in a disgusted tone as he motions for Karnin to follow him, "His father Oreian is rather a toady for an overlord...a lazy leech that travels from fortress to fortress imposing on others so that he does not have to provide for his own upkeep...not only does his heir apparent Jonin think that he is above most others...but he has a reputation for being cruel to those under him...besides he is a snob...he called you a homeless upstart and a nobody."

"Did he now?" Karnin asks, and then he shrugs and says almost too calmly, "Too bad he's not still here...I'd a liked to discuss that with him."

"Probably for the best that he is not then although I would have liked to see his reaction to your pledging to my father...Jonin thought that he should have routed you all out and jailed you a long time ago...that and my sister's infatuation with you would have probably put him over the edge," Corlean remarks, and then he sees Calphin coming towards them and so he says, "Just telling Karnin about that little twit of Oreian's."

"Who...the great Jonin?" Calphin inquires with a wide-eyed expression, and then he adds in mock wonder, "The man of legendary breeding...the one with the new fortress that has not five but six whole guest suites with their very own pools?"

"The very one," Corlean replies with a nod.

"Greatest arse sucking swani that ever existed," Calphin says with a snort.

"Swani?" Karnin repeats.

"Let us just say that a swani does not care much what it is as long as there is a hole on it somewhere that he can put his prick in," Calphin explains.

"Ah...I see..." Karnin replies with an amused nod.

"Yes well he has sent a formal request to my father to come courting," Corlean informs him.

"No," Calphin replies in mock horror.

"Yes...believe it."

"Courting who...Ann?' Karnin angrily asks, for their attitude seems rather casual to be speaking of this supposed sycophant courting a sweet innocent like Ann.

"Well I doubt little lord suck arse wants to court the cook's girl," Calphin sarcastically replies.

"He is not the only reason that my father is sending her to *Nithian* for a time...but definitely high up on the list," Corlean replies.

"Yes...for some reason Jonin will not come there," Calphin says with a shrug.

"Yes well... having someone threaten to snap your prick off has a way of doing that," Corlean mentions with a snort.

"That was years ago...when he was only an obnoxious little puke," Calphin replies, and then with a mocking hand flourish he adds, "You would think that he would have gotten over that now that he is an obnoxious big puke."

"I know I'm gonna regret this but...why'd you want a snap off his rod in the first place?" Karnin tentatively asks, for Calphin is in some ways much as Karnin would imagine his mother Andina would be if she were a male with a killer's skill set, and therefore the why of it that he would threaten to unman someone could be any one of a variety of odd things.

"That was a long time ago...I really do not remember anymore," Calphin replies.

"Yes you do," Corlean states as he turns them down a small corridor to the right.

"Some things one does not care to remember," Calphin warns.

"I for one cannot forget it," Corlean responds, and then he stops mid-stride and tells Karnin, "Calphin and I came upon Jonin peeking at his mother."

"She was...busy with my father at the time," Calphin adds.

"Ah...I see," Karnin says.

"You know Corlean...now that I think on it Ann had best be careful that she does not wait so long to do her picking that Oreian's little pervert is the only one left to pick," Calphin points out.

"Yes well he is going to have a tragic accident before that ever happens," Corlean pointedly replies, and then sets off down the corridor once again.

"Call me if you need help with that," Calphin offers as he and Karnin follow.

"You know some might think your joking about your sister's future being ruined by a bad match in poor taste," Karnin states a bit heatedly, for in his book there is nothing at all funny about Ann being married off to some loser.

"It would be if I were joking...which I promise you I am not," Corlean replies as he ushers them into a room that Karnin has not yet been in.

"You better be...a man in your position's got a think a the whole picture," Karnin pauses in the middle of the room to say.

"Are you advising me Karnin?" Corlean asks as he also stops, and when Karnin only shrugs he adds, "So what is the whole picture then?"

"Your decisions affect a lot a people...you got a keep your hands clean," Karnin tells him, and then he glances over at Calphin and adds, "You too."

"Well that is just downright depressing," Calphin retorts, and then he asks, "What about you Karnin...you are a lord now too."

"Ah well...I'm not an overlord's heir apparent...besides...everyone knows my hands ain't clean," Karnin replies.

"So...which one of your killers would you pick for a job like Jonin?" Calphin asks him as they once again begin walking across the room.

"Probably Ahnin," Karnin candidly replies, for Calphin has been spying on them for years, and so there is no need to lie about it.

"The one with the dead thing in his pocket?" Calphin asks, and when Karnin nods Calphin adds, "Yes...I can see why you would pick him...he has the look...where did you find him by the way?"

"Same place as everybody else," Karnin cryptically replies as the men stop in front of a rather ornate desk with a glass top situated near one of the room's two large windows.

"Now then Karnin...my father was very generous to you," Corlean informs him as he reaches down and flips a switch on the desk.

"Was he..." Karnin absently asks as he studies the topographical map being displayed on the desk's top.

"He was," Corlean replies, and then he rattles off as he points to the various landmarks on the map, "He has entailed everything from the marsh edge nearest *Onyat* one hundred forty-five miles south to where my father's territory borders that of what is currently overlord Tok's territory...and then west two-hundred and fifty miles to the corner where the three territories meet here...and then north north-east along overlord Devoot's boundary seven-hundred miles to the edge of the northern ice flow...which would be here...east one-hundred miles to the marshes again...and then south six-hundred and seventy-five miles to the starting point near *Onyat*."

"That is generous..." Calphin absently says as he leans over the map.

"Yes well it is all our territory's dry lands," Corlean responds with a shrug that Calphin seems to understand the meaning of because he nods rather sagely or so Karnin thinks, but then again Karnin's brain is reeling from this unexpected revelation, and so he is still processing when Corlean continues, "The land has been entailed to *Onyat*...which has now been officially titled to you...but there are still a few conditions...no selling...transferring or apportioning off the land in barter...you can of course set a piece aside and let one of your favorites to build a secondary fortress upon it...but that must be approved and if it is then he would become a vassal of my father not yours...and the title to his fortress and lands would be separated from *Onyat*...but other than that as long as you and your heirs remain our vassals this is your land so you are responsible to set patrols to make certain that no one uses your land to strike at the marshes or to do the marshlands damage."

"I wasn't expecting this much land to care for...I'm gonna be hard pressed right now to find enough men to leave behind at *Onyat* to secure it," Karnin says a bit taken aback by Marsle's generosity.

"My father said to tell you that he will delay your actual taking title of the lands south of *Onyat* until such time as this business with Tok is finished...he will explain all that once commander Torli arrives," Corlean tells him.

"Alright..." is all that Karnin can find to say.

"You seem a bit...off lord general," Calphin comments.

"Lord general?" Karnin repeats.

"Yes...my father thinks it best if you retain the general part," Corlean tells him.

"So that no one forgets that you have a big arse army," Calphin explains.

"Shadow...four...two...four to *Laraqua* watch guard," a familiar voice suddenly crackles from the communications device on Corlean's hip.

"*Laraqua* watch here...go ahead Shadow," another voice replies.

"We're approaching your warning buoy," Karnin hears Ahnin inform him.

"Copy that...I have you on my screen...come ahead Shadow," the watch guard instructs.

"Copy come ahead *Laraqua*," Ahnin acknowledges.

"Master Cogen drop the house field now," Corlean clicks a switch on his device and says.

"Copy that powering down house field," the security master's voice replies.

"Overlord," Corlean presses another button and says.

"I heard...we are already on our way to the dock," Marsle's voice replies.

Without a word the three men turn and hasten outside, for it will only take the runner a few minutes to reach them, and they do not want to miss seeing it come in. On a more personal note Karnin is rather thankful for the interruption, for his mind is still a bit panicked from suddenly realizing that he has taken on a lot more responsibility than he thought he had although he supposes that he should not be all that surprised since that has been the way this trip has gone so far. Still when they step out onto the dock area and Karnin sees Marsle he feels a flutter in his gut. After all the man is going to want a copy of his defensive plan for his new lands, and although he has given Karnin a reprieve as far as producing it that will not last long, but he cannot worry about that now. His head must be clear when he tells Torli that he will not be staying with him after they take *Filon Bora*.

Karnin therefore takes a few calming breaths and surveys the dock taking note of who has come out and where they are, which is pretty much everybody Karnin thinks as he sees the crowds of marsh folk gathered near the various dockside entrances to the fortress. As one would expect Andina, Janissa, and Aquaous along with several of the fortress's women have come out to see the spectacle, but they remain well back in a group apart with several men at arms nearby. Karnin also notes that there are a few armed security guards scattered at various strategic points on the dock as well, but given the recent incursions he is not surprised by it. Unfortunately, the one person that Karnin does not see is Ann, and he sincerely hopes that she is watching from above, for he thinks that it would be a pity does she miss seeing the runner's grand entrance Karnin hopes as Torli's sleek vehicle silently glides into view.

"Well overlords what'd you think?" Boro asks.

"I am thinking that I have a bit of catching up to do," Marsle replies and then he asks, "Is this yours Karnin?"

"I'm afraid that ownership's never really been decided between us overlord," Karnin replies.

"Would you like it to be?" Marsle inquires with a sly grin.

"What's mine's yours overlord," Karnin replies with an agreeable nod.

"I am certain that I can make the commander see that you will need it now that you are a marsh lord," Marsle assures him as he studies the way the vehicle gently comes to a halt in front of the dock and then silently begins to rotate in place.

"Yeah...about that sir...don't you think lord general's a bit much?" Karnin asks.

"That is nothing," Slolar complains without taking his eyes off the vehicle.

"You should hear Slolar's official title...takes at least two breaths to get it all out," Corlean advises.

"Thought you all didn't stand on titles?" Karnin asks.

"Yes well...that does not mean that we do not have them..." Calphin absently replies as his eyes study the vehicle.

As the men on the dock marvel at the ease with which the runner's pilot turns the vehicle broadside and then brings it to within a few inches of the dock inside the runner Torli orders the blast shields rolled up, for he does not want it to seem that he has come with anything in mind except retrieving his men. Needless to say he has already made certain that the storage covers are locked down on everything of importance that Ahnin does not need to maneuver the runner, for he sees no reason to let the marsh folk gauge his vehicle's weapons capabilities if he does not have to. Actually Torli questions the wisdom of letting them see what they just did even if the overlord's spy has already seen it. Marsle would not be told no though and so Torli had little choice. Besides Torli could not in good conscience make Boro endure a long ride on a crawler not after hearing how sick he has been.

So the marsh men have now seen that the runner is something that they could use, and so Torli supposes that he will find out if Boro's insistence that they still follow the old honorable ways is true. There is nothing else for it he thinks as the blast shields roll up. The men gravitate to the windows then to see firsthand what they have been told is a proper marsh fortress, and when they do they are rather awed by it. Until now most of them never imagined that something as grand as Marsle's fortress could exist within the confines of the marshlands. Then there is the sight of so many marsh folk in one place, which is oddly fascinating. In truth the sight of so many grayish-skinned, black-haired people staring at them with their rather odd eyes is downright unnerving.

"I'll be damn...it's him alright," Cerl says when he spies Boro standing on the dock.

"He looks...old..." Gorg quietly notes.

"Well that's because he 'is' old...he's got a be at least what...forty?" Ahnin asks Torli.

"Forty-six," Torli replies in a subdued voice.

"That's not exactly ancient magic man," Seasle points out for forty-six is considered still well within a man's prime even if he is a land man.

"He's also been pretty sick they said," Torli absently tells them as he studies the group on the dock, but at the moment he is more concerned with what he sees going on there than he is with Boro's presence, for that Marsle has placed armed guards at strategic places around the dock sends a prickling sensation down his neck.

"Personal blades only," Torli announces.

"What good'll blades do against hand weapons...?" Gorg begins.

"Enough...look out there...the guards're all placed at places vulnerable from the water," Torli points out, and then he adds as he strides towards the door, "It's not us they're worried about."

"The marshes aren't as peaceful as they'd like us to believe eh," Bro remarks.

"Cerl you're with me...the rest a you'll remain with the vehicle," Torli instructs.

"But commander..."

"You'll not step one foot onto Marsle's dock unless you get an invite from the overlord or one a his representatives," Torli orders, and then much to their relief he says, "Which I'll try to get for you as soon as I can work it in...but I'll tell you...the man that embarrasses us's gonna offer up his balls on the way back."

With that Torli commands the door open, and when he does on the exterior of the vehicle the door's outline suddenly materializes from what seconds ago appeared to be a seamless side of metal. As the door begins to move Torli nervously straightens his shirt, and brushes a lock of unruly hair from his eyes, for he wants very much to make a good impression not only on Marsle, but on Boro as well. The truth is Torli finds that he is more anxious about being reunited with Boro than meeting the most powerful of the marsh overlords, for the last time that he saw Boro Torli was a rather sickly boy not yet into his manhood. Now that he has reached his majority Torli hopes that Boro will not still see that wreck of a boy, for Torli thinks that after all that has happened since that long ago day when he said goodbye to Boro to have him still find him wanting would be rather devastating.

"Glad to see you made it commander," Karnin says as the opening door reveals Torli's form.

"Thank you general," Torli replies somewhat nervously or so Karnin thinks.

"Relax," Karnin softly says as he sends the men in the runner a covert 'all is well' signal, but he can see that Torli is still a bit on edge, and so he turns to the waiting group of marsh folk and says, "Overlord Marsle may I present commander Torli."

"Welcome to *Laraqua* commander," Marsle says, but although Torli tries to hide it Marsle can see that his attention is understandably divided.

"Thank you overlord Marsle...*Laraqua*'s quite magnificent," Torli replies and then forces his attention away from the man standing to the rear of the group.

"You already know overlord Bimian I have been told," Marsle says, but when he takes note of the fact that Boro has gone quite pale he runs through the remainder of the introductions with the least amount of fuss and then says, "And of course you know my house guest here."

"Indeed I do," Torli replies, and when Marsle steps aside Torli walks over to Boro and says with a great deal more emotion than he had intended to, "You're surely a welcome sight...uncle."

"And you boy," Boro responds, and with a wavering smile he embraces him and then says somewhat gruffly, "Glad to see you filled out...you were such a scrawny thing."

220

"Let us take this inside shall we...where it is cooler and we can all talk in comfort," Marsle suggests, and then he calls, "Berto!"

"Yes overlord."

"See to the commander's men...will you," Marsle replies as he leads them away.

"Of course overlord," Berto calls after him, and as he dubiously eyes the group of land men standing just inside the door of the vehicle Han saunters up to him.

"The fourth one there's the one you got a keep out a the kitchens," Han loudly tells him, and much to the amusement of the other men in the runner Berto settles his eyes upon Seasle and nods.

Chapter Eleven

The night is dark and swathed in shadow, for even though the sky is clear and alive with twinkling stars the planet's two moons have yet to make their nightly march. Soon though the larger of the planet's moons *Ofren* will make its dazzling appearance, and when it does it will eclipse the sprinkle of stars and transform the landscape with its eerie silvery light. Not long after that *Ofren's* smaller sister *Gofren* will peek above the horizon and follow in *Ofren's* wake adding its own yellowish glow to things. The deep darkness that now blankets the land will then flee receding to the most sheltered places of the world. Until it does however the road north to *Onyat* will be cloaked in inky blackness, and although one day soon that fact will be used to conceal the movement of men and machines south it only serves to slow the progress of the men heading north towards home tonight.

The truth of it is that the men have chosen to run at less than top speed, for their vehicle's near silent glide field gives little notice of its approach, and without the benefit of the moon reflecting off its metal hull it is unlikely that anything in the road would see it coming in time to get out of its way. Such care for the wildlife although admirable does make for a long tedious trip Torli notes as he sits staring at the runner's camera monitors. Then again the slower speed is not the only factor contributing to the dragging minutes. No the main reason is sitting at the rear of the runner sleeping like a babe without a care in the world he adds with a rather heated glance in Karnin's direction. The rest of them well they are probably glad that he is, for even though they do not know all of what took place behind closed doors at *Laraqua* they heard

222

enough once they left the marsh fortress for home to know that he and Karnin are on the outs again Torli thinks with a sigh.

Of course despite the tension between their two leaders the men were talkative enough when the journey first began for they are to a man glad to see Boro again. However as time went on and the miles clicked off Boro tired and they all decided it best to let him rest a bit. It was not long after Boro fell asleep that they decided to join him, and now everyone is snoring in their seats. Well except for Han who is as usual awake tending the runner's controls. Torli for his part rarely sleeps anymore, and so that he is still awake is not unusual, but tonight it is more than just the typical aches and pains that has him restlessly shifting in his seat. No this time it is a cumulative thing with too many issues to even list. The new found quiet has helped though, for as he passed the time watching the shadowy trees wiz by on the camera monitors some of the tension finally drained from his body, and for the first time since he heard the all of what Karnin had done Torli thinks that he may be able to be within arm's reach of him without trying to strangle him.

As it was when Torli first heard that Karnin had pledged himself and *Onyat* to Marsle he wanted to give up and just walk away from this whole business. Then he remembered what it cost Boro to get them this far and Torli knew that he could not let him down. Still it angers Torli that Boro orchestrated Karnin's alliance with Marsle, but Torli will let it go. He owes Boro his life after all, for without Boro's intervention he would have been dead before his tenth birthday. Karnin played a role in it too, but he did not do it for free no Boro had rewarded him and the others quite nicely for it. Apparently Karnin's services can still be bought, but instead of food this time it is a fortress and some land. Yes nothing has changed with Karnin except the price Torli concludes with a sarcastic sneer.

That thought sends Torli into a tailspin; for he cannot resolve the conflict between the loyal friend that he has always believed Karnin to be and the man who deserted him for a title. The Karnin Torli thought he knew would never have done that. He would never have stolen the runner from him either and he would never have agreed to split their group up. No Karnin's motto has always been that they stick together no matter what. Now it appears that Karnin has become what he has always said he despised; a loner like Merl who puts his own wants ahead of everyone else's.

Perhaps Karnin hates Merl not because he is a loner but because he sees himself every time he lays eyes on him.

With a sigh Torli checks his thoughts, for deep down inside he knows that Karnin is not a selfish lout not to the level that Merl is at any rate. Still what Karnin did was rather 'Merl-ish', and so he must bear some of the responsibility for what happened between them a few hours ago. As he was after a rather heated argument Torli had pulled a hand weapon on him and threatened to shoot him with it. Fortunately Boro intervened, but Torli was beyond all reason by then and so he tossed in a parting comment to the other men over Boro's shoulder that basically said that he was not the only one who got screwed they did too, for Karnin had given away their freedom for his new title, which pushed Karnin's buttons just as Torli knew that it would.

"Listen you...each and every one a them'll get a choice in it...a choice I might add I didn't get offered," Karnin had pointed an angry finger at him and clipped out between his teeth.

With that Karnin had stalked off to the rear of the vehicle to sulk while Torli had promptly plunked his arse angrily in this seat and tried to calm down as he had promised Boro that he would. After a lot of cursing and a few kicks to the seat opposite him Torli had managed to exhaust his demons at least for awhile, and so he was able to keep his word not to go after Karnin, but the fact that Boro had set Cerl and Bro to make certain that he did not played some role in that. Now that he has had some time to dwell on it Torli realizes that he behaved badly. Actually Torli thinks that he knew he was being an arse even as he was doing it he just could not seem to stop yelling once he started. Now he is regretting his loss of control, for he is feeling the usual exhaustion that such rages always bring, and with it a bit of nausea and depression as well. The worst part is that he is feeling smothered as if the air is too thin. As if the walls are closing in...

"All stop," Torli suddenly stands and says.

"But commander..." Cerl protests a bit uncomfortably.

"Don't argue Cerl," Torli warns.

"The lord general's not ordered it..." Cerl stands and replies with the face of a man who regrets what he has been forced to say.

"I see," Torli testily remarks.

"You heard the commander...all stop," Karnin's voice quietly says, for he has been waiting for Torli to want out he always does, and then he appears next to Torli's seat and says, "Let's go then."

224

With that Karnin turns and strides to the door, for Torli's rages always end with the need for some fresh air although of late that has gotten worse, but Torli is stressed beyond reason at the moment. Who would not be Karnin asks his self as he watches Han go to the controls to bring the runner to a halt. Torli slowly gets up then and joins Karnin at the door, but neither man even acknowledges the other, and it is easy enough to see that the tension between them has not been abated much. While Karnin and Torli stonily wait to disembark the other men exchange a few uncomfortable glances with each other, for even though no one is going for anyone's throat at the moment the men know from experience that that could change with one wrong word. They therefore gather around behind the two men with the intentions of accompanying them outside, but to their displeasure when the runner comes to a stop and the door opens their plan to be on hand to intervene is quickly dashed.

"Wait here," Karnin says over his shoulder.

"I'd be neglecting my duty if I didn't point out that it'd be Tok's great fortune if that gang a renegade tookas catch you both out..." Cerl tells him, for tookas have a rather large range, and although they seem weird and doppick they are very deadly pack hunters.

"I'd welcome a good fight with a tooka right now," Torli clips out and then hops out the door.

"Keep alert," Karnin instructs as he grabs the hand weapon that Cerl holds out to him and quickly goes after Torli, for it is obvious that Torli is well and good into one of his moods, and he is often somewhat reckless when they come.

"He always like this?" Boro slowly gets up from his seat and asks.

"Who...Torli?" Ahnin asks.

"No you..." Boro sarcastically answers him back, and then he impatiently adds, "A course I mean Torli boy!"

"I missed being yelled at by you Boro," Ahnin tells him with a grin, but then he adds a bit more seriously, "Torli's always been kind a...moody...but he hasn't been well lately."

"What're you talking about weirdo?" Seasle demands, for only a week ago he had watched Torli put three men on their backs with a fighting stick, and in Seasle's book sick men do not do that.

"What Karnin's done might a pushed him a bit over the edge Boro," Cerl says as he pushes his hair behind his ears and turns his eyes to him, and when he does Boro realizes that he has never really seen Cerl's face unobstructed by a curtain of hair, for he would surely remember that eye.

"Okay...everyone take a good look and be done with it," Cerl gruffly says, for he has decided that the time has come to trust them with his secret.

"That's a real beaut you got there Cerl..." Seasle points out and then he reaches over and waves his hand in front of Cerl's deformed eye before he says, "You got a dead eye there."

"No kidding genius," Cerl clips back.

"How'd it get like that?" Gorg asks.

"When'd it git like that?" Orn asks.

"It got like that long enough ago that you didn't hear about it when somebody poked it out dumb arses...now get your eyes or 'eye' on them monitors there and start watching what's goin' on out there," Han grumbles out from the controls.

"You knew..." Ahnin softly accuses as he takes over one of the monitors.

"So what...so'd you..." Han quietly replies.

"Why'd you wait so long to tell us about it Cerl?" Gorg loudly demands as he steps up to the bank of monitors.

"Didn't come up," Cerl retorts as he joins him.

"You mean to tell me none a you noticed?" Boro asks with a frustrated shake of his head.

"Cerl always got his hair hanging...thought he was just trying to come across like some wild man or something...you know...to intimidate everybody," Seasle informs him with a shrug.

"That eye'd a been more intimidating if you ask me," Gorg states.

"So why'd you show it to us now after all them years a hiding it?" Seasle asks Cerl.

"It's time," is all Cerl replies, which is apparently enough of an explanation, for the men all nod and grunt their understanding.

"Let's get back to my question eh boys," Boro says somewhat impatiently, for he would like to finish the conversation that he was having before they noticed Cerl's blind eye, and so Boro turns their attention back to it by asking, "Now...what's this about Torli being pushed too far?"

While the other men fill Boro in on Torli's increasingly agitated behavior of late outside the runner Karnin manages to catch up and fall in step with Torli. It goes without saying that when he does Torli sends him a rather hostile glance, and then increases his pace a bit just to let Karnin know that he does not want his company right now, but Karnin simply ignores his little snit. The reason is very obvious at least to Karnin whose mind has not flown off to the land of nins, for it is as dark as pitch out here, and therefore an extra pair of eyes may make all the difference between seeing an assassin standing in the tree line or not. Besides no matter if it were bright as day Karnin would not let Torli wander around alone not with his head as screwed up as this latest bit of childish behavior that he is doing now says it is Karnin thinks as he begins to jog, for every time Karnin has caught up with him Torli has just walked faster until it has become a foot race.

"You do know they're watching us...don't you?" Karnin asks as he jogs along on Torli's heels.

"Then stop following me," Torli snaps back at him.

"You're acting like a damn babe Torli."

"What'd you care...I'm not your problem anymore...am I?"

"No...you're not my problem...you never been my 'problem'...you're my cousin...the only blood kin I got and more importantly...you're my friend," Karnin tells him with a great deal of feeling, for he truly means what he has just said.

"I'll always be that...look...I'm not sure how to explain this but...everything's wrong...it's all wrong," Torli says somewhat desperately or so Karnin thinks.

"You want a hit me...I'll give you one free shot?" Karnin suggests with a shrug.

"It won't help," Torli replies with a shake of his head.

"Listen..."

"No for once you listen Karnin...not just nod and say it'll be alright but really listen," Torli stops to rake a hand through his golden brown mop of curls and says, but when he does Karnin does not like the hopelessness that he sees in his eyes.

"Speak then," Karnin carefully replies.

"You a all people know I's depending on us staying together...you must've known how I'd feel if you pledged yourself to Marsle," Torli stares off into the distance and says.

"Yeah... it crossed my mind...but Marsle'd every right to take not only *Onyat* but everything in it...our transports...weapons...everything...where'd that a left us and everyone else who came there to help us?" Karnin asks him.

"Together as we've always planned..." Torli replies somewhat despondently, and when he does Karnin's gut wrenches a bit, for he can no longer hear the man he knows in Torli's voice.

"Yeah...together dangling on a noose or worse...we'd a been outlaws...fair game for bounty hunters...well me and the others...you he wouldn't touch...you he'd a shipped off to stand charges before the other overlords and Boro as well," Karnin tells him, for Torli must understand that what Karnin did was the only way to make everything that they have done to this point legitimate.

"They would've given me Tok's seat...I'm the rightful heir to it..."

"It would a took too long...Tok would a dug in and by the time we got him out *Filon Bora* would a been a pile a rubble," Karnin explains.

"I can't bring *Filon Bora* back from what Tok's done to it without you Karnin...I can't and I won't," Torli replies and then walks off, but Karnin has no intention of letting Torli forget that five years ago he was confident that he could be an overlord without anyone's help, and so Karnin goes after him.

"What's got into you Torli...I know you're nervous about all that's coming...we're all feeling it...but you never run from nothing that I know a?" Karnin softly inquires.

"I don't know...I feel like I'm losing it...I don't sleep...I can barely eat...I think I'm going mad Karnin," Torli tells him, and then with a shake of his head he adds, "In time I'll be as daft as my mother was...crazy just like Galwor...I can feel it...my mind just...slipping away..."

"No...you're just tired..." Karnin tries.

"I'm sick...in the head..."

"Don't talk like that..."

"It's time to talk about it...it's time to face up to it..."

"I said stop it Torli," Karnin grinds out, for something about the way that Torli is talking scares him, but just then *Ofren* makes its appearance, and its eerie light makes Torli appear just as insane as he insists that he is, which unnerves Karnin and drives him to consider desperate measures.

Back in the runner while Karnin and Torli are having their discussion in the middle of the road Han stands alone at the runner's control console watching its monitors and sensor readouts for any sign of trouble. Oh at first he had plenty of company, but then the other men got so involved in filling Boro in

228

on Torli's ever increasing instability that they all sort of drifted away. Han only called them twits in his head and let them go, for he is more than capable of keeping an eye out on his instruments without them. It is therefore Han who first notices the telltale signs that something is wrong with Karnin. As it is Han knows Karnin better than even Boro probably does, and he has learned over the years that one can judge Karnin's mood by the stiffness of his spine, which once the moon rises he can see is about as rigid as he has ever seen it. That does not bode well Han thinks, but he barely gets that thought formed before something happens that he was not expecting at all.

"Ah nuts...crap..." Han suddenly blurts out and then promptly heads for the door.

"What's the matter?" Seasle asks as Han hurries past him.

"Karnin hit him...in the face!" Han tosses over his shoulder as he hops out the door.

"No..." Gorg says to no one in particular.

"Crap..." Seasle mutters as he hops out after Han.

"Gorg you're on the sensors," Cerl orders as he follows Orn out.

"Ah...why's it always got a be me?" Gorg complains.

"Cause your low man that's why...now get them eyes on the sensors," Bro tells him with a point of a finger.

"Keep sharp Gorg...nobody's guarding our backs but you," Boro hears Ahnin quietly tell him and then head for the door.

"He never broke his promise in all these years then?" Boro stops Ahnin to ask, for when Torli first came to him Karnin had promised him that he would never hit him in the face.

"No...this ain't good Boro," Ahnin replies with a serious expression that Boro seldom sees on him.

"No it ain't..." Boro mutters as he limps towards the door.

As it was Boro was expecting Karnin and Torli to get into it over what happened at *Laraqua*, and so he was prepared to hear a few disquieting things about Torli's moods, but he was not prepared for Karnin to lose his cool. Karnin rarely does that. No he is the cold calculating one or so Boro thought at least. Now it appears that he may not be, but then again Torli has always known how to push his buttons. They are dolts the both of them Boro thinks as he accepts Ahnin's help down to the ground. Boro no sooner gets his feet firmly under him when a battle cry rings out, and Ahnin takes off towards the group of men gathered on the road ahead.

"You lousy bastard!" Boro hears Torli shout, and with a sigh and a shake of his head Boro hobbles after him.

When Ahnin reaches the group of men he is just in time to see Torli kick Karnin's legs out from under him sending him sprawling onto his back in the dirt, but before Ahnin can shoulder his way through to intervene as he intends Torli leaps upon Karnin and begins hitting him anywhere that he can land a fist. Ahnin therefore hangs back until he sees how this is going to shake out, for in his opinion when men settle their own disputes it sticks better. Unless one of them has obviously decided to let the other one beat him to death Ahnin adds with a frown as he watches Torli pummel Karnin, for even though Karnin is covering up and blocking he is not fighting back. Torli on the other hand appears to be oblivious to that fact, but that is not surprising since he is completely taken over by his rage or demons or something dark and nasty Ahnin thinks as he nervously fingers the bird's foot talisman in his pocket.

As it stands Ahnin is quite correct about Karnin, for Karnin's plan is to let Torli wear himself out after which he will be more open to logical conversation. Karnin soon discovers that he has miscalculated how much punishment his body can take. Perhaps it is more because he has underestimated how much abuse Torli can dish out. Whatever the cause Karnin finds that it is all that he can do to protect his face, for Torli seems determined to bloody it. That is understandable but damned inconvenient, for protecting his face opens up the rest of his body to Torli's punishing blows. It goes without saying that it is not long before Karnin begins to question the wisdom of allowing Torli free reign. Actually Karnin regretted setting him off as soon as he did it, for he knew that Torli would see it as yet another dishonorable betrayal, but he was desperate to bring Torli back from whatever dark place he had gone. Guilt over having done that flees before the pain of several repetitive blows to his left kidney, and it is not long after that the two are rolling around on the ground in earnest like two errant boys scrapping over the last piece of pie.

"No...let them fight it out," Boro commands when Ahnin makes to intervene.

"Torli'll kill him Boro," Cerl worriedly says, for Torli is in a rage like he has never seen before.

"Ha...good one," Seasle replies with a laugh, for even though Karnin does not have Torli's finesse he is a crafty streetwise fighter with more tricks than Torli even knows, and so Seasle sends Cerl a cocky smirk and says, "I'll give you two to one that Torli can't kill him."

"You're on," Cerl points a finger at him and says.

"Let me get this straight...you two're actually gonna bet on whether or not our commander kills our general?" Han grumbles out.

"Does seem a bit wrong somehow," Cerl admits.

"Okay two to one that Torli gives in first," Seasle renegotiates.

"Done," Cerl tells him.

"I'll take a piece a that," Han interjects, and when the men who are not involved in the bet shake their heads in disgust Han indignantly tells them, "Hey Karnin was gonna toss me off that damn marsh crawler into the swamp for no good reason."

"You're not gonna get a piece a the action Ahnin?" Boro asks him as he watches Karnin flip Torli off him with a foot to the chest.

"I never wager...bad juju..." Ahnin absently replies.

"Just as well...they're both gonna lose in the end," Boro tells him, but Boro is actually not as certain about that as he would like Ahnin to believe. As it stands Torli and Karnin's collective fathers were the epitome of twins, and identical right down to their hot-headed dispositions and inability to accept defeat with any kind of grace.

"Damn it all you've blinded me Karnin," Torli suddenly gasps out as his swelling eyes finally take away the last sliver of his sight and as he staggers back and weakly falls onto his backside he adds, "And I think your face broke my damn hand."

"Yeah well I'll be pissing blood tonight thanks to you so I guess we're even then," Karnin complains and then spits a wad of blood onto the ground and adds, "And I might a lost a tooth."

"What now?" Torli asks as he tries to slow the flow of blood from his nose with the heel of his good hand.

"Well I for one'm too damn tired to hit you anymore," Karnin tells him and then winces as he reaches into his pocket and takes out a wad of cloth, which he shoves into Torli's hand and then suggests, "I say we go patch ourselves up and polish off a bottle a Marsle's high class spirits...for medicinal purposes."

"Will it stop my face from hurting?" Torli asks in a nasal voice.

"Two or three swigs and you won't even know you got a face," Karnin says as he struggles to get to his feet.

"Let's go then," Torli replies, but when Karnin reaches down to grasp his arm Torli angrily bats it away and then struggles to his feet.

As Karnin watches Torli stagger away it suddenly occurs to him that Torli is about as stubborn and pigheaded as any man could possibly be. Well he supposes except for himself, but even so he could learn to accept help a bit more graciously Karnin thinks as Torli staggers and then wanders off in the wrong direction. With a sigh Karnin decides to just let him go, for he sees that Han is even now using his hand held monitor to check the runner's sensor display, and so if anyone or thing is about Han will see it. Besides Torli is not likely to get very far since he is headed for a big tree. That realization sends a wave of déjà vu down Karnin's spine, for this has happened before a long time ago. As one might expect Karnin then wonders if it will end the same and a few seconds later when Torli walks right into the nearest tree he has his answer. The collision sends Torli sidestepping off balance, but he manages to stay on his feet. Soon he is underway again right on course for another tree, but this time he goes down, and when he cannot seem to get back Karnin calls it.

"You okay?" Karnin asks after he limps on over.

"This damn...cramping...damn it all..." Torli angrily clips out between his clenched teeth as he rubs his lower back.

"Come on...let's go get that bottle...and let Ahnin rub it out for you," Karnin tells him and then hauls him to his feet.

As they hobble towards the runner Karnin quickly schools the worry from his face, for the men have already gotten enough to think about today without adding to it, and so he will let them think that Torli is just a bit beat up for now. Apparently it works, for when they get within earshot of the other men Seasle loudly compares Torli's swollen face to that of a bloated carcass that they had all seen lying along the road on the way to *Laraqua*. As one might expect of him Seasle then tosses in a suggestion that Torli get inside before the flesh eating bugs move in, but since Torli is temporarily blind not deaf he hones in on Seasle voice and delivers an elbow to his ribs in passing. The men of course jibe Seasle all the way back to the vehicle, but despite that Boro thinks that their collective faces are anything but amused, which comes as no great surprise really. After all they have just watched the two men who they are preparing to entrust their very lives to try to kill each other. Not a spectacular way to instill confidence Boro thinks as Ahnin and Cerl help him back inside.

Soon they are underway once more and as the vehicle clips along no one says much of anything for quite some time although not because of Karnin and Torli's little spat necessarily they are used to that. No this silence is caused by the reason behind this particular argument, for each man knows that he will have a decision to make at some point, and none of them really wants to make it. They are worldly enough young men to know that if Karnin has pledged his fealty to Marsle then they will be doing the same if they stay with him. Of course that is only if they choose not to stay with Torli instead, for that option is open to them as well. All in all it is a grim realization, for choosing Karnin over Torli or Torli over Karnin seems like an impossible choice to make. It is also downright unfair to have to, for until this very moment none of them ever imagined having to choose between them at all.

Therefore when Karnin stops and plunks a bottle of spirits on the table in front of where the men have congregated they are not sorry at all to see it, for many a good idea has been spawned at the height of a good drunk; or so most men will say especially ones as young as they are. As is the usual case the spirits soon do their job, and with their tongues thus uninhibited it is only a matter of time before egos clash and a rather heated discussion erupts concerning the merits of pledging to Karnin who has *Onyat* and all its lands and is aligned with a powerful overlord versus Torli who will soon have *Filon Bora* and several other fortresses and actually be a powerful overlord. As it turns out though one man amongst them is totally unconcerned about having to make a choice, for he already has, and he has chosen not to choose at all.

"Ah you're daft..." Cerl insists when Ahnin unveils his plan, which he has decided to call the 'neutral principle'.

"No law says I got a pledge to anyone," Ahnin returns, and then he adds, "I'm gonna be a free agent...whichever one needs me most at the time's gonna get me."

"More likely they'll flip for who gets stuck with you," Seasle tosses at him.

"Am not," Ahnin settles his rather unusual parti-colored eyes on him and suddenly comes out with.

"Am not what?" Seasle asks.

"Gonna join the *Filcet* arse!" Ahnin hotly says, and then he jumps to his feet and points a finger in Seasle's face and warns, "Don't ever say that again!"

"What's he talking about?" Gorg asks in confusion, but when he notices the somewhat disturbed frown on Seasle's face he points a finger at him and says, "He did it again didn't he?"

"No..." Seasle defensively replies.

"Your cage's too easy to rattle...you know he's just guessing don't you?" Cerl asks with a snort.

"Yeah well it creeps me out just about's much as that dead eye a yours does," Seasle replies with a shudder.

"The foot sees all..." Ahnin suddenly whispers from the darkness.

"Knock it off Ahnin!" Seasle angrily demands over Ahnin's amused laughter.

"Alright...quit scaring the children Ahnin!" Karnin calls out, and then he replies to the question that he sees in Boro's eyes by saying, "He's uncanny good at reading people...apparently Seasle's an open book."

"I see," Boro replies, but Karnin does not miss the way that his eyes stray to Ahnin before he asks, "Now where were we?"

"You were saying my father was first to come out...so...my father got the overlord's daughter...damn...that don't seem fair," Torli replies with a nasal slur.

"I'm afraid that's the way it works," Boro replies.

"Damn," Torli says, and then he hands the bottle to Karnin and says, "Sorry 'bout that."

"They couldn't both come out at the same time," Karnin points out with a shrug as he takes a sip from the bottle, and after he wipes his mouth on the back of his hand he asks, "How's your face?"

"What face?" Torli replies with a lopsided smile, and then he says, "You know I'm thinking that Marsle's a very clever man who's not likely to make poor decisions...so why'd you think he gave Karnin all that land...I mean I'd imagine that his other vassals're gonna feel a bit slighted that he accepted a land man as a vassal and then made him the largest land holder amongst them?"

"Ah well none a Marsle's vassals'd want dry land...why do you think it was vacant?" Boro suggests as he shifts into a more comfortable position in his seat and then he adds, "The lands he gave to Karnin also border what's soon gonna be yours...which isn't a coincidence you know."

"He took a big risk doing that...I think I must be missing something," Torli states, and then he settles his swollen eyes suspiciously on his uncle and says, "Somehow Marsle didn't come across as the type to risk much for little."

"You got that right...he's a crafty old bird that one," Han tosses in.

"I'm assuming those big ears a yours heard something while we were there," Karnin inquires.

"Well it seems that lord Corlean were away from his wife for a long enough time for her to grow a babe...rumor's that Marsle sent him south to try an patch up some old feud with the southern marsh folk...but he come back with noithin'," Han says and then he glances back at Karnin and adds, "That trip must a been pretty important 'cause he nearly missed the birthing...which's a real big deal to them."

"What's her name...the one who told you all that?" Cerl asks, for Han's harmless nicey-nice appearance has always had a way of loosening tongues; female tongues.

"I'll bet she had big breasts and a tight little..."

"Hey...watch it...Lienn's a nice girl...there weren't no tight anything going on," Han indignantly says, and then he tells them with a sigh, "But she was real nice ta look at in a weird kind a way her being all shiny and pale an all."

"None a that sounds like it's got anything to do with Marsle Han," Bro notes.

"I'm getting there," Han retorts.

"Get there soon," Karnin leans back in his seat and says.

"Well...seems that lord Corlean wasn't the only house guest that southern marsh overlord'd invited... Lienn said that she 'accidently' overheard him tell the overlord that someone named Dor's there...says t weren't too happy 'bout that 'cause he called the southern marsh lord a foul name that Lienn wouldn't repeat."

"He didn't tell me about Dor being there," Boro knits his brows and thoughtfully says.

When Karnin hears Dor's name he recalls the conversation that he had had with Bimian and Goberan concerning Torli's origins, but he keeps silent on it. Now is definitely not the time to give anyone a reason to question Torli's paternity. Besides, in Karnin's opinion Goberan was only trying to gauge his commitment to Torli by seeing how easily he could seed doubt into his head. Needless to say he failed miserably there although he he did make Karnin question the depth of Bimian's involvement in all this. Karnin therefore decides to open up the topic of Dor a bit just to see how Boro reacts, for at this point Karnin has no idea how far Boro is in when it comes to arranging things.

"According to Marsle's map...Dor's lands border the southern marsh overlord Sertten's fringe lands," Karnin points out as he takes another sip from his glass.

"Yeah and Torli's border Dor's," Boro says.

"And now mine border Torli's," Karnin says with a wave of his hand.

"It seems Marsle's either built a bridge to strike from or a buffer zone to hide behind," Torli concludes, and Karnin is rather pleased to see that all the pain they both suffered came to some good, for he did not even try to correct the idea that Galwor's lands belong to him.

"Perhaps," Boro replies and then tosses a sealed specimen bag onto the table and asks, "So which one a you does this belong to?"

"Not me," Karnin replies as he picks it up and examines the contents through the clear bag and then he tosses it to Cerl and says, "But I bet I know whose it is."

"Hey I's wondering where that got to," Gorg says, and then he snatches the bag from Cerl and adds, "I thought it was long gone...where'd you find it Boro?"

"Calphin gave it to me and asked me if I knew who its owner was," Boro replies as he shoots him an impatient glance, for apparently Gorg puts a lot of stock in his appearance so much so that it makes Boro wonder just where his propensities lie.

"Wait a minute...how'd he get it?" Seasle cocks his head and asks.

"That damn fish man's been in our barracks that's how," Han angrily replies as Karnin and Torli exchange a worried frown.

"Right under your stupid noses...says Orn snores so loud that as long's he saved him for last he could've slit all your throats and none a you would've heard the other one go down," Boro replies.

"Yeah but how'd he git at us in the first place?" Orn asks a bit spooked that some fish man was watching him while he was sleeping.

"I'm wondering if any a you noticed all the standing water holes in Marsle's fortress?" Boro asks.

"There're hundreds a them...I assumed they're there to keep the humidity level up," Karnin replies.

"True in part...but they're used for other things as well...the most important a which's as bolt holes in case the fortress's breached," Boro informs him, and then he explains, "Each person within *Laraqua's* got several assigned bolt holes...if the command's given to evacuate that person'll go to whichever one a his or her holes they've been told to use and go head first into it...he or she'd then swim through the connected tunnel and come up a mile or so away...it's actually quite ingenious really...even if the attackers know a the bolt holes...which they do since all marsh fortresses use them...they've no way a knowing which set a holes Marsle's people've decided to use...makes the odds a escaping a lot better."

"The water supply," Torli concludes with a disbelieving shake of his head.

"But he would a had to hold his breath for thirty minutes or more..."

"That'd be nothing to him Seasle...some marsh folk can go without filling their lungs for hours," Boro explains.

"Damn..." Cerl mutters.

"But why go to all that trouble to take a hair brush...I mean it's an awfully good brush and all but...?" Gorg dubiously asks.

"For the same reason that he took the rest a this stuff," Boro replies and then tosses several more bags containing various personal items onto the table.

"Wait a minute those're mine," Karnin says as he tentatively claims one of the bags.

"Calphin's rather good...this's my shirt...the one I's wearing when Bro accidently cut me on the practice field," Torli says as he picks up another bag with a rather dirty off white shirt inside, and after he holds it up to peer through the hole left behind when someone cut out a piece of the bloody section he settles his eyes directly on Boro and suspiciously asks, "So what exactly're they looking for?"

"Or is it who?" Karnin cocks his head at Boro and says.

"Yeah well they were hesitant to tell me that...and since I'd pushed Marsle as far as I dared already I let it go," Boro tells him, and then he adds, "A course it's pretty obvious that they were doing genetic tests a some kind."

"I think they might a been looking for Dor's genes," Karnin says, and then he tells them about the conversation he had with Goberan on Bimian's crawler.

"Yeah I remember that," Boro admits, and then he explains, "I was fostered out in exchange for Goberan and didn't come back to Obron's keep until he fell ill and my sister sent for me...Dor'd been recalled home by then."

"Alright then let me get this straight...this Calphin took the risk a getting caught out on dry land to steal samples from us all so that they could see if any a us were one a Dor's bastards?" Gorg asks.

"That'd be a logical explanation," Boro states.

"Rather convenient for overlord Marsle to get Dor's love child under his control," Cerl cocks his head at Gorg and suggests.

"It would since Dor's made a pact with the only people out there that'd really threaten him," Torli agrees as he also glances over at Gorg.

"Yeah other marsh folk," Bro adds, and then he too turns his eyes to Gorg.

"Why're you all looking at me like that?" Gorg asks and then he says in surprise, "Me!?"

"Yeah you Gorg," Boro agrees, and then he tells him, "But you're not Dor's...you're not Dor's at all."

"If not Dor's then who else's..." Karnin begins but suddenly pauses and swivels in his seat to scan Gorg's face before turning back to Boro and asking, "Is that even possible?"

"A course it's possible...we all crawled out a the same hole after all," Boro replies.

"The *Morian*..." Torli absently comments.

"But he looks so...normal," Karnin gets up and crosses to where Gorg sits and says.

"I talked to that healer a theirs...the old woman...she and Calphin's sister did the testing..."

"She's got the most enormous blue eyes you ever did see," Han absently inserts.

"Yeah like you were appreciating her eyes," Ahnin mocks with a snort.

"Stow that the both a you," Boro orders, and then continues, "The old woman was very reluctant to even talk about it...all she'd say's that such'd happened in the past during the warring times...but the results're always very unpredictable as to what you'd get...when Calphin handed me that hairbrush all he'd say's that he'd consider it a personal favor if I'd keep an eye on its owner's safety until such time as he'd a chance to speak to his family."

"Save me..." Cerl mumbles with wide eyes as Seasle whistles softly.

"You're all nuts!" Gorg loudly announces, and then he points a finger at Boro and says, "He's making a damn joke...and it's not funny at all Boro!"

"Damn Gorg you're part fish man!" Seasle teases.

"Don't say that!" Gorg demands.

"Gorg..." Boro begins but Gorg only tosses the hairbrush onto the table and angrily storms off to the rear of the vehicle.

"Let him alone for a time," Karnin requests when Ahnin makes to go after him.

"Damn...what a shock eh," Bro says, and then he asks somewhat hesitantly, "So... he got any...marsh folk...qualities at all?"

"You tell me," Boro replies, and then adds, "You all grew up together...ever noticed anything different about him?"

"Well...he's a bit taller and slighter in the hips than most men," Seasle says, and then he adds, "But Bro and Orn aren't exactly put together like most men either."

"What 'bout all that washin' up he does... he sure likes water a lot..." Orn offers in a low voice.

"I'm just clean you whoreson!" Gorg shouts, and then he adds, "You might try a bit more a that you smelly bastard!"

"Ah above average hearing," Boro notes, and then he pointedly adds, "Marsh folk 'ave a great advantage over land folk when it comes to hearing and sight."

"Gorg hit that guard a Tok's with a rock from the end a the street that time...you remember...the one that was trying to beat out what little brains Merl had?" Seasle points out.

"Yeah...it was damn near dark too," Han adds.

"Okay so I hear and see better than the rest a you...so what...that doesn't make me a marsh man's son," Gorg slowly walks forward and says, and although he still seems resistant to the idea Boro notes that the possibility of being part marsh folk does not bother him nearly as much as losing his sense of belonging does.

"Tests for paternity're seldom wrong these days Gorg...especially when they're done in the marshes," Boro carefully says, and then he adds, "It's not the end a the world you know...I for one could've done with a bit a natural resistance to the rot."

239

"I'd just be happy knowing who my father was...even if he turned out to be a marsh man," Ahnin adds.

"Yeah anyway..." Cerl seconds.

"You gots yourself a whole family now Gorg...you lucky dog you," Orn tells him.

"You mean you lucky water dog you," Seasle comes back with.

"Hey somebody get a bucket so we can see how long he can hold his breath!" Ahnin suggests.

"Yeah I know who's going down the damn crap hole next time it gets clogged!" Bro tells them.

"Hey that's going too far," Gorg tells him with a disgusted grimace.

As the men jibe at Gorg's new found paternity it becomes obvious to Boro that they have no intention of looking down their noses at him, but Boro had doubted that they would. As Ahnin had said not too many of them even know who their fathers were. In truth Karnin's gang has always been very generous as far as taking people as they come, for they all were on the receiving end of someone's prejudiced mindset at one time or the other and that made them determined never to do such to any other human being. Well except for those who had earned their contempt Boro adds, but then a frown settles onto his face, for there is one thing that Nao-Nao told him that he still has to address, and it is not something that Boro is very eager to do. Regrettably the time has come for it.

"There's one more thing," Boro softly says, and after a short pause he adds, "One a you's sick."

"How sick?" Karnin quickly asks.

"Very," Boro replies, and then he says, "If left untreated he'll not live more than a few more years...and those'll not be pleasant ones."

"Who?" Karnin asks as the room suddenly falls silent.

"The condition's not genetic...nor's it caused by a bacteria or virus...it's caused by getting low dosed with poison over a period a years or a few high doses given within a few months if you don't care that someone notices...it works at the microcellular level and so leaves a rather distinct signature marker in the gene strand that comes out like a red flag during genetic testing," Boro says.

"Boro fer the love a all that's livin'...just say who!" Orn insists as Ahnin comes to stand next to Torli.

"Before I do know that treatment'll render the poison inert and so no further damage'll be done...but treatment takes several months and if it's halted before the full course the poison'll once again begin to do its work," he informs them as he sends Ahnin a curious look, for it is almost as if he already knows, which sets Boro's alarm bells to ringing.

"Okay we got that...who Boro?" Karnin demands.

"Well..." Boro begins as he sets two bottles containing a light blue liquid on the table in front of him, and then with an ironic chuckle he points to one of them and says, "This one's mine...and this one's unfortunately for you...Torli."

When Boro slides the vile across the table to him Torli merely sits there staring at it unmoving, and an uncomfortable silence falls in the vehicle, for as one might expect no one knows quite what to say. Ahnin as usual seems to know what is needed to break the spell, for when he puts a comforting hand on Torli's shoulder it seems to bolster him up enough to reach down and pick the vile up. As Torli turns the vile over in his hand the other men hold their peace, for they are not certain how he will react to such news as this. No not a man there except Boro perhaps has any idea how he would feel after being told such a thing, and so no one even remotely knows what to say to him now.

"There's more," Boro meets Torli's eyes across the table and says.

"Yeah a course there's more...you I can understand uncle but I've been out a Tok's reach for a long time now...or so I thought," Torli replies in a monotone voice.

"Wait a minute...you think one a us's giving it to you!" Seasle shoots to his feet and angrily says.

"Not someone here in this vehicle...I'd trust all a you with my life," Torli replies, but then he notes the way that his uncle is eying Ahnin, and so he adds, "All a them uncle."

"Could it just be residuals from long ago?" Karnin asks as his mind quickly tries to recall the names and faces of the other men in his army, for despite Boro's suspicions Karnin's gut tells him that Ahnin is not their poisoner even though his unusual skill set supports it.

"It could be...but it isn't...the tests say Torli and I've both been dosed within the last year," Boro tells him.

"Why didn't you tell me something was as wrong as that?!" Karnin angrily asks Torli.

"Yeah well I didn't know," Torli replies, and then he sends Boro a worried frown and asks, "So how sick're you uncle?"

"Not nearly as sick as you...not from the poison at any rate...I knew Tok'd been wanting me dead for a long time...so I rarely ate or drank anything I didn't 'ave control over," he replies.

"You absolutely certain that you got dosed while you were at Galwor's keep then Boro," Cerl quietly asks.

"Yeah...without question."

"Tell me Boro what's this poison do exactly?" Torli asks.

"It's a designer poison...disrupts the brain...but then Ahnin here can tell you all about it if I recall..." Boro states, for he remembers Ahnin's penchant for such things.

"Probably could if I'd a designed it," Ahnin replies as he takes the vial from Torli's hand and holds it up to the light, and then he hands it back to him and sends Boro a heated stare as he says, "Which I didn't."

"Yeah well...keep your scary looks for someone who still gets scared boy...I'm beyond that these days," Boro retorts, and then he turns his attention back to Torli and tells him, "It's rather cleverly done...in the beginning its small things...fleeting pain...muscle spasms...stuff a man tends to explain away...eventually though the brain becomes involved...and it's just a matter a time before the mind falls to it then...but neither a us's there yet Torli."

"My mother wasn't so lucky."

"No she wasn't Torli...nor was Galwor and who knows who else fell to it as well through the years," Boro tells him.

"So...Tok's got one a his own amongst us then," Torli absently says as he inspects the vile again.

"It appears that way," Boro tells him as his eyes wonder over to where Ahnin now sits sulking.

"We need a plan to ferret him out," Gorg narrows his eyes and says, and the others all nod and grunt their agreement.

"What we need to do's nothing," Torli closes his fist on the vile and says.

"Ah but you see...somebody's tryin' to kill ya," Orn says as though talking to a simpleton.

"Yeah Orn I get it...and if any a you think to treat me like some sick old lady I'll bust your balls," Torli warns, and then he explains, "But the best way to catch this person's to pretend we don't know what he's doing."

"Bait him in..." Ahnin's voice quietly says.

"Who?" Orn asks.

"You been stealing Torli's lunch or something?" Seasle asks.

"Did not," Orn indignantly replies.

"He's just naturally stupid," Gorg offers.

"Yeah...hey wait a minute fish breath..." Orn indignantly complains.

"Enough all a you!" Karnin stands and angrily shouts, and then he throws at them, "This's not a joke..."

"Karnin..." Torli says.

"So if you can't say something helpful..."

"Karnin..." Torli calmly says again a bit louder than before.

"Then just shut your damn..."

"Karnin!"

"What!"

"Perhaps our fathers weren't crazy after all," Torli tells him with a shrug.

"That's what you're gonna say?" Karnin asks in disbelief, and then he leans towards Torli and asks, "That's what you're worrying about...not oh...say...whether or not you're gonna survive the cure perhaps?"

"Oh I'm gonna survive it," Torli tells him and then he snatches the vial and the bottle of spirits off the table and says, "I got a date...with Tok...and I'm damn well gonna keep it now."

With that Torli walks over and moodily plunks down in a seat near Ahnin and after taking a swig from the bottle he turns to Ahnin and softly says something to which Ahnin nods. Torli then hands him the bottle of spirits and reclines back in his seat and closes his eyes. A few seconds later his even breathing tells them that he has fallen asleep, which is probably the first time that any of them has seen Torli go out that easily in a very long time. Whether or not that is a good sign none of them are willing to even hazard a guess. Karnin figures that even though the truth was not an easy thing to hear it still gave Torli peace of mind to finally know what was happening. Knowing is half the battle after all. The other half will come in the next however many days.

"How long's it gonna be before he'll be able to move south?" Karnin turns back to Boro to ask, but when he does he notes that Boro is once again studying Ahnin, and so he quietly adds, "I'd trust him with my life Boro."

"Would you trust him with Torli's?" Boro counters with.

"Yeah..." is all Karnin replies, for to offer explanations would make Boro think that he might have doubts about him, and so he changes the subject with, "So...how long?"

"In a couple months so long's his treatments aren't interrupted...the curative works pretty fast," Boro replies, and then he adds, "But unless he's gonna let one a you lead his men it's gonna be a lot longer before he's back in fighting form."

"How long's 'a lot longer'?" Karnin asks somewhat impatiently.

"A year...at least," Boro replies.

When Karnin hears Boro's reply he slumps back in his seat in frustration, for even though Torli has already had his hopes for a trial by combat dashed by Marsle he will never sit in a transport while his men fight. That is simply not in his nature to do. They will therefore have to wait for him to get his strength back before they go south. It will mean standing down the men who are even now packing up to move, but Torli is what this is all about, and so stand down they will. Who knows maybe when nothing comes at him for that long a period of time Tok will think that no one is coming at all especially when he hears that Karnin has pledged himself to Marsle? With a resigned sigh Karnin leans his head back against the seat and closes his eyes, for there is only one choice here. As he sits there what his mother used to say when things seemed to have gone awry suddenly pops into his head, for she always insisted that bad things are often a gift in disguise, and with the sincere hope that she is right Karnin opens his eyes and gives Boro a resigned nod of agreement.

Chapter Twelve

As the men move through the darkness their black leather suits are difficult to distinguish, for the night is dark and their movements are designed to blend in with the slight breeze that is blowing across *Filon Bora's* overgrown buffer zone. Luckily for Karnin and his team Tok has gotten very careless indeed, for he has allowed his men to lazily neglect the clear cut areas intended to make it possible to spot anyone trying to sneak into the inner keep. As a result the grass between the perimeter wall and the inner keep is thigh high and easy enough to traverse without being seen on a dark windy night like tonight. He will have to remember to thank Tok for that when he sees him Karnin thinks as he uses the cover of the next gust of wind to crawl a bit further through the grass on his belly. Working in this manner it is not long before Karnin and his team slither their way close enough to the inner keep to get eyes on the next goal, which at the moment is the rear service door.

As Karnin lies there in the grass studying the door through his night vision eyepiece he begins to think that they might actually pull this off without a single hiccup, for just as they found in the gate house the men who should be on guard duty here are apparently busy elsewhere. Most likely abed with their women just like the others were Karnin thinks as he waves his team on. One by one the men rise up and silently duck into the cover of the shadows at the base of the inner keep, and when no alarm goes up Karnin wonders if perhaps this is just a bit too easy. Ahnin is apparently thinking the same thing, for after several minutes pass without sighting a guard he frowns and pulls out his bird's foot talisman to give it a kiss. No one scoffs at him like they usually do though, for tonight every man here has done some ritual or put a whatnot or the other in his pocket for luck. Even Karnin has his mother's lucky pendant tucked away in his breast pocket.

To this point their charms seem to be working rather well, for Torli's field buster had opened a hole in the fortress's perimeter field just as they had hoped that it would, and apparently they came through the field and slammed the door quickly enough to evade detection. That or the watch guard was asleep and missed it. Whatever the reason they made it across the outer buffer zone to *Filon Bora's* perimeter wall with no trouble at all. Being that Ahnin is their best freehand climber he was logically the one to go up the wall and secure a line for the rest of them. Since perimeter walls actually require little to no maintenance *Filon Bora's* were still as smooth and slippery as the day that they were constructed. Even so with the aid of his sticky gloves and shoes Ahnin scaled the one in front of them in good time. Everyone else went up with the aid of the rope that Ahnin cast down even Bro whose large size makes climbing a bit of a chore. There was a tense moment when Bro was nearing the top and a man happened along, but Ahnin took care of him before he could raise the alarm.

Once everyone was up Bro tossed the unconscious man over his shoulder and they moved on to the gatehouse where they found the guards just as Boro had told them they would at this time of night, more specifically drunk and passed out next to whatever woman they had taken last. Securing them had therefore been quite easy. Actually their women put up more of a fight than they did. Well until one of them recognized Karnin and called a halt to the kicking and scratching. After a hard look Karnin realized that the woman was Nilly who had worked in his mother's house of pleasure back in the day. That came as a bit of a surprise since Nilly was well beyond the age when a women in her profession retire from working the sheets. Actually nearly every woman there was in that age group. As one might expect Karnin asked her if they were independent women, for that would explain why they were still servicing customers. Nilly only smiled and said that they all worked for madam Bitha in the village.

At first Karnin did not think very highly of the madam for making Nilly service the guards at her age, and knowing a lot about the business he felt entitled to say as much. In reply Nilly only shook her head and said that she and the other ladies had volunteered to come. It seems that the madam was told that if she

246

did not provide entertainment for the guards she would find herself and her girls living in the streets. Everything made more sense then, for the older women would know all the little tricks of the trade to keep their selves safe. Nilly then asked the inevitable question and after a brief discussion they decided to tell her why they were here. To say that they were overjoyed to hear that Tok was finally going to be charged for all the crimes that he has committed through the years is an understatement. It was obvious that they hated Tok. One of the ladies even went as far as stating that she would not lift a finger to save Tok's prick were it the last one on earth, which is a pretty big statement for a woman to make whose livelihood depends on pricks.

So it is that they left the ladies there in the guardhouse with Bro whose job it is to keep the gate under his control. Karnin did extract a promise from the ladies before they headed out that they would let Bro do his job, for it was obvious that they were wondering about Bro more specifically if things in the down low matched his rather larger than average stature. After getting them to agree to wait until after this whole mess was done to find out, which was Bro's idea actually they left Bro to man the gate and the women to watch the guards who were stuffed unconscious into a closet trussed up and gagged. Well to lounge about and eat up the guards' provisions at any rate, for the men are heavily drugged and so will not need tending to for a long time. Still someone might come looking for them and who would know better how to make a man forget his duty than Nilly and her friends?

So now they are standing near the next hurdle waiting for the time to tick by, and as Karnin waits he dares to hope that they will be able to take Tok tonight while he sleeps. Karnin is not the only man thinking that though. What more fitting way for Tok to learn that his cousin Torli did not fall to his poison than having it told to him when he is rousted from the overlord's bed that he killed his way into? However as Karnin impatiently checks his timekeeper yet again that hiccup that they had all been waiting for shows up in the form of a lone man who staggers over and plops his arse onto a stool near the door. As Karnin studies him he thinks that the man seems familiar somehow, and after a few seconds of pondering he suddenly realizes why. He therefore taps Seasle and signs to him the man's identity, and when he does Seasle grins and sends it on to Cerl who then signs it to Ahnin. Needless to say Ahnin immediately whips foot out of his pocket and mouths some sort of prayer to it, which the other men all agree with doing, for the way Drunk Dim drank he should have been dead a long time ago, but not only is he still kicking he is on the rear door tonight. Surely that is just too much to be coincidence?

After a few seconds of stunned staring Karnin decides it best to cut this trip down memory lane short before someone gets spooked, and so he keys Ahnin's headset to get his attention. When Ahnin turns his way Karnin gives him the signal to take old Dim out, which does not make Ahnin happy, for Drunk Dim is a legend after all. Before anyone can object though Karnin holds up his wrists to tell Ahnin to just subdue him. After all the man is not much of a threat he is drunk and nodding on the stool. Besides they owe him a few favors, for many a night had they stole something that he was supposed to be guarding right out from under his drunken nose. Apparently nothing has changed there Karnin thinks, for when Ahnin creeps over and grabs him from behind old Drunk Dim simply passes out cold. Ahnin therefore simply tosses him over his shoulder, rights the toppled stool, and then hauls him back to the other men who all chip in to truss him up. The men then give Dim an injector to keep him out, and after they stuff a gag into his mouth they stash him in the tall grass.

By the time they have finished with Drunk Dim the moment to move is upon them, and so Karnin signals Seasle and Cerl to the door with three headset clicks. As the two men slide along the wall Cerl readies one of his throwing spikes, for his job is to protect Seasle's back while he gets the door open, which is a job that a throwing spike will accomplish quite well so long as you do not miss, which Cerl never does. Cerl soon finds that his throwing skills may be put to the test though, for just as Seasle is stepping to the side to set off the charge that will pop the door's mechanism it suddenly slides open catching him out with very few options other than to flatten his body against the wall and hope that whoever is coming out does not spot him. Then there is the banger that he just set dangling there for any idiot to see Seasle adds as his hand slips round the hilt of his fighting knife.

From his hiding spot in the shadows Cerl slowly raises the throwing spike positioning it in such a way so as to be ready just in case he has to toss it, for Seasle is totally exposed by the light coming from the open door. Even as he does he steels himself to wait until he is absolutely certain that blood must be spilt, for making that kind of a mess is the very last thing that he wants to do. Nothing says 'sound the alarm' better than a pool of blood. Then again no one might think a thing of it in this damn place Cerl reasons as he waits to see if Seasle will be able to dispatch the man without his help. Once again though the fates take-eth and then they give-eth, for even though someone does come out it is not a group of men coming out to get some night air while they toss down a bottle or play a barter game, but rather one lone man in a disheveled uniform.

As the man shuffles out Karnin thinks that he surely has to be the worst guardsman on Tok's payroll, for he does not even bother to check the area around him, which is an action that even children do automatically. This particular man simply walks on out and with a loud belch he just stands there scratching his balls and staring out towards the outer barracks. As Karnin and the other men watch him they begin to wonder if he is even more incompetent than old Drunk Dim if such a thing is even possible. Then again it could just be that his mind is preoccupied with other more urgent matters, for after giving his balls one last scratch he shuffles a few feet away from the door and hurriedly undoes his pants totally unaware that death lurks only few feet behind him. So it is that as the man sighs in relief as men are wont to do when pissing Seasle quickly closes the distance between them and cleanly breaks his neck with a quick twist of his head.

As the man's body falls to the ground Seasle quickly shoves one of his own throwing spikes into the door's track to keep it from closing when its open sequence times out, and while he does that Cerl comes forward and drags the body out of sight. Tidying up being done Seasle then steps over and takes his banger back off the door's control panel, for he would have someone find it. Besides a man can never have too many bangers Seasle adds as he stuffs the explosive into one of his suit's pockets. After peeking inside Cerl motions the all-clear to the others, and he and Seasle then slip inside and take up guard positions near the door to cover Karnin and Ahnin. As Karnin steps through the door he takes the opportunity to glance up towards the fourth row of windows on the top floor, and when he does he silently curses, for there is a light shining in Tok's quarters.

Unfortunately if Tok is still awake taking him will be more difficult, but more importantly it will take all the fun right out of it if he is Karnin thinks with a frown as he slips into the inner keep and hunkers down next to Ahnin. Hopefully Tok just passed out with the light on or perhaps he is afraid of the dark nowadays. After all the rumors coming from *Filon Bora* recently say that Tok has gotten rather paranoid in the past year and a half, which is kind of ironic since Tok had taken a lot of pleasure in feeding Galwor's fears and phobias. Fortunately for Karnin and his men Tok did not beef up his security the way most men who see assassins around every corner would do. Well not outside the inner keep at least. No Tok being the cheap, selfish bastard that he is only increased the safety of the inner keep where his illustrious arse lived Karnin thinks as he reaches down to retrieve Seasle's spike and allow the door to close.

The men sit still then listening for a few seconds, and when Karnin is satisfied that the way is clear he motions his team forward. They quickly move down the corridor then and make their way through the first floor of the inner keep with the precision of a well-practiced brigade silently dropping any and all of Tok's men they come upon, for Boro had warned them that Tok only kept his most loyal men near him in the inner keep. Well those and the group of mercenaries that he hired to protect him Karnin thinks as he reaches down and rips the company patch off the sleeve of the man laying at his feet. Apparently the rumors were right. Tok had bought himself a few new friends if one could call them that. What he paid them with is the question, for mercenaries do not work for just room and board. Although as unskilled as these particular ones are they might have Karnin thinks. That is unimportant though, for there will be no mercy given to any fighters good or bad here in the inner keep. Leniency will be reserved for men like those in the outer barracks and guardhouse, for they had no choice other than to serve Tok.

At first the overlords balked over that particular portion of Karnin's plan, for they were uncomfortable with simply killing Tok's men in the inner keep without due process, but overlord Devoot's general Teneset encouraged them to allow it. Actually Karnin was rather impressed by lord Teneset, for he pointed out that based upon the information that they were able to glean the majority of the men near Tok are not from *Filon Bora* nor are they from any of the territory's other fortresses either. That leaves only the *Filcet* or the free lancing mercenary types neither of which have any given rights beyond what they have contracted for. All in all it was a very persuasive point, for the 'somebodies' of the world despise assassins of any kind for obvious reasons. No good speech

250

goes unpunished however, and the overlords rewarded Teneset for his by making him their representative at Tok's trial, which Teneset graciously accepted. What else was he to do?

Teneset's job will not begin until *Filon Bora* is taken and secured, which the overlords have left up to Karnin to get done. He therefore puts his mind on what lies ahead rather than what has already gone by, but it goes without saying that is easier to do now that they are confident that they have left no one behind on the first floor to come to Tok's aid. Not that any of them would have Karnin concludes as they creep up the emergency stairway. When they reach the second floor only silence greets them, and so they get to work. By the time that they are climbing the stairs to the third and final level Karnin has decided that Tok has gone completely mad. As it turned out with the exception of two startled cleaning women who they locked away in one of the rooms for safe keeping the entire second floor was deserted. The whole thing has left Karnin and his men shaking their heads in disbelief, for to assume that stacking the ground floor would prevent any infiltration above is a rooky mistake. Even so it is still possible that Tok has stacked the third floor where his apartment is as well, and so as they head up the stairs again he quietly reminds the others to stay focused.

When they reach the third floor while they do not find men crawling everywhere they do find a few men sleeping in one of the rooms at the far end who judging by their uniforms and badging are most likely members of Tok's personal guard. Besides them though the only others on the entire floor are the two proper bodyguards dancing attendance on Tok's door. Unfortunately for them neither one was a light sleeper Karnin thinks as he reaches down and yanks the communications device from the hand of the closest of the two dead men. After a moment's consideration Karnin decides to abandon the hope of taking Tok while he sleeps, for they cannot take the chance that he is awake in there. He would hear them breaking in and call for help. No Karnin thinks that it is time to see just how incompetent Tok really is.

With a rather predatory expression Karnin keys the COM device and after respectfully apologizing for disturbing him he tells Tok that word has just come from the control hub that a messenger from overlord Dor has come knocking at the perimeter field unannounced. As one might expect Tok curses resoundingly and then calls first Karnin and then Dor several foul names, but despite

251

his mood he does tell Karnin to let the man pass. Before Tok can sever the COM Karnin quickly informs him that the watch guard has already done that, and that the messenger is downstairs waiting. When he adds that the man was ordered to deliver his message directly to overlord Tok and no one else Tok sets off on a rant that lasts long enough for Karnin to begin to worry that he had pushed it too far. In the end though, after Tok has run out of foul things to call everyone he tells Karnin to muster out his guard.

Karnin and his men exchange a few disbelieving looks then, for surely no one is that dumb so as to believe that any messenger overlord's or not would be demanding to deliver a message to him of all people in the middle of the damn night. Then again perhaps there is something going on between Dor and Tok that no one knows about just yet. Regardless of the reason why Tok has just agreed to open the door to them it is a gift that Karnin and his men are only too happy to accept. One must take their perks where one finds them after all. Therefore, with a rather lighthearted shrug the men gather up the two dead guards, and after they shove them out of sight of the door they fade back into the shadows to wait for Tok to walk right into their waiting cuffs. A few minutes later Tok's voice blares out over the COM device asking if a man named Bandin has arrived with his escort yet.

"Yeah overlord..." Karnin keys the confiscated COM device and gruffly mumbles out.

"I'm coming out," Tok replies and then promptly hangs up.

"Thanks for the warning," Karnin quietly mutters as they all ready themselves to rush the door when it opens.

So it is that when the door slides open a few seconds later, and Tok lumbers out he is immediately set upon by Ahnin and Cerl who wrestle him back into the room. Seasle then sets about closing the door and rekeying the lock, and while he does so Karnin places the cold metal of his blade against Tok's throat, which immediately makes him rethink continuing to resist. With Tok under the control of Karnin's knife point Ahnin and Cerl disarm him and then cuff and shackle him to his own bed. Well, after chasing the woman that Tok has cuffed to the bedpost from it, for Tok was apparently making ready to strip her and sample her wares when the COM about Dor's messenger came in. It is her lucky night, for she is much too fine for the likes of Tok Karnin thinks as he takes in the way her thick reddish-brown hair cascades round her. Yes quite a nice little package indeed he adds as he watches her

252

scamper back from them, for when she does she shoves her hair back and reveals one of the nicest cleavages that Karnin has seen to date.

Unfortunately she apparently does not think herself fortunate to have Tok's plans interrupted, for she chooses not to heed Karnin's warning to take herself off somewhere. Instead the silly woman grabs a short blade from one of the room's side tables and points it at him. All things told Karnin finds that rather disappointing, for to look as sweet as she does, and still be as perverse as she would have to be to actually want Tok seems like such a waste. Karnin's faith in the fates is quickly restored however, for defending her overlord is not at all what the lady has in mind, and without warning she dives for the bed. As she does she cites her various reasons for wanting to plunge her small blade into Tok's black heart at the top of her lungs all of which seem to revolve around his being the most despicable, stupid and disgusting degenerate in existence. Fortunately for Tok Cerl is able to grab her before she makes good on her threat, but to their amusement the woman immediately tries to poke a finger in one of Cerl's eyes, which since it is his good one earns her a few rather choice words.

A brief struggle ensues in which Cerl gets a few kicks in the shins as well as one of Seasle's infamous chuckles, but to Cerl's credit he keeps his temper in check. After all she obviously did not ask to be here Cerl thinks as he grasps her wrists and tucks them behind her so that he can wrap his arms about hers. This time it is the woman who curses, and when she does a wide grin spreads across Seasle's face, for he always appreciates an imaginative curse when he hears one. Cerl on the other hand is less than pleased to have his parentage slandered the way she is doing, and he therefore takes a peek down the front of her shirt as payment for his bruised shins and pride. She wears herself out rather quickly then, and when she is calm enough to hear him Cerl tells her that a greater justice awaits Tok than to be so quickly dispatched as she would do, which to Karnin's satisfaction manages to both please her and terrify Tok all at the same time.

"Hey you got a spare bottle out there," Karnin keys his headset and calls breaking communications silence to cryptically signal Bro in the gatehouse that they have achieved the first stage.

"Naw only got enough for my shift," Bro's voice acknowledges Karnin's message with the prearranged response.

253

"Thanks for nothin'," Karnin keys his headset and replies, and after he severs the COM he sarcastically asks Tok, "So...how you been Tok?"

"You got no right to come in here like this!" Tok shouts, and then he adds, "You'll never get out a here with your balls still hangin!"

"Ah well that's where you're wrong," Karnin replies as he stalks closer to him, and then he pokes Tok in the chest with the tip of his knife as he says, "It seems that your lackeys down there all suffered a...similar fate to the one this lovely little handful thought to dish up to you...let's go...we'll deal with him later."

"You whoreson...you'll pay for this!" Tok rants as the men file out.

"Feel free to shout all you want," Ahnin tells him as he gestures for the woman to precede him out, for judging by the hateful glances that she is sending Tok's way they cannot leave her here alone with him.

"You're dead ...you hear me woman!" Tok spits out at her, and when he does she stops to call him a filthy bastard, but even though Ahnin reaches back in and pulls her out the door she still manages to pull off a shoe and toss it at Tok's head before the door slides shut on him.

"Who're you?" the woman draws herself up and asks Karnin after Ahnin pulls her over to where the others are waiting.

"Why I'm nobody...stay here with Ahnin and you'll be safe," Karnin replies, and then he turns to Ahnin and says, "Nobody goes in there got it."

"Let Seasle stay...why do I got a do it?" Ahnin calls after him as he strides away.

"He better be alive when I get back Ahnin!" Karnin calls over his shoulder as he disappears down the back stairs.

"Who're you people?" the woman asks when Ahnin turns around.

"Better question's...who're you my pretty?" Ahnin gives her a disarming smile and asks.

"Anjet...my name's Anjet," she absently replies as she watches Cerl and Seasle follow Karnin down, but when Ahnin reaches out to touch her hair she jumps like a startled animal.

"Don't touch me," she tells him, and then points the small dagger at him that in the shuffle they neglected to relieve her of.

"He beat you didn't he?" Ahnin gently asks, for he could see blood peaking through the luxurious fall of her hair, and then he notes that the hand holding the knife is shaking, and so he adds, "I promise you I won't do anything but look at it...come now turn and let me see it."

"I don't need your help...I can take care a myself...just...go away," she replies as she backs away from him, but she soon backs herself right into a chair, and when she glances back to see what she has bumped into she finds the dead eyes of one of Tok's guards staring up at her.

"Now don't go hysterical on me lady...alright?" Ahnin calmly says when he sees her eyes go wide at the sight of the dead guard, for despite her tattered and filthy clothes she has the distinct lilt of the upper crust, which would make it a bit more likely that she has never seen a dead man before.

Ahnin gets a surprise though, for whereas he expects the feisty thing to scream or get a bit panicked when she finds a dead guy at her feet, he does not expect her to suddenly pass out cold. With a curse Ahnin hurries over to her, for she went down rather hard, but as soon as he touches her and feels how warm she is he rolls her over to check her back. What he sees there makes him curse a second time, and with a heated expression on his face he goes back inside Tok's room and breaks his nose with a well placed punch. As he stands over Tok his palms itch to wrap themselves around his damn neck and squeeze, for Tok did more than just bloody the woman's back he ripped it to shreds. Regrettably killing Tok is not an option, and so he tells Tok that the punch was from the lady, and after he stresses how very numbered his days are Ahnin goes back out into the corridor before he decides to throw caution to the wind and cheat the executioner.

As Ahnin returns to the woman's side he tells himself that she is not his problem, and when that does not work he points out that he has a job to do, but of course none of that will make him simply leave her lying here what kind of creep would do that? Ahnin therefore splits the difference and after he checks to make certain that she has no broken bones he pulls her up, and tosses her over his shoulder. He then goes in search of a safe place to stash her until tonight's takeover is complete. She is sick after all, and that combined with the fabulous temper that he glimpsed in Tok's apartment makes her a danger to herself. As a matter of fact Ahnin thinks that if she were not unconscious right now she would be

255

trying to get away from him, and in her condition she would not get far either. No she would only get herself dead, and so he must secure her for her own good he thinks as he quickly carries her off down the corridor.

While Ahnin is searching for a place to lock up his female bundle of trouble forty miles east of *Filon Bora's* village Torli is on the verge of doing the same thing to Gorg before he incites a damn riot. Gorg can be glad that he understands why he is so beside his self Torli thinks as he eyeballs him. Yes any man would be frustrated if after he finally earned a place on Karnin's first assault team he was promptly kicked off of it and reassigned to Torli's ground forces. Sympathy for that evaporated several hours ago, for Gorg did nothing but pace and complain all the way from *Onyat*, and after spending many hours watching him fidget and repack his day pack Torli begins to question the wisdom of thinking that Gorg could make the transition to a foot soldier at all. No foot soldiers need a healthy dose of patience, for fighting men are in it for the long haul, and not quick-in quick-out the way Karnin's first assault team operates. Ground troops are the ones who must make the takeover stick by securing the real estate often a single foot at a time.

"How much time yet?" Gorg paces over and asks for what seems like the hundredth time.

"Soon Gorg," Torli replies from the seat where he is quietly sitting with his eyes closed.

"How can you just sit...I'm all...wound up!"

"You'd best learn a bit a restraint," Boro tells him without opening his eyes, "And a bit a wisdom...a man needs to rest his body and take the time to prepare his mind before a battle."

"Battle?" Gorg asks a tad angrily, and then crosses his arms on his chest and says in a disgruntled tone, "The real battle's already happening and I'm stuck here!"

"Yeah well welcome to the world a being somebody," Torli sarcastically snaps at him, but then he sighs and adds, "I promised your father that you'd not be on the first assault team...it's the only way that he'd agree to let you be here...and without his agreement Marsle wouldn't a let you come at all."

"My new 'father' and I're gonna have a long talk I'll tell you that," Gorg promises, and then he says, "I'm not some snot-nosed boy to be told what to do."

"Ha…you've got a lot to learn about fathers boy," Boro tells him with a snort.

"I liked it better when I was a nobody," Gorg sullenly says and then turns and paces back down the aisle.

"Ah you're breaking my damn heart," one of the other men in the transport grumbles.

"Hey…some a us're trying ta sleep here," another man complains.

"Alright pipe down," Torli softly commands, for keeping his men calm and composed while they wait for the signal to move in is his chief objective at the moment.

"Hey village patrol when ya coming in ta relieve me?'" Bro's voice suddenly squawks from the transport's COM center, and when it does Torli gives his new first man Barndon a nod.

"Ah don't get your balls in a bunch we're coming," Barndon replies.

"Put me on to the other two vehicles," Torli then commands as he stands and turns to face the soldiers that fill his transport.

"Aye sir," Barndon acknowledges, and after he throws a few switches he tells him, "You're on sir."

"Alright listen up men," Torli says to the men sitting in his troop transport, but they are not the only ones who hear him, for his voice suddenly rings out in the other two transports as well, and after a short pause to allow the men to come awake he instructs, "The rules're simple…you'll give quarter to any and all who ask for it in the outer barracks and village…but under no circumstances do you let anyone slip through the noose…each brigade's got its contingency for securing their prisoners…those a you charged with securing the noncombatants will do so with the least amount a force…surprise's our best advantage and so we'll maintain silence until everyone's in position…stick to the plan…your life and the lives a your comrades depend on it…it's gonna be a long night so take a crap or a piss or whatever you need to do…we move in as soon as word comes that the control hub's ours."

The men come alert then, for if the lord general is going for the control hub now they will be fighting within the hour, and in order to be ready they must make the switch from idle mode to full fighting trim. That involves not only seeing to their physical needs, but to their mental ones as well, for a man who goes into battle with the wrong mindset will most likely not be around to enjoy the victory celebration. In truth more than one man has contributed to his own death by unresolved misgivings. Whatever doubts that Torli's men may have concerning this particular mission whether or not Karnin and his team have the ability to gain control of *Filon Bora's* beating heart is not one of them. No they have the confidence in each other that comes with having been raised and trained together, and so the men waiting in the transports know beyond question that Karnin's team is just too good and wants it too much to fail.

Lord Teneset and his men who are waiting out of sensor range on the north road in their own transport being a bit more seasoned are understandably less certain of Karnin's ability to takeover *Filon Bora* with an inside assault. Actually they have been skeptical of it from the very beginning not necessarily because they do not think that Karnin and his men have the proper skills. Their years of spying on them whenever they ventured out of *Onyat* have told them that they do, but more so because they are only four men. Well that and the fact that no one has ever successfully taken a modern fortress from within there are simply too many safeguards against it. Oh a few have tried but the only thing that they managed to get for their trouble was hung. That would be a huge pity, for Karnin has the makings of a good leader. Needless to say if Karnin should happen to get killed in there tonight overlord Devoot will be overjoyed, for those damn *Filcet* on his payroll have told him that the man is a threat to him. No if Karnin succeeds Devoot will be livid, which is yet another reason to hope that Karnin pulls this off Teneset thinks with a smirk.

Time will soon tell the tale of that though Teneset adds when they overhear Bro's coded call. After Teneset exchanges a few dubious looks with his men he orders his pilot to head towards *Filon Bora*, for they are some fifty miles from the fortress, and unlike lord Torli's new fangled machines his old transport will take quite a bit longer to get there. Hopefully they will arrive before the whole battle is done and over Teneset thinks as he feels the transport lurch, for he is supposed to bear witness to the fair and lawful takeover of *Filon Bora* not necessarily for lord Torli, but rather for the airing and deciding of his claim to it. Teneset must therefore be there to accept the fortress in trust for whoever wins the tug of war for it although that has pretty much already been decided. Still he must go through the proper motions to make it stick he thinks as he lays his head back and closes his eyes.

As Teneset makes his way towards *Filon Bora*, in the fortress's inner keep Karnin, Cerl, and Seasle are back on the first floor again quickly making their way through its dimly lit corridors. Their goal this time is the inner keep's main entrance, for that is where they will find the fortress's main control hub. It goes without saying that they already had eyes on it when they cleared the first floor, but for obvious reasons they left it undisturbed until the proper moment for it came, which it obviously has. That will only hold true if no one pops out of the woodwork, for even though they made certain that no one came into the inner keep since they cleared it by recoding all the entry locks it is entirely possible that someone has managed to elude their sweep. Therefore when they manage to reach the control hub without anyone trying to stop them they are relieved.

They are also very much on the clock now, and so Karnin foregoes taking a few minutes to savor the moment opting instead to send Seasle in without delay. The grin on Seasle's face when he does tells Karnin that he has no complaints about being rushed. As it is there is only one thing that Seasle likes to do better than blow things up, and since there is not a willing woman in sight Seasle is more than happy to go blow the door open. Seasle must admit that if he had to choose between sex and blowing something up it would be touch and go. Actually Seasle would like to be doing both at the same time, but he knows that is just a fantasy not because he could not blow something up while he was screwing, but more so because he has never met a woman who would agree to such a thing. More is the pity he thinks as he slips over and sprays blackout film on the lens of the camera watching the door. After that Seasle is all business, and because he is it takes him less time to set enough charges to breach one of the most secure doors made than it would take a less talented explosives man to mine a privy door.

Needless to say Seasle could set these charges blind, which is not just an idle brag since he has actually practiced doing it in total darkness just in case he would ever have to. Even so Seasle has yet had the opportunity to prove to the other men that he could actually ply his explosives trade during a real deal situation, but life only likes to throw stuff at you that you are not prepared for. If you practice in the dark it will be bright light and if you think you will need two charges you are going to end up one charge short Seasle thinks as he calmly makes his way back to where Karnin

259

and the others are waiting. Life is truly a bitch Seasle silently adds as he pushes a button on the transmitter in his hand, which in turn sends the trigger pulse to his charges on the door. With a loud bang all five of Seasle's charges blow in unison sending the door's keypad careening down the corridor where it crashes into the wall across from them, which although a bit overdone is a good sign, for the keypad must be completely disconnected from the security system in as abrupt a manner as possible to prevent it from transmitting a distress. That would in turn initiate an automated lockdown that only some cutting gel and a lot of time would be able to defeat.

"You showing off these days?" Karnin asks with a droll expression as the men draw their hand weapons and rush the room.

"All or nothin'…" Seasle retorts as he slips in front of Karnin and with a huge shove forces the door open, but when he does the men see someone dash out from behind the control console.

"Take him out," Karnin orders as Cerl raises his weapon.

"No wait!" Seasle shouts as he turns he shoves Cerl's hand up causing his shot to harmlessly thump off the ceiling.

"Cease fire! " Karnin commands, for as the person at the console dives for cover Karnin realizes why Seasle countermanded his order, and so he barks a bit irritably, "Come out boy!"

"I ain't gonna come out if you're gonna shoot me…I ain't stupid you know," comes the boy's sassy reply.

"We won't shoot you …you got my word on that," Karnin tells him.

"Ha…nobody round here's got a word worth takin'," the boy sarcastically replies.

"Cocky little bastard eh," Seasle points out with a grin.

"Now listen you…if you don't come out I'm gonna come over there and get you…and if I do then by all that's known I'm gonna do worse than shoot you," Karnin threatens.

"Okay…okay…" the boy begrudgingly says, and then Karnin sees his face peer out at him for a second before he stands up with a hand weapon pointed directly at Karnin's chest.

"Now see here boy…you put that down," Seasle points an indignant finger at him and sternly says as Karnin and Cerl dive for cover.

"Seasle get down you idiot," Karnin calls out to him.

"What now then eh boy...you gonna kill me?" Seasle asks him, and then he adds, "If you do my two friends there're gonna kill you back...you ready to die then boy?"

"Well...when Tok learns that you guys got in Ponet's gonna kill me anyway cause I fell asleep an didn't see you on the screen there...so..." he replies with a shrug, which makes Karnin shake his head in disbelief, for according to Boro Ponet is Tok's security master, and therefore that he would have a boy manning the security hub is beyond belief.

"Why'd Ponet leave you in here alone?" Karnin cannot help but ask from where he is taking cover.

"He always does at night...he ain't got enough a men..." the boy replies with a shrug.

"Yeah well Ponet and all the rest a those nasty bastards're dead and Tok's all tied up to his own bed post so you're makin' your own choices now," Seasle tells him, and then he says, "Last chance boy... put the weapon down."

"Don't work anyway," the boy replies with a shrug as he tosses the weapon to Seasle, and then he asks, "They all really dead or's you just making that up?"

"You know you're awful damn cock-sure for a scrawny boy," Seasle says to him, and then he asks, "So what'd they call you besides pain in the arse?"

"Mostly that," the boy replies.

"I can believe it," Cerl agrees as he gets up.

"But my mama named me Alda before she up an died," he steps forward a bit hesitantly and says, and when the light hits his face Karnin sees the gash on his forehead, and so he steps over and rips a strip of cloth off the hem of Alda's ragged shirt and hands it to Seasle and mumbles, "Wrap his head and then tie him up Seasle."

"But Karnin..." Seasle quietly begins to protest.

"For his own sake Seasle...put him in the corner over there out a sight," with that Karnin puts the problem of Alda aside, for they have a schedule to keep, and so he says to Cerl, "Get the field down."

"I can do that," Alda pipes up as Seasle winds the cloth around his head, but when he sees Seasle take a couple of tie strips from his boot and realizes that Seasle plans to tie him up he says in a panicked tone, "I won't do nothing...I promise...I can get the field down in a second...just don't tie me up...please sir...please."

"Karnin look at his wrists," Cerl quietly points out, for Alda has scars similar to Torli's, and so how he got them is not a mystery, "You can't Karnin...look at him."

"He's not exactly obedient...he'll get himself or one a us killed Cerl..." Karnin softly argues, but then he makes the mistake of glancing over at the boy, and when he sees that Alda is trying very hard not to cry he relents and sternly says to him, "Listen boy...you go over there and you stay there do you understand...if you even think to disobey me not only'll I tie you up...but I'm gonna stuff your sorry self into one a those cabinets over there...you get it?"

"Y...y...yes sir...I'll do what you say," Alda nods and then quickly goes over to the corner, but as he sits down Karnin sees him swipe a hand across his eyes. Needless to say Karnin pretends that he did not see it, for there is no use embarrassing the poor kid.

"Field's down in...three...two...one..." Cerl calls out from the control console, and then he adds, "I got about thirty seconds to give it the verification code before the alarm's triggered."

"Hey you out there I just found a bottle I forgot about," Karnin keys his headset and says.

"Lucky bastard," Bro's voice comes back.

"Nothin' in the way a getting' a good drunk on now," Karnin replies.

"Sure goes down good eh," Bro replies with the proper coded words that tell him that he is still in control of the gatehouse.

"Yeah too bad bottle's half gone won't last but thirty," Karnin orders.

"Life's bleedin' hard ain't it," Bro replies.

"Cerl?" Karnin anxiously asks as he severs the communications link.

"Damn thing won't take any a the codes Boro gave us," Cerl tells him as he slaps his hand down on the console in frustration.

"Boro?" Alda meekly asks, and then his dirty tear streaked face peers around the corner and says, "They said he's dead."

"Well they're wrong," Karnin absently replies.

"How'd you know Boro?" Karnin hears Seasle ask.

"I's his armor boy...but one day he just...left...then Tok...he come to Boro's house in the village an made me come back here," Alda says in a somewhat subdued tone, and then after a second's pause he says, "Ah...I got Ponet's code."

"I ain't got nothing to lose now...give it to me then boy," Cerl anxiously demands.

"Six...six...six...five...five...five...four...four...four..." Alda tells him as he stands up.

"You messing with me boy?" Cerl demands as he pushes the hair from his face and lets Alda see both his eyes just to make it clear to him that he is in no mood for games.

"No honest..." Alda stutters out, for one of the man's eyes is staring at him and the other one is just sort of there doing nothing, which Alda apparently finds fascinating in a weird sort of way because he says somewhat absently as he cocks his head and stares, "Ponet's real stupid and couldn't remember anything harder..."

"Finish it out Cerl," Karnin commands somewhat urgently, for if the field stays up Torli will assume that there is a problem and fall back, which will pretty much blow their quiet takeover.

"Well that's the code alright...verification complete...field's coming down in three...two...one...go," Cerl instructs with a nod to Karnin.

"Hey you out there," Karnin keys his headset and calls out.

"What'd ya want now," Bro replies in mock irritation.

"Damn bottle's gone already," Karnin tells him.

"Yeah mine too...gonna be a long night," Bro responds with the proper words.

"I'm very glad you were here Alda," Karnin tells him after he clicks his headset off.

"I'm glad Boro ain't dead," Alda says.

"He's gonna be very happy to see you...come see," Karnin says as he motions for Alda to come over to the console.

"What's that," Alda asks in wonder as three large blimps suddenly appear on the security screen.

"That's our army boy," Seasle tells him from the door where he is keeping watch.

"And that one right there," Cerl says as he points to the center-most blip, "That'd be Boro and your new overlord coming."

"I hope he's better at it than stupid Tok," Alda blurts out, and then he grins boyishly and adds, "Be hard not to be cause Tok sure sucks at it."

"By the innocence a babes..." Seasle mumbles.

"Hey...who you callin' a babe," Alda indignantly demands, but no one replies, for Karnin and the other men are riveted to the sensor screen.

"Here they come," Cerl states as the three blips blow through the village in single file.

"It's begun..." Karnin anxiously notes when the three blips suddenly come to a stop in the vicinity of the outer barracks, for that is where Torli and his invasion force will disembark.

"He's right in the thick a it now," Seasle notes as he rearranges his headset so that he can hear the chatter of the battle a bit better.

"Yeah..." Karnin acknowledges evenly enough as he listens to Torli bark out orders.

As Karnin and the other men anxiously listen to the chatter on their headsets up on the third floor Ahnin hears it as well, and when he does he knows that he must make some decision right now as to where to leave the woman. So which shall it be the cold, damp, blue bedroom or the cold, damp green one he debates, for they are the only two decent enough to leave her in. Actually he would rather make her a bed in a closet than put her in either of those two even, but that option is not available. No it must be either the blue or green. After all damp and cold is better than riddled with bugs that have come to feast on the semen covered sheets of the red and purple rooms. Green it is he decides when he notes that the remnants of the woman's shirt are that color. That decided Ahnin wastes no time carrying her into the selected room, for now that the invasion has begun anyone with an inclination to save Tok will soon make an appearance. He must not be burdened down with this woman if someone shows up.

With a decisive nod Ahnin quickly crosses the room and carefully lays her on her stomach on the somewhat shabby but relatively clean bed, but when he goes to get up she whimpers, and Ahnin knows that he cannot leave her without doing something for her. He therefore takes out his medical kit and removes one of his three pain injectors, which he then presses against her bare upper arm. Ahnin then carefully pulls the thick fall of her reddish-brown hair away from her back only to wish that he had not, for looking at Tok's handiwork only makes Ahnin want to go in there and beat him until he looks the same. It goes without saying that Ahnin is now fighting to stay sitting, for he knows that if he gets up before the anger that he feels passes he will surely kill Tok, and he was specifically ordered to keep the bastard alive.

Ahnin therefore focuses on the sound of Torli's voice in his headset, for he is what this night is all about after all, and when he does his anger turns to determination. Yes Tok will get his just deserves soon enough he tells himself. With his head back in the game Ahnin is once again able to do what he needs to do and so he covers the woman's back with a medical shield bandage to keep out any dirt until she can be tended to later. Ahnin then covers her with one of the bed's threadbare blankets and walks out, for he cannot allow his emotions to get engaged not now he decides as he goes out and pulls the door shut. Doing so gives him pause though, for with the locking mechanism popped anyone could simply pull the door open even the woman although she may be too weak to do so. Still the only way to keep the lady safe both from herself and from anyone looking for trouble is to seal her in. There is a downside to doing so, for if there is a fire or anything she will not be able to get out, but he knows that there is no other choice for it.

With a less than pleased expression on his face Ahnin takes out his welding kit and after he removes one of his seals he places it into the door's track. When he triggers the device a short burst of white hot energy erupts as the device spot-welds the door to its track, and after Ahnin checks to make certain that it has burned itself out he heads back down the corridor to Tok's door where he melds back into the shadows to watch and wait. All in all the next thirty minutes are relatively boring, for the only sound interrupting the dead silence on the third floor is the battle chatter coming from Ahnin's earpiece. At one point when the squawk on his headset tells him that the battle is winding down something draws Ahnin's attention, and he slowly reaches down and clicks his headset off to listen for the sound to repeat itself, which is does. Yes someone is coming Ahnin thinks as he narrows his eyes to slits to reduce their shine and then he silently draws a long narrow blade from the sheath strapped to his thigh.

It is not long before the dark clad form of a man appears, and Ahnin can tell by the way he walks that he is no ordinary guardsman, for he moves with the soft footsteps of a man used to sneaking about. Ahnin therefore tenses to spring at the first opportunity, for men who sneak about are usually doing so to either steal or kill. Either way he is up to no good. Ahnin therefore draws back his knife intending to give it a toss at the first opportunity. As it turns out the man is not the best of sneaks, for he walks right under the emergency lighting giving Ahnin a perfect target. His doing so also gives Ahnin a glimpse of his face, which is lucky for the man, and with a disgusted shake of his head Ahnin quickly flips his knife and cracks the man on the head with its hilt when he comes by. As he cuffs his prisoner's hands and shackles his feet Ahnin frowns, for he had come close to killing the stupid fool and it would have been a pity to ruin what may turn out to be the most interesting catch of the night. With a snort of amusement Ahnin slaps a piece of tape over the unconscious man's mouth and then just to be mean he drags him back and dumps him between Tok's two dead bodyguards arranging things in such a way so that their lifeless eyes are staring right at him.

"Hello Merl...Gorg's gonna be real happy to see you..." Ahnin stares down at him and mumbles with a smug laugh and after he sheaths his knife he once again takes up his post in the shadows.

Chapter Thirteen

As Torli steps from *Filon Bora's* outer barracks with Gorg his eyes scan the darkness of the courtyard looking for any sign that someone may have escaped their sweep, but the sun is only just rising and so the courtyard is deep in shadows still. Of course it does not help that at some point in the takeover someone decided to shoot out the spots. Someone who may very well still be here Torli reminds himself as he gestures for his men to fan out and search the courtyard. Sure enough not long after his men disappear there is a commotion somewhere to Torli's left, and a few minutes later two of Torli's men materialize out of the darkness dragging a cuffed and shackled man who they unceremoniously dump at Torli's feet. One of Torli's men then yanks the prisoner's head up to see if Torli recognizes him, for Torli was old enough when he left *Filon Bora* to remember its people. Not this one though Torli thinks as he shakes his head no and then waves the man away. Torli's men then drag him off and hand him over to Teneset's fighting men who have already taken possession of the prisoners in the outer barracks, for until the grievances filed against Tok are decided lord Teneset is technically in command. He has therefore sent his own men to secure all the critical areas of the fortress.

Lord Teneset however is still in his transport with his bodyguards, for his vehicle is flying the colors of the *Overlord En Officianada,* which makes Teneset the man to kill if you want to stall off the investigation that he has been sent here to oversee. Teneset will therefore not come out until the final sweep of the fortress has been done. That will be very soon now Torli supposes when his headset begins to squawk with the voices of his various captains reporting the completion of their assigned search areas. Once the last of them has been heard from Torli then keys his headset and notifies lord Teneset's senior most bodyguard Tandar that the courtyard and inner keep have been cleared. Not even a minute later lord Teneset emerges from his rather shabby looking transport surrounded by his four bodyguards. Apparently Teneset is just as anxious to get this over and done as the rest of them are Torli thinks as he signals to his men to move on to the next stage, and without delay they head off to secure the fortress's perimeter until such time as its security field comes back up.

As Torli's men jog off he and Gorg cross the courtyard to where Teneset stands with his guard, for it is obvious that Teneset is waiting for him. Apparently Teneset intends to personally make certain that no one from *Onyat* gets involved in the search for the evidence that Boro says is here. As it turns out Tok is not just a sick cruel bastard he is a full blown homicidal nut case, and according to Boro he collects trophies to help him revel in the pleasure of his foul deeds. While that is disturbing to say the least it is also rather convenient for Torli since he lacks the proper evidence needed to make his accusations against Tok stick. That is why Torli has made certain that everyone understands the importance of abiding by Teneset's rules. Everything from here on out must be above board and beyond question as to its authenticity if they are to have any chance of unseating Tok from the overlord's chair. Without that Torli's claim will probably not stick. After all Torli is only Galwor's nephew while Tok bastard or not is Galwor's only living son. They must therefore be careful that no one with anything to gain or lose from the situation gets anywhere near the evidence until it is formally presented.

Teneset for his part is glad that lord Torli sees the importance of showing a bit of patience now that the fortress is under their control, for he has strict orders from overlord Devoot that lord Torli must prevail. Why Devoot has decided to back Torli is anyone's guess since Devoot has more in common with Tok than Torli. Perhaps Tok has something on him Teneset muses as he watches lord Torli walk across the courtyard. That would be a nice find Teneset thinks. At any rate just because lord Torli is wise and disciplined beyond his years does not necessarily mean that his cousin Karnin is. That is why Teneset has already had Karnin and his men rounded up and escorted down to the main entryway. It is nothing personal of course, but they are all young and thickheaded, and Teneset will not allow their impulsive natures to negate lord Torli's claim, for it just so happens that Teneset is of the same mind as his overlord when it comes to who should be in the overlord's seat here. How convenient Teneset adds as he puts on a more diplomatic face.

"Congratulations lord Torli...your men performed admirably," Teneset tells him as they begin walking.

"Thank you lord Teneset...but we couldn't 'ave done it without the lord general's team," Torli responds.

"Oh I think you could've...perhaps not so easily though," Teneset tells him, but then he pauses and says, "Just so you know...overlord Tok's filed a complaint...well...he's filed several...but one in particular involves one a the lord general's men...seems the man punched him in the mouth while he was in his custody."

"Why?"

"Something to do with a woman."

"A woman?" Torli repeats, and then he asks as though afraid to hear the answer, "Which one a Karnin's men was it?"

"Ahnin...you do understand I got a go through the motions for now?" Teneset inquires, for he wants no trouble with lord Torli, and he wants even less with the lord general.

"I do...where's he at?"

"I'd Kinbe take him down to the tank but...well...Kinbe said he just couldn't leave him there it was that foul...so he's keeping lord Boro company in my transport for now...think he'll stay there?" Teneset asks him for Teneset has no doubt that this Ahnin is talented enough to escape a normal guard.

"He give you his word?" Torli asks him in reply.

"Yeah...until Foot says otherwise," Teneset replies with a perturbed expression.

"Then he'll stay put...Foot's the smart one," Torli tells him with a grin, but then he sobers and asks, "You tell Karnin yet?"

"Yeah he knows...I expect he's waiting inside to try to talk me out a it," Teneset tells him, but when Torli sends him a questioning glance Teneset shakes his head no and says, "If Karnin's man a done that to any other overlord he'd already be dead no questions asked...maybe Ahnin needs some time to think on that."

With that Teneset turns and continues walking leaving Torli and Gorg with no choice other than to follow. Gorg for his part thinks that he would rather be anywhere but where they are headed, for Karnin will be downright livid about this business with Ahnin. Hopefully the lord general will not end up shackled to Ahnin before it is all said and done. The reality of it is that Ahnin is in a lot of trouble. Striking an overlord is a death sentence, and if the evidence is not here to remove Tok from the seat he will demand Ahnin's life. Tok will not get it though, for there are many ways to sneak out of *Filon Bora* and they know them all. No if Tok somehow manages to worm his way out of this then Ahnin will just disappear until Tok dies, which with some help will be more sooner than later Gorg thinks as he follows Torli inside. Just as Gorg figured Karnin is there waiting for them, and even though he seems relaxed enough, that glimmer in his eyes says otherwise.

"Nice work lord general," Teneset says pleasantly enough as he approaches the place where Karnin waits with Cerl and Seasle.

"Thank you lord Teneset..." Karnin replies, but Teneset can see that even though Karnin is obviously angry he still takes the time to send an assessing glance Torli's way to assure himself that his cousin is unscathed.

"Before you say anything Karnin...your man's cooling his heels keeping lord Boro company in my transport...that's where he's gonna stay for now," Teneset tells him.

"I see...alright lord Teneset...that's where I'll leave him then...for now," Karnin replies in a matter-of-fact way, but Teneset has no chance to reply to what is obviously a challenge, for just then his COM device squawks.

"Lord Teneset...this's Kinbe..."

"What you got Kinbe?" Teneset asks as the other men gather round him.

"More an we'd hoped for..." Kinbe replies.

"Bag it and tag it all...then bring it down to the transport...do not rush it Kinbe...everything needs properly documented," Teneset tells him, and after Kinbe acknowledges his orders Teneset turns to Torli and says, "Go get some rest lord Torli...sounds like you're gonna need it."

"I'd rather get this settled now lord Teneset," Torli replies much to Karnin's displeasure, for Torli should not even be considering dealing with Tok until he has rested.

"No...it's been a long night...today everyone rests and prepares...we'll settle this tomorrow," Teneset pretty much orders and then promptly turns and walks away.

270

"I'd like to see my man lord Teneset," Karnin calls after him, and when he does Teneset does pause and turn to him, but what he says is not exactly what Karnin wants to hear.

"Not now lord general...everyone's tired and tempers're short," Teneset tells him, but then Tandar leans over and says something to him, and Teneset adds, "But he seemed concerned about the woman...seems she's injured and her pain meds'll soon be wearing off...Sandon here'll take you up to check on her...come lord Torli...lord Gorg...we'll drop you at your vehicle."

With that Teneset walks off, and when he does his bodyguards politely gesture for Torli and Gorg to precede them, which after a brief exchange between Torli and Karnin they do. After all what would be the point in refusing with Teneset holding all the cards Torli thinks as he walks away? Teneset for his part has his reasons for hustling lord Torli off, for Teneset has learned over the years that the best way to keep young and overly cock-sure men who are pumped full of adrenaline from overstepping their selves is to limit their opportunities to do so. Splitting up the ring leaders also helps he adds. At the moment though Teneset feels somewhat responsible for Karnin and his rather unpredictable men, for they have actually made his job here much simpler, and so he will stick his neck out for this Ahnin as a thank you. Besides a little goodwill goes a long way, and it appears that Karnin is going to be his neighbor permanently so long as he does not go and let his new found title get him into trouble.

At any rate bailing Ahnin out is in reality a minimal risk, for Tok is already a dead man he just does not know it yet. Actually no one knows it yet except Teneset and the overlords and lord Boro of course, for lord Boro has been sending evidence out of *Filon Bora* to overlord Bimian for years in an attempt to build a case against Tok although no one must ever know that. No that would only give Tok a good reason to point a finger at Bimian and accuse him of interfering in his right to govern his own territory, which is one of the most serious crimes that an overlord can commit. As it is by the rules set down in the *Pact of the Overlords* an overlord can mistreat and murder his own people for sport all he wants so long as he does it on his own land, but he cannot abuse another overlord's folk now that would be crossing the line Teneset sarcastically thinks as he exits the inner keep.

After Teneset and his remaining three bodyguards disappear into the courtyard Karnin stands contemplating his options for a few minutes, which in the end he concludes are rather limited at the moment. Ahnin has dug himself a hole this time, and all that needs done now is for someone to shove him into it. Fortunately it sounds as if Kinbe has found the evidence that they need to undo Tok's succession to overlord, and if that happens then Ahnin did not strike an overlord he struck a man who murdered an overlord which is not something that anyone will care much about. Tomorrow will tell the tale of that though, but in the meantime Karnin supposes that he had best check on the woman so that he can say that he did. After all she did nothing to deserve what she got from Tok. Besides the thought of her lying up there sick and all alone bothers him although the why of that Karnin decides is best to let be.

Karnin has a stop to make first though, for the woman is not the only thing that Ahnin has locked up on the third floor. With a resigned sigh Karnin gestures to Sandon to come along, and when he does Seasle and Cerl quickly fall in behind despite the impatient look that Karnin sends their way. As it is the two twits have appointed themselves his bodyguards, and even the threat of being reassigned to foot patrol when they get back to *Onyat* has not deterred them from it. In all honesty though Karnin has to accept that at some point he will have to tote a proper guard, for he is a lord now, but not those two. There is no way either of them could stay in the background and keep quiet watch while Karnin does business. The whole thought of it is laughable he thinks with a perturbed frown as he takes the stairs two at a time, but when he reaches the third floor he finds the stairwell's fire door blocked open, which it should not be. After all that defeats the door's purpose Karnin thinks as he pauses to note that what is keeping the door from closing is a regular blocking device rather than some makeshift thing.

"Kinbe's men did that...Ahnin refused to walk down so they carried him," Sandon informs him.

"He's lucky...I'd a drug him by his damn feet..." Karnin clips out as he watches Sandon remove the door block.

"That's exactly what Kinbe said," Sandon tells him as the four men begin to walk towards Tok's apartment, but as one would expect when they draw near Kinbe's guards step out to challenge them.

Sandon smoothes things over then, and when he asks one of the guards points out both the door to the room where Ahnin stashed the woman as well as the place near it where Merl is lying face down.With a shake of his head Karnin decides to stop by and say hello to Merl before he goes to check on the woman, for Karnin has found that the best way to get the truth out of Merl is to make him believe that he can talk his way out of trouble. Yes once Merl starts blabbing he simply cannot shut up Karnin thinks especially when he gets nervous. Unfortunately, the first thing that Karnin notices when he nears the spot where Merl lays trussed up is that his hands are turning blue, which to Karnin's displeasure manages to garner a bit of sympathy from him, for losing one's hands is a rather harsh punishment for any man to suffer especially a man too stupid to fall back on his brains Karnin thinks as he flips Merl over with his foot and then firmly plants it on his chest.

"Well...well...look who it is," Karnin remarks when Merl's eyes pop open, but when he reaches down to pull the tape from Merl's mouth he sees him cringe, and once the tape is off Karnin can see why, for the area around Merl's mouth is full of mean raised welts.

"Those damn arses yanked that on and off...I'm gonna kill them for that," Merl spits out.

"Spouting off right out the gate eh Merl...no apologies...like oh...I'm sorry I'm a faithless twit Karnin?" Karnin mocks.

"I couldn't stay..."

"You never could...the question a the day's why you kept coming back then?" Karnin angrily asks him.

"Couldn't find no place to go," Merl candidly replies.

"Looks like you found one this time...what're you doing here Merl?" Karnin narrows his eyes on him and asks.

"Got hired to get something back that Tok took," Merl replies.

"Like what?" Karnin demands, for Merl has not the skills to steal anything from a fortress even one as lax as Tok's.

"Just some photos...that's all..." Merl replies.

"Who hired you?" Karnin asks.

"I can't tell you..."

"You *Filcet* now...that where you went eh?" Karnin angrily grinds out as he puts a bit of pressure on the foot resting on Merl's chest, and when he does Seasle sees Sandon send Kinbe's guards a hold sign, which is good he did for their sake Seasle thinks as he stares one of them down.

"No...I swear it Karnin...I ain't no *Filcet*..." Merl replies.

"Yeah well...you ain't one a mine either...remember what I said's gonna happen next time you just took off?" Karnin asks him.

"Yeah...I remember...but that was if I come back...which I didn't," Merl belligerently responds.

"He's got a point there," Seasle comments, and when Karnin sends him a threatening glare Seasle only responds with one of his less than apologetic shrugs.

"I suppose he does," Karnin clips out, and then he angrily adds in a rather deadly tone, "Well if you ain't back then you ain't my problem Merl."

Merl being the arse that he is gives Karnin a cocky reply about being able to deal with his own problems, which Karnin rewards by reaching down and shoving the tape over his mouth again, for there is absolutely nothing that Merl could possibly say that will change the predicament that he has gotten himself into. Besides if he cannot speak then he cannot push anyone's buttons and get beat up or strangled Karnin concludes as he grabs the short connector on Merl's foot shackles and unceremoniously drags him over to where Tok's dead bodyguards lie covered by a sheet. With a twist Karnin flips Merl on his side to face the two dead men, and then pulls the sheet off and when he does Merl's eyes go wide, for even though he awoke with those dead eyes staring at him several hours have transformed them from a glassy blank stare to a milky one that makes Merl's skin crawl.

"Take a good look...that's the future staring at you Merl," Karnin throws at him and after he checks his cuffs he then promptly walks away.

Needless to say Teneset's guards have begun to suspect that Merl has probably earned the lord general's anger, for Merl has proven to be an abrasive big-feeling young man. It is not that though it is the fact that judging by what they have seen he has not earned the right to be so. Actually the two guards think that they probably should have known that Merl was going to be a problem, for when he woke up the first thing that he did was to throw a tantrum. It was sort of funny at the time, for Merl had kicked his feet and made threatening sounds like he actually believed that he could intimidate them or something. Even so they still feel a bit sorry for him now, for the lord general comes across as the kind of man that one does not want to cross. Actually the lord general was coming across as a rather cruel man as well, but then they saw him reach down and loosen Merl's cuffs a few notches before he strode away. That made them wonder if perhaps the lord general is not as bad a sort as he is putting on.

Karnin on the other hand wishes that he was the bad kind of sort who could simply write Merl off and walk away, but something about him pulls at Karnin's gut it always has. Yes Merl is like that favorite child the parents dote on and give every advantage to only to have him turn out worse than all the rest of the kids put together Karnin thinks. One day Merl is going to come to a bad end, and if he will not tell Teneset who hired him this may be the moment that he does. Unfortunately Karnin will probably try to salvage his sorry self although he will not trade getting Ahnin out of trouble for Merl. Thinking about Ahnin only makes Karnin angrier, for unlike Merl who has a shortage of thinking cells in his head Ahnin has more than his fair share of brains, and so he was well aware of what the consequences were going to be for doing what he did. On second thought Karnin thinks that perhaps he will barter for Merl's release and leave Ahnin sweat it out for a time. Maybe then he will stop thinking that he can do whatever he wants to Karnin thinks as he spies Ahnin's seal on a nearby door.

With a sigh Karnin stops in front of the door and then motions to Seasle who steps forward and sets about freeing the door with a small hand cutter that he pulls from one of his pockets. With a snap and a spark the little tool makes short work of Ahnin's seal cleanly severing the bead sealing the door to its frame within a few seconds. Before he can shove it open though a shriek rings out, and so panicked does it sound that all the men in the corridor immediately duck and turn expecting to see someone murdering Merl. Much to their consternation what they see is that Merl has apparently tried to escape using what Karnin and his men refer to as the 'step through' method in which a man cuffed with his hands behind his back actually contorts his body enough to pass his cuffed hands down around his feet, for once the arms are in front it does not take a whole lot of effort to free the feet. It is a move that requires strength, flexibility, and precision none of which Merl obviously has, for he has gotten stuck in a most awkward and painful position.

"Here I thought that damn woman was gonna be the biggest pain in my arse tonight..." Karnin mumbles as he walks over with the other men to stare down at Merl in disbelief.

"Excuse me lord general but...you want us to help him out?" one of Teneset's guards asks, for if Merl stays in that position too long his dislocated shoulder will most likely turn into a more serious tear.

"No...the lord general's got his own men Avin," a voice says behind them and when Karnin glances over his shoulder he sees Kinbe standing there, and judging by the expression on his face he is not amused by the situation.

"Aye sir," Avin immediately says and then goes back to his post.

"Uncuff him Cerl...pop his arm back in," Karnin commands with an impatient gesture, for if there is one thing that he cannot stand it is a snob, and Kinbe comes across as a rather judgmental bastard.

"I'll help you..." Sandon tells him and surprisingly enough Kinbe says nothing about it, but as Karnin watches Sandon work he understands why, for once Merl is uncuffed Sandon pops his shoulder back in place like a professional.

"You a healer Sandon?" Karnin asks him.

"Always good for a man in my line a work to know the basics," Sandon replies.

"My men say your friend here was sent to steal something from overlord Tok lord general," Kinbe comments as he walks over.

"Yeah apparently so," Karnin responds

"Must a been some minor lordling or something...you know...someone too poor to hire quality," Kinbe remarks with an amused grin, but when he does Merl treats him to one of his murderous looks, and with a disbelieving shake of his head Kinbe asks, "He mentally all there?"

"Yeah well that's the question I been trying to answer for years," Karnin crosses his arms on his chest and replies as he watches Cerl reach down to recuff Merl's hands, but then Merl does what he always does; he reacts without thought.

"I'll kill you Cerl!!" Merl pulls the tape from his mouth and yells before lunging at him.

It goes without saying that Merl's decision to take the few seconds needed to remove the tape before trying to get at Cerl turns out to be a poor decision on his part especially since the man who he is attacking is one of *Onyat's* more talented fighters. In truth someone as good as Cerl only needs a few seconds lead time to thwart someone else's game plan especially when the man is as easy to read as a children's book Cerl thinks as he sees Merl's eyes dart towards the corridor. So it is that when Merl makes his move and tries to run Cerl simply sticks out a long leg and trips him up. With a disgusted shake of his head Cerl tries to drag him back, but Merl is apparently not done yet, and so a short scuffle ensues.

Through it all no one makes any move to intervene, for neither Kinbe nor Karnin have ordered it mostly because it does not appear to either of them that Cerl needs any help.

There is also the fact that Merl is one of Karnin's men and Karnin outranks him Kinbe notes, for he can tell by the way that Karnin and his men are interacting with this Merl that he is still one of them or so they feel at any rate. All in all Kinbe finds that rather interesting since Merl obviously has no loyalty to them. He also brings nothing to the table Kinbe decides when the skirmish is rather short lived, but then again Cerl's grappling abilities are above average. The stupid fool still struggles though, which makes Kinbe wonder if he truly is a bit short in the head, for he does not seem to realize that the fight is over. That would explain why they all feel the need to show some sort of special leniency for Merl Kinbe concludes, but when he glances over at the lord general Kinbe finds that Karnin's dark eyes are watching him and not his two men. That is also noteworthy Kinbe thinks, for it says that Karnin has enough confidence in his men to take the opportunity to size up the competition.

"You do that again and I'll break your damn neck Merl," Kinbe hears Cerl say.

"Cuff him back up Cerl," Karnin orders as he slowly turns his eyes back to his men.

"Come on Karnin...cut me a break this once..." Merl pleads.

"Give me one good reason why I should even remotely do that?" Karnin comes back with.

"Okay don't then...I don't care..." Merl snaps out like a spoiled babe.

Even though Karnin would not take such lip from one of the others he finds that he cannot give Merl the punch in the face that he so thoroughly deserves, for Karnin knows that he had a hand in creating the disaster that Merl is. To be honest Karnin holds his own self mostly to blame for Merl's having been given one too many chances growing up. The problem is that Merl is the youngest amongst them, and as the babe of their group he was coddled and protected a bit too much for his own good. So much so that Merl still thinks that the world revolves around his wishes. That is unfortunate, for at twenty-three he should be a great deal wiser than he is especially after surviving on his own for so long now. Then again even a fool gets lucky once in awhile.

"You know one day I'm not gonna be there to rescue you Merl," Karnin angrily tells him as he hands Cerl a pair of ties, which Cerl then swaps the cuffs out for.

"Thanks," Merl says, but even though his tone tells Karnin that he is sincere enough, the crafty shift of his eyes also tells him that Merl thinks that he has just been handed his freedom.

"Shut up," Karnin retorts and with that he simply walks away.

"You think leaving him like that's wise?" Kinbe asks as he follows Karnin over to the door that they were getting ready to open.

"Merl's got less pain tolerance than a two year old...he won't push that shoulder far enough to get out a them ties," Karnin tells him, but when he hears Seasle talking to Merl he falls silent to listen.

"Gorg's gonna be mighty glad to see you," Seasle crouches down and tells Merl, and when Merl makes a lot of pissy sounding noises Seasle reaches down and pulls the tape off and asks, "What's that?"

"I said I ain't scared a Gorg," Merl snaps at him.

"Actually it's lord Gorg now...oh...and lord general Karnin too just so's you know," Seasle informs him.

"What...they get married or something?" Merl asks with a sarcastic snort.

"No...Boro made Karnin swear to overlord Marsle...and Gorg's got a new papa," Seasle replies with a rather ornery grin, for he knows that Merl has always been jealous of those amongst them who actually know who their fathers are.

"Yeah right...so what's his name then?" Merl asks with a dubious expression.

"Lord Goberan...Gorg got an uncle what's an overlord too...it's a shame Gorg probably hates you now...you could a sucked onto to a piece a his new found fortune," Seasle leans his head down and tells him, but when he does Merl angrily tries to head butt him, and Karnin takes that as his cue to interrupt their little chat.

"You two all caught up now?" Karnin tosses at them.

"Oh yeah..." Seasle replies as he stands up, but when he does Karnin sends him an impatient stare, and so Seasle adds a less than convincing 'sir' to it.

"Gorg's still a bastard," Merl petulantly says.

"Yeah...but I'd rather be a rich bastard than a poor...well...you..." Seasle replies and then reaches down and literally 'slaps' the tape back over Merl's mouth.

278

Without further ado Seasle walks over to where Karnin stands by the now sagging door, and attempts to force it open. He soon discovers that when the door went askew it jumped the track and wedged itself cockeyed in its frame. Seasle being who he is immediately asks Karnin if he wants him to blow the door off to which Karnin replies with an impatient no adding his usual 'twit' at the end. Seasle is undaunted by it, for Karnin's 'twit' remarks are sort of his own brand of endearment or so Seasle thinks, and in truth they actually are. Seasle therefore moves a bit so that Cerl can help him, and with the aid of a break stick that Kinbe just so happens to have on him they eventually succeed. With a creak, a groan and a hastily called 'stand clear the door' the portal then comes down with a loud bang.

Inside the room when the drugs that Ahnin administered to her began to wear thin the young woman stirred, but she was just too exhausted to open her eyes let alone get up. Besides the bed where she is lying is the most comfortable thing that she has known in a very long time, for Tok has made her sleep shackled to the foot of his bed ever since she arrived in this forsaken place. The thought of Tok brings back all the pain and the fear that she has endured at Tok's hands, which is amplified all the more by the thought that they may soon come to take her back to him. Worse yet they may send her back to the man she had fled from in the first place. That particular worry quickly does what she was unable to do without it, and she drags her legs over the side of the bed trying her best to ignore the wave of pain that burns itself across her back and leaves her panting. As she sits there fighting the nausea that courses through her gut she suddenly realizes that there is a sound that she has been ignoring. To her horror she pinpoints it as coming from the door, and in a near panic state she forces herself to her feet. Unfortunately just as she does the door comes crashing down revealing the outline of a man, but then someone is screaming, and in her delirious state she does not even realize that it is her own voice echoing in her head.

"Don't...please," the young woman begs Cerl who is more than glad to defer his position to Karnin when he shoulders his way by.

"Take it easy now...no one's gonna hurt you..." Karnin tries, but she only shakes her head and holds her hands up in front of her as if doing so could somehow ward him off.

"She don't hear you Karnin..." Seasle mutters behind him, for the way her eyes shine in the light filtering in from the corridor tells him that she is not really living in the here and now.

"We came to help you lady," Karnin says as gently as he can.

"I'm sorry...I'm sorry...please don't ..." she pleads as she backs away from him.

"I'm not gonna hurt you," Karnin reassures her as he steps over to the wall to turn on the lights. As he hits the button it occurs to him that she might go into hysterics of a different sort when she sees him in his ominous looking black assault suit, for to her he probably looks like the specter of death or some such dire thing.

"It's you..." is all she whispers when the lights illuminate his dark clad form.

"Yeah...we met earlier...remember?" Karnin replies, but much to his frustration his words do not seem to reassure her, which he cannot blame her for all things considered.

"Please don't send me back..." she pleads, and when she does Karnin assumes that she is talking about Tok, and so he feels fairly confident that he can reply to that without having to eat his words later.

"I won't...now...you need to let Sandon here look at your back," Karnin tells her.

"No...stay away...I'm not going with you..." she warns in a high pitched voice.

"Lord Karnin...wait..." Sandon warns as he steps in front of him to keep him from approaching her, for something is not right about her, and if it is what Sandon thinks it is then stressing her further is the worst thing that they can do.

"Easy now lady...no one wants to hurt you..." Sandon tries in a soft voice as he slowly approaches her, but as he does he can see by the way her eyes are darting about that she is far away living a nightmare induced by the one thing that all persons trained in the healing arts fear the most.

"No...father please...please don't...I'll be good..." she hysterically pleads, and when she does even Kinbe is moved by it, for that any female should fear her own father so much as to make him a part of a nightmare induced by what is most likely a deadly high fever is sad indeed.

"Stop Sandon...you're scaring her..." Karnin commands, but before he can take control of the situation he sees her sway on her feet, and it is all that Sandon can do to get an arm under her to soften the fall.

"Who're you?" she turns her face up to Sandon and asks in a hushed voice.

"I'm Sandon..." he replies.

"Promise me...promise you won't send me back to him...please..." she practically begs, and when she does Sandon is tempted to say what she wants to hear, but he knows that he cannot.

"Please..." she begs rather desperately.

"No one's taking you anywhere," Karnin steps in and replies for him.

"Thank...you..." she replies so softly that Karnin has to strain his ears to hear it, and then she seems to let go, for her eyes roll back in her head, which alarms Karnin considerably.

"Hey you....don't you go anywhere...you hear me!" Karnin shakes her and says a bit more commandingly.

"Bring her to the bed..." Sandon instructs and when he does Karnin does not take offense to his doing so, for Karnin is more than willing to admit that Sandon knows more about healing than he does.

As Karnin gathers her up and walks her over to the bed Kinbe studies his rather grim expression with a great deal of concern, for he seems to care more about what happens to this woman than the circumstance merit. Kinbe supposes that since Karnin hails from *Filon Bora* it is possible that he knows her. At this point in his musings Kinbe sees Sandon roll the woman over and push aside what Kinbe thinks is a rather uniquely colored long length of hair to reveal a large blood soaked medical patch. That is not what makes Kinbe unable to think on the lord general's odd behavior though, but rather what peeling away the patch reveals, for the back of the woman's shirt has been reduced to shreds that are now stuck in the bleeding and oozing stripes that crisscross her back. Kinbe now understands why a man with as much savvy as Ahnin seems to have lost his head when he saw this and at that moment Ahnin gains a rather important ally in his bid for freedom. Yes Kinbe thinks that he would have punched that bastard Tok in the face too, but of course he would not have left him alive to file any damn charges.

It goes without saying that Kinbe is not the only man there thinking about meting out a bit of justice for the lady, and their thoughts on it range from knocking out every tooth in Tok's miserable head to flaying the skin from his decrepit body. Then there is Seasle who obviously thinks that blowing his parts off one at a time might be just the thing, but that is what one gets from someone who lives to blow things up. Sandon for his part forces such thoughts from his head before they form, for he cannot take the time to indulge in that if he is to save this woman's life. Sandon therefore gets to work trying to extract the pieces of her shirt that will still come out of the lady's wounds comforted by the knowledge that Tok will soon be dead and unable to harm anyone else. After all it does not matter how he gets made dead so long as he is dead. Unfortunately dead may be what this poor woman will soon be as well he grimly thinks, for he can feel the heat radiating from her back beneath his hands, and Sandon knows how quickly infection can put even a big healthy man in a box.

After a few minutes Sandon abandons his efforts to clean up her back, for the rest will require tools and some sort of liquid, but more importantly it will take a great deal of time. That is something that the lady does not have, and so he sets about removing her outer garments so that he can assess the rest of her. At this point Kinbe does take control from the lord general, and with a shooing gesture he herds the other men out into the corridor. The other men go without argument, for to a man they believe that the woman deserves more than a bunch of bachelor eyes ogling her wares no matter what her station in life turns out to be. After several nerve racking minutes Sandon sounds the all clear and when they troupe back inside they find her lying on her stomach covered by what they assume is Sandon's emergency blanket. The news although good does not really make anyone feel better, for even though she has no broken bones nor does she have any of the telltale signs of internal injuries everyone knows that her back is enough to do her in all by itself.

As if things are not already grim enough the woman suddenly whimpers and her body begins to convulse rather violently, and when she does the blanket comes away and the men standing round the bed get a glimpse of a generous set of hips and thighs before the view is blocked. Kinbe on the other hand sees something that the other men do not or if they do they assume is a bruise or a birthmark. Kinbe knows that it is not, for he has seen that mark on another woman once a long time ago. Kinbe however keeps his own counsel about it, for it is not something that anyone should know about at least not right now he thinks as he steps out into the hallway to bring Teneset up to date as to the woman's condition. As far as for the mark on her leg Kinbe will not even speak of it over a secure COM, for if she is who Kinbe thinks she is then this whole business could get a lot more complicated rather quickly. How much so is not something that Kinbe will even presume to decide. No having to make those sort of decisions is part of the price for a fancy title, and since Kinbe does not have one he will let Teneset choose the lady's fate Kinbe decides as he returns to the room.

Chapter Fourteen

On the morning of the second day since the taking of *Filon Bora* Torli stands on the fortress's roof watching the sunrise, and as he does he cannot help but feel vindicated even though in reality he has not been. Well not yet at least. Today however is the day for it, and no matter how it turns out he will always be grateful for this moment even if it has fallen short of his dreams. Unfortunately that is what happens when one goes through the proper legal channels. One becomes a somebody who must follow the rules that govern the titled men and women of the world Torli thinks as a light breeze picks up a few stray curls of his shoulder length golden brown locks and makes them dance. With a resigned sigh Torli pulls the tie from his hair and lets the wind take it, for sometimes one just has to let the inevitable happen, and having his unruly locks tangled by the wind seems to be how things are supposed to be so why fight it? In the end the wind will win, for it is a force that no one can ever truly control.

Yes many people think that they can control things not meant to be controlled. Things like the weather or the future. Boro tried that, and he nearly died for his trouble. The reality of it is that even though it appears as if Boro has succeeded he did not get everything that he wanted. The man who gave his health in an effort to find justice for others will never get any for himself. Not directly at any rate. Neither will Torli's mother and father and the countless others who Tok murdered over the years, but then again how many times can you kill a man? That thought brings back the memory of the day that he had met his cousin Karnin, for Karnin had said something quite similar when he offered to kill Tok for

Torli. Torli had told him that he had to kill Tok in a certain way. Dead is dead what does it matter how he gets that way Karnin had said, and it seems that when all this is done that is exactly how things will go down. Tok will die for another crime at the hands of an executioner, but even though Torli's vengeance will not be as sweet as it could have been Tok will still be dead, and his reign of terror ended. That will simply have to be enough Torli adds as he hears the tread of a familiar pair of booted feet approaching.

"It's time Torli," Karnin stops behind him to say, but when he does he sees Torli close his eyes and tip his face up to catch the warmth of the sun's first rays, and so Karnin remains silent until Torli has finished his little ritual.

"For what it's worth..." Torli eventually says, and then he turns to Karnin and tells him, "You did the right thing swearing to Marsle."

"Yeah I know...but it's good to know you finally come round to it," Karnin replies with a grin.

"Don't let it go to your head," Torli tells him, but then he goes all serious and adds, "No matter what happens in there you keep your hands clean."

"That damn Teneset's not giving me much choice there," Karnin replies with a perturbed expression.

"That's lord Teneset's job," a now familiar voice advises.

"A good bodyguard's seen and not heard Kinbe," Karnin remarks just because he can.

"Ah well I ain't your bodyguard my lord...you got two a those already although quite frankly sir they need a bit a work," Kinbe tells him with a pointed glance Seasle's way.

"Not gonna argue with you there," Karnin agrees which earns him one of Seasle's 'mean looks', but Karnin does not even bother to comment on it since it would be rather pointless, and so he turns to Torli and somberly asks, "You ready?"

"As ready as I'm ever gonna be..." Torli replies and after he binds his curls up again he takes one last deep cleansing breath, squares his shoulders, and sets off across the roof for the lift.

As Torli strides along Gorg and Karnin fall in behind him while Seasle and Cerl flank the group watching for anything that is out of the ordinary. Kinbe for his part signals to his four men who are guarding the perimeter around lord Torli, and they trot over to take the head and tail of the group of men, for it is Kinbe's job as the temporary security master of *Filon Bora* to make certain that everybody stays hale and whole until this business concludes. Sometimes that is an easy task to do Kinbe thinks as his gaze falls upon the young soon-to-be overlord, and sometimes a bit trickier he reasons as his eyes fall upon the lord general. Then there is the downright distasteful Kinbe adds, for he must also protect Tok's sorry hide from anyone seeking a bit of premature vengeance. That is the unfortunate truth of life, for there is a balance in the universe, and for every really good thing there is its counterpart bad. It is just how it is Kinbe adds as they reach the lift.

Kinbe's four men peel off then to cover them while they board the lift, and as the lift door closes Kinbe keys his COM device to tell his men waiting on the first floor that they are coming down. So it is that when they reach the first floor Kinbe's men pick them up, and the formation then makes its way to the fortress's main eating hall, which has been cleaned up and arranged to accommodate today's proceedings. Therefore when they enter Torli finds it much changed from the day before, and so he pauses just inside the door to take it all in. As his eyes travel from the gallery swarming with *Filon Bora's* good folk come to watch their future decided to the conspicuously placed cameras hanging from the room's vaulted ceiling Torli thinks the place is just as he always pictured a high tribunal would be. Yes pompous and sterile he thinks as he sees Barndon approaching.

Barndon stops in front of Torli and after he gives him a respectful nod he hands him a document reader. As Torli pages through the documents presented there he inquires if Barndon prepared them and when Barndon tells him he did Torli puts his mark to them without bothering to read them. As it was Torli was with Barndon when they were drafted, and so Torli already knows that what lies upon the pages are his various complaints against Tok, for the law requires that the complaint Torli brought before the overlords be reaffirmed today. That done he then takes a seat amongst a large contingent of his fighting men who are seated in a somewhat shadowed corner of the room where he can observe the tribunal as inconspicuously as possible.

As Torli watches Karnin and his two bodyguards seat themselves near the front of the room he has to admit that his cousin is every bit the lord of *Onyat* today. That thought makes Torli wonder why it is that he never considered the possibility that Marsle might want to acquire him rather than jail him, for Karnin is an outstanding asset. A natural born leader who will fit into the role of lord without a hiccup Torli thinks, but then he smirks at the irony of that, for Torli always thought that Karnin would be one of his assets one day. Now he sees that his vision there was rather narrow. When all is tallied up though Karnin deserves what he has been handed for a number of reasons the least of which is that he did not leave him in that alley to die all those years ago. Luckily Boro chooses that moment to limp in and take a seat next to Karnin, which shifts Torli's attention from that dark day so long ago back to the here and now. A few minutes later the accused makes his noisy entrance.

"This ain't goin' nowhere an when everthin' gets dismissed I'm gonna bring me own charges!" Torli hears Tok's voice belligerently say, and a second later he is escorted to a seat at the center of the room where he stops to survey the crowd. He apparently spies someone who he knows, for he suddenly points an angry finger at a man sitting amongst the village folk and bellows out, "You useless coward...get down here Ponet and defend your overlord!"

Even though Tok's words do not get the expected results as far as he is concerned the man who he so conveniently points out does get up and move, but only with the help of a few of Kinbe's men. As it turns out Kinbe has been hunting for Tok's security master, and under other circumstances Kinbe would have thanked Tok for saving him the trouble of having to go through the village house by house to find him. It goes without saying that Tok does not get that he maybe should not have pointed Ponet out, for the man may have come to attempt a rescue, although judging by the way the man carries himself Kinbe rather doubts it. Still appearances can be deceiving and no one here knows that better than Kinbe. He therefore orders Ponet cuffed and shackled before they haul him off to join the other questionable prisoners waiting to be sorted out.

"You got no right to take my man whoever you are," Tok complains.

"Ah well...I'm responsible for the security a this fortress until the *Overlord En Temporada* leaves it sir," Kinbe responds.

"Yeah well this whole thing's a waste a my time and his," Tok grumbles out, and then he points an angry finger at Kinbe and commands, "And you better address me proper...it's overlord Tok!"

"As you wish...sir," Kinbe says, and with no further comment he gives Teneset's crier a nod.

"Make way for lord Teneset a *Dorelon Bodon*...vassal a overlord Devoot...appointed *Overlord En Officianada* of the *Eastern Central Lands* by the overlords Devoot, Marsle, Krenot, Bimian, Sertten, Dor, Cantil, Caramu, Quincy, Pobin and Oreian who as the law requires have requested this investigation!" the man calls out, and when he does the crowd gathered to witness this event sees a tallish land man with neatly tied back brown hair and piercing light brownish-green eyes enter flanked by his bodyguards.

"We've met before...I assume you remember me sir?" Teneset asks as he comes to stand near Tok.

"I remember you Teneset..."

"Good...then we'll get right to it so we won't waste any more a your valuable time," Teneset responds interrupting whatever else Tok was going to say, and then Teneset rattles off in a matter-of-fact way, "The charges're rather long to list...but the gist of it is that you've been accused a murdering and or ordering the murder a the late overlord Galwor...his three legitimate sons...a couple a his illegitimate ones...his sister and her husband...so on and so forth...plus various other attempted murders one a which's the blatant and intentional poisoning a the late overlord Obron's lady wife's brother lord Boro as well as doing business with the *Filcet* for the express purpose a contracting lord Boro's assassination."

"You're daft...I ain't never killed no one outside the law," Tok replies, and then he demands, "As fer Boro...he ran off cause he conspired against me...and so if he's gone and got his self dead too damn bad...I'm only sorry it wasn't me who offed him."

"Yeah well...we'll explore lord Boro's complaint when and if we get to it..." Teneset responds, and when he does Tok sends him a rather hostile glance that clearly says that he gets the implications behind Teneset's words, for if he is convicted of killing overlord Galwor he will be executed without delay making all of the other charges rather moot.

"Yeah well we'll get to it Teneset...and when we do I want them charges I filed read," Tok demands, but after his eyes search about a few seconds he angrily blurts out, "Where's that bastard what punched me...he better not be gone Teneset!"

"He's in my custody sir and I assure you he's not gone," Teneset replies somewhat frostily.

"I'll believe that when I see him with my own eyes," Tok clips out.

"Very well...go get him Kinbe," Teneset orders, and when he does Kinbe nods and makes his way out only to return a few minutes later with a casually dressed and rather carefree looking cuffed and shackled Ahnin who much to Kinbe's displeasure sends Tok a challenging little grin in passing.

"I want him tried now Teneset!" Tok insists as Kinbe shoves Ahnin into a seat along the far wall, but when Teneset only shakes his head no Tok shoots to his feet and angrily says, "I got rank here and this's my fortress...you'll do like I say!"

"I'm sorry sir but at the moment your title and authority've been...suspended..." Teneset informs him.

Being told that he no longer holds any sway in what he considers his own territory is apparently the last straw for Tok, for it sends him into one of his infamous rages. With clenched fists he advances across the room towards Teneset who to his credit calmly stands his ground. Of course there is no real need for him to do anything else. Teneset is sporting four bodyguards and one Kinbe today, and therefore it is doubtful that even one of Karnin's killers could get through all of them let alone a lumbering ham-fisted man like Tok. So it is that when Tok comes within striking distance of Teneset Tandar steps in front of him, which only makes Tok all the more determined to hit somebody. Unfortunately the many years of easy living have taken their toll on Tok, and so the fist that he throws at Tandar's face does not set any speed records. Tandar therefore simply deflects the blow and tells Tok to step back, but Tok is not finished playing the fool, and so he hooks a punch to Tandar's gut. This time Tandar does not just deflect Tok's blow he follows it up with a hard two-handed shove to Tok's chest that sends Tok stumbling backwards right into the arms of Kinbe's guards who catch him up and escort him back to his seat.

"I'd suggest you not do that again sir," Kinbe stares down into Tok's reddened face and warns to which Tok replies by belligerently spitting at Kinbe's feet.

"Let's get this done shall we," Teneset commands in a rather bored fashion, and then he turns to his communications man and asks, "Are we transmitting?"

"Aye sir," Teneset's communications man replies.

"Then we'll start...bring in the evidence," Teneset orders as he makes his way to his seat.

The next six hours are rather eye opening for anyone who does not already know what Tok is capable of, and in some ways even those who do find themselves taken aback by Tok's sordid hoard of trophies. Even Boro is rather shocked, for the evidence that he stole and sent out to overlord Bimian consisted of biological samples from Galwor and a few injectors containing the poison used to kill him that Tok had failed to dispose of properly. As it was Boro had heard a rumor that Tok was a trophy taker, but he never imagined that his cache would be as big as it turned out to be. Boro also never imagined Tok's hoard to be as gruesome as it is either he thinks with a disgusted shake of his head when Teneset holds up a properly bagged and tagged jar with an eyeball in it. When Teneset then reads the tag attached to the jar a feminine wail is heard and the crowd erupts in anger, for the eye once belonged to the seventeen year old daughter of the village baker who had disappeared many years ago.

Teneset is forced to pause then until order can be restored, but in time things quiet down enough for him to present the find-of-the-day to the overlords who are watching Teneset's transmission of the proceedings from the comfort of their fortresses. The fact of the matter is that when Teneset holds up the jar with two testicles in it even overlord Devoot is offended although in his case more so because he finds it unimaginable that Tok could be so stupid as to keep something like that than from any sort of disapproval of the act that procured it. Then Teneset reads the label, and when he does Torli's heart begins to race, for the testicles belonged to overlord Galwor. As if that were not good enough Tok had dated the sample bottle, which is far beyond anything that Torli thought that they would get from Tok's trophy stash. So much so that he subconsciously rises to his feet in anticipation when Teneset announces that they were able to successfully do both toxicology and genetic testing on the testis.

Unfortunately when Torli's golden brown head slowly rises above everyone else's Tok spots him, and the eyes that Tok turns on him are so filled with hatred and loathing that it leaves no doubt in anyone's mind who sees it that Tok knows exactly who Torli is. Teneset then announces that not only did the testing confirm that the testicles did once grace the late overlord's crotch, but also that Galwor had a lethal level of toxin in his system that day. As if that were not enough Teneset then adds that the tests also revealed that the testis were taken while Galwor was still alive, which as one might expect causes the room to erupt into a confused mass of curses and pointing fingers. In the midst of it all

Kinbe quickly puts eyes on lord Karnin, for he would not have the lord general or his men take advantage of the disruption to do something stupid especially since the overlords are watching, but apparently doing stupid things is Ahnin's mission in life Kinbe supposes when he notes that Karnin and his men have not moved from their seats.

Kinbe then swivels his gaze to Ahnin, for if there is one thing that he has learned in the last few days it is that there is more to Ahnin than meets the eye, and even though Kinbe has yet to figure out what it is he does know that the man bears watching. So it is that when Kinbe turns to check on Ahnin he sees his head come up like a predator scenting the wind, and for some unexplained reason when Ahnin's eyes fix themselves on someone in the crowd Kinbe finds himself sending his guards to apprehend him, but before they can get there the man shoots to his feet and sends a knife careening across the room towards lord Torli. With a shout Kinbe tries to alert lord Torli, for he knows that he is too far away to intercept the blade, but he hopes that perhaps one the men nearby or lord Torli his own self might still thwart it. When all is said and done Kinbe need not have worried, for when the knife nears its intended target a hand suddenly comes up and simply snatches it from the air.

As one would expect Kinbe quickly closes the distance and grabs the knife catching hand's wrist fully expecting to see blood dripping from its palm. To his surprise the newly crowned young marsh lord managed to grab it by its handle, which is either the luckiest grab ever or one of the best display of reflexive skills that Kinbe has witnessed. Either way the young man deserves to keep the thing Kinbe decides as he takes the knife from Gorg and gives its blade a quick check with his poison sniffer, for even though tipping their blades with poison is a trademark of the *Filcet* it is an easy thing for an amateur killer to copy. The knife comes up clean, and so Kinbe then does what is often done amongst fighting men; he presents it back to Gorg hilt first with a nod of acknowledgement.

Kinbe then turns his eyes to Teneset who signs to him that he should take the assailant out and secure him for now, which Kinbe immediately heads off to see to. However as he goes he gives Ahnin a quick check just to make certain that he is still there, and when he does Kinbe finds Ahnin's odd eyes studying him. Actually that stare of his is rather disconcerting, which is exactly what Ahnin intends it to be. Yes Kinbe gets why Karnin is determined to get the man back, for his oddness actually works rather well for him so long as one has not dealt much with odd people. Luckily Kinbe has met several strange people in his lifetime some even more so than Ahnin, and so as good as it is Ahnin's attempt to rattle him is wasted Kinbe thinks as he motions for his men to bring the assailant down from the gallery.

"I think now'd be a good time to adjourn to allow the overlords to decide whether or not the evidence has merit..." Teneset announces, and when the folk gathered quiet down he turns to Tok and asks, "Before we do...you got anything you want a offer in your own defense sir?"

"Yeah...I ain't never seen none a that stuff before...I'm being framed...your damn evidence's nothing but a plant so's somebody can rob me a my damn birthright," Tok grinds out between his clenched teeth, and then he tosses in, "I want them tests done again...with people who ain't yours."

"Are you suggesting that overlord Caramu's lab techs botched the tests sir...or perhaps you think they doctored them up?" Teneset asks.

As Teneset waits for Tok to reply he hopes that Tok is feeling trapped, for Teneset can see by the expression on Tok's face that he realizes Teneset knows that he has something that belongs to overlord Caramu. Apparently Tok is not as dumb as he acts since he also gets the fact that Teneset has not told anyone about it yet. Yes Tok knows that he is dead no matter what he does now, for if he pushes things with the evidence Teneset will simply tell Caramu what Tok has been up to, and no matter if Tok gets off all the charges he will not enjoy his freedom long. No one crosses Caramu like Tok has done and lives long, for overlord Caramu is a ruthless man who keeps a few professional killers on his payroll for just such occasions. On the flip side if Tok does not formally protest the evidence then the overlords will find him guilty of 'killing his way to the seat' and if that happens he will also be dead. The question now therefore becomes how it is that Tok wants to die and more importantly who he will decide to take down with him when he does Teneset decides.

In actuality Teneset does not really want to make good on his threat to inform overlord Caramu that Tok has apparently stolen his daughter, for doing so would expose the lady's presence here. Besides knowing how Caramu can be he would probably blame the poor woman, and she has suffered enough already. Needless to say Teneset would prefer to forget that he ever saw her here, which is actually his standing order to Kinbe and the other men who may have knowledge of her. She will at least have some peace for a time Teneset thinks, for as far as he can tell he and his men are the only ones who actually know who the lady upstairs is. How long it will be before that will end is anyone's guess. With a sigh Teneset wonders not for the first time how women bear their lot in life, for they have a rather thankless place in the scheme of things although some have it better than others. Still it is how things are Teneset concludes as he turns his mind back to the business at hand.

"Anyone got anything to add?" Teneset asks with an all-encompassing gesture, but when his only reply is silence he nods and authoritatively states, "We stand adjourned until there's a verdict then."

With that Teneset walks out to his transport with his bodyguards, and when he does his communications tech sits down before his portable transmissions station to transfer the feed signals connecting *Filon Bora* to the various other overlords to the vehicle. While the COM tech works Kinbe has his men escort Tok to a secure waiting area set up in a nearby room where he finds food and drink as well as a bed and a washroom, for regardless of the suspension of Tok's authority, until the overlords render their decision he is technically still a sitting overlord. As such he is entitled to certain comforts and considerations although many present would argue that point, which is one of the reasons why Teneset made certain that there was food and drink available for the regular folk as well. Judging by the satisfied faces that he sees around him it was a clever move on Teneset's part Ahnin thinks as he sits in his chair along the wall observing.

As time continues to pass Ahnin begins to wonder if Kinbe has perhaps forgotten about him, for he did not even leave a guard to keep an eye on him. At least not one that is being obvious about it Ahnin thinks as he carefully studies the people milling around the room, and when he does he finds a pair of rather pretty brown eyes studying him over the cup of whatever it is that she is drinking. Much to his surprise Ahnin finds that he is quite taken by her, for she is beautiful and bold, and when Ahnin sends her one of his seductive smiles she does not put on any coyish pretenses. No instead she cocks her head at him and then laughs. No not a laugh really more like an amused smirk he thinks, which Ahnin finds rather intriguing, for that she is not easily put off is of a certain. At this point Ahnin sees a big brute of a man walk over to her and after he gives Ahnin a rather hostile glance he hurries the woman off, but as they go Ahnin gets a chance to peruse her diminutive form. To say that he is not disappointed by what he sees is an understatement, for even though she is slight she has hair past her arse and the body of a goddess.

"You best get your eyes off that," a familiar voice warns.

"Ain't no law against looking Seasle," Ahnin retorts.

"That ain't your 'just looking' face," Seasle remarks, and then offers Ahnin a bite of the hand pie that he is eating, which Ahnin eagerly accepts, for he did not eat this morning mostly because Kinbe wanted him to.

"So..." Ahnin begins but then pauses long enough to take another bite of the pie that Seasle holds up to his mouth before he continues as he chews, "She married to the blockhead there?"

"Nope...but he ain't the one you got a worry about...she got an uncle by the name a Bonin what raised her that the blockhead's scared a," Seasle tells him as he holds his cup up to Ahnin's lips.

"Pussy," Ahnin comments with a snort.

"So...they treatin' you good?" Seasle asks.

"If you don't count that Kinbe made me piss with one hand on a long lead then yeah...they're treating me pretty good," Ahnin replies.

"At least he let you piss so you wouldn't disgrace yourself," Seasle hears someone say behind him, and when he turns to eyeball whoever it is he finds Kinbe and Karnin standing there.

"That's more an you'd a got from me magic man," Karnin tells him.

"How long you gonna be mad at me this time...sir?" Ahnin gets to his feet and inquires.

"That depends on what it's gonna cost me to get your sorry arse out a trouble...this time," Karnin sarcastically comes back with, and then after thanking Kinbe for treating his man better than he deserves he walks off with a 'let's go Seasle' over his shoulder.

"This time?" Kinbe inquires as he watches Karnin leave the hall.

"Yeah...well he gets mad when any a us act 'impulsively'," Ahnin tells him, and then he grins and adds, "He's mad at me a lot."

"I can believe that," Kinbe states as his COM device squawks out that Teneset is ready to reconvene the tribunal.

Kinbe therefore signals to his men, and when he does some of them begin circulating through the throngs of people announcing that they should take their seats while others set off to summon the lords and their men back to the forum. Not surprisingly once word goes round that a verdict may be ready the room becomes charged with anticipation, for *Filon Bora's* people are hoping that this inquiry will spell the beginning of a new and better era for *Filon Bora.* Logically enough they are also a bit anxious as to who will take the seat if Tok is put out of it. Hopefully the rumor that the man the assassin tried to kill during the trial is lady Myna's son will turn out to be true, for if it is not then Obron's bloodlines have played themselves out. The overlords will then be free to place anyone they want to in the seat. Still after years of Tok's harsh ways most folk would be willing to pledge to almost anyone who is not him.

The object of their disgust is brought in then, but this time Tok finds no chair waiting for him, and the possible reasons for that apparently do not escape him, for he immediately casts about for some way to save himself. Of course he finds none, and so he racks his brain for some way out of the web that he has spun over the years, but nothing comes of that either. He therefore does the only thing left to him, for if he is to die then he will take someone with him. Unfortunately he has no way to take the man who deserves it most, for he has no case against Boro nor does he have anything against Myna's brat who should have died months ago damn him. He does have the means to get at them both in a roundabout way he thinks as his gaze narrows on Ahnin. Yes and the lord general too. How perfect Tok thinks as his eyes slide away.

"Tok...bastard son a the late overlord Galwor..." Teneset formally begins, but Tok wastes no time interrupting him, for if he is to have his vengeance then he must not allow Teneset to announce the verdict before he says his little speech.

"Wait!" Tok loudly calls out, and when Teneset sends him a rather withering stare he says, "Before you get to what those nosy bastards decided I want my charges read...while I'm still around to hear 'em."

"Very well...lord Boro...you stand accused sir a manufacturing rumor and propaganda designed to overthrow your lawful overlord," Teneset announces, but then he casually walks over to stand a few feet from Tok before he states, "That'll be continued...if it's decided you're not lawfully seated then no crime's been committed even if his lordship did it."

"Yeah I kind a figured that...read his too," Tok remarks and then sends Ahnin an evil stare, but when a few seconds of silence pass without Teneset complying Tok locks eyes with him and belligerently adds, "No matter what they decided...I's at least a lord when he hit me...and I want my due."

"Very well..." Teneset replies, and then he clasps his hands behind his back and slowly walks over to stand in front of Ahnin and instructs, "Stand."

"I know the charges lord Teneset," Ahnin says as he gets to his feet, but when he does Kinbe gives him an elbow in the gut.

"Check that attitude," Kinbe demands, but the truth of it is that he just wants Ahnin to shut up before he digs the hole deeper.

"My apologies," Ahnin replies, but much to Kinbe's displeasure he then adds, "I freely admit that I hit him."

"What's he doing?" Seasle leans over and hisses out to Cerl, for even though the punishment for striking a lord is not death it can still very harsh.

"He thinks he's being chivalrous," Cerl points out, and when Seasle sends him a perturbed expression he adds, "You know...he's taking one for somebody else."

"I know what the word means..." Seasle hotly retorts.

"Pipe down both a you..." Karnin demands and something in his tone makes even Han sends him a concerned frown.

"Karnin you can't interfere..." Cerl warns.

"Yeah...I know that Cerl...but you two carping over it ain't gonna make it go down my gullet any easier so shut up," Karnin responds.

"That's a guilty plea Teneset...you know the law...punishment's mine to mete out," Tok's voice drones out then, which effectively recaptures Karnin's attention.

"You're a fool Ahnin," Teneset leans towards him to softly remark.

"Make sure it's not for nothing," Ahnin returns in like kind.

"You're quite right...sir..." Teneset tells Tok in a normal voice all the while angrily eyeballing Ahnin, but then he turns away and adds, "But as the *Overlord En Officianada* what that punishment'll be's for me to decide."

"The minimum's ten lashes...in public...by my own hand Teneset...I'll be satisfied with that," Tok tells him rather smugly.

It goes without saying that Teneset would rather hand the whip to a few of Tok's victims and let them flay Tok with it than let Tok use it on Ahnin, but he cannot. No the one thing that Tok knows how to do well is manipulate the law, and he has constructively tied Teneset's hands with it. Therefore since there is nothing else to do but get it done as quickly as possible he gives the order to 'stretch him out' meaning to bare the convicted man's back and 'stretch' him over the whipping rail, which Tok had relocated from the courtyard to the gathering hall some years back so that he could watch the beatings while he ate his dinner. With a grim face Kinbe complies, but this time he does not order his men to do it, for he will not make them take part in this distasteful thing. Besides Ahnin might try to run when things get too bad and they will Kinbe thinks as he takes Ahnin by the arm and leads him over to the whipping rail.

After Kinbe divests him of his shirt Ahnin puts on a brave face and after he kneels he voluntarily lays his body over the rail, but as Kinbe is locking the neck bar down as is often the case when nerves set in Ahnin begins to question his choice to play the martyr. Then the reality of his situation sinks in and he realizes that he was always going to end up here, and since there was never a way to avoid it he might as well go out with his dignity intact he thinks. He therefore shores up his courage, for he knows that this will be rather brutal he has seen Tok's work before, which ironically enough is why he is in this position in the first place. Full circle he thinks as he tries to reach his right pocket, but he cannot since he is still cuffed on a belt, and so he resigns himself to having to do this on his own. At that moment however he feels a hand slip into his pocket and then the familiar feel of Foot in his hand, which he is grateful for, and so he looks up and momentarily locks eyes with Kinbe to let him know that. Then the first strike comes and when it does it drives all thought of Kinbe from Ahnin's mind.

The blows come one after the other then although rather slowly so, for Tok takes his time pausing long enough between the lashes to savor the moment, which only prolongs the pain of the whole thing. Ahnin for his part does alright at first, for even though it is painful it is bearable, but somewhere after the third lash the pain no longer eases between them anymore, and Ahnin is forced to dig deep in order to continue denying Tok the reaction that he is craving. Ahnin is determined to beat Tok out of this one last sick pleasure, but he must admit that when it begins to feel like his skin is gone he does ask the powers that be to let him pass out, which is a mercy that for whatever reason they deny him. After that everything seems to run together, but in the midst of the waves of pain Ahnin hears a commotion, and then there is a longer than usual pause. He would not find out until later that it was Torli trying to intervene. Of course Teneset prevented it, but Tok obviously recognized him, for he made some remark about Torli remembering what stealing his seat cost his friend.

The remaining blows were more vicious than Ahnin ever imagined they could be, and they nearly broke him. When all was said and done Tok did not get a whimper from him, which Ahnin counts as a victory of a sort. Unfortunately Tok is not in the mood to give credit where it is due, and the fact that he could not make Ahnin fold infuriates him to the point where he throws caution to the wind. With a bestial growl Tok raises the whip intending to give Ahnin a couple more stripes for his cheek. After all they can only kill him once Tok thinks. The blow never falls though, for Kinbe suspected that Tok would do as much and so was ready to intervene. Actually it is all that Kinbe can do not to give Tok that extra lash, but he knows where his duty lies and with whom, and so he settles for relieving Tok of his whip and ordering his men to cuff his hands behind his back. While all that is going on one of Kinbe's men releases Ahnin from the neck bar, and when he does Ahnin tries to get up, for he would like to leave the hall under his own steam just to piss Tok off. Needless to say he finds that he cannot. Something odd happens then, for someone pulls his head up by the hair, and he finds the very same pretty pair of feminine brown eyes that he had been so taken with earlier only inches from his face.

"You're nuts you know," she surprises him by saying, but then she takes some of the sting out of it by softly telling him, "I know why you did it though...now get up."

"That's...easy for you...to say..." Ahnin manages to get out between his clenched teeth.

"Omon help him get up," the woman turns her face up and says.

"He's a damn criminal Lizzet...let someone else help him," a deep voice replies.

"You're such an arse sometimes," he hears his little heroine say.

"Aw...come on Lizzet..." he begins to retort when he is interrupted.

"Move idiot...afore I mash you like a bug," Ahnin hears another big voice say, but this one is familiar to him and the next thing he knows he is being hauled up to his feet by Orn who then half walks half carries him out.

As Karnin watches Ahnin go by he gets a glimpse of the damage done to his back, and when he does he feels an anger bubble up inside of him the magnitude of which he has not felt in a long time. At the moment though he is unable to pinpoint whether he is angrier with Ahnin for playing the hero or with Tok for being the demented bastard that he is. Perhaps it is more the situation, for no matter what Ahnin chose to say or not say he was destined to have his back laid open. That is the least that one gets for striking a man with a title Karnin tells himself as he watches Teneset say something to Sandon who nods and quickly walks out presumably to see to it that Ahnin gets the proper care until such time as the healer can be summoned back. Poor woman she has only just gone home after a long day and night vigil with Tok's mysterious prisoner. Karnin quickly cuts that line of thought short, for thinking of the woman unsettles him, and that is not something that he needs right now he thinks as he checks to make certain that Torli has gone back to his seat, which Karnin sees that he has.

"Now that's done we'll hear the verdict..." Teneset begins but he is once again interrupted by Tok.

"That was good...where's that whore a mine...I got a boner as big's my fist," Tok blurts out with a bark of laughter.

"Shut him up," Teneset angrily orders.

"My pleasure sir," Kinbe responds as he walks over and forces a gag stick between Tok's teeth and secures it, and in truth Kinbe is relieved once it is done, for if Tok spills it about the woman upstairs all that Ahnin has and will suffer in the weeks to come will be for nothing.

"The next man who interrupts me's gonna spend the night in the damn tank," Teneset warns, and then he takes a deep breath and rattles off, "Tok...bastard son a the late overlord Galwor...the overlords've come to a unanimous decision...they find you guilty a patricide and although they went no further since it was not necessary they asked me to note that they fully believe you responsible for the deaths a the late overlord Galwor's other children as well as his sister lady Myna and her husband lord Edbon as well as the attempted murders a lord Torli and lord Boro...that being said you're overlordship a this territory's been annulled...and you're to be given a traitor's death at the earliest convenience...which I deem to be now...Kinbe."

With a nod Kinbe draws his fighting knife and walks over to Tok who has begun to struggle in a panic as a man who knows that his death is eminent is wont to do, but Kinbe's guards are well trained and so they force Tok to his knees with a few well placed kicks to the backs of his legs. As Tok kneels before him Kinbe tells him that he should prepare his soul to face the justice of those on the other side waiting for him, and with that he grabs Tok by the hair and slices his throat. A traitor however is not intended to get a merciful death, and so the cut that Kinbe makes is shallower than he would use if he were intending to kill a man outright. So it is that for the next fifteen minutes the room stands in silence as Tok slowly bleeds out, and when it is over and Tok lies dead in a pool of his own blood no one present is left feeling that justice has not been done.

Needless to say Torli would have preferred to kill Tok his own self as he had always planned that he would, but as it turns out Karnin was right dead is dead he thinks as he walks over and yanks his mother's signet ring from Tok's dead finger. At this point Teneset orders Tok's body to be taken to the incinerator without delay, and when he does his men unceremoniously roll Tok into a body bag, and then set about cleaning up the mess. Once the area has been wiped clean and sterilized they toss the bloody waste into the bag with Tok, and after they zip it shut they haul it away. The aftermath sets in then, for as is always the case in such situations although the people are relieved that Tok is finally gone they are still somewhat troubled by the process, which is why Teneset does not delay the final portion of this tribunal long.

"Lord Torli...son a lord Edbon and lady Myna...grandson by blood a the late overlord Obron...and nephew a the late overlord Galwor...please step forth sir to be recognized," Teneset requests. When Torli steps out of the crowd a ripple of excitement passes through the room, for even though when they saw the glorious mop of golden brown curls on Torli's head they suspected that he was of Obron's line to have it officially confirmed is still a thrilling moment for them.

"I'm lord Torli," Torli responds as he comes to stand before Teneset.

"I'm pleased to tell you that overlords're in complete agreement as to your status sir," Teneset states. Actually that the overlords have managed to find common ground for the second time today is a moment to remember Teneset sarcastically thinks, but he only says, "I've been authorized to name you as the *Overlord En Temporada* a this territory...as custom dictates your overlordship'll be finalized at a ceremony to be held in six months time...do you accept sir?"

"I do," Torli responds, and when he does Teneset thinks that he is a bit pale, but who would not be having second thoughts when faced with the prospect of taking on the wreck that twenty-five years of collective incompetence has created Teneset reasons.

"By the power given to me I therefore declare this tribunal officially closed and my duties here discharged," Teneset announces, and when he does the people literally pour forth to offer their thanks and congratulations to their new overlord, which Torli accepts a bit more graciously than Gorg who becomes increasingly agitated by the pressing crowd.

"Relax lord Gorg," Teneset stops next to him to say, but when Gorg only frowns at him Teneset adds, "There're a lot a eyes watching the crowd."

"Yeah...but if anyone's gonna avenge Tok now's the time," Gorg replies without taking his eyes off the sea of faces surrounding them.

"I think you already thwarted that plan," Teneset tells him, but Gorg is not convinced of that, which is the sign of a good bodyguard.

Too bad Gorg is a lord, for he would have made a good candidate for the new overlord's security team, but his father is not likely to approve that Teneset thinks as he steps over to stand next to the new *Overlord En Temporada*. When he does his own bodyguards position themselves around him, and in turn around lord Torli, which is not as generous as lord Gorg might think although Teneset would most likely have done the same thing even if his reputation were not on the line. In this case he has decided to settle in and wait until the crowd disperses on the off chance that lord Gorg's misgivings turn out to have some basis in fact. After all it would not exactly be a feather in his cap if after everything that has transpired someone simply walks up and kills the new overlord right under his nose Teneset reminds himself with a rather bored expression as he watches an old man stop in front of the *Overlord En Temporada* and then kneel to offer his fealty.

As he watches lord Torli help the old man to his feet Teneset thinks that young overlord will do well here, for he is beyond exhausted and this is not the proper forum for taking fealty yet he does so for the old man who is obviously no longer able to understand that. It is a kindness where one is needed, and judging by their indulgent looks it is one that many of the other folk approve of. Smart Teneset thinks as his eyes locate the lord general who he notes is standing a short distance away with his men. It goes without saying that they are not just standing there doing nothing, but rather are watching the crowd for anyone who does not seem to belong. Another smart one Teneset thinks, and not for the first time since he met the lord general does Teneset thank the powers that be that he is not his enemy. Well not yet at any rate but give it time Teneset thinks, for in time Teneset is certain that overlord Devoot will find a way to piss Karnin off like he does everyone else.

Chapter Fifteen

As Ahnin begins to find his way out of the drug induced sleep that he has been in for the last day and a half it is the fresh smell of soap that he notices first. That and the soft smoothness beneath his bare chest make him feel content to just lie there and experience it. Unfortunately at some point he begins to feel the burning warmth in his back, which is such a contrast to the cool crisp sheets that he is lying upon that it annoys him. Still he is just too tired and comfortable to do anything about it. After a time though the heat in his back begins to do more than annoy him, for it feels as if some beast is gnawing upon it, which is a situation that understandably rises to the level of having to do something about it. On the other hand his mind is still muddled and so he cannot seem to figure out what that something should be. Ahnin therefore decides to just let it be. After all how much could one little beastie eat anyway his doped up mind tells him?

However the slight discomfort in one small portion of his back soon spreads, and as Ahnin lays there trying to make sense of that the discomfort morphs into pain. So sudden is it that Ahnin has no time to think he simply reacts, but when he reaches back to bat away the things chewing on his back he finds that his arms are too short to reach them, which confuses him since he has always been able to scratch his own back before. Needless to say he keeps on trying, for as is often the case with people in a drug induced state he somehow believes that a repeat of the same action will somehow get him a different result. It goes without saying that in his state of mind it never occurs to him that his arms are tethered to prevent the very thing that he is trying to do. Then again in the twilight place where Ahnin's mind is currently dwelling he does not even recollect the why of it that his back hurts.

"Ahnin..." he hears someone call, but he is busy right now trying to figure out how his arms shrank like they obviously have, and so he tries again to knock away the annoying thing on his back only to have the same results and hear the same voice say a bit more insistently, "Ahnin wake up now."

"I'm busy," he hears himself reply, and then he mumbles, "My arms shrank...I got a stretch 'em back out."

"Damn...I want some a what he got," Ahnin hears a familiar voice say.

"You got a get a back like he got first stupid," another familiar voice retorts with a snort of disdain.

"Naw...I'll just skip to the juice," the first voice says.

"You'll end up like Bella you do that," a different voice states, but for whatever reason this one Ahnin is able to put a name to.

"Cerl..." he calls.

"Yeah..." Cerl replies and then walks over to crouch next to Ahnin's sickbed so that he can see his face.

"I's just dreaming the weirdest thing," Ahnin opens his eyes and tells him.

"No doubt...you're pumped full a pain killers," Cerl tells him, and when Ahnin frowns he says nothing, for it is best if he works out what happened to him on his own, which he quickly does.

"How long?" Ahnin asks.

"A day and a half," Cerl replies.

"Damn...I missed it then..." Ahnin complains, but then Cerl sees him flinch, and it tells him that clarity is about to rear its ugly head.

"Yeah you did...but it got filmed for posterity so you can still see it," Cerl tells him.

"Karnin still mad at me?" Ahnin asks as he closes his eyes against the growing pain coursing through his back, and when he does Cerl glances up at Karnin who is sitting in a chair next to the bed.

"He is," Karnin answers and then inclines his head to tell Cerl to step back away, and with a resigned expression he and the others go to stand in the doorway while Karnin tells Ahnin what he has decided with regards to his future.

"I really screwed up this time huh?" Ahnin asks, but then he makes the mistake of trying to move, and it feels like the skin on his back splits from top to bottom.

"Lie still...you'll make it bleed again," Karnin directs as he reaches over and lays a restraining hand on Ahnin's shoulder.

"You know nothing I said would a spared me this," Ahnin tells him after the pain subsides.

"Yeah I know..." Karnin replies, but Ahnin just rushes on.

"I know you think I'm crazy Karnin...but I'm not...the woman...you know...the one we found in Tok's room...she got a tattoo...she belongs to somebody..." Ahnin tells him.

"You know I don't hold with that Ahnin," Karnin reminds him, for at one time it was common practice for the owners of houses of pleasure to actually purchase girls for their establishments who they would then tattoo to let everyone know that they were property, which is a barbaric and dehumanizing practice in Karnin's opinion.

"Yeah I know you don't...but you didn't put it on her...question's who did," Ahnin points out.

"And you know who magic man?" Karnin asks, for that would make this rather simple since all that would be required then would be to pay her owner off.

"No...but there can't be all that many houses in the village doing that anymore," Ahnin says as he carefully slides his arms under the pillow.

"You'd be shocked at how many still do," Boro interjects from where he, Torli, and Gorg have come to stand in the doorway with the others, and then he adds, "But we should be able to track it down...what's it look like?"

"I don't know...I never seen it actually...how about you tell me what it looked like when you saw it magic man," Karnin leans his forearms on his knees to say into Ahnin's face.

"I didn't...I heard Sandon and Kinbe talking about it..." Ahnin replies, but something about the way that he turns his face away gives Karnin the impression that Ahnin is not telling him the entire story.

"Well...I guess we got a see it then," Karnin bluffs, but when he goes to get up just as he thought would be the case Ahnin stops him.

"Wait...it's on her inner thigh...you'll traumatize her..." Ahnin insists.

"I got a know who to pay for her freedom Ahnin..." Karnin tells him.

"Alright...alright...it was a crest," Ahnin admits.

"A crest," Boro repeats, and then he adds, "Are you sure?"

"Kinbe seemed pretty sure," Ahnin replies.

"We're gonna definitely need to see it then," Cerl says from the doorway.

"No...we're...not gonna see it...only one a us's gonna see it," Karnin possessively tells Cerl, which causes more than one eyebrow to be lifted at him, but Karnin merely shakes his head and says, "Don't read more into things than there is."

"Sounds like what is's more an I thought it was," Seasle comments, but then he adds, "Boro ought a do it...he's the least scary one."

"I'm gonna assume that was a compliment," Boro testily says.

"Oh yeah," Seasle quickly replies, but the wicked grin that follows belies the truthfulness of that.

"No one's gonna look at that poor girl's thigh," a feminine voice chastises, and then the healer woman from the village worms her way through the group of men at the door and walks across the room with her assistant in tow.

"We got a find out whose stamp it is somehow Enna," Seasle tells her.

"Enna?" Ahnin asks, for he has been locked up and now laid up and so he has not yet seen her.

"Yeah...it's me," Enna replies as she leans down so that he can see her face without moving.

"You grew up," he turns his head on the pillow and says.

"So'd you..." she replies, for she remembers Ahnin from the old days when she herself was a young apprentice who Boro had paid to stay at the cave and care for Torli, but then she remembers what they were talking about and so she straightens back up and sternly adds, "Like I said no one's gonna bother that poor girl."

"How we gonna find the right guy to pay if we can't see it?" Seasle demands.

"How about a picture...ever think a that?" she inquires as she hands Boro a reader device, but the expression on Boro's face when he sees the picture of the lady's tattoo stays the smart arse comment that Seasle has rolling round in his head, for Boro is downright pissed.

"Why that damn...he knew who she was...and he didn't tell us," Boro angrily accuses.

"He who?" Seasle asks as he saunters over to take a peek.

"Kinbe...and probably Teneset and Sandon as well," Boro responds.

"Who is she then?" Karnin asks as he gets up and walks over, and what he sees worries him, for the tattoo is indeed a crest and a rather complicated one as well.

"This's overlord Caramu's crest Karnin..." Boro carefully tells him, for he knows of the promise that he foolishly made to their mystery woman, and he fears that Karnin has finally met the vow that he will not be able to keep.

"He ain't done a very good job taking care a her," Seasle grumbles out.

"No he 'asn't," Boro agrees with a sad sigh.

"I don't care if she's Caramu's property...she's not going back to him...I promised her Boro," Karnin gives him a mutinous stare and says.

"Listen Karnin..." Enna begins, but Boro only interrupts her.

"I warned you a long time ago about doing that kind a thing boy."

"Yeah well I intend to keep it," Karnin clips out.

"Look Karnin she's not just any woman..." Boro tries, for what he must say now will not be easy for him to say and even harder for Karnin to hear, and so as he continues he watches Karnin's face very carefully just to make sure that he is truly hearing him, "She's his damn daughter."

'That's nuts...why'd a father want a mar his own daughter like some whore?"

"Because Caramu's a damned ego maniac Seasle...makes his own wife kiss his feet when she greets him...he uses his daughters as bargaining chips...tattoos his seal on their inner thighs so that every time the men he gifts them to screws them they're reminded a where their allegiance lies...I promise you he's gonna want her back," Boro replies.

"Teneset didn't want a send her back to him...neither'd Kinbe...that's why they didn't say anything," Ahnin's muffled voice says.

"You sure a that Ahnin?" Boro asks.

"Yeah..." Ahnin lifts his face from the pillow to reply, which is good enough for Boro, for even though he has no idea how Ahnin manages to get his information he is a canny man who never claims to be sure of a thing unless he has verified it.

"That's convenient ain't it...I mean...if her papa don't think Teneset knew she's here then Caramu won't come after him," Han breaks his silence to point out.

"Yeah...he's gonna come after us instead," Seasle tosses in.

"You sure she's his daughter Boro?" Karnin quietly asks.

"It's a known fact that he brands his wives and daughters...and it's his crest...it all just fits too nicely," Boro tells him, and then he fills in a few of the blanks for them by saying, "His first wife was said to be a real beauty...had the oddest shade of reddish hair that she gifted to both her babes...one a them was a daughter...she sort a dropped off the radar some years back...everyone thought her papa'd offed her in one a his infamous fits a rage like he'd done her mother."

"What's her name...the daughter?" Cerl asks.

"Anjet apparently," Boro replies with an annoyed glance.

"Maybe she run away from him then," Seasle suggests.

"Possibly..." Boro replies with a shrug.

"Her papa might not even know she's here," Cerl offers.

"Yeah...unless Tok tried to ransom her," Seasle suggests.

"Yeah well...she's going to *Onyat*..." Karnin begins, but he is quickly interrupted by the voice of reason.

"Karnin...before you do something stupid I need to tell you something..." Enna interjects.

"It's not stupid to give a crap about another human being...I'd think you'd know that healer," Karnin snaps back.

"Don't you talk to Enna like that..." Boro warns.

"Look...I'm sorry Enna...it's just that I can protect her at *Onyat*..."

"Marsle's gonna get me kicked out a my damn seat before my arse even warms it if I let you take her to *Onyat*...all we worked for'd be for nothing then..." Torli interrupts him to say, and then he walks further into the room and adds, "She stays here until we find out what's what."

"If she's run off maybe her papa ain't looking for her...maybe he's thinking she's just too much trouble," Seasle suggests.

"I doubt it...Caramu'd never let some woman best him...and that's how he'd see letting her defy him without retaliation from him," Boro responds with a negative shake of his head, and then he adds, "He'll keep looking for her until he finds her...even if he doesn't want her back."

"I remember hearing once that he keeps *Filcet* on retainer," Torli states.

"He used to...top shelf talent...but whether or not he still does I couldn't say...not much news comes out a Caramu's territory," Boro tosses in.

"Listen...all a you!" Enna suddenly blurts out, and when everyone turns to her in silence she tells them, "Anjet wasn't in very good condition before Tok started beating her...it's what I came to tell you...she's not doing well at all...and I'm not sure she can pull out a this," Enna tells them as she lays a sympathetic hand upon Karnin's arm, for she does not really care how illogical it is to have a tender for a complete stranger that Karnin does is apparent.

"You know where I'll be if you need me," Karnin grimly says.

"If she dies here there's gonna be an inquiry Torli," Boro warns him after Karnin has gone.

"Yeah...I know uncle...but I can blame any and all unfortunate things on Tok for a couple more days," Torli replies, and then he adds, "So we wait."

"We'll probably know by morning overlord," Enna tells him, and then she gestures to her step-niece and says, "Come Lizzet...we got a full schedule today."

When Ahnin hears the name Lizzet his eyes pop open, for it is the name that he remembers hearing at the tribunal after Tok had finished whipping him. Actually Ahnin is rather surprised that he remembers hearing it, for what happened after that point is a jumble of disjointed memories that he cannot seem to get in the right order. Well all except for when Omon the beast showed up. Yes he remembers that quite clearly, for it was right after that ridiculous ogre called him a criminal that he learned her name, which reminds Ahnin that he owes the man something for that insult he thinks with an angry frown. Yes something rather nasty and long lived that will hit him right where it hurts the most he plots.

"Uh-oh...he's planning somethin'," Ahnin hears Han remark.

"Yeah...he's got the face on," Seasle concurs.

"So...whose offended Foot this time?" Cerl asks with a worried expression, for he thinks that he has a good idea who that would be.

"He called me a criminal," Ahnin reminds him.

"Don't want a spring this on you all at once or anything...but you got convicted and flogged...so technically speaking you're a criminal now," Seasle informs him matter-of-factly.

"That's beside the point," Ahnin retorts.

When Ahnin makes that remark Seasle, Cerl and Han think that they know exactly what the point is or rather who, but they decide not to say anything about it at least not to Ahnin. No Ahnin's infatuation with Enna's step-niece is just what they need to budge Karnin's stubborn arse off the decision that he has made. As it is Karnin intends to leave Ahnin here when they go home to *Onyat* to as he put it 'sort himself out', but the knowledge that Ahnin may get into trouble again if he does may just make Karnin reconsider. It is a long shot, for Karnin is not easily dissuaded once he makes a decision, and he has been concerned about Ahnin's reckless nature for some time often referring to him as a possible weak point in the team. The other men see it a bit differently. They see Ahnin as an asset that they will never be able to replace if he takes his skills elsewhere, and they think that Karnin should make a few allowances for his odd behavior because of it.

As Karnin's men are plotting a way to change his mind about Ahnin, Karnin is sitting next to the bed of the woman who he now knows is the daughter of one of the most despicable overlords on the land. To be fair though Caramu is not the only ruthless bastard with a title although he is one of the most notorious for his intolerant behavior and imaginative and often painful punishments that he metes out or so Calphin and Corlean had said. As it turns out the belief that the marsh folk pay little to no attention to what happens on the land is incorrect, for Corlean and Calphin knew a great deal about what all the major players were up to there. They did not care much about it but they knew. More importantly they were more than willing to share that information with Karnin. As a result Karnin is well aware that if Caramu ever finds out where his daughter is he will either take her back and make her pay for the rest of her days for crossing him or kill her on the spot. Anything else would be unacceptable to him. The saddest part is that despite what he said earlier Karnin knows that if he is to keep his promise to Anjet then he cannot take her to *Onyat* it would be too obvious.

"Karnin..." he suddenly hears, and when he glances down he sees that Anjet's eyes are open.

"Yeah...I'm here..." he replies as he slides onto his knees so that he can look her in the face.

"I'm gonna die this time..." she weakly informs him, and when she does her lack of emotion scares him.

"You giving up then?" he asks a tad bit angrily.

"Why shouldn't I?"

"Because I don't want you to...I mean...I've only just met you...I'd like to get to know you," Karnin tells her and when he does he realizes much to his worry that he means it, which is illogical as all get out and totally unlike him.

"No you don't..." she counters.

"Yeah...actually I do," he insists.

"Why..." she asks but then she begins to cough, and the sound of it is deep and hacking, which Karnin knows from experience means that lung sickness has set in.

"Because you're beautiful...and brave...why wouldn't I want a get to know you?" Karnin tells her as he reaches over and wipes the bloody spittle from her mouth, but he can see that she is too exhausted to talk anymore and so he picks up her hand and says, "You rest...I'm not going anywhere."

"Thank you..." she mumbles as her eyes close, and a few seconds later Karnin can tell by her breathing that she is asleep.

Unfortunately, when Karnin tries to let go of Anjet's hand she stirs a bit, and so he decides to give her a little more time to fall more deeply into sleep before trying to disengage his hand from hers again. In the meantime though he might as well be comfortable he thinks, and so he simply turns his body round and sits on the floor with his back against the bed rails and the hand holding Anjet's slung over his shoulder. That is how Torli finds him some two hours later when he decides to stop and check on the lady. With a shake of his head Torli gestures for Gorg to wait outside with Seasle and Cerl who are out in the makeshift waiting room passing the time by handing Enna sterilized injectors to reload and label. As Gorg goes to join them Torli walks over and carefully sits down on the floor next to Karnin, for he knows that there is no reason to wake him. Karnin has always been a light sleeper, and sure enough only seconds after he sits down Karnin lets him know that he is awake.

"You lost overlord?" Karnin quietly asks.

"No...sometimes it's good to remember where you came from," Torli responds.

"True…" Karnin agrees with a wistful smile, for when they were growing up they had no chairs or beds, and so one of the first things that they had always said that they would do when they 'got rich' was to never sit on the damn floor again.

"How's she doing?" Torli asks as he carefully watches Karnin's face, for Karnin is a bit of a sucker for a sob story, and this particular lady's is even more blubbery than most.

"She's hanging in there…sorry I didn't help out with the prisoners Torli…" Karnin tells him.

"Don't be…they were easy enough to decide on…" Torli replies, but then he suddenly asks, "You still gonna leave Ahnin with me?"

"Yeah…he needs to sort out his head…" Karnin responds.

"I'm not sure any amount a time's gonna help there…Ahnin's…well…Ahnin," Torli says with a shrug.

"Ahnin's gonna end up dead he keeps going like this," Karnin replies.

"This's the first time he's actually got caught by his own doings…maybe that'll do what all the years a you carping at him didn't," Torli says, but Karnin never gets to object to Torli's use of the word 'carping', for the hand that he is still holding over his shoulder is suddenly jerked from his grasp, and the lady is up and out of the bed running before either Karnin or Torli can get up off the floor.

"Anjet wait!" Karnin calls as he bolts after her, but she does not make it far before her body betrays her and she collapses onto the floor.

"Don't papa…please…please let me out…it's dark…please…" she deliriously mumbles as Karnin carefully gathers her up and puts her back on her side on the bed.

"Here now…it's okay now," Karnin softly tries to reassure her, but she just keeps mumbling the same thing over and over until quite suddenly she falls silent, which scares Karnin more than the delirium did, and so he shakes her a little and says, "Hey you…don't you dare…Anjet!"

At this point Enna rushes in and takes control of the situation, and after a brief examination she tells them that Anjet has fallen into a coma. Of course Enna does not say the words, but everyone including Karnin knows that a 'from which she may never wake' is in there somewhere. It is at this point that Karnin forces himself to consider the possibility that he may not get the chance to ever really know this woman. That particular thought fills him with what he can only describe as deep regret, for there is something about her. Some sort of nameless thing that makes her the woman that Karnin knows he will never be able to forget, which could not have come at a worse time Karnin concludes. He has no room in his life for that sort of thing right now. He has too many people looking to him for leadership these days to walk around mooning over someone who he does not even know, but then he glances over at Anjet lying there, and his gut wrenches.

As Karnin stands watching Enna connect up all the tubes and lines that will keep Anjet's body functioning Karnin wonders if doing such is the right thing. There are those who would say that the fates determine whether or not a person lives or dies, and so to try to thwart the will of the powers that be is wrong. That belief is simply too bleak, for it assumes that she is destined to die, and Karnin simply will not accept that without a fight anymore than he did when Torli nearly died in the cave all those many years ago. No if the fates want her they will have to work for it and as long as her mind stays intact she has a chance he thinks as he watches the squiggly lines scrawling across the brain wave monitor. Unfortunately there is no such monitoring device for the mind, and so there is no way to know if Anjet's has survived the ravages of the fever until she wakes up. If it has not then keeping her brain and other organs functioning will have been for nothing, for the mind is the spark of life without which a body is just a body regardless of whether or not its heart still beats.

Now however the only thing that Karnin can do is to wait. Therefore when Enna has finished Karnin settles into his chair by Anjet's bedside once again, for he will stand vigil with her now until this is decided one way or another. Needless to say Karnin is hoping for a good outcome, but he is too world-wise to kid himself into believing that he can will away Anjet's death although he is a firm believer that she can if she still has enough strength left to do it. Time is the only thing that will answer that though. Fortunately or unfortunately depending upon one's perspective they will only have to wait ten or so hours. Enna was pretty clear about that. So it is that they will know by morning whether or not the machines will be switched off to allow Anjet to take over her own functions again or to let the body go that she has no further use for. Karnin can only hope that his presence will in some way help her.

As the night wears on Seasle and Cerl eventually wander in to stretch out on the floor near the door and get some shuteye, for

313

they will need to be well rested come morning especially if this night turns out badly. As is the usual case when the team is away from home Han keeps tabs on everyone throughout the night. Well everyone except Bro, for he has been temporarily assigned to Barndon of all people. Han supposes that is because Bro is good at remembering things and Karnin wants him to learn more about the rules that govern the operation of a fortress. Now that Karnin is a fancy lord *Onyat* will be expected to be run like a proper fortress whatever that is. In the end it does not really matter so long as they do not try to change up his department. That ain't happening Han decides as he settles into a chair in the corner of Ahnin's room to keep an eye on him for awhile.

Torli for his part takes his leave soon after Karnin settles into a chair next to Anjet's bedside, for he has things that he needs to see to, and he must also make certain that he gets a bit of rest his own self. As it is no matter what happens here tonight he will still have a full schedule to see to tomorrow. Even fuller if he must COM overlord Caramu to inform him that his daughter has passed Torli grimly adds. As if that is not enough as he walks along with Gorg and Boro his headset beeps and he hears Barndon's voice say in his ear that they have just received a request from one of overlord Caramu's vassals a lord Bortten to speak via COM with whoever is now in charge of *Filon Bora*. As one might expect that gives Torli pause, for he had hoped to have a bit more time to sort all this out before one of Caramu's people came searching for Anjet. Then again overlord Caramu's lab techs were here for Tok's trial, and so he should have considered the possibility that one of them may have heard it rumored that some unknown woman was found here.

"Damn," Torli says, and after he explains what is going on to Gorg and Boro he says, "I suppose I should tell Karnin."

"No...let Karnin be Torli...what you do now's yours to decide...it's your arse on the line after all not Karnin's," Boro reminds him.

"Yeah...he's got enough to think about already anyway," Torli agrees, and then with a decisive nod he starts walking again, for he knows exactly what he needs to do.

"You're not gonna give her up're you?" Gorg asks as he brings up the rear.

"I can't lie about it Gorg...well...not blatantly...but I can pick and choose a bit...so I'm just gonna describe the lady...say she's been unconscious since we took over...and end with a...sorry but the healer's don't give her much chance," Torli tells him.

"The overlord's gonna want a send someone Torli..." Boro points out.

"Yeah well...he better send somebody who's 'ad the pox then...she's got an odd rash," Torli responds.

"That's blatant you know?" Boro points out.

"Okay maybe I got security problems...no that'd only make him want a get her out a here all the faster..." Torli responds with a bit of frustration.

"Just tell him no," Gorg tosses in, which earns him an impatient glance from both Torli and Boro, but he only shrugs and adds, "You're the overlord...this's your territory...tell him you'll take his request under consideration...that's what they all do."

"He's right...no overlord worth his salt'd let some little puke lord tell him what to do," Boro says with a chuckle.

"Yeah...he'll take what information I decide to give him and be glad for it," Torli decides as the three men head for the third floor where the entrance to the watch tower and COM center is.

As Torli heads up to put lord Bortten in his place Karnin is dozing in his chair next to Anjet's bedside while two rooms away Ahnin lies awake trying to work up the courage to get up from the bed, for he has to piss, and he is damn sure not wanting Han to help him do so. He would never hear the end of that. Unfortunately ten lashes seem to have reduced him to a sniveling pansy, for he finds that he fears the pain that moving would bring, which frustrates him like nothing could. It is not like he has never been in pain before he has on more than one occasion, and he even broke a couple ribs a few years back, which anyone will tell you is one of the most painful things that you can do. Now that he thinks upon it though being flogged is by far worse. Still pain is just a part of life he tells himself as he moves his arm enough to untie the tether restraining it with his teeth, but no sooner does he have it free than a shadow engulfs him, and when he glances up he sees the outline of a small form standing there.

"What're you doing?" she asks in a rather miffed way, but then she turns on Han like a small beast and demands, "And what're you doing...you're supposed to be watching him?"

"I ain't his mama," Han defensively says.

"I got a piss alright," Ahnin tells her as he reaches over and unties his other arm.

315

"That's what Enna sent me in for..." Lizzet tells him and then holds up the portable pisser in her hand, which gives Ahnin pause, for even though he objected to Han putting his mitts on him Lizzet here is another matter altogether.

"Hurry up then...I really got a go," Ahnin tells her, and he must admit that when he does he cannot help but smile what man would not?

"Yeah...okay," she replies, but then she tosses the portable pisser to Han and says rather smugly, "Hurry up...he got a go."

With that Lizzet turns on her heel and walks out leaving the two men to figure it out on their own. Just as he deserves for thinking himself so damn clever she thinks. As if she would ever allow herself to be trapped into touching any man's penis that she did not want to touch. The problem is that she sort of wishes she had. Only out of curiosity of course she assures herself, for this Ahnin person is very different from anyone that she has ever met before. As a matter of fact he is different from anyone that she has ever seen before and she has even seen a marsh man once. Lizzet is therefore curious as to how he measures up to other men. Not that she is a slut or anything she has yet to choose what man she will bestow her virginity upon, but she has seen men naked before. Tok's men sometimes paraded around that way when they were trolling for a good time, but none of them ever bothered her uncle Bonin's place. They were afraid to.

"That was fast," Enna notes when Lizzet emerges from Ahnin's room.

"His friend's helping him," Lizzet replies.

"Too bad...all the village women'd a been jealous as all get out that you got a glimpse of what he's got under his clothes," Enna tells her, and then she shrugs and adds, "Oh well...one a them'll find out I'm sure...he's gonna be here until the banquet."

"Good for them," is all Lizzet replies, but Enna only secretively smiles, for Lizzet has done nothing but sneak peeks at the man since she first saw him.

Quite frankly Enna would rather Lizzet explore what Ahnin has to offer than 'Omon the Moron' she rhymes to herself with an eye roll. Although Lizzet has only just turned eighteen and Ahnin well he must be at least Karnin's age, which would be twenty-eight or twenty-nine so he might be a bit mature for her just yet. Even so if they did mesh Enna thinks that she would not be more pleased. There has always been something special about Ahnin. Some little something that makes him standout from the crowd. Well other than that weird foot thing of his. Besides pickings are very slim here at *Filon Bora*, for Tok and his goons subverted or killed off a large portion of the younger men, and the older men are married or really old. Oh well if Lizzet cannot snag one of the better catches like Ahnin perhaps one of the new men that Torli brought with him will attract her attention. That would probably be best anyway, for Bonin would most likely not approve of Ahnin especially if he meant to take Lizzet to *Onyat*.

As for the top two prizes well Torli would be all wrong for Lizzet. Oh he would spoil her shamelessly but that is not exactly what Lizzet needs. No she needs a man who will keep her in line with a clever mind and firm but loving hand not one she will walk all over, and Torli needs some soft sweet creature who will love him unconditionally. That is certainly not Lizzet. Karnin on the other hand may be a bit too rigid, for he is strict and set in his ways, but that is why they are all still alive today. Even so he and Lizzet would make each other miserable. In the end though Lizzet will choose who she wants when she wants that is how she is, and Enna can only hope that he does not turn out to be Omon. Omon is a heavy handed big mouth who will end up getting Bonin thrown in lockup or worse for murdering him when he does or says something stupid to Lizzet.

Oh well no use worrying over it time will tell the tale Enna reminds herself as she gets up to go check on Ahnin who she finds sighing in relief. It goes without saying that Han is nowhere near him at least not right now at any rate, but Enna suspects that he did help Ahnin line things up before he fled back to his chair. Enna being a mature woman knows enough about male pride not to comment on that. Instead she waits until Ahnin is finished, and then takes away the portable pisser and wipes his penis with a towel all in one well practiced move. So slick is she at it that Enna is already headed out the door before it occurs to Ahnin to thank her. Enna's amusement fades rather quickly once she emerges from Ahnin's room, for she must now check on her other patient, and she finds the prospect of doing so rather depressing. Then again finding herself in a position where her best efforts may fail to save her patient has always made her feel at a loss. This time is no different she tells herself.

Unfortunately Enna knows that this time is very much different, for most of her anger is not centered on her own failure, but rather

317

upon that of those who should have looked after Anjet. After all she is an overlord's daughter. She should have been pampered and spoiled and yet she has been so deprived of the very basics of decent life for such a long period of time that her overall physical condition is no better than a old washer woman's. Whoever is responsible for that has earned Enna's eternal contempt and perhaps one of Ahnin's infamous curses as well. Maybe that one that Ahnin claims will make a man's balls shrivel. Yes that way that father of hers will not sire anymore unfortunate children, for Enna holds him ultimately to blame for Anjet's neglect. He should have loved her she is of his own body. He is an unnatural man she decides as she makes her way into Anjet's room.

As Enna prepares to tend her patients throughout the coming night Torli stands upon *Filon Bora's* roof watching the sun dip below the horizon, for watching the great star's comings and goings has been his ritual for many years now. As the last vestiges of the sun's rays fall several beams strike *Filon Bora's* inner keep transforming it into a beacon in the gathering darkness or so Torli thinks. Tonight however his mind finds no solace in it, for his chat with lord Bortten had made his blood nearly boil from his veins. To his credit though Torli did not lose his cool with him although he did take a great deal of pleasure in telling that big feeling bastard that he was not yet ready for visitors and that someone would COM him when things were secure enough at *Filon Bora* to permit inter-territorial travel. The absurd man had actually tried to reply to that but Torli had hung up on him before he could. One would think that a man who seemed so intent upon getting the lady back as soon as possible might treat the man who has her with a bit more respect than lord Bortten showed him. It matters little in the scheme of things though, for Bortten is not going to get her back regardless of how much sucking up he does. No the only difference that lord Bortten's lack of manners made was that Torli will now feel completely guilt free about lying to him if it comes to it.

Is that how it starts Torli wonders? Is that how a good man is subverted by power? First one guiltless lie then another, and the next thing he knows his conscience simply cocks up its toes? Torli checks his thoughts at this point, for they are getting a bit overly dramatic. The truth of it is that he has always known that being at the top of the food chain would occasionally require a few well placed lies or 'diplomacy' as the upper crust prefers to call it. Hopefully none of the 'diplomatic decisions' that he will be forced to make will cost him his soul Torli muses as he closes his eyes and tips his face to catch the last of the sun's warmth. Regrettably not even that pleasure will stop the past from breathing down his neck tonight, and Torli knows that the moment has come to face it. Yes it is time to let the past out of the dark hole that it has bored into his soul and into the light.

He therefore allows his thoughts to travel backwards to the moment that he has tried to forget about. Soon he sees himself as a boy holding his mother's hand as they flee through the corridors of *Filon Bora's* outer barracks, for there had been a plan to escape Tok, and that night was the night. Sadly just as they were drawing near the point where someone would be waiting to take them to safety they had gotten caught. Torli's mother quickly threw herself into the guard's path and told Torli to run, but he did not, for the man who had caught them had always been kind compared to the others. In his young heart Torli truly believed that he could be convinced to let them escape. That day the guard had not been moved by Torli's pleas, and although Torli could see the anger over having to do so in the man's eyes he said that he must take them back, for Tok would kill him if he did not. He also had his own family to think of.

So they were returned to Tok, and Tok had made certain that Myna would never get the chance to run again, for he chained her to their bed where she remained until life mercifully left her in her sleep several months later. Before she passed however, Tok had used Torli to make her life even more a misery than it already was, and when he hurt Torli he made certain that she knew he did so only to punish her. That was the sticking point, for Tok would not have been able to use him to hurt her if Torli had run like she had begged him to. Torli has always believed that if he had runaway that night his mother would have forced the guard to kill her rather than go back, for her life with Tok had been unbearable. She would have known that it would only be worse after her attempt to flee him, but when Torli refused to go even that avenue of escape was taken from her as far as she was concerned at any rate.

All of that is history now though. The stories that she used to make up to pass the time and ease Torli's pain, the tears, the screams, the whispered I love you's in the night when Torli was afraid all of it over and done a long time ago. The fact of it is that Torli's mother might have been a bit simple in the mind, but she was also the most courageous person man or woman that Torli has

319

ever known, and the kindest. That is how Torli wants to remember her. As she was before things went so terribly wrong. Back when she was young and free, and for the first time in a very long time when Torli thinks of her he smiles. He can almost see her running through a field of flowers in utter abandon like the fey thing that everyone said she was. She had a love of life, and Torli is rather glad to find that the sweeter memories of her are still there, for it tells him that it is time to forgive the young boy who did not understand that leaving her might have been a kinder thing than staying turned out to be.

"You sticking around for a few days Gorg?" Torli asks without opening his eyes.

"If you want me to," Gorg replies.

"Yeah...I'd appreciate it," is all Torli replies.

"No problem..." Gorg comments, but then he turns away and asks, "You think it's nuts to kind a wish I'd a never found out who my father was?"

"No...not at all..." Torli responds with a chuckle that he explains away by saying, "I've found myself wishing I could roll the clock back a few years myself."

"You'd think we'd be happy with our good fortune wouldn't you?" Gorg asks as he steps next to Torli at the rail.

"I think we're happy about it Gorg...it's just that change's hard," Torli explains.

"Yeah...so...how long can I tell my new father I need to stay then...a few weeks...a month...a year maybe?" Gorg asks.

"A few days no more Gorg...you can't put it off forever...besides...you're coming back for the banquet remember?" Torli tells him.

"Oh yeah...that's right," Gorg responds with one of his boyish grins.

The two men stand in companionable silence then each lost in his own thoughts, but when the darkness closes in a cool breeze begins to blow. Of course neither man is cold, for they are used to the seasons of the northern country, and at *Onyat* the temperate weather has been gone for several weeks now. The sudden flash of light in the distance does make the guards standing round the roof get a bit anxious to get inside though, for the wicked storms at *Onyat* roll in over the hills and mountains quickly and beat on one hard. Here in the south where the land is flat though one can see a storm coming when it is still nearly an hour away. The men around

Torli should know that, for to a man they hail from *Filon Bora*, but then again they have been in the north for a long time now. Long enough to forget how the weather works here although judging by their somber faces not long enough to forget the reason that they left here in the first place Torli thinks with a resigned sigh.

Chapter Sixteen

Six days after *Filon Bora* fell to Torli and his allies Karnin's runner and one of the three transports that were brought down from *Onyat* sit in the courtyard being prepped for the road. As it is Karnin has stayed here as long as he dare, and now he must return home to get his lordly affairs in order. After all Marsle expects him to live up to his part of the bargain, which was to secure and protect the lands that he had so generously bestowed upon him. That is not something that Karnin can do when such a large portion of his men are sitting on their arses in Torli's fortress. Besides Torli's people need to know that he is in charge here not his cousin with the army. Karnin must therefore take his army on home and leave the new overlord to sort things out. As one might expect that prospect makes Karnin rather nervous. The truth is that it is going to take some time to get used to not being the one responsible for Torli anymore, but now that *Filon Bora* is clean and reasonably secure the time has come for him to let Torli go he thinks with a sigh.

Allowing Torli to be his own man does not mean that Karnin intends to just walk off and let him fend for himself alone that was never going to happen no matter what. No Karnin polled the men before they ever left *Onyat* to see how many had families here who they would like to rejoin. The number was not extremely high but enough wanted to swear their oaths to Torli to make Karnin feel comfortable about leaving. Well as comfortable as he was ever going to feel Karnin amends. *Filon Bora's* people will eventually see that Torli is a man worthy of their loyalty, and Torli will be as safe as anyone is in this world then. Actually Karnin doubts that it

322

will take long at all for *Filon Bora's* good folk to come to love Torli, for he is a good man. Besides after having experienced Tok's rather warped reign Karnin supposes that most of them would gladly swear to Drunk Dim. They would have to wait a few weeks until he sobers up though Karnin thinks as his eyes wander over to what is now *Filon Bora's* drying out barracks. Yes the fact there is not an empty bed to be had in there is a testament to how very badly Tok failed his people. It is his legacy.

Thinking of Tok's incompetence only points out how very capable Torli is, and with a little chuckle Karnin realizes that he has been worrying like an old woman for nothing. Torli is more than ready for this the last few days have confirmed that. Moreover this whole business has proven to Torli that he has what he needs to take the reins of overlord, and as his confidence has grown he has begun to show the promise of leadership that Boro has always believed he possessed. Still Karnin feels a pang of regret that he and Torli will now go their separate ways. True *Onyat* is only a few hours away, and Karnin already has plans to return in a few weeks for the celebratory banquet, but even so one rather important chapter in both of their lives will end today when he goes out the front gate. That however is the natural progression of things. Boys grow up and leave the nest to find their own way. Well some of them do Karnin thinks as he watches Seasle hand over what looks to be a peace-offering pie to Han.

Ah but Karnin's hesitancy to move on to the next phase of his life is not the only thing making him wish for another day here. Would that it were Karnin thinks as he glances up at the row of third floor windows for the fourth time today. Why he feels an attachment to her is just as great a mystery as why he keeps checking to see if she is at the window when he knows that she is still too sick to get out of bed. Hopefully when he gets home to *Onyat* whatever insanity he has contracted will leave him. To Karnin's displeasure thinking that only bothers him more. Perhaps if their parting had been a bit better he would feel more at ease, for Anjet was rather emotional about his going, and she did not hold back that is for certain. No she let him have it, and after she was finished telling him that he was just like every other man she had ever known promising things and then never holding to it she tossed in that he had no honor. Karnin must admit that one did sting a bit, but to his credit he did not react to it. No he just let her blubber and cry until she wore herself out enough to hear what he had come to say, which took awhile but eventually did happen. Hopefully she will remember it, for she was very played out.

All in all though Karnin is confident that Anjet will understand his position once she lets herself, for she is an overlord's daughter, and so she has been around the upper crust long enough to know about duty and the limited choices that it sometimes gives a person. Then there is that new promise that he allowed her to extort from him Karnin reminds his self. That should help her feel better about things, for she got more than just a simple promise. The whole thing is actually ridiculous, for now if Torli decides to send her back to her father Karnin will be honor bound to kill him for breaking the promise that Karnin extended to her on his behalf. As one might expect Torli was not all that pleased to hear about that, and Boro well quite frankly Karnin is hoping to get out of here before he learns of it. Perhaps it is a good thing that he must leave, for if he stays who knows what else he might promise her.

Promises however will not protect her from someone with as long a reach as overlord Caramu has though, which begs the question as to why he could not seem to find her here at *Filon Bora*. In Karnin's opinion Caramu did not know that Anjet was missing at all it is the only logical answer. After all Caramu is an overlord with deep pockets and he employs several of the *Filcet's* better assassins who should have been able to find her especially here. *Filon Bora* is after all a logical place to look, for it is the closest fortress to Caramu's border. It would also have been an easy place to search when Tok was in charge, for his security measures were practically non-existent, and so anyone could have sneaked into the place. No the only reason that lord Bortten could not find her is because he never asked Caramu for help in doing so. The reason for that is that he was the one who lost her in the first place. Yes the overlord gave lord Bortten a valuable commodity to guard and he let it get away. If Anjet would not be hurt by it Karnin would tell Caramu his own self and let him take care of snotty lord Bortten. The man thoroughly deserves it.

As it was sending Caramu a COM was one of the suggested remedies they tossed round yesterday for the problem that Anjet presents, but that one died a quick enough death mainly because of Caramu's obvious lack of fatherly love for his female children. Unfortunately no other workable plan could be concocted until they knew how lord Bortten played into things, and there was only one person who could tell them that. Karnin, Torli, and Boro

324

therefore went up to Anjet's sick room to talk to her about it. When they asked her how she came to be here at *Filon Bora* Anjet fell back on her original frail female plea of 'I don't remember', but Karnin suspected that she did. He was convinced of it, and her reaction when lord Bortten's name was mentioned made him certain enough of it that he badgered her into tearfully admitting that she had indeed run away from Bortten's fortress. Unfortunately when they asked her why her father sent her there in the first place she began weeping in earnest, which damn near broke Karnin's resolve to insist that she tell them. Luckily they were able to get enough of the story to piece it together.

It seems that she had displeased her father and he sent her to the farthest point away from his person namely to lord Bortten whose fortress *Afenean Condo* sits near his territory's border with what is now Torli's. She then managed to escape the place, which makes one wonder what kind of fortress Bortten is running in the first place. At any rate somehow Anjet made it on foot over the border and was picked up by one of *Filon Bora's* patrols who delivered her to Tok. At first she thought things would be alright, for even though Tok had locked her into one of the bedrooms until he 'sorted it out' he had fed her and made certain that no one touched her. All in all she saw little of him and she had begun to think that he was arranging for someone to come fetch her. When days turned into weeks something changed, for one night he had had her brought to his bedroom where he had beaten and then raped her. By this point in the interview Anjet was so overset that she was shaking uncontrollably. The scariest part was that she had not only stopped weeping, but she had stopped reacting with any kind of emotion at all.

As one might expect Enna tossed them all out then, and they went without complaint, for it was obvious that Anjet would not be able to tell them anything else she was just too ill and traumatized. Unfortunately, they were still left with many unanswered questions although the consensus amongst them was that Anjet could not have answered some of them anyway. The main one being what had changed to make Tok suddenly decide to kill her? The only thing that anyone could think of was that Bortten had refused to pay Tok to get her back or more disturbing Bortten had paid Tok to get rid of her in a permanent way. Yes it all fit rather neatly, for it just so happens that Tok would have had to go through Bortten's fortress *Afenean Condo* to communicate with

Caramu. Bortten of course would not want his incompetence to come to light, and Tok was just sick enough to help him make certain that it never did.

After some thought on it they decided that why Tok did what he did is rather irrelevant, for it would not change the situation. They then put their heads together once more to come up with some workable plan. All that mattered was that they find some way not to relinquish custody of Anjet's person preferably a legal one that will stick. As simple as it sounds it turned out to be a hard order to fill. Then somewhere amongst the sips from the bottle Gorg had what he said was a moment of clarity, which then led him to the brilliant conclusion that if someone married Anjet all her problems would be solved. Needless to say his statement earned him a few rather nasty retorts at first, but the longer they sat there mulling it over sipping on the bottle the more they began to think that Gorg might have just hit upon something that they could work with. In retrospect Karnin thinks that it was more likely a matter of blood alcohol content than the actual content of the plan itself that made them think it worthy enough to consider.

In all fairness though some of what was said did have merit, for in the eyes of the law if they could prove that Anjet had consented to a marriage all her father could do then was to demand that she divorce and if she refused his only other avenue would be to disinherit her. On the other hand her husband he could bring up on charges, but if the man who married her was in a high enough position the best that Caramu could hope to get was an apology and a few recompense tokens. All in all it seemed like the beginning of something workable the only sticking point being who it is that Anjet should marry. Most everyone thought Torli being an overlord now would be the best candidate. Karnin must admit that stuck in his craw a bit, but even if he was the marrying kind, which he is not he could not wed Anjet. His rank is not high enough to protect him or her from a man like Caramu. Besides only overlords can wed without permission, which Karnin is not likely to get from Marsle considering who Anjet is. Then in the midst of all the debate the oracle who until now had remained silent spoke.

As it was Ahnin had against Enna's wishes dragged his beat up self down to Torli's makeshift conference room under the guise of saying goodbye to 'the only family he has in the whole world'. When that did not gain him the invite back to *Onyat* that he was obviously angling for Ahnin being Ahnin did not stomp on back to the infirmary in a huff as a man is wont to do when he has embarrassed himself he is much too stubborn for that. Instead he limped his self across the room to the couch where he could sigh and make pained noises like a child in the punishment corner does. Yes Ahnin excels in his ability to get beneath one's guard Karnin admits, for even though he will deny it forever Ahnin's pathetic act did make Karnin feel bad. Not bad enough to let him come to *Onyat* but bad enough to drink a bit more than he normally would. The result of that was entertaining an idea that when all was said and done sounded rather stupid especially when it was the babe on the couch who pointed it out to him.

To be fair it was probably good that he did although Karnin thinks that when his head cleared he would have seen all the holes in their 'plan'. It goes without saying that when Ahnin interrupted what Karnin thought at the time was a rather brilliant argument for Torli wedding Anjet to point out that whoever married her would earn a place on Caramu's list of people who he would like to see dead being big strong half-drunk men they blew it off. Then Ahnin's over thinking brain tossed in that it would not be beneath Anjet's father to use his own daughter to get even with them, and since he keeps some of the most skilled assassins the *Filcet* offers on a retainer the odds that he would choose to go that route are rather good. All in all it was a reminder for everyone that only bad ideas are found at the bottom of a bottle Karnin thinks as he triggers his headset to acknowledge Han's report that the vehicles are ready to depart.

In the end the idea that marriage would somehow set the lady free morphed back into the tired old idea that they had already kicked around and rejected namely faking her death and hiding her in a place where her father's spies would not find her. Needless to say since that plan had already been explored before there was little support for it this time round. Boro still insisted that faking her death would simply be a waste of time and effort saying that without a body Caramu would not be convinced that she was dead, and everyone had to concede that he was quite right about that. Then the oracle put his opinion into words and said that it would be better if they just said that she ran away then they wouldn't need a body. It was plausible Ahnin had insisted. After all everyone knows that Tok bled his territory dry, and so that Anjet could manage to get out of *Filon Bora* is not all that farfetched especially since she had already managed to escape from lord Bortten.

Karnin must admit that Ahnin's suggestion had an appealing side to it, for if they went that route they could rat out lord Bortten, and then perhaps Anjet will get some small bit of justice. As it stands there is no doubt in Karnin's mind that Anjet did not run away because Bortten was treating her well or anything. Ahnin's plan however had the same exact flaw that all the others that came before it had namely that Caramu would send his *Filcet* dogs out to hunt her down, and they still have no safe place to hide her. They had already eliminated *Filon Bora*, *Onyat*, and Boro's guardian fortress *Arrel Tamell* on the grounds that they would be too obvious. Torli's most remote fortress *Obdon Bora* had also been previously discounted since it lies very close to Devoot's territory. Living at *Onyat* on Devoot's doorstep had taught them one thing about their neighboring overlord, and that was that he spies on his neighbors on a regular basis.

By this time in the discussion everyone's level of frustration was rather high, and so when Boro stated that without a safe haven for Anjet they could not even entertain the thought of helping her most everyone agreed. Except for Gorg who angrily announced that he will go on the lam with her and keep her safe his own damn self, which although it was rather laughable did make the rest of them feel like heels for giving up. Once they were done describing the kind of killers that Caramu had on his payroll Gorg understood why even the most seasoned fighters amongst them would not choose the route that he had suggested. Gorg being Gorg refused to give up though, and he then suggested that the marshes would be an ideal place to send her. After all land men do not go there often, and the marsh territories seldom involve themselves with land affairs so the odds of Anjet running into anyone who might recognize her there was practically none.

That set them all to thinking rather hard mostly about why it is that none of them thought of that. In the end other than the worry that Anjet might contract the rot no one could really see a serious down side to sending Anjet into the marshes to hide. In truth Gorg had made a good case for it, and since he is a marsh lord now he actually has some connections although they may be a bit too new to strain them in the way procuring an invite for a fugitive land woman might do. Gorg then offered to speak to his father about it, and since Karnin already knew the man was honorable he encouraged the others to let him. Why not there was not much to lose and it is possible that Goberan might actually agree although

Karnin thinks it unlikely. Why should he after all? Anjet is nothing to him.

At that point they adjourned with a temporary plan in place. It was a simple plan that in hindsight seems a rather poor showing for an entire night of plotting, but sometimes simple works best. So it is that Torli will put off anyone asking about Anjet by telling them that her health is still too poor to have visitors, and when that runs its course he will use his upcoming banquet or whatever such thing as he deems needed to keep them at bay. Then when Anjet is well enough to leave *Filon Bora* they will sit down with her and explain her choices to her. Hopefully by then they will have at least one feasible option to offer her. What is important though is that she has a say in it, for that is the one thing that she has never had, and Karnin intends to see that she gets a chance to choose her own destiny this time. Well unless of course she chooses to return to that demented father of hers. He has no intention of letting her do that he adds and then turns and walks up the ramp to the runner door without a backward glance, for he is not expecting anyone to come see them off the goodbyes were all said last night.

Something makes him pause at the door to look back though, and when he does he sees Torli standing with Boro near the main entry to the inner keep. Karnin should have guessed that Torli would still come, for he is a creature of habit, and he has always been there to send off anyone who went anywhere. It became a sort of ritual with them. Torli would stand with his stoic face and wave and Ahnin would do some sort of blessing. That memory no matter how warm and fuzzy only serves to remind him that Ahnin is upstairs lying on a bed with his back shredded, but he has always been a quick healer, and so his back is well on the mend already Karnin assures himself as he raises a hand in farewell. After it is returned he quickly goes inside, for there is no purpose in delaying and getting everyone all emotional about it he thinks as he stows his daypack in the storage compartment near his usual seat, but as he does it he looks out the window and glances up, which apparently does not go unnoticed.

"We can wait if you want a go say goodbye," Cerl startles him by quietly saying behind him.

"I said my goodbyes to her yesterday," Karnin retorts a bit testily.

"I's talking about Ahnin," Cerl replies.

"I don't got much to say to him right now Cerl," Karnin replies, and then he adds, "He's on the mend...he'll soon be his old obnoxious self again."

"And that don't worry you...just a bit?" Cerl asks, and when he does Karnin cannot help but smile some, for he may have a point.

"What'd you suggest?" Karnin asks him.

"Let him babysit Merl," Seasle pipes in, for Torli had actually decided to accept Merl's pledge, and although Karnin thinks that he is making a mistake Torli is within his rights to do so.

"Nope...it's time Merl take care a his own self...and Ahnin as well," Karnin replies.

"We better be good Cerl...he's liable to dump us off somewheres too."

"If I drop your arse somewhere it's gonna be when we're passing *Big Rock Crack* Seasle."

"Ah now my feelings's hurt," Seasle responds with a dramatic sniff as Bro announces that the door is coming closed.

As the runner makes its way towards the gate a sullen expression passes across Karnin's features, for he does not feel good about leaving Ahnin here, but he still thinks that he has to do something to make an impression upon him. After all there is no longer any option to go free agent as Ahnin has often threatened to do in the past when the two of them butted heads. Ahnin swore an oath to him and through him to Marsle, and whereas Karnin might release him he is not certain that Marsle would allow it. Ahnin is just too valuable to the team, and after this little jaunt to *Filon Bora* Marsle will be even less likely to let Karnin cut anyone on his team loose. Still Karnin will find a way if after his time of exile with Torli that is what Ahnin really wants, which he may since he has eyes for Enna's niece. That worry is for another day though he adds with a resigned expression.

No sooner has he decided to lighten up than his mind does a flip to the dark side again, for his thoughts wander to Anjet. That only serves to irritate him, for he is twenty-nine now, which is much too old to be obsessed with some girl he cannot have. Besides he has a steady girl that he is very comfortable with. Well he supposes that she would be his mistress now that he is a lord. Yes he has a mistress who is young and beautiful and smart. In truth they are both quite satisfied with the arrangement Karnin tells himself, but unfortunately Bernta's face is not the one that passes across his mind's eye. No it is Anjet's panicked face trapped within some hellish nightmare from the past that he sees. The depth of the emotion that thinking of the lady's plight instills in him shakes Karnin a bit, for it makes no sense whatsoever. How could he possibly have fallen for anyone no matter their circumstances in such a short period of time, and with a shake of his dark head he wonders when exactly it was that he lost his damn mind?

"But Karnin....who's gonna chase away the darkness if you go?" Anjet had gazed up at him with those fevered eyes of hers and asked.

"Oh yeah...that's when..." Karnin mumbles with a snort of derision, for his heart had damn near broken in two, and he had done the first thing that popped into his head.

"Here..." he had replied as he pulled off the necklace with the charm that had once belonged to his mother, and as he hung it round her neck he had said with a shrug, *"My mother said this's made for her by an old healer to ward off the evil eye some village woman put on her...personally I think all that's crap...but I'd pretty good luck since I started wearing it so..."*

"What a dumb arse..." Karnin mutters with a disbelieving shake of his head, for he is rather embarrassed by how awkwardly he had behaved, and that he had given her his mother's charm was so very little-boyish that he cannot help but mumble, "Idiot."

"Hey...what'd I do now?" Gorg remarks from the seat across from him.

"Not you..." Karnin responds.

"Should I ask?"

"Not unless you want a walk to the dock."

"Want me to put him out for you," Seasle's voice offers from the rear of the runner.

"Don't forget he's related to that damn sneaky Calphin now," Cerl reminds him, which does give Seasle a moment of pause, for Calphin is not someone who he would wish to cross if he did not have to, and with a disappointed pout he concedes with a mumbled 'damn fish people'.

"Speaking a marsh folk...look what I got," Gorg announces as he reaches into his pack and pulls out a wrapped bundle which he carefully lays before him on the table.

"That what I think it is?" Seasle asks as Gorg begins to undo the bundle.

"Yep..." Gorg replies, and when he does the other men gather round to stare reverently down at Gorg's cache of sweet trees.

331

"What you want for one?" Seasle asks.

"What you got?" Gorg comes back with.

"Han got a pie," Seasle offers with a shrug.

"Hey...that ain't yours to barter with..." Han complains from the controls.

"Yeah but I paid for it," Seasle reminds him.

"That don't make no difference...you gave it to me," Han responds.

"I got a bottle a last year's berry brew..." Bro triumphantly says as he plunks the item on the table in front of Gorg.

"I don't know Seasle...I think Bro's gonna be hard to beat," Karnin points out with a dubious shake of his head, for last year was an exceptionally good year for berry brew.

"Come on Han...how about just half?" Seasle walks forward and nearly begs.

"No!" Han firmly replies.

"We'll split it...yeah?" Seasle suggests.

"Pies's enough for me," Han replies with a disinterested shrug.

"But he's got sweet trees..." Seasle whines.

"They'll rot your damn teeth out your head," Han comes back with.

"Yeah well...yours're gonna get knocked out..." Seasle threatens.

"Just like you...can't win so you want a beat somebody up," Han replies, and as he turns the runner onto the road he keys his headset and says, "Nuts to transport nine...nine...nine."

"Go ahead Nuts," the transport's pilot replies.

"We'll catch up Phantom," is all Han says, for he had already told Hornten that the runner would be going to the dock to drop Gorg before heading to *Onyat*.

"Copy that Nuts...catch us if you can," Hornten challenges.

"Ha...runner'll be on you before you get to *Big Rock Crack*..." Han sarcastically replies as he turns the runner's nose towards the dock, for the runner is twice as fast as the much larger and more cumbersome transport especially with it as loaded with men and gear as it is, and so Han feels confident that he can drop Gorg and reach Hornten's position before he gets to the narrow canyon that marks the halfway point to *Onyat*.

"You're on," Han hears Hornten reply, and it is only after Han sends the runner cruising off at a fast clip that he glances back at Seasle again, but when he sees that he is sulking in his seat watching Bro suck on one of Gorg's treats he calls back, "You give me one a those sweets for half a pie Gorg?"

"Yeah...okay..." Gorg replies, and then hops up and carries the bartered for item to the front of the runner where he hands it to Han.

"Pie's in the box over there..." Han tells him as he inclines his head towards one of the runner's built in overhead storage boxes, and when Gorg has the pie out Han adds, "You can keep the whole damn thing you give me one for that pouty babe back there too."

"Won't never learn nothing you keep giving in to him you know," Gorg points out.

"Ah well...can't seem to help it...I mean...look at him," Han replies and then casually turns to openly study Seasle.

"Yeah...kind a like that cute little gandet kit that Ahnin tried to tame for a pet," Gorg reminds him with a nod.

"What...the one that nearly tore his damn face off?" Han asks with a snort of amusement.

"Yeah...that's the one," Gorg replies, and as Han mulls over Gorg's comment Seasle gives him one of his predatory looks after which Gorg says, "See...can't tame a wild thing."

"Yeah...but if you keep its gut full it won't chew on you in your damn sleep," Han leans over to him and mumbles, and as he turns back to his control console he calls out, "Got an extra sweet tree Seasle!"

"What you want for it?!"

"What you got?"

"Fish breath got a pie," Seasle retorts with an ornery grin.

"That's lord fish breath to you," Gorg corrects.

"Don't want pie...what else you got," Han replies.

"Minute ago pie was good enough for you."

"Changed my mind."

"You're worse an a woman," Seasle complains, and then he adds in a high pitched mocking voice, "Faster...harder....not that fast...not so ruff you damn beast."

As Karnin sits listening to his men banter and barter with each other he smiles a bit, for some things never change, and in an odd way the constant bickering amongst them is rather reassuring especially now when he is feeling Torli's absence. With a sigh he settles back into his seat and lets the gentle hum of the runner's propulsion system lull the tension from his body. As is usually the case when the knot in his neck eases clarity comes, and he soon finds that he has relaxed enough to examine the past weeks from a different perspective. A short while later he thinks that in retrospect he is not as nervous anymore about being the lord of *Onyat*. After all he and a group of nobodies had just attacked and taken one of the largest fortresses in the world, unseated a sitting overlord and placed one of their own in his chair all with the blessing of every other overlord and lord in existence. Not a bad day's work.

As if that were not enough of a confidence booster there is the fact that not only is he returning to *Onyat* a free man, but he is doing so because he now owns it. That little perk he never saw coming although he most likely should have. All in all things had turned out better than expected for them all. There is one problem with accomplishing everything that you set out to do plus some though Karnin thinks as he gives in to the heaviness of his eyelids. How to top it he adds, but as he dozes off the face of a certain young lady with the most glorious fall of reddish-brown hair passes through his mind, and he suspects that the fates have already chosen what his next great quest will be. Unfortunately there will be no personal gain in that one, for if she is to be free she cannot be with anyone in the public eye, and that would not be him. That fact will make it a hard sell as far as Marsle is concerned, but maybe that is the challenge in it Karnin reasons. Only time will tell...

THE END

Coming Soon!

Book Two in the Quest Saga

The Quest To Save The Despot's Daughter

Glossary

Afenean Condo – (Af **nē** an **Con** dō) guardian keep of the *Western Central Land Territory* that lies near the border of the *Western Central Land Territory* and the *Western Southern Land Territory*

Ahnin – (**A** nin) of the land; joined Karnin's band at *Filon Bora* as a young teen after the man who had raised him Coras died, nicknamed 'magic man'; known for his superstitious nature, deadly fighting skills, knowledge of poisons and healing, and his uncanny ability to 'read' people

Alda – (**Al** duh) of the land; Boro's armor boy at *Filon Bora*

Alenio – (Al **ēn** ē ō) the transition of a newborn marsh babe from a creature subsisting solely in water to one who breathes air that must be performed within the first few hours of life outside the womb

Alitin – (**Al** i tin) of the marshes; the last *King of the Northern Marshes*, father of Tair, grandfather of Marsle, builder of the original fortress of *Laraqua*

Andina – (An **dēn** uh) of the marshes; *Lady of Mori*, wife of Bimian, *Lady En Tenda of the Central Marshes and Fringe Lands*, mother of Calphin and Aquaous, eldest sister of Cantil overlord of the *Southern Coastal Marshes*, known for her rare blue eyes

Anel – (**A** nel) of the marshes; Corlean's lifelong friend and *Aqualean's* steward

Anjet – (**An** jet) of the land; daughter of Caramu and Millit the lady of *Sero Dolan*

Annitequea – (An ni **teq** wē uh) (Ann) of the marshes; daughter Marsle and Naona, sister of Corlean

Aqualean – (Ah kwuh **lē** an) the marsh fortress that Corlean built and presented to his wife Aquaous as her wifing gift

Aquaous – (**Ah** kwā us) of the marshes; daughter of Bimian and Andina, sister of Calphin, wife of Corlean, mother of Milin, healer and lady of *Aqualean*, known for her rare blue eyes

Arrel Tamell – (Air **rel** Ta **mel**) guardian fortress of the *Eastern Central Land Territory* that lies near the border between the *Eastern Central Land Territory* and the *Western Central Land Territory*

Avin – (**A** vin) of the land; one of lord Teneset of *Dorelon Bodon's* fighting men

Bandin – (**Ban** din) of the land; captain of Tok's personal guard

Barndon – (**Barn** dun) of the land; steward of *Filon Bora* after Torli took the overlord's seat

Bella – (**Bel** luh) of the land; camp woman at *Onyat* known for her shrewd and rather heartless nature, mother of Polie

Berto – (**Bur** tō) of the marshes; *Laraqua's* steward

Big Rock Crack – also known as *Rock Crack*, *The Crack*, or by the more colorful *Arse Crack* it is a natural gorge situated not far off the modern road that leads from *Filon Bora* to *Onyat*

Bimian – (**Bim** ē an) of the marshes; overlord of the *Central Marsh Territory and Fringe Lands*, father of Calphin and Aquaous, husband of Andina, elder brother of Goberan

Bonin – (**Bo** nin) of the land; Enna's husband, brother of Bort, uncle of Lizzet, one of *Filon Bora's* metalers often referred to as Bo-Bo behind his back

Bornan – (**Bohr** nan) of the marshes; one of Andina's pet's (Onot) handlers

Boro – (Bohr **ō**) of the land; Jubiet's brother, Galwor and Myna's uncle, lord of *Arrel Tamell*, Torli's great uncle who recruited Karnin to help him smuggle those who Tok had reason to kill out of *Filon Bora*

Bort – (**Bohrt**) of the land; husband of Nadina, father of Lizzet, brother of Bonin, killed with his wife at *Filon Bora* by Galwor's guards for hiding two loaves of bread from them

Bortten – (**Bohr** ten) of the land; one of overlord Caramu's vassals, lord of *Afenean Condo*

Bro – (**Brō**) of the land; one of Karnin's men known for his great size who joined their band as a young man when he came to *Onyat* pedaling stolen goods for the lord of *Dorelon Bodon* Osgo

Caldin – (**Cal** din) of the land; Torli and Karnin's first cousin and the rightful lord of *Obdon Bora*

Calphin – (**Cal** fin) of the marshes; son and heir apparent of the overlord of the *Central Marsh Territory and Fringe Lands* Bimian and his wife Andina, brother of Aquaous, husband of Janissa, father of Corlon, lord of *Miowna*, known for his rare blue eyes

Cantil – (**Can** til) of the marshes; overlord of the *Southern Coastal Marsh Territory*, brother of Andina

Caramu – (**Care** uh moo) of the land; son of Haldis; father of Tomlan, Anjet, and Sonter plus several other illegitimate children, overlord of the *Western Central Land Territory*

Cerl – (**Surl**) of the land; one of the original members of Karnin's band of boys and Karnin's heir apparent who is known for his shaggy hair

Cint Oota – (**Sint Oo** tuh) considered the true consummation of a marsh marriage it is the biological bond between a marsh woman's and a marsh man's bodies that occurs after conception and renders the marsh woman unable to bear children to any other man

Cogen – (**Cō** gen) of the marshes; *Larauqa's* security master

Corlean – (**Cohr** lē an) of the marshes; son of overlord Marsle and Naona, heir apparent of the *Northern Marsh Territory and Fringe Lands*, husband of Aquaous, brother of Annitequea, lord of *Aqualean*

Corlon – (**Cohr** lon) of the marshes; son of Calphin and Janissa, heir apparent of *Miowna*, grandson of overlord Bimian and Andina

Cronen – (**Cro** nen) of the marshes; member of overlord Oreian's traveling entourage

cuke – (**cūk**) a large black slug-like water snail resembling a sea cucumber that is often eaten by marsh folk pickled and brined although it is an acquired taste

Debon – (**De** bon) of the land; Karnin's father who was the youngest of the lord of *Obdon Bora* Bornal's identical twins

Devoot – (De **voot**) of the land; overlord of *the Eastern Northern Land Territory*

doodle frog – (**doo** dil **frog**) a brown amphibian that inhabits the marshes known for its loud human-like scream

Dor – (**Dohr**) of the land; overlord of *the Eastern Southern Land Territory*

Dorelon Bodon – (**Dohr** e lon **Bō** don) the *Eastern Northern Land Territory's* guardian fortress between both the *Eastern Central Land Territory* and the *Northern Marsh Territory's Fringe Lands*

Drunk Dim – of the land; one of *Filon Bora's* guardsmen who was given the nickname by Karnin and his gang of boys because he was dim-witted and normally drunk on duty

Edbon – (**Ed** bon) of the land; Torli's father who was the eldest of the lord of *Obdon Bora* Bornal's identical twins who inherited the title of lord of *Obdon Bora*

Enna – (**Ē** nuh) of the land; healer Boro brought to the cave when she was an apprentice to nurse Torli back to health who later became *Filon Bora's* primary healer and married Lizzet's uncle Bonin

Fendora – (Fen **dohr** uh) guardian fortress of the *Central Marsh Territory and Fringe Lands'* that lies in the marshes near its borders with the *Eastern Central Land Territory,* the *Northern Marsh Territory and Fringe Lands*, and the *Southern Marsh Territory and Fringe Lands*

Filcet (The) – (**Fil** set) a group of high priced assassins also known by the slang terms 'ghosts' or 'eyes'; who have a reputation for their high standards with regards to the quality of their assassins, and their near spotless record when it comes to fulfilling their murder contracts

Filon Bora – (**Fī** lon **Bohr** uh) the seat of the overlord of the *Eastern Central Land Territory* and its guardian fortress that lies near its border with both the *Eastern Southern Land Territory* and the *Central Marsh Territory and Fringe Lands*

Galwor – (**Gal** wohr) of the land; son of Obron and Jubiet, father of Tok, uncle of Torli, overlord of the *Eastern Central Land Territory*

gandet – (**gan** det) a predatory small cat-like animal notorious for its cunning hunting abilities that primarily dwells on land although it often extends its hunting territory into the marshes in the cold season when the marshes are frozen over

gifting day – the anniversary day of one's birth

Goberan – (**Gō** bur an) of the marshes; younger brother of Bimian, husband of Renya, father of Slolar and Gorg, lord of *Fendora*

Gofren – (**Gō** fren) the smaller of the planet's twin moons described as having a yellowish glow and the last of the two moons to rise at night as well as the last to set in the morning

Gonia Nona – (**Go** nē a **No** nuh) *'Sweet Nothings'* a marsh treat composed entirely of the hardened sweet nectar of various flowers that are a traditional gift given from one person to another in celebration of some occasion of importance or in thanks for some extraordinary favor done

Gorg – (**Gohrg**) of the land and the marshes; son of Lilit of *Filon Bora* and lord Goberan of *Fendora*; rescued from a cage that his mother's father-in-law locked him in to die when he learned that Gorg was not his son's child

Grolin – (**Gro** lin) of the marshes; *King of the Northern Marshes*, father of Alitin, grandfather of Tair, great grandfather of Marsle, builder of the first marsh keep known as *Laraqua*

Han – (**Han**) of the land; the first member of Karnin's original gang of thieves and the oldest, *Onyat's* master mechanic, weapons and gunnery master, and vehicle pilot training master

heir apparent – next male in the line of succession for a lord's or overlord's seat

Hornten – (**Horn** ten) of the land; one of the older more experienced of *Onyat's* security men who occasionally acts as a transport or runner pilot although his primary duty is personal security

inner keep – referred to as the 'heart of a land fortress' the inner keep consists of a defendable central building of several stories that houses the fortress's defensive weapons usually upon its roof as well as the lord of the fortress and his staff and their families and serves as a safe haven for all the fortress's occupants in times of trouble

Janissa – (Jan **ni** suh) of the marshes; wife of Calphin, mother of Corlon, lady of *Miowna*

jim-jon – a rat-like creature that can often be found inhabiting dwellings, frequenting garbage piles, and raiding gardens and food stores that are known for their ability to quickly overpopulate their environment as well as their fierce sounding bluff of lord screeching and teeth chattering when threatened

jitty – (**ji** tē) an open marsh transport vehicle designed to seat one or two men that is propelled by the use of water in a similar fashion as a jet drive motor uses

Jonin – (**Jo** nin) of the marshes; overlord Oreian's obnoxious son and heir apparent nicknamed 'pasty face' because of his rather sallow skin color

Jonlean – (Jon **lē** an) fortress built by Jonin the heir apparent of the *Northern Coastal Marsh Territory* not far from the *Northern Marsh Territory and Fringe Lands'* northernmost fortress *Lanoua*

Jubiet – (Joo bē **et**) of the land; Obron's wife, mother of Galwor and Myna, eldest sister of Boro, grandmother of Torli

Karnin – (**Kahr** nin) of the land; bastard son of Ornea and Debon, lord of *Onyat* and first cousin of overlord Torli

Kinbe – (**Kin** bē) of the land; Teneset's second in command who served as the temporary security master of *Filon Bora* in the interim time when Tok's overlordship was being contested by Torli

Krenot – (**Kren** ot) of the land; overlord of the *Western Northern Land Territory*

lady – title carried by the wives and daughters of a lord or an overlord as well as the females who hold the fortresses of *Mori* and *Sero Dolan* in their own right

Lady En Tenda – (**La** dē En **Ten** duh) the formal title given to the wife of an overlord

lambis – (**lam** bis) a type of small fish commonly eaten by the marsh folk smoked whole often as a snack

Laraqua – (Lah **ra** qwuh) the seat of the overlord of the *Northern Marsh Territory and Fringe Lands*

Lizzet – (Liz **zet**) of the land; daughter of Nadina and Bort of *Filon Bora*, niece of Bonin who raised her from the age of two after her parents were both killed, Enna's step-niece

lord – title carried by the vassal of an overlord who has been given charge of a fortress as well as all successive legitimate male children of said vassal's line

marsh crawler – a large marsh vehicle that consists of a platform equipped with a forward open air sitting and satellite control center, a large cabin for lounging, eating, and sleeping, and a smaller cabin that houses the vehicle's drive and security systems all of which is supported by four legs known as 'risers' that propel the vehicle by moving up and down in a walking motion

Marsle – (**Mahr** sul) of the marshes; overlord of the *Northern Marsh Territory and Fringe Lands*, father of Corlean and Annitequea, husband of the late Naona

Merl – (**Murl**) of the land; one of Karnin's boys who was known for being unreliable and loyal only to his self

Milin – (**Mil** in) of the marshes; son of Corlean and Aquaous who is known for his rare blue eyes

Mont – (**Mont**) of the land; Karnin's stepfather

Mori – (**Mohr** ē) the oldest and most historically significant fortress in the marshes whose title and lands have been held exclusively by females since the fortress's construction in ancient times; *Mori's* charter was redone during the negotiations that led to *The Pact of the Overlords* and as a result *Mori's* vast lands were divided amongst three of the newly drawn territories in an effort to preserve it and to limit the power of its lady although the lands remained entailed to *Mori*

Morianite – (**Mohr** ē an īt) a marsh man or woman who hails from the fortress of *Mori*

Morian Sea (The) – (**Mohr** ē an **Sē**) the ancient marsh name for the vast sea that encompasses the portions of the world that are not marsh or dry land

Myna – (**Mī** nuh) of the land; daughter of Obron and Jubiet, Galwor's sister, Boro's niece, Torli's mother, said to be rather childlike in her thinking

Nadina – (Nuh **dēn** uh) of the land; wife of Bort, mother of Lizzet, killed with her husband at *Filon Bora* by Galwor's guards for hiding two loaves of bread from them

Naona – (**Nā** **ō** nuh) of the marshes; wife of Marsle, *Lady En Tenda* of the *Northern Marsh Territory and Fringe Lands*, mother of Annitequea and Corlean who was killed when she slipped and fell off the front of the marsh crawler she and Marsle were traveling on

Nao-Nao – (**Nā** ō - **Nā** ō) of the marshes; *Laraqua's* chief resident healer

Nebara – (Ne **bahr** uh) of the marshes; one of *Laraqua's* healers who apprenticed under Nao-Nao

Nilly – (**Nil** ē) of the land; woman from *Filon Bora's* village who worked in Karnin's mother's house of pleasure until it was burnt to the ground by Tok's men at which time she went to work for Madam Bitha at *Bitha's House of Pleasure*

Nithian – (**Nith** ē an) the seat of the overlord of the *Central Marsh Territory and Fringe Lands*

Obdon Bora – (**Ob** den **Bohr** uh) guardian fortress of the *Eastern Central Land Territory* that lies near its border with the *Eastern Northern Land Territory*

Obron – (Ō bron) of the land; the first seated overlord of the *Eastern Central Land Territory* after *The Pact of the Overlords* was signed, husband of Jubiet, father of Galwor and Myna, grandfather of Torli

Ofren – (Ō fren) the larger of the planet's twin moons that is described as casting a eerie silvery light and the first of the two moons to rise at night as well as the first to set in the morning

Omon – (Ō mon) of the land; son of one of *Filon Bora's* meaters who courted Lizzet at the same time as Ahnin who Ahnin nicknamed 'Omon the Braun'

Onot – (O not) of the marshes; Andina's unusual pet who has enormous yellow eyes, a long fat tail, a pouch, four legs, semi-arboreal habits, and a liking for wet environments

Onyat – (On yot) the fortress that Karnin and his band of misfits built upon a portion of the *Fringe Lands* of the *Northern Marsh Territory* after their exodus from the *Eastern Central Land Territory*

Oreian – (Or rē an) of the marshes; overlord of the *Northern Coastal Marsh Territory* and known as the biggest mooch in the marshes because he spends most of his time traveling around with his entourage visiting other overlord's fortresses in order to consume their resources and conserve his own

Orn – (Orn) of the land; long time member of Karnin's band of misfits known for his large size and his winning way with the ladies, *Onyat's* security master

Ornea – (Or nē uh) of the land; Karnin's mother who worked in the kitchens of *Filon Bora* until lord Debon took her as his mistress and set her up in a house in the village that she turned into a brothel after Debon's death left her unable to provide for herself and her infant son

Osgo – (Oz gō) of the land; lord of *Dorelon Bodon* who sent Bro out to peddle goods that he stole from his overlord Devoot who eventually replaced him with the general of his army Teneset

overlord – the highest position of power in the known world held through the male line of legitimate offspring and passed from eldest son to eldest son although in the absence of any surviving legitimate male heir the title passes to the eldest illegitimate male heir, and if there are none or no specifically pre-appointed and pre-approved successor the choice of the next overlord falls to the *Counsel of Overlords*

Overlord En Officianada – (**Ōh** ver lohrd **En** Ō fi shē an **o** duh) an individual usually a lord who the overlords have unanimously chosen to represent their collective authority with regards to overseeing the investigation of a complaint or other such matter brought before the *Council of Overlords* as well as seeing that whatever disposition is decided upon by the overlords is carried out

Pact of the Overlords (The) – the accord that was signed after the last great war that divvied up all the world's lands into territories that were then given in perpetuity to the various warlords and kings; the agreement also established the rules and rights of said 'overlords' which essentially gave an overlord absolute power within his own territory with the collective body of the world's overlords known as the *Council of Overlords* being the only power able to usurp an overlord's rights if he has broken the rules set forth in the pact

personal device – a handheld computer that most people use to record and document their personal affairs and other things of interest

Pobin – (**Pō** bin) of the land; the overlord of the *Western Southern Land Territory*

Polie – (**Po** lē) of the land; born at *Onyat* to a camp woman named Bella his paternity was never really discovered although for a time his father was believed to be one of eight men more specifically Karnin, Cerl, Gorg, Bro, Orn, Han, Seasle, and Ahnin although genetic testing eventually ruled them all out

Ponet – (**Po** net) of the land; Tok's inept security master

poonies – (**poo** nēz) imaginary little marsh folk similar to faeries said to haunt the marshes near *Mori*

poppy snails – the juvenile stage of a much larger snail often eaten as a delicacy in a similar way as caviar

Quincy – (**Kwin** sē) of the marshes; overlord of the *Central Coastal Marsh Territory*

runner – a hybrid land/water war machine designed by Torli that utilizes a field generator system of propulsion and numerous thrusters for directional control; fully armored and armed with several varieties of weaponry and equipped with a full sensor array, a 360 degree array of exterior cameras and blast shields that can be lowered to allow outside viewing via several windows

Rylon – (**Rī** lon) of the marshes; one of Marsle's bodyguards

Saleni – (Suh **lē** nē) of the marshes; one of *Laraqua's* healers who apprenticed under Nao-Nao

Sandon – (**San** dun) of the land; one of lord Teneset of *Dorelon Bodon's* primary bodyguards trained in the basics of the healing arts

Seasle – (**Sē** sil) of the land; abandoned as an infant and found by Karnin's mother who nursed him alongside Karnin until his real mother came and claimed him to sell him into service in *Filon Bora's* inner keep, known for his in-your-face personality, chief demolitions expert on *Onyat's* first assault team

Sertten – (**Ser** ten) of the marshes; the overlord of the *Southern Marsh Territory and Fringe Lands*

Shack (The) – the original lean-to built by Karnin and his refugees on the site upon which they later constructed the fortress of *Onyat*

shooter – an open land vehicle that is propelled along on a cushion of air that is designed to sit a driver astride the forward facing seat and a guard man in the secondary rear facing seat

Slolar – (**Slō** lahr) of the marshes; son of Goberan and Renya, nephew of Bimian and Andina, the heir apparent of *Fendora*

snipey fish – (**snī** pē **fish**) small fish of the outer marshes whose behavior is similar to piranha

sugared kelp – a confection made from strands of a grass-like marsh plant that is brined in a sugary syrup

swani – (**swun** ē) a marsh slang term used to describe someone who enjoys sexual encounters that are depraved and unnatural

sweet tree – a marsh confection made from a branching marsh plant that has been brined in a honey-like syrup

Tair – (**Tāir**) of the marshes; son of King Alitin, father of Marsle, first overlord of the *Northern Marsh Territory and Fringe Lands* after the signing of *The Pact of the Overlords*

Tandar – (**Tan** dahr) of the land; one of lord Teneset of *Dorelon Bodon's* primary bodyguards

Teneset – (**Ten** e set) of the land; the general of overlord Devoot's standing army, lord of *Dorelon Bodon*, acted as *Overlord En Temporada* during the tribunal in which Tok was removed from the seat of the overlord of the *Eastern Central Land Territory* which was then given over to Torli

Tok – (**Tok**) of the land; bastard son of Galwor who ascended to the overlordship of the *Eastern Central Land Territory* after killing his rivals and his father for which he was subsequently removed from the seat and executed

tooka – (**too** kuh) (sci. *tookapendis*) a large land bird about the size of an ostrich and resembling the flightless prehistoric genera of 'terror birds'

Torli – (**Tohr** lē) of the land; son of Myna and Edbon, grandson of Obron and Jubiet, nephew of Boro and Galwor, first cousin of Karnin, ascended to the overlordship of the *Eastern Central Land Territory* after Tok's execution for murdering Galwor and his lawful heirs

Tosel – (**To** sel) of the marshes; one of Andina's pet's (Onot) handlers

wifing gift – the gift that a marsh man presents to his wife at a celebration held six days after the birth of their first child that symbolizes his recognition of the great gift that she has given him and the finalizing of their status as man and wife

Made in the USA
Middletown, DE
23 May 2021

40254681R00199